WILD HOPE

ALSO BY JOAN THOMAS

Five Wives
The Opening Sky
Curiosity
Reading by Lightning

WILD HOPE

A NOVEL

JOAN THOMAS

HARPER **PERENNIAL**

Wild Hope
Copyright © 2023 by Joan Thomas.
All rights reserved.

Published by Harper Perennial, an imprint of HarperCollins Publishers Ltd

First Canadian edition

No part of this book may be used or reproduced in any manner whatsoever without the prior written permission of the publisher, except in the case of brief quotations embodied in reviews.

HarperCollins books may be purchased for educational, business, or sales promotional use through our Special Markets Department.

HarperCollins Publishers Ltd
Bay Adelaide Centre, East Tower
22 Adelaide Street West, 41st Floor
Toronto, Ontario, Canada
M5H 4E3

www.harpercollins.ca

Epigraph from *Everyone Knows Your Mother Is a Witch* © 2021 by Rivka Galchen. Published in Canada by HarperCollins Publishers Ltd. All rights reserved.

Library and Archives Canada Cataloguing in Publication

Title: Wild hope : a novel / Joan Thomas.
Names: Thomas, Joan (Sandra Joan), author.
Identifiers: Canadiana (print) 2023018331X | Canadiana (ebook) 20230183433 | ISBN 9781443468640 (softcover) | ISBN 9781443468657 (ebook)
Classification: LCC PS8639.H575 W55 2023 | DDC C813/.6—dc23

Printed and bound in the United States of America
23 24 25 26 27 LBC 5 4 3 2 1

For Hazel Loewen and Heidi Harms

> *Well . . . I said to myself, you're not a child,*
> *you must be your own source of light.*
> —RIVKA GALCHEN

WILD HOPE

ISLA

ONE

Reg Bevaqua stands on a beach on Georgian Bay with a white drone at his feet. He's fiddling with the control sticks, explaining them to his son and heir. The kid is seven, how could he possibly fly a drone? But Reg is an expert, and he can't resist. I can't see Reg's wife—she must be sitting on a rock at the base of the cliff—but there's their little girl, wandering across the sand in a pink and purple swimsuit. She finds a spot she likes and squats and sets to work, tenderly burying her Barbies in the sand. The dog noses after her, a hound of some sort.

We're on a beautiful stretch of shore on the west side of the bay, very near the spot where my boyfriend Jake's family used to have a cabin. Shapely brown rocks. Terns with orange bills. Sprinkles of light on aquamarine water. A yacht is anchored a few metres out, admiring its reflection in the still lake. The Bevaquas came by water, but I climbed the rocky trail along the shoreline, foraging for signs of Jake. Now I'm crouched on the cliff above the Bevaquas, binoculars dangling around my neck. I watch as the drone lifts itself out of Reg's hands. It gains altitude fast, heading straight for me, nimble as a UFO. A chipmunk chitters a warning, and it occurs to me that Reg might be filming. But no worries, little William is at the controls, and just as the thing reaches the height of the cliff, it tilts and veers drunkenly toward the sand. Cries ring out. I lean forward to see. The drone has crashed in driftwood and rocks. Poor William—his shrill voice is full of tears.

Reg picks up his toy, frowning over it. At this point in a film, the watcher on the cliff would lift binoculars to their eyes, and that's what I do, I pull the subject of my surveillance into focus. His ear, ordinary, neat. His jaw, clamped in irritation. His *temple*, the bony crypt where all his vile ideas are hatched. I close in on his quill-like hair, his resolute hairline. Three or four years ago, when I met him, he was a mere multi-millionaire trying to take his company public, and I swear he was balding at the time. But when you get rich enough, your hair grows back out of sheer respect, right?

I lower the binoculars. The night before, Reg's wife, Eve, assured me they were totally committed to the search. "We're going to spend the day on the *Sequana*, but we'll keep our eyes open for anything out of the ordinary," she said, tucking a sleeve of rice crackers into the picnic basket I had packed for them—but in fact, nobody's searching for Jake except me. They're not even pretending. I don't know what this means, but it feels sinister, and panic rises in my chest. I inch away from the cliff, avoiding a scattering of deer turds, and lie back on pine needles and moss. Why are you doing this, Jake, I cry silently, like he's hiding from me on purpose. Near me, a bird starts up, an uninspired little song, like a gate swinging back and forth on rusty hinges. I close my eyes against the sky, a perfect sky, and sling up an elbow to deepen the darkness. I've been sucked into something I don't want to be any part of. That's how it feels—like my ordinary life has morphed into a crime drama with its crude apparatus of suspects and motives and weapons and clues. Not at all the story I had in mind for myself, but the universe insists.

Here, it says. Right here.

I lift my arm and turn my head against the moss and I see it. A shell casing. A bright brass shell casing, nestled in ground cedar two feet from my nose.

•

Rewind, go back a few weeks, to a Saturday in April when I took a train into Toronto. It was Easter weekend, to be exact. Jake and I were living in Adlington, a small town an hour northwest, where I was part-owner of a farm-to-table restaurant called The Grange. Not yet open for the season and probably closed for good. Jake had an art show in Toronto that night (not a major show, just a remount at a new artists' centre called The Ark), and I assumed we'd take the train in together. But around noon, a text from Jake's agent landed on my phone. *I only hope all the bridges he's burning are helping to light his way.*

Jake is a nocturnal animal, and he was still outside in the shed he uses as a studio. I crossed the yard and barged in. At the sight of him asleep on his futon, I felt a sharp longing to strip off my jeans and crawl in with him, into the warmth and the smells that collect under a quilt through the night. He sensed something and opened his eyes. "You're not going to your show," I said. He pulled himself to a sitting position. "No," he said. He was wearing a T-shirt, and his jeans were crumpled on a chair. The light from the skylight fell on his tangled hair. His eyes were calm, not angry or defiant. It was like he was claiming the high ground by declining to explain.

We had just endured a few weeks of awful silence, and it was, I guess, a tipping point. I tore into Jake, my voice low and ferocious, strange even to my ears. When I ran out of words, he said, "You'd leave me if I told you everything. So I think you should leave." I stared at him in shock. "Alright, Jake," I heard myself say. "Hope you have a nice life." I turned and walked back to the house, where I went straight to my phone. One of our neighbours had mentioned she was going to Brampton that day, and I called her and asked for a ride.

The train was waiting when she pulled into the Brampton station, and I got on and found a seat alone. All I had in my shoulder bag was a hairbrush and toothbrush, mascara and moisturizer. This might suggest I didn't consider that stupid kiss-off an actual break-up, but as the train pulled out, I began to grasp that it was. We were breaking up. By the time we slid into Union Station, I was fighting to hold myself together.

From the rail tracks, the city struck me as abandoned. When I walked out of the station, the towers leaning over me looked higher than ever and more audacious. I came to an intersection where you can't see sky at all, and I hesitated stepping off the curb, and then I heard a raw old voice singing "Don't Think Twice, It's All Right." A busker with thin grey braids, playing an acoustic guitar. As I crossed towards him, he gazed at me as though he saw my distress. After a minute, I fumbled in my bag and tossed a big coin into his guitar case, and he narrowed his eyes in thanks and looked away.

I kept walking vaguely northward, taking in the way light fell on the upper planes of the buildings, the pedestrians navigating the sidewalks as separately and as together as a murmuration. I walked all the way to King Street, past the first restaurant I'd ever worked at (Sheff's, now a cannabis store called Heart and Soul), past my first apartment building, past the yoga studio where I'd mastered the headstand. I walked past the condo where Jake's agent, Phoebe, had thrown a dinner party for us, just before Jake and I moved out of Toronto. That night I wore a rayon jacket and skirt I'd bought at a vintage shop—amber, I called the colour. No, it's ochre, Jake said. Persimmon. He was dressed in an old tuxedo with purple satin lapels. Was that tuxedo ironic or post-ironic (like, was he trying too hard)? That's what we'd debated as we walked to Phoebe's.

I turned away from the memory and started walking with purpose, thinking I would check out the venue for tonight's art show. It took me about half an hour—then there it was, The Ark. A red-brick and grey-shingle church, smaller and more hunched than I remembered, like its over-large dome had pressed it into the ground. It had been bought and renovated by the artists' co-op Jake belonged to, transformed into a live-work gallery for emerging artists. Its main entrance was still behind a maze of scaffolding and plywood, but the posters plastered on the cladding bore the familiar image of Jake's Rachel Carson canvas. The opening was at eight. I needed to decide whether I was going to put in an appearance, which meant making up my mind about . . . well, my entire life.

I walked for another hour, trying not to think. Finally I saw a bench under budding trees and sat and listened to the roar of the city around me. This was the way I'd spent my days when I was a kid, wandering without a plan or a destination. While my friends sleepwalked their way from one class to the next, I'd ride the subway and jump off at random stops to explore. Home-schooling, it was called. Finding a washroom was always the trick. I needed one now, and eventually I got up and started walking again. When I saw a hotel, I stepped inside, called a friendly hello to the receptionist, and made my way unerringly to the bathroom off the lobby. On the way out, my eyes fell on a bottled water vending machine in an alcove. It was entirely filled with BevAqua Blue—rows of glacier-blue bottles, backlit like a museum display.

I'd have loved a drink of water, but I would die of thirst before I slid my bank card into one of those machines. *Reg Fucking Bevaqua*. BevAqua Blue was his marquee "hydration product" in North America— he always bragged about the way he'd turned his family name into a popular brand. He wanted you to think BevAqua Blue was the source of his wealth, but the guy was only in his mid-thirties, and nobody gets that rich that fast by bottling water. It was other, sordid businesses around the world that had paid for his yacht and his ridiculous cars and his lavish properties, though he never talked about those branches of his empire.

I knew Reg Bevaqua through our restaurant. We offered a high-end *menu complet*, and the customers we called regulars tended to patronize us once a year. But we fed Bevaqua constantly because Adlington was en route to his lodge on Georgian Bay and he fell into the habit of using The Grange like a highway truck stop—apparently being rich entitled him to the table we kept free for extraordinary last-minute requests. It also entitled him to drop in and hang around the kitchen during off-hours, treating our barn like a petting zoo for his kids. My business partner, Sheff, was the one who indulged him. I'd never really warmed to the guy. He was sure to be at the opening tonight, in his new role as patron to the arts. Another great reason not to go. Reg Bevaqua was actually the cause of a lot of the tension between Jake and me—though is any fight between lovers ever about the issue that kicks it off?

I hadn't eaten all day, and when I turned up Ossington, I realized how hungry I was. Three weeks earlier I was still wearing my parka, and now restaurants were beginning sidewalk service. I slid onto the bench of a picnic table in front of a place called Ralph's and ordered a veggie burrito. The cornmeal shell was handmade and the cilantro was fresh, and I savoured every bite, flirting wordlessly with a little boy sitting cross-legged on his bench. He was munching a hamburger he held in both hands. From time to time, his parents exchanged amused looks with me. *Raised by Wolves*, their kid's T-shirt said. The sky was an evening blue now, and the last of the sun fell warmly on us. The little family left and I sat on, drinking ginger ale and trying to decide what to do. I was wearing black jeans and a narrow black sweater and my favourite boots, a good-enough look for an artists' party, but I could feel the sweat and oil on my face from a long day of walking, and my hair had lost its bounce. Sheff had an apartment in Chinatown. He was in Spain at the moment, and his keys were in my bag. I could go over there and shower and do my makeup, making a late and more impressive appearance at the art opening. Or I could take the subway to my parents' place, blow off the party altogether.

Don't think, I said to myself. Just stop thinking.

The sun, orange now, dropped towards the earth. It touched the grey skyline and sank into it, and then it flashed a brilliant goodnight. The second it vanished, I got up and started walking again, back in the direction of The Ark.

Darkness, or what passes for it in the city, had fallen when I arrived. By the front steps of the old church stood a tall, long-haired guy in a vintage suede jacket, perplexed by the scaffolding. "There has to be another entrance," I said, and he followed me around the side of the church. And there was, a massive door with an iron ring in the middle. "Cryptic," I said. The guy held the door open, looking at me with interest.

In the foyer, a woman with a phone to her ear was counting people off for an elevator, and the tall guy and I just missed the cut. We waited side by side without speaking. His hair was shoulder-length and blunt-cut and he was clean-shaven, which gave him (I thought) a Renaissance look. Then we were on the third floor, in the common area. Jake's agent, Phoebe, who was on the board of the co-op, stood by the elevator, greeting guests with high cries. She always picked her clothes with the bold intentionality of a costume designer, and she was wearing a beautiful silk kimono in semi-abstract flowers, her breasts glowing like ostrich eggs above the lace bodice of an ivory silk slip. We mimed kisses at each other. Her smile faded when she saw I was alone.

"No?" she said. "You couldn't talk him into it?"

"Nope."

For a long time, Phoebe's relationship with Jake was strained, as a consequence of his not producing anything. Then she called and told him the co-op wanted to remount *Dreaming the Future*, and though he had doubts about their motives in asking him, he said yes, and it seemed that he and Phoebe might get back onto a good footing. But they had spent the last few months pissing each other off.

"Is Reg Bevaqua here yet?" I asked.

"No." Her eye shadow was a *trompe l'oeil* of twin butterflies. "He called this afternoon. He was looking for Jake's number."

"What?"

"Yeah, he wanted to get in touch with him. Maybe they'll show up together."

"Yeah, I don't think so."

But it was weird.

By then the long-haired guy in the suede jacket had moved on, and I walked into the party alone.

So this was The Ark. Jake had been in a few times to tour the place, but I'd never made it. Contrary to my earlier impression, it was *enormous* when you saw it from the inside, not built on a human scale but dreamed up to attract and house some supernatural power. The nave had been divided horizontally into three floors, except at the front, which was left open so you could stand by a plexiglass banister and admire the full beauty of the stained-glass window. Phoebe had told us that the church had had to be deconsecrated before they could buy it, and I looked over the banister and pictured a priest in a brocade robe walking up the aisle swinging an incense censer, chanting, the devil be with you henceforth. Not that I was religious, but wasn't it strange that they'd want to whisk all traces of sacredness from a building where people were going to continue to gather?

I heard music and turned to see a woman lifting a violin to her chin. And then I spied my busker from that afternoon! There he was, tuning up, his guitar case open at his feet. I drifted over, charmed that buskers had been invited into an indoor party and amazed that he was one of them.

"Hey, it's you," I said.

He flashed me a noncommittal smile. His teeth were obviously false. "What do you want to hear? I take requests. From my true fans."

He was old, the age of my grandfather. "You know that Peggy Lee song? 'Johnny Guitar'?"

With no preamble, he began to sing it in his plaintive voice, plucking a chord and adjusting his pitch up a little. His guitar case caught my eye.

Foreign coins were spilled across the wine-red velvet. I crouched to study them.

"Take something," he said out of the corner of his mouth during a guitar bridge.

So I did, holding it up to show him. A coin with a head like a Roman bust. *BRASIL*. He nodded in approval, and I slid it into the front pocket of my jeans.

The loft was filling up fast. It was dotted with thrift-shop sofas, and at the back stood a bar and a folding auditorium table displaying supermarket sushi and other room-temperature delights. Jake's big canvases hung on the walls, two to a side. I decided to get a drink before I checked them out, and I joined the bar line, trying to be unobtrusive as I scanned the room. I didn't really expect people to recognize me. When Jake and I were together in Toronto, I worked every night and was more of a rumour in his circle than an actual presence. I saw no sign of Reg Bevaqua. An ordinary-looking man, a little beefy, a little overdressed, his hair cut in a high fade, but you tended to notice him because of the hum of excitement that rose up around him. I began to wonder if the famous artist and the famous patron were both going to stiff the party.

Someone said my name, and I turned. A guy behind me in the lineup. His hooded eyes, the dark eyebrows that toggled at the bridge of his nose—I totally knew him, but from where? He gestured for me to step back and join him.

"So. A cash bar in a house of Our Lord."

I should have said, excuse me, who are you? but he was so casually familiar in his manner that I would have felt like an idiot. He asked me if I was just in from the country for the night, and I raised my shoulders in a shrug.

"Looks like you've got a pretty good thing going up there. You have an acreage, right, not just the restaurant?"

"You've eaten at The Grange?"

"As if. I Googled you a while back. You know, killing time at three a.m. So, Isla's moved into the ownership class, I said to myself."

Oh. Swim club, when I was sixteen, half my lifetime ago. I was still blanking on the guy's name but I could picture him with wet hair and goggles. He always made a point of sitting with me on the way to inter-city meets. The bus would be pushing through the morning dark on the 401, our teammates slumbering around us, and he'd be jackknifed into the seat with his knees as high as his shoulders, lecturing me on the exploitation of the workers.

"I'm carrying a third of a massive mortgage," I said, "if that puts me in the ownership class. And actually, the property's on the market right now. We don't plan to reopen this spring."

"Oh. Why is that?"

"Just—a lot of shit going down."

"Well, good," he said. "You can start doing something useful."

"People have to eat."

He flashed me one of his mocking looks. "Do they have to eat the way you feed them?"

What he was doing here?—I couldn't remember how the artistic class fit into his politics. We'd arrived at the front of the line. The bartender was pre-pouring beer into red Solo cups, and my old friend swivelled towards me. But before he could get the words out, I'd scooped up two beers, dropped a twenty on the bar with a quick *keep the change*, and dashed into the crowd. I paused only to offer a cup to my busker (who took it thirstily), and then I made my way to the left gallery.

Dreaming the Future. The first time I met Jake was the night, five years ago, when this show opened in a Bloor Street gallery. Four huge canvases, in which each subject's interior life hangs like a rich tapestry around them. Rachel Carson, Ayn Rand, Margaret Thatcher, and Eunice Newton Foote (a nineteenth-century scientist nobody'd heard of, chosen because Jake was still trying to defy his long-deceased father). To most viewers, these paintings suggest a classical inspiration, like Henri Rousseau's nude reclining on a sofa in a forest with its fauna and flora vivid in her dreams. But I knew it was not Rousseau who'd inspired them, it was a series of Annie Leibovitz photos. A fashion shoot from *Vogue*, Jake confided in me, one day early on, when we were exchanging embarrassing and even humiliating stories in the way you do to celebrate your trust in each other. "*Vogue?*" I said. "Annabelle had a copy," he said (Annabelle being a previous girlfriend). "She stole it from a spa."

Remembering that afternoon, the two of us naked on our sunlit bed, I felt my eyes burn. I perched on the upholstered arm of one of the couches, willing the tears not to fall. If we truly stepped into the chasm that had opened up between us, everything would have to be revised. Everything. Not just this show, but all our private moments. And I wondered what we would do with confidences like that, with that trust, whether, to escape the pain of our breakup, we would switch sides and join the ranks of the people who despised us for our secret failings. I sipped my beer and waited for my tears to subside. I was readying myself to look, to be disarmed the way I always was by Jake's work. Finally I got up.

Ayn Rand. She sleeps in a bedroom crammed with massive and opulent furniture, and on the brocade coverlet of her bed, a cigarette burns down in her fingers. She's lying in her dream, a world of towers. They rise around her like cacti in the desert, each tower with a solitary person visible in the balcony or window, isolated as on a pinnacle. I looked at her white face and felt chilled. Her skin is chalky, and her mouth, slightly open, made me think of a death-mask. Another figure crouches on her balcony, peering yearningly through the barred window. It's Ayn Rand herself, watching Ayn Rand sleep, at least that's the way I read it. I thought it was brilliant, I thought Jake's vision of her pernicious ideas, of her power and where it would lead, meant even more now than when I'd seen this painting at Jake's opening. I stepped back and ran my eyes across the other canvases. This was what struck me: none of these dreams were good. All of them were terrifying, the dreams of the figures Jake admired and the dreams of the figures he abhorred.

The lights dimmed just then, and the party shifted into a new phase. Music had begun to pour out of massive speakers mounted on the walls between the paintings, drowning out the buskers. I watched my busker stoop to lay his guitar in its case, and then I sensed someone beside me. The tall, long-haired guy I'd come in with. Instantly I felt better. We couldn't talk for the noise, but he gestured towards the paintings and touched his hand to his heart. Raw human voices poured out of the speakers and filled the loft, singing broken phrases. Not real lyrics, but something you might improvise in the shower. Their voices overlapped, and the sound was strangely powerful, like the shared intimate longings of everyone at that party. After a minute, the voices faded and instruments took over, and the guy put his fingers on my wrist and led me between groups of people into the middle of the room, where the bass and percussion thudded in my breastbone. He touched me lightly, turning me a quarter-turn, and a scream of electric guitar blasted my ears. It was eerie—we were standing at the border where two sound fields collided like weather systems. *Weird*, I mouthed. I was shaken by the size of him so close to me. Desire clattered through me. It broadsided me, that surge of lust when I was hurting so much about Jake, but there it was. I hadn't slept with anyone else since I met Jake, and I hadn't slept with Jake in months.

We pushed back through the music to the edge of the room and stood watching the party, and I tried to pull myself together, though it wasn't easy, standing right beside the guy. His height was *excessive*, I thought, though he held himself so as not to dominate. His face was bony but compelling—I thought he resembled the image on the Brazilian coin in my pocket. People I assumed to be tenants of The Ark had started voguing their way through the crowd. All wearing masks, spectacular papier mâché masks, fashioned with drama and cunning. They were animals, I saw, some decorated with glow sticks artfully installed as antenna or eyes or whiskers. Art could be this, I thought. It could be this happy celebration. My problems with Jake had weighed me down for a long time, and I was sick to death of it. We were like embattled *elk*, who might have given up the fight but couldn't split because their antlers were tangled. By getting on the train that afternoon, I had broken free. I could quit trying to imagine myself into Jake's head.

The long-haired guy and I stood and watched the party for a long time. We glanced at each other occasionally and smiled, and I found myself adjusting the negative space between us, not touching him, of course, but opening myself to the possibility. A tall woman in a charcoal dress stood in a group near us, and I realized that I knew her. It was Mary Attica. She was Phoebe's star client—her curriculum vitae featured the Venice Biennale—and she was by far the most prominent artist I had spotted that night. She must, like Phoebe, be on the board of directors. My companion knew her too, he reached out a hand and she turned. They stepped warmly towards each other and exchanged kisses. I had met her more than once with Jake, and she seemed to remember as she ran her wide grey eyes over me in greeting. Her greying hair was swept up into a knot, and she held herself like someone who felt the usual signifiers of modesty would be disingenuous and even disrespectful to her work. I knew how much Jake admired her talent, and I wondered whether her creative energy had survived the last few years, which had taken such a toll on his. She and the guy in the suede jacket began to talk, mouth to ear, as you had to in that space, and she kept semi-including me in the field of her vision—clearly she thought the two of us were together. By then the human voices had resumed, massed now into a churchless hymn, like the dirge sung by miners descending into the earth, and I heard them and realized that I was drifting in a direction

I was going to regret, and felt shocked at how mindlessly I had surrendered to that drift. I made an excuse-me gesture, lifting my empty beer cup, and headed for the bar, where I bought a shot of JD. This time the bartender gave me an actual glass, and I carried it over to the banister, and that was where Phoebe found me.

"Well? Is it awesome?" she said.

"It's lofty."

"It's down to you, you know. It would never have happened without you. I should make a speech."

"Oh, please," I said. "But what's up with Bevaqua?"

Phoebe made a helpless gesture. What event on Reg Bevaqua's calendar could mean more to him than a chance to soak up the adulation of a mob of impoverished artists? And Jake, I thought sorrowfully. He had very few chances to see his work celebrated. I lifted my eyes to the soaring dome, where wooden trusses arched like the limbs of an elm tree, and naked bricks held each other up in defiance of gravity, and I felt completely unmoored. This fateful day was about to end, a day in which I had declined to think and refused to plan, and I was baffled as to why I was here. I thought again of the farewell party Phoebe had thrown for us five years ago. It was October and chilly, but nevertheless we took our aperitif, a couple of bottles of Prosecco, up to the rooftop garden. The sky was indigo, smeared with bright clouds the exact colour of my skirt and jacket. Twelve or fifteen of us on the rooftop, the city laid out around us in the dusk. We raised our glasses, calling cheers, and I remember turning to Jake, and his face suddenly being unfamiliar to me. In that moment, I saw that I did not know him at all, I understood how profoundly I did not know him, and as I clicked my glass to his, I was as terrified and thrilled as you might be at the top of a bungee jump when you grasp the height of it for the first time.

Death metal warped around us now, a maelstrom of noise, and the crowd seemed to give itself over to it. Phoebe touched my arm and I leaned close to her, and her voice fluttered warmly into my ear. The only phrase I made out was "arrested development." For a second, I thought she was talking about Reg Bevaqua. Before I could react, the lights went off, all the lights in that huge vaulted room. The music buckled like a wall of bricks as darkness fell upon us. A single scream sprouted in the silence. The dancers with the glow sticks came into their own, scattered tableaux of blacklight theatre. The darkness felt alive with human energy. Shrill voices, nervous laughs. Acoustic guitar chords, mellow and warm. A rough old voice singing "Johnny Guitar."

In the distance, an exit light.

It was my chance to escape and I took it. Without a word to Phoebe, I darted towards the exit, weaving my way between dim clumps of partiers. I saw a corridor, I saw shadows moving along it, and I joined them. A lot of people were leaving, looking for the stairs. We found a spiral staircase of white-painted metal, and I lifted my phone and shone its light on the steps as we clomped our way down. I was slightly dizzy when I emerged into the ordinary noise of the street. People were laughing, looking around as if reluctant to end the night. Among this crowd was the guy in the suede jacket, and I felt the shining tug of inevitability.

"Anybody interested in sharing an Uber up to the north Annex?"

He didn't look at me as he said this, but I was not fooled.

"I'm going that way," I heard myself say. "But I don't do the internal combustion thing." This was more an aspiration than a fact, and I'm not sure why I said it.

He let out a surprised laugh. "How did you get here?"

"I walked."

"Want some company walking back?"

I was still clutching an empty bourbon glass. A low stone wall surrounded the church. I reached over and placed my glass on the ground behind it, and we set off up the street.

TWO

The Marxist in my swim club once told me a joke. Two young fish are swimming along a stream when they meet an older fish. "Morning, boys," the old fish says. "How's the water?" The young fish ignore him and swim on by. "What the hell is water?" one of them says to the other.

That joke was my only real take-away from those long-ago conversations on the swim bus. Back when I was sixteen, I got it, I vaguely knew I was one of those fish. But it takes a certain amount of distress in your life to break you out of your trance, doesn't it. Whereas Jake—he had a different relationship to the world than I did, I'd always known that. He knew it as dangerous, to him personally. So he paid more attention. Having a happy childhood (as I would say I did) is a huge gift. Assuming life will treat you well, that you can do what you want, that you're not going to be punished for simply existing and enjoying yourself—it's a gift, but it's still something you have to get past, if we consider consciousness a good thing.

I would call my parents countercultural—they didn't own a television or a car, they seldom ate meat, and we never travelled because, back before it was a thing for most people, they had a serious case of what Swedes call *flygskam* (shame of flying). But they were not exactly political. Their decision to home-school me, for example, was not based on ideology. They were just skeptical of schools, in spite of the fact that both had graduate degrees and were employed at universities. My mother was a researcher in mycology, spending her day bent over slides of moulds and mildews, or trays of yeasts and mushrooms, a job that suited her perfectly because she was always a little baffled by people. In grade nine she'd had to have her long black hair cut off because a bully sitting behind her in art class had scrawled white glue through it, an incident she frequently relived and tried to understand (He thought it was funny?). My father, an occasional lecturer in psychology, resented having squandered his youth, the years when his brain was a receptive sponge, in boredom and conformity. So when I was six and reading everything in sight, they let the Department of Education know they'd be responsible for my learning.

At the time, my father was working in a home office, so that was convenient for home-schooling, although he was mainly focused on writing a book and found it hard to deal with another sentient being even breathing in his space. It was fine, our house had lots of private corners. Turned out that, like my mother, I had the disposition of an autodidact. As I got older and could go out on my own, I became a haunter of libraries, a devotee of museums, an off-path explorer of parks, a curator of trivia, a voyeur of other lives. I loved many corners of the city, but two especially. On a cloudy afternoon, while police cars pelted up Bloor Street and an old woman cried out her story at a streetcar stop, I would cross the gorge into Rosedale, a thief stealing into the enclave of the rich. Up their silent streets I'd wander, under the ministering trees, past stone mansions with their turrets and dormers and gables and green-painted doors. Everything about those houses moved me. I thought of them as good, separate from the money that bought them. Gazing at their diamond-paned windows, I was gazing into the way people were meant to live, transformed by money into their best selves, mastering the Goldberg Variations on a grand piano, reading and speaking Italian or Portuguese, spiritually transported by morning sunlight falling through casements onto polished floors. And I adored Chinatown, where a medicine and diet and cosmology totally different from mine was laid out in trays—open-mouthed dried geckos, hairy nuts, red sand in vials, twigs sliced like brown-edged coins, all labelled with gorgeous and cryptic characters that I translated to mean *there is no way into this for you*. I'd hear people speaking Cantonese or Punjabi or Arabic on the subway, and feel a stab of pain, realizing I'd never penetrate that elaborate labyrinth of sound, and that furthermore, these were just a few of the thousands of languages I would never learn. It made me crazy, I ached for an eye that could take in everything. I understood why people invented gods. My world would widen and widen, but it would never widen enough.

I was a classifier of words, a collector of factoids, a secret pedant. There are details that gleam with a special light, and those are the ones I went after. I kept hardcover notebooks where ideas, sketches, diagrams, statistics, rants, haiku, etc., interbred promiscuously. My parents loved looking through my notebooks. "Isla thrives on independence," they always said. Did I? Let's just say I was shaped by it. I see myself sitting on a bench near a pretzel cart. The lunch crowd has drifted on, the pretzel maker stands sucking on a cigarette. A thin woman strides by in a business suit and Nikes, lost in her thoughts. They knew what it was all about, they knew their role in it. While I, invisible, sat watching them, wracked with longing. Knowing things from reading is a kind of knowing, but what are facts without a narrative?

Not that I can't see how lucky I was. I had a much better time than Jake, for example, whose dad was a federal cabinet minister, who went heli-skiing as a kid, who went sailing in the Caribbean and rambling along Las Ramblas, but who had to fight for every narrow millimetre of freedom to be himself.

When I was thirteen, we talked seriously about my going to real school. My father's book, *Too True: The Wonder and Terror of Conscious Living*, was published and my dad took a sessional teaching gig at the university. In the end, my parents left the decision up to me. I had friends from the neighbourhood, plus a few from the swim club I joined around that time, kids my age who regarded me with pity and envy and sometimes brought their homework over, dumping a welter of daily planners, reading journals, memos, thumb drives, inhalers, gel pens, and other school paraphernalia onto our dining table. My father would drift in and spend a few minutes interrogating them about their day, and their vacuous answers always re-radicalized him. I remember one night he put on Pink Floyd and we danced around the kitchen, singing out our aversion to school in the voices of Cockney children.

How could I deny my parents their little rebellion? I said I'd do high school on my own, and my parents made their first serious effort to work up a reading list. It moved systematically through history, focusing on a different century each semester. I was eager for the sixteenth and seventeenth (having seen *As You Like It* on stage and *Romeo and Juliet* on screen) but it was the fifteenth that turned out to be fateful. One day that spring, a book called *On Right Pleasure and Good Health* fell off the library shelf and into my hands. It was an English translation of a 1470 culinary treatise written in Latin. Its pages were full of delights. A recipe for hashish meatballs. A method for roasting quail eggs on a miniature spit made of a sewing needle. Every education has its lodestones, and *On Right Pleasure* was instantly one of mine. I started cooking dinner for my parents every night, correlating our meals to the historic period I was into. Food became the vehicle for everything: biology, botany, geography, chemistry, history, literature. I published my findings in a blog I called *Comestible*. When I was sixteen, I pitched a food column to a national teen magazine. I offered to create a monthly recipe with a lively sidebar tracing the provenance of its ingredients. To our astonishment, they picked it up, so then, like my father, I knew the excitement of casting my voice out into the world.

The June I turned eighteen, the Department of Education awarded me a high school equivalency certificate, overlooking the fact that a unified theory of life still eluded me. We planned a celebratory dinner out. I chose a tapas place on King Street West—its owner-chef Lionel Sheffield was sizzling hot at that time—and we reserved a table. My father ordered a bottle of white and a bottle of red, and my mother (who had spent an hour twisting her hair into a French roll for the occasion) made a speech. "Every generation is supposed to have things better than the last. That's how we define progress, that kids will be richer than their parents. That's not going to happen with you, Isla, because of the real estate bubble. But your generation has already surpassed ours in other ways. In empathy and respect for others. You have, you know, and we take no credit for it."

Cheers.

They were baffled by the menu. "Yikes," my mother said. "*Shiso. Koji. Teff.* I don't even know what language this is." She looked helplessly up at the server. "Isla here is a food person. I think we'll just let her order."

Our server smiled shyly. "Are you Isla Coltrane? I recognized you from your photo. I always read your column, and I always try your recipes."

So *that* was cool, like a drizzle of black truffle oil glamorizing the whole evening.

Our first dish was two beautiful honeycomb morels sautéed with shallots, which we meticulously divided into three portions. When it was time for the second, a pale, slight man wearing a toque appeared beside our table. Lionel Sheffield himself, a pioneer of the small-plate movement, offering us a personalized special! I had recently featured octopus in my monthly recipe, mentioning how, because of its sophisticated nervous system, the octopus was designated an honorary vertebrate in the UK and covered by the law forbidding cruelty to animals. "Nevertheless we eat them," I marvelled in my column. On the sea-green china saucer Lionel Sheffield placed before me, an octopus the size of a child's hand lay tangled, its suckers like rows of miniature snap buttons, garlanded with red (ginger) and green (seaweed). Sheff had prepared this dish as a compliment to me. He asked me to taste it and tell him what I thought. I sliced off a tender tentacle and identified a hint of smoked paprika, which had not been in my recipe. The dish was of course far better for it. Our eyes met in recognition. "Who are you cooking for these days?" he asked. I had been accepted at U of T, intending to go into science (though I didn't know what field), but that was the end of that. If my parents were disappointed, they never said so to me.

I worked at Sheff's for six or seven years, first in prep and then as a line cook. During those years, the small-plate craze took over the city, but Sheff maintained his place as the king of the innovative hors d'oeuvre. His kitchen was a true subculture, populated by maverick figures who rarely infiltrated the daylight world. I held my own, and I learned technique from Sheff, and continued writing my column until the magazine (which had a quota of youth columnists) cut me loose. But that very month, a literary agent approached me about shaping my food writing into a book. We dreamed up the idea of *The Omnivore's Alphabet*, using some of my columns and a bunch of new material. We featured whole foods (*Abalone. Bulgur. Chanterelles.* Not *Aioli. Biryani. Cannelloni.*) For the letter O I wrote a new piece on olives because I had watched a documentary in which an octopus dismantles the water filtration system in its tank, and also turns a light off and on for its own amusement. What I knew in my head about the octopus suddenly moved into my gut, and I regretted ever having placed this fantastic creature in the context of the human diet. *X* was the tricky one, of course. What would I have done without *Xoconostle*, a prickly pear cactus from which you can make a delicious sour salsa? My agent found a publisher, and they commissioned an illustrator, and *The Omnivore's Alphabet* came out just before Christmas the year I was twenty-two. It was spun as a playful romp through the gardens and forests of the world, the hot gift for young foodies, and I did some TV spots and made a bit of money. Did it whet my ambition for more success/attention/fame? Not really. It made me think, okay, Isla, you've got that out of the way. Now you can do whatever you want.

I moved to my own apartment, and in a gesture of independence from my parents, I bought a TV. I really had no idea what I wanted, and so I just kept cooking for Sheff. Too long, probably. I guess this was partly because of my childhood isolation, which left me feeling somehow outside the conversation. I stayed because the sit-down staff meals we had before opening were the fun hour of my day (family dinners, we called them), and because our wordless camaraderie on a busy night was as exhilarating as playing in a band, and because the travel Sheff arranged for me, the internships I did (in Manhattan, in Cumbria, and in the Madrid kitchen of one of his friends) were opportunities anybody in the restaurant industry would kill for. I was still with Sheff when he sold the restaurant on King and set up a low-overhead catering business so he could sock money away for his next enterprise. I got my driver's licence so I could drive the van, and I was in charge the night we catered an event at the Galbraith Gallery on Bloor, the opening of a show by an artist named Jake Challis. "Isn't he a politician?" I asked the first time Sheff mentioned the opening. "No," Sheff said. "That was his dad. Jack Challis was a cabinet minister, he's dead now. The kid is only about thirty. There's a lot of buzz about this show."

I had dated an artist the year before and found his world interesting, so after a winter of doing corporate gigs, I looked forward to this one. Walking into the gallery to get our buffet set up was a little like stepping into the pages of a lushly illustrated children's book, but I didn't have time to really look. I met the gallery manager and got the portable grill going in the service room, and once the servers were circulating with platters of seared scallops and satay beef and those tiny lamb chops with their own obliging handles, I picked up a plate of mini-samosas and started circulating as well. Sheff was not technically working the event, but he had come to work the crowd, dressed in the bespoke suit he brought home from a trip to Hong Kong and a bolo tie he'd picked up at the Calgary Stampede. I ran into my old boyfriend, Zolan, who greeted me with the same detached fondness I felt for him. Scarfing down samosas, he told me about his new project, digital collages of Tinder profiles. Two of his friends joined us and talked enviously about the impending announcement of a huge art prize, for which Jake Challis was considered a front-runner. Near the entrance, dressed in a black suit with a dark grey T-shirt, his straight dark hair parted in the middle, the artist himself held court.

The minute the rush was over, I grabbed a chance to take in the show. Four huge oil canvases depicted influential figures and their dreams. The first was the naturalist Rachel Carson. She lay in a bed of ferns, her sleeping face both somber and luminous, and birds filled the sky. Jake Challis's style was not what I knew as hyperrealism. It was almost impressionistic, dabs of transparent colour guiding your eye to areas of the canvas that were immaculately detailed. The scene was tender, it had an interior radiance that suggested the world was good. But what seemed to be a pool of brackish water near the bottom of the canvas was really a welter of bird carcasses. I didn't see this at first, but then I did, and my eyes stung. In the beautiful articulation of the birds' feathers was a world of loss.

I turned to move on and there was the artist himself—in fact, he was watching me intently. It was as though we had stepped into the antechamber of each other's unconscious mind. I wanted to say something about the picture, but his face was filled with so much emotion that I just gestured towards the painting and said, "Thank you." He said, "No. Thank *you*. I saw you checking it out. I just—"

He paused, and before he could go on, someone else was there, bringing him a drink, and that was that. But for the rest of the night, I was entirely tuned to Jake. I knew where he was at every moment. I was taken with his listening posture and the quickness of his expressions. When, around eleven o'clock, the energy in the room shifted and the joy went out of it for him, I knew. The crowd thinned, the last of the stragglers drifted out, and as we cleaned up, I was aware of Jake standing in deep conversation with an attractive woman with long hair bleached to platinum. When I stepped into the gallery ten minutes later, he was alone.

"You're not out celebrating?" I said.

"I'm on my way. I had to talk something over with my agent."

His agent. She looked like a buyer for Saks Fifth Avenue. Whatever, she was gone, and he was still there, holding my eyes warmly.

It was absurd to think he might be waiting for me. But I went into the service room, where Charlie, one of our crew, was packing up the grill, and said, "Want to drive the van back to the warehouse and do the cleanup?"

"*Cool*," he said, deftly catching the keys.

I had a nice jacket with me and I threw it on over my uniform skirt. Jake was in the foyer now. He did not try to disguise his pleasure at seeing me ready to leave.

"I'm walking over to meet my friends at the King's Head," he said. "Do you feel like coming?"

We set off up Bloor Street. The King's Head was two blocks away. It had rained during the show, and car lights wavered like spilled paint in the puddles. We walked fast and without speaking. Jake was good looking, but it wasn't that—I had to remind myself not to stare as I tried to work out what it was that appealed to me so much. Most people would assume the attraction between us was sexual. Well, yes, of course. But not only. We came to the corner, and his friends were crammed against the windows in an alcove of the pub. They were watching for him, they jumped up and mimed an exaggerated welcome. We stepped into a lineup, and in the brief privacy of the entrance, between two sets of doors, Jake looked right into my eyes and said, "You know—it's great to have this show, but I'm never sure people get what I was going for. I've kind of stopped seeing the paintings myself. And then I watched you take it in, and it was like you gave it back to me."

Oh, it was a moment. It's the premise of a romance novel, isn't it, the celebrated artist and the serving girl. Of course, there wasn't really that sort of gap between us. The instant connection we felt—there were reasons for it.

Right from the start, we were amazed and amused by a hundred tiny coincidences. Jake had grown up in Rosedale, though not on one of the streets that had so fascinated me when I was young, and now we lived just one subway stop apart (well, he didn't live anywhere, but the studio where he crashed was a few blocks from my apartment). He had worked as a waiter at our major competitor's, Belgard, while he was painting *Dreaming the Future*. We shared a passion for a weird old British television series called *The Singing Detective*. We both ate honey with our grilled halloumi, we both played Go, we owned the same brand of bike, we adored a Talking Heads concert video from our parents' youth. I was charmed by the fact that we both had a naked baby picture of ourselves on display, and it began our years-long debate about the difference between ironic and post-ironic. When I told Jake about my amazing little terrier Plato, he claimed his childhood dog was named Socrates. And amazingly, my new boyfriend knew and loved my father. Jake did not go to art school until the year his own dad died of a heart attack (these two things were not unrelated). Before that, he did two years towards a humanities degree at U of T, and his first psych class was with my dad. He enjoyed it so much that he read my dad's book, enrolled in two of Dad's courses the next year, and declared a double major in psychology and English. He shared my enthusiasm for my father. We were identical twins separated at birth!

I'd been in relationships before, of course, but never felt like this, crazy-sensitive to everything in the world, my nerves lit up like fibre optics. No doubt Jake's work was part of what turned me on. Darwin had dominated my nineteenth-century reading list. I knew about the male satin bowerbird, and the elaborate courtship bower he builds, chewing up a certain kind of berry that makes a blue dye and using a piece of bark like a brush to paint the floors and walls. He is ecstatic at the prospect of love, intoxicated, and it all comes out in art. There's no adaptive advantage to this enterprise—except that female bowerbirds really dig it.

I asked Jake when he'd made the decision to go into art, and sure enough, it had something to do with a woman.

"The summer my dad died, I met a girl who was applying to fine arts. She was working on a portfolio, and I didn't have a job that summer, so I started doing the same thing. And then I got in and she didn't."

"You literally never thought of yourself as an artist until you met her?"

"No."

"But you said you always used to carry a sketchbook around."

"Honestly, it wasn't the fact that I drew or painted. That was just something dorky I did. Like, I don't know—being super-fast with a Rubik's Cube. Art was more—it was what I saw and how it made me feel. I would take the canoe out around the bay in Lake Huron where my grandparents' cottage was, and poke along the shore, and just be in a daze. It was like a drug or something, I would see this whole new meaning in everything. I'd lose all track of time, and then I'd come home a little embarrassed, as if I'd jerked off in the canoe or something."

"Maybe you did."

"Oh, probably, sometimes."

One afternoon I took the subway out to Parkdale to talk to my parents. My mother was in the backyard, digging up her begonia roots, and I reached in to help her knock the dirt off them and told her about Jake's show. While other artists were programming animatronics, I said, or mapping out bee dances, Jake was painting pictures that people felt they understood, pictures that thrilled you with their beauty even as the story they told might break your heart. Without the slightest hesitation,

I used the word *love*. "It's like, I fell in love with him for his art, and he fell in love with me in the same instant. For my reaction."

I could tell she didn't like this. "Sounds like it's all about him," she said.

"No," I said firmly.

"Well, it's a danger with an artist. That's all I'm saying."

I saw where she was going. "He's not narcissistic," I said, "if that's what you're thinking. A narcissist will never be a good artist. They only see themselves, they never really see the world." This was something I had been figuring out in my mind. "The night of the opening—it wasn't just that I told him I loved his work, and so he was flattered. Everyone tells him they love his work! It was that I really *saw* his work, the truth he was going after, and he was drawn to me because that truth matters to him. It wasn't just that I got his meaning, intellectually. I *felt* it, it hit me really hard. And he could see that."

"Alright," she said steadily. "That's wonderful."

I stayed for supper and we talked some more. My dad remembered Jake as a student, and they were curious about Jake's family, because of course they knew who his father was, the industry minister who poured so much into oil sands development. Jake had told me quite a bit about his dad, who he always called *Old Jack*. Old Jack was a petroleum engineer who did his graduate degree at Penn State and was working for Exxon in the US when Jake was born. They came back to Canada when Jake was about six, and a year or two later, Old Jack ran for parliament and won his first election. As a kid, Jake was dragged door to door in all his dad's political campaigns. My parents tended to mingle only with their own kind, and the son of a Conservative cabinet minister seemed very exotic to me.

"He must have grown up talking politics," my dad said.

"No," I said. "They never talked politics, because there's nothing to debate. People on the left are soft, or lazy, or crazy. Deluded, dangerous.

When Jake was ready to go to university, his dad could only accept two careers for him, law or business. So Jake didn't go to art school until after his dad died."

My dad said, "No doubt Jack Challis wanted his family to be role models of conservatism. Demonstrate a good work ethic and, you know, reap the rewards."

"No," I said. "I think he was just a controlling prick."

We were carrying dishes to the kitchen just then, and my mother put her platter down and reached out to hug me. "Well, Isla, I wish you every joy," she said. And then I felt like a total idiot because, come on, I had known him a month.

It was a very sweet fall. Jake did win the Hubbard Prize—it would support him for several years. We met up and went for a celebratory cycle along the lakeshore. I remember the sun pouring yellow light onto the lake, and sculls from the rowing club snagging up the surface into satin pleats. We stopped and bought souvlaki from a food truck and sat to eat it on a slope under a maple tree. Tzatziki oozed out of our folded pitas, and we let it fall in gobs on the mat of red leaves. Jake had shoved his sunglasses up to the top of his head, and in that light his eyes were greenish blue with shards of brown in them. I took in his sockless feet, his bony ankles with sparse and wiry black hairs, his worn cycling shoes that (I knew from watching true crime shows) had a tread-wear pattern as distinct as a fingerprint.

"Maybe you'll be able to afford some new shoes now," I said.

"You think?"

"How long have you had those?"

"I bought them at Marathon on Spadina on April 22, 2008. About four in the afternoon."

"What?" I laughed.

"I had an exam that afternoon," he said. "In your dad's course, Deviance and Conformity. It was a brute, but I did okay. I respected your dad for how hard his exams were. It was my last one, and after I handed my paper in, I cycled over to Marathon and treated myself to new cycling shoes. The clerk was really pushy, and I almost walked out. Instead, I left my old shoes on the floor under the chair in—you know, a petty gesture of defiance. Then I cycled home. My mom met me at the door to say that we needed to go to Ottawa. My dad had had a massive heart attack in the foyer of the Parliament building. At four-thirty that afternoon. So, just as I was cycling up Spadina in my new shoes."

He said all this quite matter-of-factly. After a minute he slid down and lay with his head in my lap. Above us, huge leaves arranged and rearranged themselves, playing with the light. I ran my fingers over his hair and forehead and cheekbones, tracing the moving shadows.

"It was one of those days," he said. "You remember every single little thing about it, and you always remember the date."

That day, the day we had souvlaki on the lakeshore, was September 27, 2014.

THREE

Lionel Sheffield's charisma was a bit of a mystery. He was skinny and hairless and monochromatic, his eyes such a pale straw-green that they were basically no colour at all. The night we celebrated my high school grad in his restaurant, I saw keen interest in those eyes: I was the eager young acolyte he'd been waiting for. I was eighteen then, and I took him to be in his mid-thirties, a hard-living thirty-five-year-old. In the two weeks between the night he made his way to our table with a platter of octopus in his hand, and the day I showed up in his kitchen, dressed as instructed in kitchen blacks, a romantic dream seized hold of me, in which wise mentorship blossoms into love, as it often does in novels.

It took me a week in Sheff's kitchen to get that he was gay (well, I didn't get it, people finally got tired of watching me make a fool of myself and told me). It took me another week to stop feeling like something had been stolen from me. But it took me only a day to realize that he looked at everyone who worked for him with keen interest and even delight, and as I hand-julienned a mountain of carrots, hour after hour, the orange sticks threaded with my blood, I began to wonder bitterly whether he actually knew us apart. Oh, the little tricks I played to get him to notice me! I cooked him rare treats, I sought him out with ideas and gossip, and deftly he stepped aside from all of it. "You hired me under false pretenses," I complained once, trying to sound like I was joking. "I thought you thought I was special."

"Everybody here is special," he said.

I never knew him to offer an opinion on anything other than food and the restaurant business. I never knew him to read a book or a magazine or to talk about a film. In those days, I had no idea where he lived, or who he lived with, or what he did during the day. Once he left his driver's license on the order desk, and I was astonished to discover that he was *fifty-two*. He wasn't old for his age, he was just old. He gave you so little of who he was that when the breeze blew the curtains apart and you glimpsed something behind them, that private information glowed like the Ark of the Covenant. Yet somehow his unwavering privacy freed him to give you his whole self. As he taught you to fillet a fish, he was completely present. In the perfect economy of his gestures, in the way he read and responded to your doubts and hesitations. You could tell how fully he inhabited his body just by watching the grace of his feet. Focus is the salient quality of a chef, he told me. Thirty orders will come at you in ten minutes. It's all timing, it's all choreography. You're as absorbed as a high-wire juggler, you have the muscle memory of a figure skater. You can't let anything break your trance.

I listened with my whole self, because I wanted to be good at it but also because getting food right seemed like getting life right. And of course, I still yearned to be special to Sheff, I yearned to be trusted. Eventually, I realized I was both. Everybody else drifted on, or he fired them for cutting corners, or for being moody and prone to rage, or for not showing up, or for showing up drunk or high, or (in the case of a line cook named Leonard) for being observed *licking* a steak just before plating it. But I hung in, and with time I was the one in charge when he took his long winter holidays. I was sometimes restless, but I stayed because I hadn't learned all he could teach me. But still, mastery and boredom were always duking it out. People come back to you over and over for the thinness of your veal saltimbocca, and for the Marsala deglaze you drizzle over it, and they don't appreciate you changing it up. I'd be pounding my hundredth saltimbocca for that week, and I'd think about my Uncle Peter, my dad's younger brother, who went to meditation retreats where he would sit on a cushion eight hours a day, reciting a mantra and moving dried peas from one dish to another. Occasionally, he promised me, you broke through the soul-destroying tedium and into bliss.

When I turned twenty-five, the pastry chef made a fig and orange cake for me and the whole staff stayed after cleanup to get me drunk. Make a wish, they said as I blew out the candles, and I yelled, "I never want to make another fucking saltimbocca as long as I live." The next day, Sheff called me into his office and showed me the website of a business he had visited outside Boston. That was when I first heard about his dream, a farm-to-table restaurant in the country, open only in summer, serving a *menu complet*, different every night. A premier restaurant where we could serve food grown on our own land. This dream had consumed him for a long time—he named the restaurant "The Grange" before it actually existed.

"What do you think?" he said. "Want to be my partner?"

"Why do you want to move to the country?"

"Because real estate is cheaper. And it makes dining an event for city people, having to drive out to a rustic setting. You pair with a farm. Everything you serve is fresh."

"You still plan to serve meat?" I asked, because that was a conversation I was having more and more often with friends.

"Yes," Sheff said. "Animal protein has been a staple of the human diet since humans swung through trees. It's all about producing it in a healthy and sustainable way." As I turned this over in my mind, he added, "You can charge, say, $150 a plate with wine pairings, and work like a fool for six months and lie on a beach for the other six."

I asked him if I could think about it for a few days, and an hour later, I went back to his office and said yes. The money from my book was pretty much untouched. We decided I'd be a one-third part-owner, Sheff two-thirds. Sheff's ambitions might have been fundamentally commercial, but this enterprise was never about money for me. The Grange seemed like a solution to questions I was asking myself at that time. It promised not just novelty but challenge, and excellence, and beauty. It promised right pleasures and good health. I was acquainted with the joy that kicks in like a drug when you create something, when you take what is mundane and crack it open to reveal its brilliance, when you add to the daily stockpile of human good. I had experienced it, but not often enough. Here was the promise of more.

In the months when Sheff and I began to look seriously for property, I was absorbed in getting to know Jake. I worked most evenings, and our typical date was not a noisy bar but a one a.m. assignation at my place and a slow, lazy morning, baked apple pancake in my kitchen for breakfast. Or Jake would meet me at closing and we'd walk over to his place and spend the night there. My apartment was more comfortable, but I loved going to his studio. It was on the third floor over a barbershop on Spadina, in a block full of art studios. The building wasn't zoned for occupation, but you saw a lot of its tenants smuggling bags of groceries up the stairs. They cooked in microwaves, slept on judo mats, and their cats prowled the hallways. Jake kept his personal things in stacked-up plastic Coke crates and had a wooden storage cupboard for art supplies, but these systems were inadequate and, in spite of his best efforts, had pretty much broken down. I loved the clutter, the rolled-up posters, brushes standing in clay jugs he had made himself, easels, stretched canvases propped against the walls, and prints and sketches tacked up everywhere. It thrilled me to look at his work.

He had a huge blank canvas leaning against a wall. He said he stretched it the day the movers took *Dreaming the Future* out of his studio, as a gesture towards *his* future. Other than painting an undercoat of a colour I would call "celestial," he had not put a brush to it.

I had learned from Zolan, my old boyfriend, never to ask an artist what their work is *about*. "Can you already see what it's going to be?" I asked instead.

"To an extent," he said. "But that doesn't mean much. If you can envision it, can you therefore create it? That's what I haven't figured out." He lowered himself onto his mat and gestured towards the blank canvas. "Maybe I'll just show it like that," he said. He went on to tell me about an art show in Paris in the 1950s, an exhibition that exhibited nothing. It was called *Le Vide*. Attendees stepped through a blue curtain and milled around in an empty gallery and were served cocktails of Cointreau and gin with a shot of methylene. They gazed for an hour at nothing, and then went home. A thousand people came. It was a sensation.

"Methylene. It turns your pee blue."

"Yes!" he said, impressed that I knew this. "They peed blue for a week, and I guess that sustained their excitement about the show. What is art, right? It makes my work seem really conventional."

He had tacked up studies of the figures in *Dreaming the Future*, done in acrylic on paper. It was news to me that artists did that sort of preliminary work, like experiments in a test kitchen. Of the four subjects in the show, the only one I'd never heard of was Eunice Newton Foote. Jake said that John Tyndall was always called the world's first climate scientist, but Eunice Foote was actually five years ahead of him in establishing that CO_2 traps heat. She experimented with CO_2 because she was trying to explain the past—in the Eocene, when the earth was so hot, was it because the atmosphere had more carbon in it? In Jake's painting, she is dreaming about the future, the ice shelves melting, and Jake said he sometimes worried that using Eunice Foote in this series was a stretch because there was no evidence that she ever extrapolated to the actual effects of burning fossil fuels in the industrial age.

"Well, that's the prerogative of an artist, isn't it?" I said, studying the image. Eunice Newton Foote has fallen asleep with her head on her work table, with beakers of CO_2 in front of her. What she saw, what it meant—it's all there, in the slump of her shoulders.

"This is the painting I wish my dad could have seen."

I already had a sense of the narrow line Jake had walked, trying to please and trying to defy his dad at the same time. "Was he proud of how talented you were?" I asked.

"No." Jake lay back on his mat. "But maybe I got the last word on that one. When he was dying, I was sitting by his bed and I found myself drawing him. Like, just mentally making a sketch. I've always felt shitty about that."

"I thought he died on Parliament Hill."

"He had a massive heart attack on the Hill. He was walking through the foyer of the House when he collapsed, and there were tons of people around, and they did CPR. But he was clinically dead for at least five minutes before the paramedics arrived. Maybe ten. He didn't have a pulse. Then they took out cables and jump-started his heart. It's pretty bizarre. Who knew you could restart a heart after that long?"

"Scientists can get a recently excised pig's heart to beat in a glass beaker. It's made of what's called excitable tissue."

"Really? Well, I guess that explains it. They kept him alive for three more days." *Alive*—he made air quotes. "But eventually, the doctors were not seeing brain activity, and they asked to take him off the ventilator. And then he kept on breathing. Until late that night. I was sitting with him when he died. Or, when he died again."

"You were alone with him?"

"Yeah. Everyone thought he was stable, and my mother went out for a break."

"Wow. That must have been hard, Jake. You were, what, twenty?"

"Yeah."

This was early days for us, we were still feeling each other out. I wondered how often Jake had talked about that painful experience. I wanted to ask him more, but I couldn't read his expression—he looked almost defiant, like he was daring me to ask. "You must miss him," I said, chickening out.

He made a scoffing sound. After a minute, he said, "I wish I could say, 'Congratulations, Dad. Your plan worked.'"

"What do you mean?"

Jake had been sprawled on his mat, and he got up and walked across the studio to a work bench, and leaned against it. I sensed he was going to share something big with me, a shameful confession of huge proportions. His dad had been charged with fraud, maybe, or sexual misconduct. "You might not have followed the politics closely," he said, "but my dad was one of the main mouthpieces of climate denial in the 1980s. He worked for Exxon on their disinformation campaign. Then when he went into government, he kept up the good fight. Tar sands development, fracking. Lots of government subsidy for the industry. He knew what was coming, they all did, and he wanted to make sure we creamed off all the profits we could while we still had time. When I caught on, our relationship was, well, I guess you would call it broken."

I was astonished by this. You never actually consider individuals making these sorts of world-altering decisions, people you almost know. "How old were you when you figured this out?"

"Thirteen, fourteen. I was in junior high."

He told me how in science they were learning about greenhouse gasses and their impact on climate, and he sat in class feeling superior to the teacher, because his dad was a petroleum engineer and a politician, and he knew the real story of climate change, the way liberals and socialists were exaggerating the threat in order to put regulations on business. He decided to pick a science fair project that would refute what he was learning in class. He started researching and he was soon terrified by what he learned, and ended up doing his project on permafrost melt in the Arctic. He built a model of Arctic lands in a huge aquarium, placing crushed ice under soil and volcanic rock, inserting tiny temperature sensors at different depths. Then he set a heat lamp on one side and charted the melting trends and the sinking of the soil. He displayed photos of the crazy lopsided sinking of Gold Rush buildings in Dawson City. He researched and charted the release of methane gas as permafrost melts.

He met my eyes and made an enough-about-me gesture. "I'm guessing your science fair project was on pig hearts?"

"I didn't go to school, Jake."

"Right, of course."

"So, how did your project do at the science fair?"

"Got top prize. Second at the regionals."

"Hey, you super-geek. What did your dad say while you were working on it?"

"Nothing, he was in Ottawa. He came home the day of the fair. I was pretty excited—I guess I thought we would have a conversation about the ideas I had put together, and that he would actually be proud of me. And he hardly spoke to me, he was all cold about the prize. It's crazy. I was so freaked about it all—freaked because it seemed that the way we saw the world, the things my family believed, what my father said in public, that it was *wrong*. I guess I was still hoping he could resolve it all for me. But it must have looked to him like I was challenging him in public, and then my main feeling about winning was shame, about pissing off my dad. Isn't it bizarre, that I was the one feeling ashamed?"

"At the time, did you think your father actually didn't know the science? Or was that when you realized that he knew, and he was misrepresenting things on purpose?"

He thought for a long minute. "I remember being hurt that he just looked at my display board, at my model, but he didn't read the text. He didn't ask me a single question. At the time I thought—okay, so he knows more about all of this than I do. But I couldn't quite see how both of us could be right. I guess I was like a lot of people are right now, you know, knowing it's true but hoping it's not. Eventually, it was clear to me that he was never interested in the facts. The ideas he spouted were based on something else. Not on science. He and his cronies had a system that was working spectacularly well for people like them, and they weren't going to change it, no matter what it cost. And now, of course, it's come out that those oil and gas dudes knew all about the effects of CO_2 for decades, and worked hard to gaslight the public."

So much contempt in his voice when he talked about his dad! It didn't make me think he had left his dad behind, exactly the opposite. My own childhood felt so simple in comparison to his. I mean, the future is scary as fuck for everybody, but it was kind of baked into the conversations in my home. We talked about it a little but not a lot, as befits very hard matters of mortality. Then we carried on, and that was a kind of security. Only take on a problem if you feel you can solve it, might have been the thinking. I felt awe for the kid Jake had been, a kid who didn't make things easy for himself.

In that moment, sitting cross-legged in the smell of linseed and turpentine, I saw love as a dark door I had to enter. But it was open, and I didn't question for a moment whether I was going through it.

FOUR

It was hard to think of leaving Toronto just as this astonishing thing was happening between Jake and me. But the new restaurant would be shut down from October to April—maybe the two of us could get a place together in the city. How could he not welcome a rent-share, given that he'd have it to himself all summer, given that he was currently sleeping on the floor and cycling to his mother's house to shower?

The fourth property Sheff and I looked at was in the little town of Adlington, a perfect distance from Toronto—close enough that its golf course and stables drew people from the city, but far enough that driving there you might end up behind a tractor taking its time on the highway or a straw-hatted Old Order Mennonite man with a horse and buggy. No fast-food chains, by municipal decree, and only one restaurant: Steve's Casual and Fine Dining, where each laminate table had a rotary file of jokes and riddles to get you through the wait. Adlington was vintage rural Ontario: baskets of petunias dangled above shop doorways on the main street, hydrangeas tumbled over the steps of red-brick houses, and kids played on the road in front of vinyl-clad bungalows on the edge of town. A pretty creek ran along its southern boundary, and on the bank of that stream stood the house we immediately called The Grange. Big, beautifully-proportioned, built out of limestone from the region. In 1876, by a railway magnate. Its two additions, a sunroom and a conservatory, had been carefully designed to preserve the house's symmetry. Its brick basement would make a wonderful pantry and wine cellar. Its morning room, dining room, library, and salon had the original casements and ceiling coves. Beautiful arched windows everywhere. We'd have to put in a commercial kitchen and bathrooms, but the dining areas were in wonderful shape. "You just give these floors a quick refinish, and you are good to go," said the agent.

Sheff and I followed him up the wide front staircase. The current owners had very little furniture. I spied signs of children, not plastic squalor but homemade things, a kite, a skateboard. The master bedroom had been turned into a classroom with three old-fashioned desks spaced out across it. On the ceiling the kids had tried to paint a luminous solar system with the ceiling light as the sun. I say tried, because I knew from my own efforts as a kid that you can never get it to scale. They'd also painted murals of fantastic animals right on the walls. "Who are these people?" I asked the agent, feeling an instant affinity.

Kurt and Annalise Altenbach, he said. They had immigrated from Germany about ten years before. They bought the house and the land next to it, a thirty-acre hobby farm, and started an organic CSA (Community Supported Agriculture) business, every week heading into the city in their truck and dropping crates of produce on the doorsteps of their subscribers. They also sold honey, eggs, sausages, pickles, preserves, and produce from a roadside kiosk. But they couldn't make a go of it. They had a huge mortgage and they'd defaulted on it. It was sad, he said. They were good, hardworking people, and they gave it their best shot.

I don't think the organic nature of the enterprise mattered to Sheff, except as a marketing angle: he had an instinct for trends in the zeitgeist he could take commercial advantage of. But the quality of ingredients in your mouth was important to him. "Do you think they'd be interested in running the farm for us on a contract basis?" he asked as we stood in their kids' classroom.

"I could sure ask," said the agent. "If you feel they are the right fit. They're still here because the bank hasn't seized their assets, the livestock and machinery. I guess everyone agreed that a working farm would make the sale more attractive."

Sheff and I stood looking at each other in silence. We were doing the math. Sheff's goal was one hundred diners with fifteen square feet per diner, spacious enough to allow for private conversation, close enough that diners felt like they were having a shared experience. This property offered almost two thousand square feet of useable space in four rooms. It was perfect.

The agent read our expressions. "Let me show you something that's going to seal the deal," he said, leading us back to the staircase.

The back of the house opened onto a terrace. Beyond it was pasture enclosed with a rail fence, and the original barn, made of unpainted vertical boards with a fieldstone foundation. And then the little orchard, and the pond, and the green ridge of the escarpment. The terrace would be stunning for pre- and post-dinner drinks.

"We'll need a stonemason," Sheff said. "We'll need a landscaper."

"Live music," I said. "Alvvays."

"Millennials don't have the money to eat here," Sheff said.

Okay then, we'd have Carlos Montoya pouring out of a speaker under a wisteria trellis. I didn't care. I loved everything I saw. Sheff and the agent went inside, and I stood on the terrace for a long time, picking up whiffs of manure from the barn and watching a flock of mallards settle on the pond.

If you can envision it, can you therefore create it?

Three days later, Sheff and I sat in a realtor's office in Guelph and signed the papers. I was only twenty-six. I was immensely proud to be able to write a cheque for a one-third share of the down payment: the money from my book, some current savings, and fifty thousand dollars my parents gave me, money they had put aside for when I wanted "to settle down." My parents invited Jake and me over for dinner to celebrate.

I was uncharacteristically nervous, leading Jake into my parents' living room. I saw things I rarely noticed: the scraggly and dying plants on the windowsill, the coffee table strewn with newspapers and journals fanned with yellow sticky notes. I hadn't met Industry Minister Jack Challis's wife yet, but I was fairly sure her hair was not grey-streaked and pulled into the ponytail that had worked well for my mother and Jane Goodall for forty years, that she did not exclaim *yikes* two or three times in every conversation. I hoped Jake would look past that to her unfailing kindness and her forthrightness. I so wanted us all to be okay with each other. Strangely, Jake was nervous too. He had an intent expression I'd never seen on his face before. It was a revelation to me, that lack of confidence, and I wondered if my parents' hearts would go out to him for it, or if it would make them distrust him.

My father greeted him with unusual friendliness. "I wasn't sure you would remember me," Jake said. "Your classes were huge."

"You wrote the best student paper on Jungian symbolism I ever read," my father said. Jake's eyes met mine, and I understood that he had never written a paper on Jung. Yet he did not correct my father. I opened my mouth to say something, but he gave his head a minute shake.

We poured the wine Jake had brought and sat in the living room. My parents had gone to see *Dreaming the Future*, and my mother told Jake warmly that she loved it. She said, "I thought the pictures interacted in interesting ways. The way nature is depicted, or not. Ayn Rand—there's nothing alive in her picture, is there. Except the people in the towers."

"That woman saw nature as humanity's foe," my dad said.

"So Rachel Carson's nightmare is Ayn Rand's dream," my mom said.

I could see how pleased Jake was with that observation. The Malbec was excellent. Evening light came in through the blinds and lit up the dust along the edges of the hardwood floors, but I knew we were going to be fine. If my parents would only back off.

"Have you started a new project?" my dad asked, leaning back and crossing his ankles.

Poor Jake, he was helpless in their hands. "I prepped a canvas, but it turns out it's not big enough. I find myself picturing a frame about three stories high."

"How would you paint something that big?"

"I'd have to build scaffolding. I don't know where I would do it. I need a studio with a higher ceiling. I'm like Isla these days, all I think about is beams and joists and load-bearing walls."

He was trying to pass the conversational baton to me, but my mother was having none of it. "In the meantime, how do you spend your days?"

"Trying things out in my sketchbook. Thinking. Well, *thinking* . . . I'm not exactly thinking. It's more a matter of staying open. To, I guess, a vision. If that doesn't sound too grandiose."

"I can't imagine it. Weeks of waiting for inspiration. Standing and staring at a blank canvas."

"I've got a wrestling mat in my studio. I don't need to stand."

"Great metaphor," my dad said.

"Actually, dreaming up metaphors takes up the biggest part of my day."

"Such as?" my mother had to ask, although I knew her to be incapable of grasping metaphor, the way some people are colour-blind.

"Well, yesterday I pictured tying a rubber tube around my arm, and palpating the muscle." Jake demonstrated. "Like, trying to find an artery I could drain."

"Yikes," my mother said.

I couldn't take any more. I jumped in and invited them to raise their glasses to my new venture. This property in Adlington had everything we had dreamed of and more. The house was gorgeous, the farm had an organic certification, and there was a little pond that we hoped to stock with trout. "Beehives?" asked my mother.

"Why not?"

"Will you serve meat?"

"Yes, we will," I said. "Our cattle and pigs and sheep will wander the fields in happy consort, no antibiotics and no avermectines polluting their flesh. Fungi will flourish on their dung and earthworms will feast in it, aerating, fertilizing, and hydrating the soil. As for the flatus, we will feed the animals angelica and shepherd's purse so they don't release as much methane."

"Flatus?"

"Farts, a layman might call them." I had spent the last two weeks reading, nurturing my vision. We were going to be part of the new wave of omnivores who want their meat rare, wild, and gamey. More woke than the vegans, part of the animal world, living by the law of the tooth and the claw.

My father went to the kitchen to put the finishing touches on something he called Cajun stew, vegetables and pulses simmered in the slow cooker to the colour of desert camouflage gear. I dressed the salad and sliced rye bread from the corner bakery. "We are just lost without Isla," my father said when Jake and my mother came to the table. "She looked after Christine and me throughout her childhood. We called it home-schooling."

I told them about the home-schooling family in the big house in Adlington. The Altenbachs, who I still hadn't met, had begun to seem like the key to everything. I loved that they were European. I saw them walking behind a plow, cultivating land as a spiritual practice, just like their ancestors in the Middle Ages.

"Sheff and I are going up to meet with them on Wednesday," I said. "They're still living in the house, so we have to make up our minds about each other fast."

Jake knew the country around Adlington. It was on the way to his grandparents' cottage on the Bruce Peninsula. I had no intention of taking him along when I drove up for the meeting—I didn't want the distraction—but, strangely off-balance at my own family's table, I found myself turning to him and smiling invitingly.

"Hey," he said. "I'd love to."

"You could make a day of it," my mother said. "Stop at one of the lakes."

"Gracie Lake," Jake said. "I'm a big fan of Gracie Lake."

When I arrived at the farm on my own, having dropped Jake down by the creek, Annalise Altenbach was out in the little orchard with five or six pigs moseying around her. She was wearing work boots and shorts, although it was late fall and not a warm day. Her hair was eccentrically braided into eight or ten pigtails, all pulled back into a single elastic. Her features were straight and perfect, and in the direct way she looked at me, she dared me to be superficial enough to think of her as beautiful. I remember feeling sad as I approached her: Sheff and I represented the failure of their dreams. I caught on fast that she did not need my pity and did not even notice my sympathy. Her life was her own to live.

Between the orchard and the pasture was a rail fence, and in the pasture five tan cows and three white sheep grazed, the friendly beasts from a nativity scene resting through the off-season. Annalise had led the pigs out to the orchard to clean up hazelnuts that had fallen from three nut trees. The pigs entranced me. They were black with beige saddles. I could not stop admiring those dapper and athletic creatures as they feasted on the windfall that crunched underfoot, their piggy tails expressing their joy at living their best lives. A month ago, Annalise said, these pigs had cleaned up the fallen apples.

"That's very cool," I exclaimed. "They are part of your labour force."

She smiled, showing perfect teeth. "So are the chickens," she said.

"The chicken coop is on wheels, and we move it around the pasture so the hens can help keep the grasshoppers under control."

A pig paused to greet me, and when I reached down, it put a mobile, intelligent snout to my palm, like it was reading Braille. "What's this cutie's name?"

"We don't name creatures we will one day eat. Well, perhaps the children do."

"They are *so* handsome."

"And they are tasty," she said. "You will taste the nuts and the apples in the meat."

"Seriously?"

"*Du bist was du isst.*" You are what you eat, I guessed. "This saying applies to our animals and it applies to us."

"We have so much to learn. I have to say—the fact that this property has an organic farm attached to it, well, that was really what sealed the deal for us."

"It doesn't." Her voice was matter-of-fact.

"What?"

"It has a farm, but the organic certification is in our name. It takes years to get certified, and the certification doesn't automatically transfer with the sale of the property."

She did not in the least try to be nice about this, and I grasped that she was someone who said what needed to be said and let her listeners deal with their own reaction.

Clearly, the stakes were high for us to work out a quick partnership.

Sheff had driven to Adlington with our lawyer and our accountant, so we were six at the meeting that morning. We sat in the room the agent had called "the salon," around a table that was actually a big door on saw horses. Kurt Altenbach was a match to Annalise in his classic good looks and self-possessed manner, although I thought he was more wary, as if he was holding back—well, who knows what he was holding back? Annalise did most of the talking for them, while he sat watching us intently with orange-brown eyes. His legs were crossed and his feet were encased in rudimentary calfskin elf shoes I thought he must have made himself. When Sheff or I spoke, a sardonic smile would chase across his face, as though we had revealed far more about ourselves than we intended. We talked through the year-round work of their enterprise: the planting and tending and harvesting of the gardens, the making of preserves and pickles, the curing of meats. Annalise said, "Kurt can augment your menu with foraged foods. He spends a lot of time on the escarpment. He's learned where to find mushrooms and berries."

Kurt spoke up then: "Lake trout. Clams. Frogs. Grouse. Deer."

Sheff and I had not talked a lot about *wild*. Our eyes met.

They had brought their tax returns to the table, and we worked through their expenses line by line. We were close to the end when Annalise pitched the possibility of running a garden stand through the summer. "You will have a hundred city people driving up every night," she said, "and we will send them home with produce for their week."

Sheff nixed this idea. "It's not a good fit with our business model. I hope the terms of your contract will make moonlighting unnecessary. How do you assess your labour costs? Annually?"

The accountant was paging through the tax forms, looking for a salary line. Annalise glanced at Kurt and named a sum so low that we stared at her, confused.

"For both of you?"

She raised her shoulders slightly.

"I think we can do better than that."

Kurt spoke up. "And the children?"

"What do you mean?"

"What would you pay the children?"

"We won't be hiring your children," Sheff said. "It's contrary to labour laws."

Kurt received this thoughtfully, a novel idea that would have to be unpacked.

When I texted Jake, he said he was in a park on Armitage Street. I drove over to pick him up. It was a playground, actually, and he was sitting in a swing. "Do you want to take the tour?" I asked as he walked to the car, and he said, "Yes. But let me show you something first." He directed me up a street lined with rusting maples, and we stopped at *his* discovery of the day: a house with a For Rent sign in the window. A small bungalow in Adlington's burbs, vintage 1965, encased in mushroom-coloured siding. "I tracked down the owner," Jake said. "She agrees it's not much to look at, but she offered to plant some hollyhocks in front in the spring." We got out, and Jake bent over beside the front steps and retrieved a set of keys hidden under a rock. He did not lead me to the door of the house but around the back to another building. It was giant, and it had a high overhead door like a garage. But it was not a garage. "She calls it a shed," he said.

We went in through a side door. The shed was lit with a skylight and smelled wonderfully of wood. It was a carpentry workshop! "It's not three stories high," Jake said. "But it's a heck of a lot higher than what I currently have." He walked towards the back and then stopped suddenly and turned around and smiled at me. His joy was tangible. It was like a huge bird with coloured feathers; it filled that whole sunlit space.

JAKE

FIVE

Annie and Letitia, Jake's two favourite people from art school, took him out to celebrate when the Hubbard Prize dropped into his bank account out of the blue. Annie was co-owner of a paper shop in Scarborough and was still tangentially part of the art scene because her shop sold hand-made paper and unique greeting cards. And Letitia now taught in an art program for inner-city children. They congratulated Jake extravagantly and ordered drinks, and then sat looking at each other, lost for chat. This was the bar they had frequented in art school, eight or ten years ago. "Do we presuppose the sanctity of aesthetics when we confront the hegemony of subjective constructs?" Annie said, and they laughed.

"Is that how we talked?"

"I don't know," Annie said. "I have no fucking idea. I wouldn't be able to write an artist's statement now to save my life."

"Me neither," Jake said. It was true, it had all fallen away.

"Didn't you have to write an artistic statement for the prize?"

"No."

"What did you have to do?"

"I didn't apply."

"You didn't apply? They just *gave* it to you?"

Alright, this was not a good start.

"Tell us about your new girlfriend," Letitia said, to pull things back. They had both met Isla at the pub the night of the opening. Annie had had a thing for Jake back in art school, so he tried to play it cool.

"She's a really interesting person," he said.

"*Interesting*." They laughed. "*Person*."

They loved that Isla was a chef, they saw her job in a different light than Jake's mother did—Barbara had once referred to Isla as "that waitress." Annie and Letitia both claimed they wished they had gone into food. The sensuous pleasures. Ritual, community, comfort, making people happy, keeping people healthy—it was all there, it was a sort of alchemy. Knowing how to make real custard. How to debone a chicken. Plating—plating was art.

"She was home-schooled," Jake said. "And she's never been to university. So she's got a unique way of looking at things, like I guess any autodidact. I love talking to her." They continued to find him funny. "We talk a lot," he insisted, "and it's like—we're always going back to first principles."

"Are the colours I see the same as the colours you see?"

"Do dogs have souls?"

"Are vegetarians allowed to eat animal crackers?"

"You guys are fucking hilarious." But he felt their affection.

"So what does she think of the politics of your show?" Letitia asked.

"You mean—"

"What does she think of you turning your male gaze on female subjects?"

Honestly, he hadn't been prepared for how big this was for everyone. It's not like he made a conscious decision, I am going to paint women. He started by painting his dad's heroes, Margaret Thatcher and Ayn Rand, thinking about the sort of world they wanted. That what we deplore is what they yearned for. Then for the counter point of view, was he going to paint Noam Chomsky? David Suzuki? Bill McKibben? Rachel Carson came to mind, dreaming in a wilderness on the verge of vanishing. She was so poignant to him. The dreams of men were always going to be tainted by unearned power. Her outsider status—it did not feel alien to him, he felt it viscerally. He almost said that. He was smart enough not to say it, but just barely. "We don't choose our subjects. They choose us," he finally said.

"Lucky you," Annie said.

"He *is* lucky," Letitia said. "He's a lucky, lucky, lucky dude."

"You think I love being known as Jack Challis's son?"

"Jake, being known as Jack Challis's son is the *least* of it."

They were right. Was there any way for him to paint the world without plundering it?

The afternoon before his opening, he'd run into David Stonechild outside the Ontario Arts Council offices where, Jake assumed, Stonechild was on a granting jury. He was Cree, the director of a gallery in Winnipeg. He wasn't a practising artist, but he was a wonderful writer and everybody cared what he thought—his criticism was fresh and incisive and it pointed a way forward. He was also a really nice guy. After they'd chatted for a bit, Jake invited him to the opening and David said that he had been planning to come.

That night when Jake first spied David Stonechild at the Galbraith, he was talking to someone Jake recognized but didn't know personally—a U of T art prof. Phoebe also noticed this conversation and swiftly positioned herself to eavesdrop. The U of T prof asked Stonechild what he thought of the show, and Stonechild said mildly that Jake Challis seemed to be having an argument with his father. The U of T prof quoted that line by Audre Lord about the master's tools never being adequate to dismantle the master's house, and Stonechild laughed, seemingly in agreement. When Phoebe made her way back to Jake, she was reluctant to report what she'd heard, but he forced her to. She tried to convince him it was nothing to worry about, but this exchange landed heavily with Jake. Not because he was afraid David was going to write about him, panning the show, but because he instantly understood that David Stonechild was right.

How deliberately he had made friends with the most outspoken leftists in his class when he started art school. He had to make sure no one questioned his politics. His old friends (Reg Bevaqua and company) had vanished in a puff of smoke. His new friends were zealous and scrappy, they had high hopes of changing the way people thought. They saw art as a project in identifying neoliberal constructs, naming them, draining them of their power. All a little cerebral, compared to the emotions that drove Jake. His friends had their progressive irony, he had his visceral wrath. How many of them had witnessed the prime minister stand up and say about their father, "We owe Canada's position among oil-producing nations to this man"?

Just like that, hearing David Stonechild's words second-hand, Jake realized what he was up against. How hard it was going to be. Can you critique the colonial-capitalist-racist patriarchy you were born into? You can't do it. You can't see except through the eyes you were given. You will speak with the intonations learned at your father's knee. You may acquire different vocabulary, you may say different things, but you'll never lose the accent.

He visited the Galbraith three times before the show closed, every time for media interviews. He had to live with the fact that he attracted more attention because of who he was. He wanted to say to journalists, "I'd love to talk to you, but this is not about my father, okay?" Phoebe advised against it. She said it would just excite people's curiosity. Every interviewer asked some version of "What would your father have thought about this show?" Jake's usual response was "I learned never to predict what my father was thinking" (a total lie. His father was nothing if not predictable). But what *do* you talk about? He was mortified at being asked to explain his paintings, their "meaning." As for aesthetics, well, the elements in his work that people remarked as beautiful—either the beauty made him a little sick, like he was in love with his own artistic gestures, or it came from somewhere entirely outside himself and he didn't want to focus on it and smudge it with his narcissism.

The whole thing set up a brutal cage match between his ego and its dark twin, self-loathing. He didn't really realize how bad it was until the day of his TVO interview, when the makeup person sat him down in front of a mirrored wall and brought the tuft of her foundation brush towards his face, and said, "What is this, hon?" It was a raw patch between his eyebrows, just above the bridge of his glasses, not as big as a nickel but bigger than a dime. Without being aware of it, he'd been picking at his brows again. This was a throw-back to middle school, when he'd scratched all the skin off not just his brow ridge, but also his elbows and behind his ears, mindlessly fretting at a body that hardly seemed to exist. When his parents noticed, they tried every incentive to get him to stop, first taking away his allowance, then his TV privileges, then his skateboard. Finally, they sent him to a counsellor named Mrs. Whitmore, an art therapist. She said that whether you drew well or drew badly did not matter in the least to the work they would do together, but she discovered that he drew very well, and she was the one who encouraged him to start carrying a sketchbook around. She had a Yoda figure on a shelf, and she encouraged Jake to channel Yoda as a benign guardian when he felt tense. "Screw up we all will," Yoda was supposed to say. "Kind let us be to ourselves and each other." Her theory was that Jake picked and scratched at himself as a pre-emptive punishment whenever he felt he had disappointed his parents. Mrs. Whitmore's cringey Yoda impressions aside, what she said made sense—although (as Jake realized now) he excoriated himself just as much when good things happened as when he fucked up, and he couldn't recall her ever explaining that. But the kindness part was good advice. After he got home from TVO that day, he gently washed off his makeup and put a small round Band-Aid over the worrisome patch to keep his fingers off it.

In sum: he was rotten at self-promotion and it was hard on him. Phoebe said, "You seem eager to debrief all your doubts when you talk to media. Try to suppress that impulse, okay? Confess to someone else. Your girlfriend."

•

Isla, with her deep blue (almost indigo) eyes and her transparent face: she was not at war with herself. If she saw something as good, she did it. She never thought about the impression she made on people. She was so unselfconscious, it was dazzling. She would stare at you as wide-eyed as a kid. She watched you because she was interested in what you were thinking and feeling, she wanted to figure it out. She was curious, self-affirming, she lived in the real world. And her father turned out to be Jake's beloved psych prof, Dr. Paul Coltrane! How amazed Jake was when this came out. He thought of Dr. Coltrane quoting Sigmund Freud: "Show me a normal person and I will cure them." And there was Isla, his own daughter, beautifully defying her father's science.

When Jake was nineteen, did he realize he was idealizing his psych prof? Maybe not, but he remembered everything the guy said. He quoted Dr. Coltrane, examined his own daily life in light of his theories. Dr. Coltrane tried to be precise in his thinking and speech. He did not appear competitive, his drives were intrinsic. He was courteous to his students, gave them the sense that they were his peers in inquiry, without pandering to them. Didn't play power games. Never tried to be hip, a hint of which would have poisoned everything for Jake. Seldom talked about himself, so that when he did, you hung on to every word.

One of Dr. Coltrane's rare stories from his student days was about being in a drama workshop when someone came to the door and announced that John F. Kennedy had been assassinated in a motorcade in Dallas, Texas. All morning the group had been improvising scenes based on prompts, and they received this assignment gravely. People cried out in disbelief, some began to sob, one guy declaimed theatrically about the absurdity of human existence, one girl fake-vomited into the wastebasket. Then somebody came in with a transistor radio, and they heard a journalist reporting from outside the hospital in Dallas. It had actually happened! They were slammed silent with the shock and just picked up their things and headed heavily for home. "What we identify as *feeling*," Dr. Coltrane said, "is to a large degree culturally determined and performative."

Jake probably wrote that line down. For two years, he scribbled down pretty much everything Dr. Coltrane said, imagining that Dr. Coltrane noticed and approved. During class discussions, he sketched. He came across an old notebook with a drawing of Isla's father and showed Isla. She was entranced. "It's him, but it's also somehow ... George Clooney," she said.

Now that Jake had met Isla, his reverence for Dr. Coltrane had only deepened. So it was a big deal to go to the Coltrane home the first time. When Dr. Coltrane got up to shake his hand, Jake felt a rush of love but also pity. He could see that time had begun to screw his old prof over: he was a shaggier, saggier version of his previous self. The living room was an extension of Dr. Coltrane's office and of his mind. Books were piled on the floor to armchair height. On the walls hung photographic prints of the pioneers of psychology and psychoanalysis in their childhood or student days. The prints were ironic and reverent at the same time: Freud as a five-year-old with his hands in his suit pockets. A boy with a hatchet—Jake thought he might be Alfred Adler. A woman with a skull tucked under her arm, men brandishing swords around her. "Karen Horney," Dr. Coltrane said, looking at Jake knowingly from under the awnings of his unruly eyebrows. Was Jake supposed to know who Karen Horney was?

Isla's parents had both seen *Dreaming the Future*, and they talked about it at embarrassing length. Dr. Coltrane did not praise the show, but he had paid very close attention to it, which was even better, right? Dr. Coltrane did not invite Jake to call him "Paul." He treated Jake with exactly the reserved warmth he'd displayed the few times Jake stopped by his office. That was fine with Jake, it was good. Of course, for all the obvious reasons, Jake remembered Dr. Coltrane way more clearly than Dr. Coltrane remembered Jake. Or he thought he did. But apparently other stuff had crossbred with those memories. Over dinner they started talking about how every generation has its *Where-were-you-when* moment, and this inevitably took them to the day John F. Kennedy was assassinated in Dallas, and Jake said something about Dr. Coltrane having been in an improv workshop when it happened. "Lad, I was eight years old in 1963," Dr. Coltrane said, not amused.

Jake and Isla rode the subway home. A concert or big game was just getting out, and they ended up sitting across from each other. Isla leaned her head against the window, resting in a little pod of well-being. Jake sought out her eyes as they approached Bathurst, and she met his with a smile but didn't make a move. So they got off at Spadina and walked up to his studio. He had never gotten over the thrill of having a studio, but he would always by choice go to her place. He might be living in his studio, but still he tried to protect it as an artistic sanctum, thinking of Picasso, who said he left his body outside the atelier the way Muslims take off their shoes before entering a mosque. But here Isla was, casting his quilt out over his wrestling mat, and how could he not be glad?

They'd been sleeping for a couple of hours when a vein started ticking like a clock in Jake's ear and woke him up. Instantly, exchanges from the dinner party returned to him, more pungent with chagrin than when they had actually happened. His incoherence about his work. Dr Coltrane calling him *lad*. The exit light over the door of his studio laid a thin red film over everything: it was the nocturnal off-gassing of Jake's shame.

He rolled to his back. And then out of nowhere, or maybe because he had been telling Isla about it, he was thinking about his dad, about the night he died. About being alone with him. Jake was playing the big man when he encouraged his mom to take a break from his dad's bedside. Go back to the apartment, take a shower. It was awful after she left; the horror-film sound of his dad's underwater breathing entirely filled the room. Jake pulled his chair as far back from the bed as it would go. He sat for maybe half an hour, looking at the figure lying on that bed, trying to comprehend it as his dad. He saw a woodcut of the scene. He saw a cyborg laid out on its back, skin waxy and white, sparse black threads stitched into the lower rim of his eye sockets for lashes. The product of a botched medical experiment. Or something that had never lived. And then it opened its eyes. They were fixed on something in the middle distance, galvanized by a thought. The head came up, turtle-like, and then fell back on the pillow. The eyes were still open, white and pale blue. The body forced out a breath, and then another. And then it didn't.

Jake stood up, astonished by the silence. In front of his eyes, life drained out of his father's white face exactly the way air drains from a balloon. In less than a minute the face was grey and wrinkled and fallen in on itself, like a dried mushroom. He stood and watched this amazing deflation, and terror overtook him. He backed away and went quickly to the door and opened it, closing it carefully behind him. He stood still a moment, his heart thudding, and then he walked in his new cycling shoes down the empty corridor to the nursing station. No one was behind the counter, so he followed the corridor to a room where three nurses sat around a table, eating salads from Styrofoam takeout containers. They raised their heads. "I think Dad might have died," he said.

As he lay on the floor of his studio, the pain of that long-ago scene filled him. He was twenty, and he'd acted like a fucking child. Not going over to the bed, not saying something comforting, not taking his dad's hand—surely any human being is entitled to a gesture of love as they die? And then afterwards, not reaching over to gently close his dad's eyes the way they do in movies, not using the buzzer to call the nurse, but instead just running away and leaving a body alone in a room a casual cleaner could have walked into. No doubt there were ancient rules about leaving bodies alone. In witnessing a death, he had moved into the realm of ancient rules. He had demonstrated that he was not up for it. Even what he said when he found the nurse: "I think Dad might have died." *I think*, when he knew for certain, so that he and the nurse made the long walk back to his dad's room in silence, she not wanting to say, "I'm sorry for your loss," because she didn't know whether the patient was actually dead. He was such a piece-of-shit loser. He rolled onto his side, and then the realization that had comforted him more than once through the years came on like a light inside him: it didn't matter. In the silence after his dad's last breath, no one saw his fear. No one was there to see it, or to judge him for it. *He had been alone in that hospital room.*

And now he was not alone. There beside him in the red light lay Isla, breathing softly in creaturely oblivion. The quilt had slipped off her shoulder and he pulled it back up, and eased his arm under it and over her sleeping body. His hand found her breast. He savoured the softness of her skin, he felt the nipple take shape. She stirred and he lifted his head to find her mouth. She smelled of sleep. This is fucking criminal, he thought, pulling her closer. She has no idea what she is taking on.

SIX

Jake and his mother went back to Toronto the day after Old Jack died, and Jake's two older sisters and one brother-in-law and two nieces arrived. A lot of people came to the house, including journalists, and his mother brought in a caterer. In the week before the funeral, the family moved around in a shaft of light, perfect versions of themselves, standing gracefully at the centre of every scene, actors who until now had always played extras in Old Jack's court. When the condolences and reminiscences flagged, his mother would say brightly, "So, have you been up to the cottage yet this spring?" or "Susan and I managed to get orchestra seats for the opening night of *A Chorus Line!*" and he learned how grateful people were to be released back to the ordinary world. Wine and whiskey flowed. At times he sensed a tenderness in these gatherings. They had all weathered an ordeal together, not (he thought) Jack Challis's death, but the life-sapping ordeal of being friends with him. "You are so lucky to have your big son with you," people said, and his mother said, "I know," and looked at him with a new warmth.

It would all be over in a week, and he'd start his summer job. *Not* the job Old Jack had lined up for him in his parliamentary office, emailing him to announce it, saying, "Nine sharp every morning. No special treatment," to which Jake replied, "Dad, thanks anyway, but I don't think I'm cut out for your office." Then came the formal job description, salary, forms they needed him to fill out for a security pass, etc. That email had been sent by his dad's assistant, so Jake wrote her back and copied his dad: "Thanks for all this, Natalie, but as I mentioned to Dad, it's not going to happen. I'm working as a consultant this summer for Revco International, doing an environmental assessment in the oil sands." Wow, it felt cool to write that! Revco International, the consulting firm where his friend Reg Bevaqua was working part time and summers so he could get into business school. Back in January, Reg told Jake that Revco had landed a huge contract with an oil company wanting to expand in the Alberta oil sands and needing environmental assessments done in order to secure a permit. "Revco's taking on summer students to do all the sociology shit," Reg said. "Up at Fort Mac and in the communities around. You'd conduct interviews about the impact of the expansion. You'd have to travel a lot." It was beyond perfect. It hinted at a possible career path, and it would stick in his dad's craw like nothing else, Jake serving the ends of the environmentalists and regulators. Because *of course* the report he would write would ultimately condemn the expansion, how could it not, and Jake would have played a role in quashing oil sands development. Pouring drinks for his dad's cronies in the days before the funeral, being plied with the usual questions about what he was up to, it struck Jake that he should have a start date by now. He didn't actually have a contact name at Revco. Reg had said, "Just give me your résumé." He tried to follow up just before exams, but Reg said, "Don't bother, it's a lock." But he should have heard by now.

The day before the funeral, Jake was looking out the living room window when Reg pulled up in his Trans Am. He went outside and they faced each other in the driveway, and Reg gave Jake's shoulder a little shove, and said, "What the *fuck*." Reg never had any idea how to behave. A lot of people were surprised the two of them were friends, which was (Jake thought) obnoxiously classist. Jesse Ketchum Public School drew kids from both Rosedale and from Upper Jarvis, where Reg, son of a car salesman, had grown up in a sagging row house. When Jake and Reg were kids, the ravine was a magnet for them, a no man's land between their two neighbourhoods, where they mucked around in Yellow Creek, made like they were tracking coyotes, spied on lovers, smoked cigarette butts. Reg didn't give a shit about a lot of the things Jake had to worry about, and it was a kick being with someone bigger, meaner, more reckless. The real question was why the Challises were so generous, taking Reg on family holidays, paying his way. Your sisters have each other, his mom would say, and it's no fun for you on your own. (You're too much of a brat on your own, she meant.) But still. Jake didn't want to be an obnoxious classist himself, but he knew that if he took Reg into the living room now to mingle with the crowd, he'd end up being embarrassed by Reg's aggressive overtures to his parents' friends.

"Come up to my room," he said.

In the bedroom, Reg went straight over to the bed and sat down. Jake took the desk chair. Laughter rose from the living room.

"That crew is taking it hard."

"They're all still here," Jake said. "They all dodged a bullet. One in four extroverts dies of a heart attack by sixty. Males, that is."

Reg stared at him, his mouth slightly open, and then he bowed his head and said, "Shit. Shit. I don't believe it." He was *crying*. Jake sat there stupidly, not getting it for a minute, that Reg was crying for Old Jack. He was crying hard. He cried the way he used to cry as a kid, like the time they were nine and climbed the garage roof at his place, and Reg gashed his leg on a broken eavestrough.

Jake got up and pulled a handful of Kleenex out of the box on his desk. He handed it to Reg, and said, "You okay, bud?", trying to judge the best proximity and posture to express concern without embarrassing Reg. "He was one of the greats," Reg struggled to say through his sobs. "He was like a father to me."

When it seemed the tears were subsiding, Jake said, "We need a drink." He went down the back stairs, musing at Reg's choice of words. At Old Jack's last political campaign, Reg had canvassed three polls, and in his victory speech, Old Jack called him up on stage to join the family and described him as "a force of nature." Terms like that were cherished at Jack Challis's old Toastmasters Club, the club little suck-up Reggie had joined last year.

By the time Jake came back with two beers, Reg was calm and had wiped his face dry. He gave Jake a wry smile and took the beer.

"Corona Light?"

"Best I could do without attracting my mother's attention."

Reg took a long swallow. They sat without speaking for a while, and then Jake asked Reg about his house. Facing the massive tuition of an MBA, Reg was nevertheless buying a house! The plan was to furnish it and rent out rooms to pay the mortgage. His voice a little hoarse, Reg filled Jake in on his progress. He had decided he would only rent to girls.

"Rhianna Telford moved in last night," he said. "You know her, right?"

"You're running a soc experiment," Jake said.

"No, I'm setting up a harem. I've got one room left. It's great, it's on the main floor. I could make an exception to the gender rule. You want to move in?"

"I don't know. I'll think about it. I'm going to be out of town a lot, right?" He meant with Revco. The research in the north.

Reg said, "Right, you're going to Ottawa."

"What?"

"Although, I guess—you won't still be going to Parliament Hill?"

"I was never going to the Hill. Where did you get that idea? The Revco job—I thought it involved travel."

"*Oh*. Yeah. No. That job. They took on somebody else."

"What?"

"Yeah, they hired a guy from York. A master's student in public policy or something."

"When did this happen?"

"I guess a few weeks ago. I haven't seen you, dude."

"Fuck. You told me it was a done deal."

"I guess you should have followed up."

"I *tried* to follow up. I asked you who to call. You said, no, no, it's all good." Reg just sat there, letting it roll off him.

"You're *really* an asshole, you know that?" Jake said. "I mean—Christ." He got up and went downstairs, leaving Reg alone in his bedroom. He tried to head for the back door, but his mother caught him in the kitchen and sent him out to say hello to a great-aunt who had just arrived. Following her through the dining room, he thought, at least *He* doesn't know I fucked this up. A while later, he looked across the living room to see Reg moving shamelessly on the minister of finance.

It was a huge funeral. The prime minister and his wife and other members of the cabinet filed in just before the family and sat in a reserved section. Everyone stood for the invocation, and while all heads were bowed, Jake pinned his eyes on the image of execution by torture hanging behind the choir, finding it (as always) philosophically repugnant but aesthetically compelling. Five hundred mourners sank into the pews at the amen, their little coughs and the rustle of their suits making a mighty cacophony in the rotunda. Jake, in his black suit and newly polished shoes, walked up three steps and across a thick carpet to the pulpit to read, "To everything there is a season," delivering a close to flawless impersonation of a confident adult. He had rehearsed the shit out of that reading, he knew the text by heart, and as he delivered "A time to cast away stones, and a time to gather stones together," his eyes fell on his high school friends, a group of them, Reg, Noah, and Jason, sitting in the same row in the suits they'd bought for high school grad, all looking soberly at him, and his voice faltered a little. But otherwise he did fine. In the endless reception line, Jake stood between his sisters and handled it like a pro, although he was aware the whole time that in not being a slouch, he was giving Old Jack something he'd refused him for years.

The prime minister. "It's uncanny, you're the spitting image. Jack Challis will never be gone as long as you're here. And now you have a family history. You make sure you talk to your doctor about it, son."

He was the third person that week to threaten Jake with a heart attack!

The prime minister's wife, with her kind face. "I am so sorry. A thousand joys, a thousand sorrows."

A little break in the lineup, and Jake said in a low voice to his sister Sarah, "What's she talking about?"

"It's a Buddhist saying. It's supposed to be *ten*. In every life, ten thousand joys, ten thousand sorrows."

From his other side, his sister Ellen murmured, "I guess the real trick is to know the difference."

Three days later his sisters left. People stopped coming, and the shaft of light moved on. The only flowers left from the funeral were two baskets of waxy purple leaves. Jake and his mother and his uncle Ron went up to Ottawa and emptied out the apartment. They stayed in a hotel. Old Jack had rented the apartment furnished, so it was only his personal things they had to deal with. All the takeout containers that he washed and saved, the tubes of hemorrhoid cream, the dusty stomach-acid pills on every surface. A DVD of the Three Tenors. A stack of crime novels. Michael Crichton's *State of Fear*, a well-worn copy of *The Fountainhead*. The enlarged photo of twenty-five-year-old Jack Challis with Ronald Regan, taken at a trade event when Jack worked for Exxon in the US. Three framed copies of that photo existed, as far as Jake knew. Two laptops, the personal one Jake had helped his dad set up, and an old clunker with a built-in CD-ROM, engraved *Property of the Government of Canada*. Someone should have claimed that one, it was crazy that they hadn't. Jake took it to his dad's assistant, who was cleaning out the office in B Block. Natalie had months of work ahead of her, preparing Jack Challis's papers for archives. Jake stood by her desk and thought, I'll never be here again. His mother would usually chat by the hour with Natalie, but that day she didn't want to linger. She said she'd had enough and wanted to go home. The next morning Jake woke up in his own bed and realized the summer was upon him.

He thought about Reg a lot in the days that followed. How tight they were in middle school, when they lived on their skateboards, on Pizza Pops, on *The Simpsons*, when their favourite slur for each other was *Micropenis*. The Monopoly games, a gang of them sprawled around the board on someone's rec room floor from noon to midnight on weekends, the savagery ramping up, grudges forming that poisoned the whole next week. You'd be standing at your locker and someone would stab you in the side with a geometry compass and say, "Asshole," and you'd know what it was for. He thought about Comstock Cove, his grandpa's cabin on the Bruce where he and Reg inhabited a parallel world for weeks in the summer, avoiding the adults as much as possible. They slept in the tent, they travelled by canoe. They built their own fires, they hunted with bow and arrows or the pellet gun, though all they ever shot was gulls. The cave they found just beyond Prospect Point, narrow, dank, and solemn, was a gift that thrilled them and spooked them. They aspired to overnight in it, maybe one night they would. They were explorers, spies, guerilla fighters with mud caked on their faces. Crouching on cliffs, jumping each other. One summer Reg laid an expert tripwire across the trail they always ran down. Jake could still feel the brutal surprise he felt as he crashed to the ground. It was always hard to distinguish terror from exhilaration. Them against the world, them against each other.

In high school, Reg started working at Burger King, and the summer trips ended. They didn't hang out as much in the years after, but the closeness was there. Reg's offence this spring, the thing about the job—it was a betrayal like the tripwire, but worse: this was the real world. This was the end for him and Reg, and that was a good thing. Jake told his mother that the job with the consulting firm had fallen through, but he didn't mention how Reg had screwed him over.

"We can look after you for next year," she said. *We*. She was sitting in the den with the TV off. "You'll need to fill the summer somehow, though," she said after a minute. "Every spring my mother had someone in to wash the walls through the whole house. It was something they always did when she was young, when they had coal furnaces, and the walls would get covered with soot. You don't need to do it these days, what with natural gas, but my mother kept up the tradition."

Jake got up and went to the wall where a print Barbara had bought in Portugal hung. He slid the frame to the side to reveal the inverse shadow on the paint.

"Oh, my goodness," she said. "Well, that's from all the candles we burn at dinner. My mother never lit a candle in her life. Except on birthday cakes." She had dark hollows under her eyes that her makeup could not cover. "Your dad used to say spring cleaning was something Protestants did instead of Lent. You know, he had a lot of insight. There is so much about your father that you won't get a chance to see. A child needs to be about thirty before they begin to know their parents for who they really are. I'm sorry you won't have that opportunity." He could tell she was digging deep, or making a speech she had already worked up in her mind.

When he didn't reply, she said, "Have you got another minute? I want to show you something." She went to her bedroom and came back with a file. She perched on the sofa beside him and pulled a single sheet from it and handed to him.

"These are our assets and investments. I got the accountant to print a summary for you and your sisters. Sarah has been asking me about the estate. She was really hoping there might be a bequest for each of you.

She feels she needs it now, when her kids are young. But your father was very firm that he and I would be named each other's sole beneficiary. He felt, you know, that you kids need to prove yourselves in the world, and money would stand in the way of your doing that. So the money will come to you later, when I'm gone."

Jake had grown more and more embarrassed as she talked. He glanced at the paper and then folded it in half, just to say, I don't give a shit about all this. She flinched at the gesture. "You know, Jake, these last years, you've been acting like you were allergic to your dad. But when you were tiny, you adored him. And he adored you—I wish you could have seen how happy he was to have a baby boy."

He had seen her cry before, but had never heard her speak in a voice so rough with feeling. He could not summon up a corresponding emotion. Maybe he should reach for her, offer her a hug, but they had not hugged since he was a kid. "Eventually you two would have found your way back to each other," she said. "Now you will have to do that work on your own."

He sat there with the folded paper in his hand, an itemization of all the money his dad had explicitly not given him. He knew he would never do the work she was talking about. He was exactly the distance from his father that he wanted to be.

His mother was bugging him to call a few of his dad's colleagues in Ottawa; she said they would take him on in a flash. It began to be hard to be in the house, and he spent long hours on his bike. He had to find a purpose before he could move ahead. This had nothing to do with a summer job, it was an inner mandate he was looking for. He was carrying around a secret: how immensely relieved he was that his dad was gone. In his own mind, he'd made the emotional break five or six years ago. Though to his surprise, his dad's death still felt like a very big deal.

People might call this grieving—but it was actually the work of sloughing off what it meant to inhabit the same world as Jack Challis. Freed from living in the shadow of his dad's self-serving self-righteousness, Jake was glimpsing brilliant possibilities. Finding a real, authentic way to be in the world. What would it mean, in concrete terms? He couldn't go back to university. His courses had all been chosen to irritate his father or to barricade himself against him.

He felt strangely weightless. He had friends from university, but he wasn't in the mood for them. He started cycling past Reg's, where evenings the Trans Am was usually parked in the driveway. It was a two-story house on a narrow lot on Arlington, just on the edge of Cedarvale Park. Its concrete facade had pebbles pressed into it, as though it had been deliberately uglified. Built-in flower boxes on either side of the front door looked to be filled with large stones. But it was a detached house in metro Toronto, and it was owned by a twenty-one-year-old!

There is a time for casting stones and a time for gathering stones together. One night Jake found himself stopping in front. The house was dark, but he wheeled his bike around to the back yard. Reg and one of his renters, Rebecca, were sitting on lawn chairs facing a fire pit, a barrel sunk into the ground. Jake and Rebecca had met a few times, and she got up and came over and put her arms around him in a gesture of condolence. Reg pointed towards a lawn chair and handed Jake a beer. He was acting a little cold. If either of them was going to be pissed off, it should be Jake. In fact, Jake felt totally at ease. Because he knew he occupied the moral high ground. He watched Reg settle back in his lawn chair and thought, fuck, it must suck to be you.

"You allowed to have open fires here?"

Reg shrugged.

"Not that anybody would call this a fire."

They were trying to burn two-by-four ends, and it wasn't working. Reg went into the garage and came back with a can of fire starter and sprayed the pieces of wood on the ground beside the barrel. "Careful with that," Rebecca said, and they started telling her about their feats with fire at Comstock Cove. Their efforts to shoot flaming arrows. The time Reg poured gasoline straight from a can onto an open fire, and the can exploded.

Reg kicked off his shoe and showed Rebecca a scar on the top of his foot.

"Oh, poor baby," she said.

So Jake, who was wearing cycling shorts, showed her a scar on his thigh.

"That's not a burn."

"No, it's from a pellet gun."

"It didn't leave a scar, you little suck," Reg said.

"You were *shooting* at each other?"

"Not directly at. Around. It was this stalking thing we did. Up on the Bruce. I guess sort of like paintball, but we used pellet guns."

"God," Rebecca said.

"I can't help it if I'm a better shot than you," Reg said.

"You're a crap shot. You were supposed to *miss* me, for Christ's sake."

"God," Rebecca said. "God, I'm glad I'm a girl."

"We're glad too," Jake said, smiling at her. It was the first time he'd felt normal this summer.

It was dark by then, and the light from the fire danced on Rebecca's face. "So when are you moving in?" she asked.

Reg had furnished his house at a bankruptcy outlet. The housing experiment was not what he'd made it out to be. Two years of speculation about Hannah and Amy was now confirmed: they had both come out, and they were together. Rhianna was in a relationship with a guy named George, who was tree-planting for three months, up north of Merritt, BC. Reg and Rebecca (of course) were sleeping together in the master bedroom at the front of the second floor. Jake's room was the only bedroom on the main floor. It had a single bed in it, a dresser and a chair. He was amused to find a formal rental agreement on the dresser, two copies for his signature. Reg's terms were month-to-month, and he had waived the damage deposit. Jake had enough in savings to cover the rent for a couple of months, even if he didn't find a summer job. Before he signed the forms, he checked along the mattress seams for bedbugs.

Rebecca worked evenings as a server at a pizza place in a strip mall. "I'll ask if they're taking on more staff," she said kindly to Jake. Reg had met her at that restaurant. When she handed him the takeout box with his leftover pizza, he handed it back and said, "You forgot something. You didn't write your number on it." Could you believe he pulled a girl like Rebecca with a move like that? During the day, Rebecca did art. She was building a portfolio towards applying for fine arts at the January deadline. A large painting on particle board sat on an easel in the dining room. People walked up a city street in the rain, carrying huge toadstools or mushrooms as umbrellas. This reminded Jake of something, some kids' book or fairy tale, but he didn't want to say so, in case she thought he was accusing her of not being original. The mushrooms were fleshy and real. The subject struck him as kind of twee, but he thought she was very talented. "Don't go into fine arts," he said. "They'll totally fuck you up."

She gave him a dimpled smile. She was a little plump, or maybe she'd be plump when she was older. Right now she was curvy. Jake got it, that the figures in her painting were all versions of her. Maybe when you looked at the world, you were just laying the template of yourself over everything, over and over. How awesome if the world really was the way Rebecca saw it through her sparkling brown eyes. Everything healthy. Everybody with her glow, like she was nourished by her happiness in herself. When Rebecca was home, her bright presence filled the house.

•

Evenings Reg worked at his dad's Honda dealership, days he worked for Revco. He was assigned to a Ganymede contract. Ganymede, the bottled water giant where Jack Challis's closest friend, Keith Lundstrom, was CEO, was facing a PR crisis due to the depletion of the Aberfoyle aquifer. There was talk of a national boycott, and Reg was running focus groups to figure out how much people knew and what sort of policy announcement or advertising campaign or product enhancement would turn their distaste around. Once when someone commented on what a great job he had, Reg said, "Jake's dad knew somebody."

This was news to Jake, and of course it pissed him off. It also got him thinking. He'd never heard Reg and his dad discuss Reg's job. He cycled home the next afternoon to pick up more of his stuff. His mother was leaving for a hair appointment so he said he would lock up when he was done.

On the floor of his closet was the laptop he'd brought home from his dad's apartment in Ottawa. He sat at his desk and opened it. The first email was dated September 2004, when Jake, in grade eleven, set the laptop up for his dad. The inbox was massive—it was clear his dad had never deleted a thing. Jake went to the outbox, did a quick sort, and scrolled down to Reg Bevaqua. God. There were maybe three hundred emails between them. Make that five hundred. The first subject line was "NOTE NEW ADDRESS," so they must have been corresponding before that at his dad's parliamentary address.

The first exchange was brief and concerned Jake.

Old Jack: "I thought my son was less than thrilled to see me when I stopped in at the riding office last night. Was he high, by any chance?"

Jake snorted. His dad and drugs! It was all reefer madness and the opium dens from Sherlock Holmes.

Reg: "He was just tired. We knocked on doors for about ten hours and Jake did most of the talking." Reg was such a bullshitter, but at least he was bullshitting in Jake's defence, unlike the time he bought two massive spliffs on the beach in Ocho Rios and set Jake up to take the fall.

His dad and Reg were close in a way that Jake had never suspected. They discussed Reg's future, his ambitions. At first Reg talked about oil and gas, but Jake's dad was steering him towards water. Water was the next oil. Think of it as a commodity. The day will come when we will trade futures in water. Reg's surname was what tipped the scales, in Reg's mind. When he started a corporation, his name would be his origin story.

Reg: "It's an old Italian name given to people who didn't drink wine. Seriously. I could make it part of my brand, that I only drink water. I'll have to stop hanging around with Jake, haha."

Jake scrolled down. There it was, a subject line reading "Work Experience." Work experience was crucial in getting into business school. They batted it back and forth over five or six emails. Reg was hoping Old Jack would use his influence to get him a spot at Ganymede, but Old Jack nixed that without saying why. He said he'd call someone at the consulting firm Revco International—Ganymede was a client, so Reg would still be close to the action, but he'd get some experience with other corporations.

A week before his heart attack, Old Jack wrote that he was hiring Jake as his junior assistant for the summer. "If I'm going to pay somebody to misfile reports in the office, it may as well be my own kid. But he seems to believe he's got a job with you folks at Revco. Will you give me a call ASAP?"

The words seared Jake's eyes. Pain tightened his chest. Like he cared or something. His dad was a prick. What was new about that?

He should have walked away at that point, but he scrolled back up and kept reading. It made him feel like shit, but he kept reading. It was just so weird that all this was going on without his realizing it. Was his dad grooming Reg for something, or did he actually like him?

Reg tells Old Jack a story about his own asshole of a father: "So last night Dad pulls the car into the driveway and then he passes out behind the wheel. That's how drunk he was. I had to drag him into the house."

Old Jack responds with stories about the abuse he suffered at the hands of *his* alcoholic father. "My dad stopped drinking when I was in grade school, but he was meaner and angrier sober then he had ever been as a drunk. When I was about nineteen, I managed to get into a bar. I wasn't used to drinking and I got really smashed. I tried to sneak into the house in the dark and I fell over the dog and landed on my keister. My dad was waiting up for me. He had his work boots on and he put them to me and left me on the floor. I was in a lot of pain the next day so I went into the hospital for an x-ray, and here the old bugger had broken two ribs."

Reg: "That is pure abuse. I thought I had it bad! I hope your father got nailed for it."

Old Jack: "It was a real turning point for me. I tried lying, but (God bless that doctor) he kept after me. He said, "You will never be your own man if you don't face up to him." Finally I agreed to let the doctor call the police and they came to interview me and my dad was charged with assault. He got a suspended sentence, but he never forgave me. You pay a price for courage."

Jake's father had never told Jake this story, but he was willing to tell Reg. He was willing to offer Reg the image of himself falling-down drunk. These last years, while hardness was gathering in Old Jack's cardiac arteries like the limescale in a kettle, it was Reg Bevaqua he was confiding in.

It was a bit rich of Jake to be hurt. He'd avoided his dad for years. At one time, they had father-son dinners out. Jake would get dressed up in a jacket and tie and meet his dad in a wood-panelled steakhouse on Bloor East. Other diners were supposed to recognize them and say, oh, isn't that touching. Old Jack started arranging these dinners when Jake was about twelve, and kept them going even after the science fair moment of truth. One of Jake's strategies, as he got older, was to perform such a parody of compliance and submission that his dad would be ashamed. It never worked, his dad took it like it was his due. By the time their filet or prime rib or porterhouse arrived, his dad would have homed in on whatever was bugging him about Jake that week. Old Jack's scrutiny—it was a sincere quest to figure out what was wrong with Jake and fix it. Gruesome for both of them. And now, the son Old Jack really wanted turned out to be Reg Bevaqua.

Cycling home, Jake thought about various uses he could make of this information. Reg wasn't home when he got there. He was out with Becky, at a reggae festival down at the Beaches. Jake heard them come in around midnight, their low voices as they climbed the stairs. At the top they turned the hall light off, and the band of yellow under Jake's door vanished. Reg and his dad were welcome to each other, Jake thought, lying in the dark. It wasn't like he gave a shit.

The next day, something was wrong with him. He felt like he was wearing a padded vest that weighed him down and impeded his movements. Sitting in the library, he started to be distracted by pains around his heart. He felt so bad that he headed home in early afternoon. When he got back to the house, Rebecca and a girl named Kerri were sitting on the front step drinking something pink. He reached for Rebecca's glass and she gave it to him with a smile. It was gin and lemonade.

"Ask Jake, Becky," Kerri said, getting up to leave.

"Ask me what?"

"Becky is doing life sketches. She's looking for models. She just drew me."

Rebecca kept her brown eyes steadily on him and as soon as Kerri was gone, she said, "What about right now?" She said she had moved her easel to the bedroom, they would have privacy there. He was still feeling pain as he walked up the stairs after her. Squeezing pains in his chest. He was having trouble breathing. "Sit down," she said in the bedroom. He wanted to say, I'm having a heart attack, but what burst out was a sob. He sank onto the bed. She moved swiftly towards him and put her arms around him, making comforting noises. He lay with his head against her breasts and the sobs wracked him.

He was seeing his dad in his last moments, seeing him more clearly than he ever had. The bony scaffolding of his head, the pathos of his haggard face, all his certainty and aggression gone. The terror and surprise. Totally oblivious to his son—the terror on his face was for himself. You're about to be extinguished, my man. It was all for nothing.

A groan escaped Jake's chest, and then another. He couldn't bear it, that his father had given up his spirit in his presence. That he, Jake, with his stone-cold unforgiving heart, was the one who'd witnessed it, the last moth of breath issuing out of his father's mouth, and then something unthinkable: no breath at all, the revolving Earth grinding to a stop on its axis.

SEVEN

If he'd grown up in a poor family and never spent holidays outside the city, would he have ended up an artist? It was a pine-scented outcropping of limestone in emerald water that did it. Out at his grandparents' cottage, he'd be walking a trail or floating in the lake, and the world would come to him so intensely that he'd almost think he'd had a seizure. Everything gleamed with—if he was religious, he might have thought it was God. It wasn't just that the wilderness made him more aware of beauty. There had been actual visitations. Once when he was maybe fifteen, he skied alone around the cove. By the end of the first hour, the air felt like mercury in his veins. Then a soft noise filled the sky. Something between a rustle and a boom. It swept across the cove like a cosmic whisper. Three times he heard it. The lake was sharing its secrets with him.

So Adlington, when Jake and Isla moved there, felt like a gift, a promise of a return to all that. Though it was two hours south of the Bruce Peninsula, and not exactly wilderness. But still, he would wake up in the night and hear distinct and separate noises in the silence, not the hum and throb of a big city. Mainly he heard dogs or trains. He never heard an owl or a coyote, but it didn't seem delusional to listen for them. He moved his computer and running gear to the shed. He bought a futon on Kijiji and threw a quilt and a pillow onto it. He invested in two big electric heaters. He loved that the shed was windowless, that it only gave you the sky. It was an event when a bird flew over. Every time it snowed, he climbed a ladder, carrying a long-handled mop, and shoved the snow off the skylight.

Of course, only a real urbanite would consider Adlington rural. But it was an escape from the city's zeitgeist. His old world was an elaborate project in denial. Nobody denied the science anymore—that project died around the time Old Jack died—but they seemed to have accomplished the higher art of denying reality. Everybody he knew (except two or three of his artist friends) was focused on sucking what they could out of a system in its death throes. In the last few years, that project had gotten more frenetic. People knew we were in freefall, but they never let on. Politics south of the border, for example, the shootings, the conspiracies: Jake's private theory was that folks were being driven crazy by terrors so awful they could never acknowledge them. They were driven crazy by all the cognitive dissonance. Here in Adlington, nobody talked about climate change either. But they did talk about the weather. Constantly.

His first Adlington friend was a three-year-old girl. One day, he walked across the yard to the shed and saw her wandering in front of their house with a vacant look on her face. No adults around. He went over and asked her whether she was with her mom or dad.

"No," she said.

"What's your name?"

"Brie."

"Brie what?"

"Brie O'Neil."

Ah. He actually knew where she belonged.

Even here there was no escaping Old Jack's long arm—Adlington's mayor, Drew Connaught, had stopped by the shed the week before, assuming he and Jake would be intimates on the strength of a roast suckling pig fundraiser he once hosted for Jake's dad. He was eager to fill Jake in on Jake and Isla's landlord, who lived in Guelph (the nice woman who first gave Jake the keys to the house had turned out to be a front). The

Town of Adlington was renting a house from the same guy, on behalf of a single mom named Quinn O'Neil. She was originally from Toronto, and she had substance issues, Drew said. She'd hopped on a bus with her three kids looking for a fresh start, and spent the first night at the Adlington Inn, where she proceeded to write a bad cheque. The police who showed up at the inn helped her make arrangements to stay in town until her court appearance. Four years and one baby later, she was still here. Drew speculated on the paternity of the youngest child and told Jake that Quinn had done time at the Grand Valley Institution. He seemed to see her as public property because she was living on welfare. She wasn't *ashamed*, that's what Drew couldn't get over. She would walk into the town hall and ask if her *paycheque* was ready. She thought society should give her a salary to raise her own kids! The taxpayers of Adlington were responsible for damages to the house. "Those little buggers can't be bothered to use the toilet," Drew said, referring to her twin boys. "They pee down the hot air registers. You can smell it from the street." "Five-year-old twin boys?" Jake said. "Christ, she must be overwhelmed."

This little girl must be Quinn O'Neil's youngest child. Everything about her slayed Jake. The smell of childhood that rose from her tousled hair. How confidently she took his hand when he offered to walk her home. She said she was three, but how tiny she was for three—he was startled when she spoke in sentences. "This is your house, right?" he said as they approached it, and she swatted his leg and said in her high little voice, "How did you know that, mister?"

He knocked on the door and a voice called, "It's open." Quinn was sitting on a saggy couch, poking at her phone. By the door was a massive cardboard crate stamped *Kraft Dinner*.

Jake let go of Brie's hand, and she wandered into the kitchen. "Your little girl was on Armitage, up by the railway tracks."

"They are free range kids being raised by a village," Quinn quipped, finally looking up.

"Well, I'm glad she let me walk her home, but you probably don't want her thinking it's okay to go off with strange men."

"You want me to thank you for not being a pedophile?" One side of her scalp was shaved and the other side chopped off with a dull blade. She had an uneven mouth and a stud below her lip that looked infected.

Jake let it drop. He introduced himself and mentioned that they had the same landlord.

"Does your place stink like this dump?" Quinn said. "The toilet's been plugged since last night, and that asshole won't pick up."

Jake knew there was no point calling their landlord, so he walked to the hardware store and bought a plunger. When he was going out the door after unplugging her toilet, Quinn said, "Hey! Leave that here!" as though he was stealing it.

He was soon taking them produce from the farm. Isla was too preoccupied with The Grange to go with him, but she was happy to send stuff over. Sometimes he watched the kids while Quinn went to an NA meeting, or ran to the drugstore when she needed something. He started tutoring the older girl, Amber. Quinn was always on the make with him, always. When he "lent" her twenty dollars, she spied a fifty in his wallet and harassed him until he forked it over. Connaught was trying to get her into a job readiness program, but she laughed and threw the form into the garbage. "Prick like that is going to see me as a parasite no matter what I do," she said. She was always trying to stick it to the mayor. She seemed determined to stick it to Jake too, which didn't seem quite fair. Why did he keep going? Good question.

"I have an appointment in Guelph tomorrow," Quinn said one day. "I need somebody to drive me."

She and Amber were sitting on the floor with a bucket of markers, colouring Cersei and the owl in a *Game of Thrones* colouring book. Her own skin had more blue in it than any skin tone Jake had ever seen. If she ever let him paint her, would he be able to capture that mixture of bravado and hurt?

"I don't have a car," he said.

"Yeah, right. You and your wife drove past here yesterday."

"Oh. Yeah. We borrowed a car. Rita's—she works with Isla. But Isla was driving. I don't have a licence."

"That's weird," Quinn said. "Why not?"

"Just never wanted to be part of car culture. Pumping carbon into the atmosphere."

"Must be nice."

"What do you mean?"

"Everything must be going good for you if you've got time to worry about shit like that."

Shit like that. That's why Jake visited her: to be reminded that his entire reality was an indulgence. From an hour away, he and his Toronto friends had begun to look like a school of identical fish, cruising in perfect synchrony through tepid waters.

Kurt Altenbach, who worked The Grange farm with the lovely Annalise, also piqued his interest. Physically the guy had an uncanny resemblance to an actor Jake had often seen at Stratford, most memorably in the role of Iago. Isla said Kurt had grown up in East Germany. His English was perfect and almost unaccented, but he spoke with a strange formality, as if each of his pronouncements was coming down from an oracle. Friendliness was not in Kurt's repertoire, but he seemed interested in Jake too. Once at a staff dinner at The Grange, he talked at length about his experiences during German unification. He had grown up in East Berlin, and he was twelve when the wall came down. He said that he and his brother walked up Wilhelmstrasse, a street that dead-ended at the wall, and watched in a crowd all day. First there were what he called wallpeckers, people with crowbars and hammers. They made a hole about the size of a human head, and people on the West side looked through it one by one and called greetings. The GDR sent a crew that afternoon and patched the hole with concrete. By the next day the government had given up, and then a bulldozer came and smashed that section of the wall wide open so Wilhelmstrasse could run through for the first time in twenty-five years.

"Wow. What an exciting thing to see first-hand," Jake said. "It must have felt like a dream come true."

"Not in the least," Kurt said. One of his favourite expressions.

"What do you mean?"

"We lost everything. I am a man without a homeland."

On an evening in late winter when snow fell heavily, Jake and Isla stood at the living room window watching Kurt ski past their house. Isla said he'd found his skis in the basement of The Grange. They were wooden, with leather straps for bindings. He skied right down the middle of the road so cars had to slow to a crawl behind him.

"He's such a provocateur," Isla said.

This was their second year in Adlington, and they had a new game, finding a one-word definition for Kurt Altenbach.

"He's actually an anarchist," Jake said. "All rules are meaningless to him, including the rules of the road."

"You're wrong. It's exactly the opposite. He's a *utopian*."

"What?"

"He is! He believes that better days lie ahead, and he's eager for them. He can't wait for all this to collapse so we are forced to eat squirrels roasted on a spit."

One day when Isla mentioned that Kurt was making sausages, Jake stopped by The Grange's workshop. Spring had come, and all that snow was turning to puddles in the yard. Kurt had a big tub of ground meat on the work table and he was working fennel seed and ground spices into it.

His thick cotton shirt and pants were a deep indigo and sewn in a style that evoked the Mao regime.

"I was going to see if you could spare some sausages for the O'Neil family," Jake said. "But I guess I'm a little early."

Without looking at Jake, Kurt turned and walked into the freezer. He came back a minute later with a handful of sausages from a previous batch, still not frozen.

"I haven't seen you around a lot this winter," Jake said as Kurt slipped them into a plastic bag.

"I've been camping up on the Bruce."

"You mean, on the trail?"

"Up on the peninsula. On the shore."

"Seriously. You camp in the snow."

"I was there most of February."

"You must have to pack in a lot of food."

"No. A few noodles. Oats. Beef jerky. I snare rabbits. I fish through the ice." Kurt turned to the sink to wash his hands. "Got really lucky this trip. A pack of wolves took down a deer on the lake right below where I was camping. I watched the chase by moonlight. After the kill, I went down and scared them off. I carved out the haunches and left the belly and ribs for them. I ate venison for a week."

He picked up the package of sausages and handed it over. Then he did look at Jake. His amber eyes dared Jake to doubt the story.

Isla was not thrilled when she saw what Jake had brought home. "You know, I'm happy to share produce with Quinn, but don't ask Kurt, okay? He shouldn't be giving away meat from the shop. It's not that I'm cheap. We're not licensed for commercial sales. We could get fined or shut down."

"No money changed hands."

"I know. But Kurt has been bootlegging hams in the village."

"Seriously?"

"That's what somebody told Sheff last fall. Sheff confronted Kurt and he didn't deny it. And Sheff thinks it's still happening."

"What are you going to do?"

"I don't know. How can we let Kurt and Annalise go, how would we ever replace them? We don't have organic certification without them."

Having launched into the subject, she complained about Kurt at length. She said he rarely came to their weekly menu meetings, and when he did, he watched them with disdain, just making the occasional comment in German to Annalise. She said that he often switched out produce they had requested—with no notice and for no reason, just to assert his superior notions of what they should be serving. She speculated that he enjoyed the killing of the animals a little too much. She said he vanished for days at a time and the rumour in the kitchen was that he was using drugs. Annalise was dependable and straightforward, but if they managed to keep up, it was because the kids often took over the routine chores. Isla worried that The Grange was in violation of child labour laws.

"Do you have any idea where he goes?"

"No," she said, like she couldn't care less.

One day they met outside the post office, and Kurt told Jake he'd found some petroglyphs out on the escarpment that weren't on any map. Jake told Kurt how much he'd like to see them. "Maybe I could go with you the next time you go out?" he said. He ripped a piece off the envelope he was carrying and wrote his cell number on it and pressed it on Kurt.

"Okay, Shatterhand," Kurt said.

"Shatterhand?"

"You don't know that story? Chief Winnetou of the Apaches? He had a white sidekick named Shatterhand. You wear your hair like him."

Ah. A light came on. Kurt was part of that movement in Germany that fetishizes North American Indigenous cultures! Accountants and dentists from Hamburg and Dresden dressing in braid-wigs and buckskins and camping in a tipi village and staging barefoot tomahawk raids on other camps. The wolf-slain deer on the frozen lake—it must have been something Kurt dreamed up back then. The blood on the snow, the wolves pacing around him, their eyes glinting in the moonlight.

Jake almost told Isla about the petroglyphs, then thought better of it. She was already a little hurt that he didn't want her company when he went out sketching. So why would he be eager to go with someone else? Why?—because hiking with Kurt, he'd still be essentially alone. The guy reminded Jake of a bear or a fox or a coyote, the way they avoid eye contact with humans; their being is other and elsewhere. And, let's be honest, Kurt had one very attractive attribute: he owned a truck.

Getting out into the wilderness was all Jake wanted to do. The whole notion of art as an argument—it was gone. Draw and paint as he had begun as a kid, as a way of seeing. Draw from the right place, as a creature of nature. Heal that breach.

This sort of practice would take time to get into. You could head out to what looked like wilderness, and humanity would intrude at every step. You'd have to edit out contrails, distant cell towers, chunks of abandoned concrete with rebar in it, cigarette butts, Kleenex melted into the earth by rain, the howl of semi brakes on the highway over the ridge, used condoms, Burger King wrappers. Even yourself—he had to edit out himself, his tendency to compose and frame and censor. Everything, even his artistic impulse, reminded him that he was separate from the scene.

But he always came back in a different place. He came back feeling more alive.

The biggest challenge in this new life turned out to be the whole cohabiting thing. He'd never lived with a woman before, and it was a lot more demanding than he'd expected. He often worked at night and came into the kitchen the next day to the smell of baking. Or to the sight of Isla kneading in a deft rhythm, the muscles in her arms shaping and releasing, her chestnut hair in a braid down her back. Holding her bread-doughy hands out of the way, turning her face for his kiss. He was surprised to discover that he did not always welcome this. Having to talk, having to respond. Living with a woman meant living with yourself in a way that was new to him.

"I don't need to talk all the time," Isla said. "I'm fine with silence."

But you still see me, he wanted to say. You think about me. You react to what I do or don't do. You turn those dark blue eyes in my direction and zoom me into existence.

And you bring into the house things I don't want in my life.

On a Friday evening he was walking across the yard from the shed when a preposterous bronze sports car rolled past. Armitage Street was full of potholes and that car's chassis had about three inches of clearance. Turned out his old friend, his old nemesis, Reg Bevaqua, was dining at The Grange, and it was his car.

"You know who he is, right?" Isla said when she came home. "That water tycoon?" She launched into a comic bit about a spaceship landing in front of The Grange, and its doors lifting like a pair of bent wings, and a guy in a deep purple suit prying himself out of it, the curve of his scalp shining through his thinning hair like a rising moon. "What is he saying to the world with that car? He's saying, I'm a fucking idiot! I peaked at the age of twelve! It's a thing with the filthy rich, you know. Elon Musk paid a fortune for a car that was used in a James Bond movie. Turned out he bought it because he believed it would actually transform into a submarine."

"You made that up."

"No. I read it online. So while Mr. Bottled Water and his wife were eating dessert, I stopped by their table and said, 'Your car makes quite a statement. Does it fly?' And he thought I was serious! 'Fly?' he said. 'No.' His wife looked a little embarrassed."

Jake had been lying on the couch, listening to music. Tiny sounds rose now from the earbuds on his shoulders. Isla went to the kitchen and put the kettle on. She had pretty much exhausted the subject, he could get away without telling her.

He had literally not crossed paths with Reg Bevaqua since the day he moved out of Reg's house. In the last ten or twelve years he'd been aware, of course, of Reg's amazing transformation into a water wunderkind. How could Jake not be aware, with his mother constantly going on about it when she phoned him? Reg had followed Old Jack's advice, he'd gone into water, he'd become Old Jack's avatar in the business world. From time to time, Jake caught glimpses of the guy on TV. He watched an interview in which Reg argued that privatizing water was a social good—the era of easy hydration products is over, we don't value what we don't pay for, etc. Reg had grown into what had always been a big body, and his hair had thinned—he looked almost middle-aged. He wore expensive suits with ease, as if he'd grown up in them, and he'd honed his bullshit to a high art. Lately his face was everywhere because his company had started lobbying for a federal contract to manage water and sewage needs for First Nations. Once, about a year ago, Jake was in Toronto at his mother's, and they caught a bit on the news about BevAqua donating flatbeds of bottled water to northern reserves. The handover of this dubious gift featured Reg Bevaqua himself, clearly still craving the spotlight. *We have a corporate mandate to be part of the solution for Indigenous people. The feds have proved they don't have what it takes.* He was packaging his greed as altruism! Well, he had learned from the best.

Isla was back in the doorway with a cup of tea. Jake knew he could let it go, but if Reg returned to The Grange and Isla discovered how well they knew each other, the whole thing would end up being way more important in her mind than it needed to be.

"Bevaqua has always been humour-challenged," Jake said as she crossed the room towards him.

Isla paused. "You know him?"

"He went to my school."

"Oh, really. Same year?"

"Yeah." And then, without intending to, he sidestepped. "What's the guy look like now?"

"Mm, like the losing suitor in a Turner Classic Movie."

That made him laugh. He got up and slipped one of the earbuds into Isla's ear and the other back into his. "Hey," she said, and she put her tea down and started dancing, and he spent the rest of the night distracting her in ways they both enjoyed.

He did come back. Turned out he had property on the Bruce Peninsula, so he'd stop in for a meal as he drove through. Jake felt a heavy premonition, hearing this. He knew, and he couldn't believe it. Then Barbara called and confirmed it. Reg had bought Comstock Cove! He had bought the Challis cottage from the people who bought it from Jake's grandpa. The harbour at the middle of the cove used to be subdivided into three modest properties, and Reg had managed to acquire all three. They were on one of the few privately owned parcels of land along that shore—he had outbid Parks Canada to get that land. Barbara had friends with a cabin at Oxenden, and they told her all about it. They said Reg had torn those little cabins down and built his own magnificent lodge. They said he had considered a modernist multi-level design that would take advantage of the cliffs, but then he changed architects and hired an explosives expert and blasted a wider footprint in the rocks for a traditional two-story lodge. He brought in a massive construction barge with a crane. Glass professionals to install his panoramic two-story windows.

"It's so interesting that he didn't buy on the other side of Georgian Bay," Barbara said. "Or in Muskoka, where most of the money is. It tells you how much his summers with us meant to him. I don't really get why you two aren't friends. If you would just swallow your pride, darling, and give Reg a call, you could be going up to the Bruce again. You used to love it there."

What the fuck. What was the douchebag trying to do?

One weekend morning, off-season, *the guy called Isla*. Jake heard her talking in a cordial but guarded voice, polite-friendly. She put the phone down and said, "Guess who that was. Reg Bevaqua! He's inviting a lot of people up to his lodge for Christmas and he wants me to cook for him. He says his kitchen is state-of-the-art, a work space any chef would die for."

"How did he get your cell number?"

"Yeah, good question."

She was sitting there musing about his offer while her eggs congealed, and he could see the appeal of it growing on her face.

"You know Comstock Cove is part of a land claim right now?" he said. "It's on Treaty 72 land. Way back, the Saugeen people gave up a million and a half acres of farmland in the south, for the promise that the Crown would keep the Bruce Peninsula free of squatters." Sometime in the last few years he had looked it up, and ended up thinking, just as well Dad lost that cottage.

"I guess when you look at it, we're on stolen land here."

"Yeah, but it seems worse somehow when the treaty was specifically about the issue of squatters." Isla looked unconvinced, so he added, "Anyway, I'm not sure I'd want to work for someone who considers water a commodity."

"True," she said, thoughtfully. "Jake, you know Karthik? Our new cook?"

"The guy who did that grouse dish?"

"Yeah, him. Well, he's really interested in Reg because of Reg's business in India." Karthik's parents were domestic workers in Pune, she said, southeast of Mumbai, but his father had grown up in the south and still had brothers farming there, in a region where climate change was causing terrible droughts. Regulations were loose in their state, and government officials were used to being bribed. Karthik said that multinationals had come in and bought up the tracts of land with the most ground water. They'd installed pumps that sucked that water up, and in consequence, the wells of farmers in the surrounding area had run dry and they couldn't grow their crops.

"And then," she said, "they pour that water into cheap plastic bottles and sell it back to the desperate people. It's just terrible. Bevaqua's company in India is called Varsha. I asked Karthik whether he really thought Bevaqua bribed officials to get the permits he needed, and he said, of course. Can he get away with that, Jake?"

"It's obscene," Jake said. "Robber barons like that welcome climate catastrophe. They can exploit it to make money."

"Like, does Canadian law not care what a Canadian businessman does in India? I asked Karthik, and he just said, 'Isla, you think there's an answer for everything.'"

"Reg Bevaqua is a total loser," Jake said. "You want to stay as far away from him as possible."

When she left for work, he checked it out. Varsha was not mentioned on the BevAqua website, and neither was India—no doubt Reg's marketing team wanted to keep the sparkle in the BevAqua brand—but elsewhere online, Jake found articles about BevAqua water-grabs in Pakistan, Nigeria, and South Africa. Theoretically, there *was* an answer to the crimes Karthik alleged Reg had committed in India: the Corruption of Foreign Public Officials Act. It was against the law for Canadian companies to bribe government officials, even outside Canada. The trick was getting evidence to prove it.

"Dad," Jake said aloud. "What do you think of your little buddy now?"

ISLA

EIGHT

By the third spring, Sheff began to say with satisfaction, "We are hitting our stride." In fact, The Grange was successful beyond anything we had imagined. There was so much demand that bootleggers were selling reservations for $500 in Toronto.

My own dreams for the place were always a little different from Sheff's, though, and I was still making up my mind about our enterprise. I loved the nights when a flamenco guitar turned a restaurant dinner into a feast for intimates. I loved being out in the salon around sunset on clear evenings, when the western light would reflect off the eastern hills, painting them a pale orange—alpenglow, I think you call that light. It only lasted a moment and I had to be on my toes to catch it. I loved creating the daily menu. And our team was a great bunch—but let's face it, there was far more life in The Grange's kitchen and cellar than there ever was in its dining rooms.

It was weird—we aspired to a locavore philosophy, but we never served locals, except for annual comps to Adlington's mayor and the MPP. Occasionally we'd book a modest couple splashing out for their twenty-fifth wedding anniversary, but mostly we became a destination for media personalities, politicians, corporate CEOs with out-of-town guests, TV actors and their agents and managers—in other words, the Toronto elite. Usually nice, individually, but often not, having purchased the right to perfection—or their idea of it, which did not always coincide with ours. They tended to be immune to surprise, bored with their options. Some of them were aspirational foodies, and you could pick up *anxiety*—that this evening was going to disappoint, that it would be less spectacular than their dinner last month in Tokyo or Ibiza, that their lives weren't on a rising trajectory after all. And yet, they weren't as savvy about food as you'd assume. They might have thought they wanted artisanal fare, but they were accustomed to exotic ingredients put together with tweezers. Their palates had been acculturated to olive oil, and they weren't prepared for croutons crisped in chicken fat. Crimson egg yolks, piggy-tasting pork. Pan-fried puffballs. Dumplings made with bone marrow (a German delicacy Annalise taught us), salads made with weeds. We aspired to use every part of our animals. Black pudding, haggis, tripe, pigs' feet—dishes like that might have had a few adventuresome takers on an ordinary menu, but they were a bust on a *menú del día*, as we learned the hard way. Our website was very clear about what you could expect at The Grange, but customers would catch a whiff of the air from the barn and ask to be moved off the terrace. I found their complaints absurd. Like the lawyer who never expected her clients to be so guilty, I hadn't realized our diners would be quite this entitled.

We'd been in Adlington three years before Phoebe ventured up the 401 in her mint-green Fiat Cabrio and appeared in the doorway of the shed. She was wearing a yellow cotton dress and red pumps with matching lipstick, her hair (black now) turned under in Rita Hayworth coils, and she had wonderful news: the Vancouver Art Gallery wanted to mount *Dreaming the Future*. She drank in our excitement, and then she embarked on a tour of the shed. When she saw the huge canvas Jake had hired two teenagers from the village to help him stretch, she walked gravely over and put her fingertips to it, consternation twisting her crimson mouth. Where would a painting this big ever be shown? We watched her in silence. We both knew the size of that canvas didn't matter, because nothing was ever going to be painted on it. Jake had told me what he intended, and his telling me meant the idea was dead. He was going to paint icebergs and high rises, the towers of the Arctic and the towers of the city, paintings that would draw their force from juxtaposition and scale. But in one weird moment, he said, the background took over and effaced the subject (in the painting in his mind, to be clear). I didn't understand. He finally said, "Oh, whatever. Some projects only work as a premise. In this one, even the premise was bad."

But abandoning an idea is progress, right? Every dead end means you can eliminate that particular tunnel in the maze.

"Jake should not be so isolated from other artists," Phoebe said, turning back to us.

"We're not that far away," I said. "He went in to the Godfrey Wang opening last week."

"And did he mingle? Did he pitch his ideas? Did people leave the gallery that night talking about Jake Challis and not about Godfrey Wang?"

"I doubt it."

"I rest my case."

"He's not competitive, Phoebe. It's the art that feeds him, not the acclaim."

"Oh, sweetie." Phoebe gazed at me, amused. "He'll never produce if he's not competitive."

And meanwhile Jake was sprawled on his futon, watching us expressionlessly.

It happened to be the day of the spring feast, and we had invited Phoebe to stay over. Spring was by far my favourite time at The Grange. All the happy reunions as our friends trickled back into town and the house rang with music from five continents and jokes in six languages. Most of the staff had travelled, some had worked in other kitchens, all had eaten new food, and I loved hearing the stories, trying out their ideas, working in quiet intimacy interrupted now and then by gales of laughter, by a spontaneous dance in the cellar. We dined on our experiments, sometimes on the terrace, from where we could see the lambs jumping in the pasture and the fruit trees in full blossom. The night before we opened, we always threw a feast for staff and friends, a last blow-out before the customers arrived, and I'd invited Phoebe.

I was coming out of the kitchen, a platter of gnocchi in one hand, a platter of roasted asparagus in the other, just as she and Jake arrived. Kurt Altenbach stood at one of the tables carving meat. He was shaggier than when we'd first met him, his brown hair matted now into proto-dreads. Phoebe tripped over to us, looking like the sexy mid-century wife who might once have been the doyenne of this mansion. I introduced them, mentioning that Kurt was our farmer. She eyed the glistening ham he was carving. "How long did it take you to raise this pig?"

"I didn't raise her," Kurt said.

"No?"

"Her mother raised her."

"Ah," Phoebe said, tilting her head. Time to drift along, Phoebe. But she persisted, a nymph drawn to a satyr. "Where do the animals go to be butchered?" God, she was delivering herself straight into his hands.

"Go? They don't go anywhere."

"You slaughter them yourself?"

"What's wrong with that? Why wouldn't I?" She shivered and he pinned her with his eyes. "Death makes you uncomfortable?"

"Of course. It doesn't bother you to put a knife to a living creature's throat?"

"Am I not a living creature? Will I not die?" He speared a crusty tidbit of ham with the point of his knife and held it out to her.

Even Sheff had paused to watch. "What does it matter to the pig if we eat it after it is dead?" he said, in a perfect impression of Kurt. But Phoebe refused Kurt's offering, putting her red fingernails up to shield her red mouth. And honestly, when you looked at her flawless skin and her gleaming hair, the idea of human mortality did seem preposterous.

I remember afterwards, stepping out into a verdant spring night, walking home with Phoebe while frogs chanted in the pond behind The Grange. She was curious about Kurt. I told her that he and Annalise had come to Canada with the intention of starting a boarding school, something I had only recently learned. "They wanted to work with troubled and at-risk youth. Kids who had lost their way would find it again through mucking out the barn, that was Kurt's theory. It never got off the ground."

"I wonder why they wanted to start their school here. Like, not in Germany."

"Yeah, I don't know."

"He's not in a doomsday cult or something?"

"A doomsday cult?"

"Well, he was talking about the skills he was teaching his own children, and I said, 'You want them to have careers in agriculture?' and he said, 'No, I just want them to be self-sufficient after the collapse.' He meant, of *civilization*."

"He was just trolling you."

"You think?"

"Yes. Don't take him seriously. He's . . . well, he's a contrarian."

"Do he and Jake spend time together?"

"Not that I've noticed."

"Well, I would try to shut it right away down if you do," she said. "That man is highly dangerous. Seriously."

I laughed. We'd come up on our house. The skylight was a square of pale yellow, so I knew Jake (who had left the party hours ago) was out in the shed. I stepped onto our driveway, and she put a hand on my arm.

"You realize how extraordinary *Dreaming the Future* was," she said. "The wall between serious art and the ordinary consumer is pretty much impossible to penetrate. But Jake put a jackhammer to that wall. It's not nothing. It doesn't happen very often. This is an inflection point for him. He could be one of those names everyone knows. Ai Weiwei or Lucian Freud. It's entirely feasible. He's at a critical juncture, and I'm not sure he's handling it well."

This was how Phoebe got when she drank, I thought. Full of wild hope and wild fear.

Clearly she overestimated my influence with Jake. I didn't actually see much more of him in Adlington than I had in the city, and I didn't see him much more in the winter than I had in the summer. I did not feel entirely welcome in the shed. It was a fine place to be, and I could see why Jake preferred it over our house, which had what you might see as bad feng shui. He often slept out in the shed, because sleep with its occult adventures was adjacent to creativity (or something). I was beginning to grasp how very important his work was to him, and I wanted to honour that. This arrangement wasn't what I had imagined of a relationship, but I accepted the challenge with goodwill. My old image of his artistic process, the male bowerbird pouring his ecstasy into art, had faded. And I sometimes worried, picturing him brooding for months over creative ideas, gradually eliminating whole neighbourhoods in the web of his hypothetical oeuvre.

Meanwhile, I needed to do another book. Those winters were the chance. Of course, I was no longer a teenage phenom, and I didn't have a new idea. I called up the agent who had represented *The Omnivore's Alphabet*, and she suggested I start a podcast to rebuild my audience. The idea of talking for an hour to invisible and possibly nonexistent listeners left me cold. Maybe I could capitalize on the popularity of The Grange—like *The Moosewood Cookbook*, which turned a restaurant in an old high school in upstate New York into a legend. I would have to negotiate that with Sheff. In the dark winter days, I mulled over a welter of recipes. We were doing some interesting things with pulses and local fungi, but it was a little early to say what The Grange's signature ideas would be.

Still, my work was methodical, in a way that Jake's was not. There's an expression about trying to catch lightning in a bottle—that was Jake. He packed up a sketching kit, and every chance he got, he hitched a ride north, spending the day on the Niagara Escarpment, or in the Forks of the Credit River, or one of the other conservancy areas to the north of Adlington. Recently, he'd begun to produce studies in charcoal, which he tacked at eye level all around the shed. He was lost in textures, and the techniques that could capture them. I could see he was grouping the sketches. He had placed the study of a limestone ledge beside the study of a marmorated stink bug, for example. He was working with patterns, with spots and stripes and spirals and waves and crystals, undulations and tessellations. Fractals. I thought he was onto something. It was really striking, seeing the same patterns in rocks and tree trunks and clouds and fungi and insects. I had no actual idea what art was, to be honest, but this series—*Why?* it made me ask, and I think that was the idea.

When I think back to those first years, they look idyllic to me. It was Jake's mother who kicked everything to a different level.

Barbara Kathleen Webster Challis. She was lovely, her hair the colour of a violin and just as richly polished, her lipstick poppy red and perfectly applied. There was something in her expression that asked, why would anyone choose to be different from me? But still, from the time we met, she extended her greatest courtesy to me: she pretended we shared the same view of the world. I thought she saw me as her best hope of managing Jake, like Phoebe did.

We didn't see her a lot. Off-season, we sometimes arranged to meet in a restaurant for Sunday brunch. One day she gently asked us when we were going to start a family. I didn't respond, because I hadn't figured out yet whether I wanted to have a child. Jake replied, though. He said something pessimistic about the future any kids of ours would have to face. A year or so later, Barbara raised the subject again, and this time she observed, "Well, *they* are not going to stop reproducing," gesturing vaguely towards the restaurant staff. "What do you mean?" Jake asked, and she said, "If people like you refuse to have children, where are the leaders of tomorrow going to come from?" That day I understood why Jake was so reluctant to visit his mother: he liked to believe that all the entitlement and elitism and racism in their home sprang from Old Jack, and he had to stay away from Barbara to maintain that illusion.

When she finally sold the big family house in Rosedale and moved into a condo, we borrowed Rita's car and went into Toronto to help her with the move. She'd been bugging Jake to haul away his stuff, all the junk he'd abandoned when he left home at twenty, and when we were done for the day, she mentioned his boxes. "It's now or they go into a dumpster."

"Excellent," Jake said. "I can make that happen."

"*No*," I implored. "At least look through them."

In a corner of the empty basement, we found four or five cardboard boxes, a very fine handmade canoe paddle, and a plastic bin piled with Rollerblades, badminton rackets, hockey sticks, and bike helmets.

"Oh, that paddle!" Barbara said, when we dropped the load in the front hall. "That was Grandpa Challis's handiwork. It's beautiful, isn't it. How skilful that man was!"

"Was he a professional?"

"He was a woodworker in England, before the war. You should see the chest of drawers he made, with its dovetail joints. I guess it's still in the cabin at Comstock Cove. Jake's grandpa sold that cabin with all its contents. People do that in lake country, they leave the furniture behind, but they usually go in first and take out items of sentimental value. Not Grandpa Challis! He prided himself on not being sentimental. This paddle is the only thing we have from the cabin. He gave it to Jake on our last trip up."

"He didn't give it to me," Jake said, plunking down his box. "I borrowed it the last time we were up. I wanted to paddle out—you picked me up at Scalloway, remember? Then he sold the cabin and I never had a chance to take his paddle back. I don't think the old geezer ever gave me anything."

"Well, you could learn from his example. He died alone, poor old fellow, because he didn't cherish family." The box Jake had carried up was an over-full legal box, and playfully, she tipped off the lid with the toe of her pointy-toed flat. "You have a real treasure trove from your childhood here. You're going to have so much fun going through it." A pile of sketchbooks and pictures slid onto the floor. On top was a framed photo, face up. Two teenage boys in swim suits, against a background of spruce, laughing at whoever was taking the picture.

"That's Reg Bevaqua," I said, feeling a shock pass through me.

"Oh," Jake said. "Yeah, I guess it is."

"You hung out together? He was at your cottage?"

"Jake and Reggie." Barbara laughed. "They were joined at the hip from the time they were five. I can still see Reggie, the first day of kindergarten. I came in to pick you up—remember, Jake?—I came in just in time to see him hitting you over the head with a big plastic truck. Oh, darling. Somehow you bounced back. You two had so much fun when you were boys."

We stood with our eyes fixed on each other's faces. Jake looked embarrassed but also defiant. I turned away and picked up my shoulder bag and the car keys. Barbara realized she had opened something up but she wasn't backing off. "Reggie has done so well for himself. I would never have predicted it. He was such a clumsy boy. Not physically clumsy, I don't mean that, but in terms of social skills. Rough around the edges, I guess you would say. And now—it's amazing—he gives a new meaning to the word *success*. I can't help but feel a little proud. Our place was his second home. And my husband was something of a mentor to him, you realize."

"I know Reg quite well, actually," I said. "He and his wife eat at The Grange."

"Oh, really! But you and Jake don't socialize with them?"

"No."

"Well, that's too bad. You boys always had such a great time together. Diving off the rocks at Comstock Cove, remember? *Jamaica*—one year Reggie came with us, and Isla, those two little demons volunteered to catch crabs for the resort's crab races, and here they fixed the races by clipping elastic bands around the legs of some of the crabs. Honestly, they were such a pair!"

"I'll have to let Reggie know that Jughead's just down the street," I said meanly. I gave Barbara a couple of the elegant cheek kisses I had adopted from her, and then I walked away from the two of them, away from those boxes and straight out to the car, where I waited in the driver's seat while Jake made three or four trips down the driveway to schlep his gear. I had talked about Reg Bevaqua constantly for the last two years. When he and Eve had their tenth wedding anniversary, we shut down for a night and catered their party. It was the only private event we ever did. I talked about that party for weeks. And my live-in lover never once let on that Bevaqua was anything more than a distant acquaintance.

He got into the car and we drove out of the city. I turned onto the 401 and we sped along without saying a word.

Finally, when we were on Highway 3, Jake broke the silence. "So, Isla. You seem a little pissed off. Do we have *rules* about what I have to tell you?"

"Rules? Is that what this feels like to you? You feel like I'm trying to control you? Because I want to know you?"

Then I *was* pissed off.

I wanted to return the car to Rita with a full tank so, on the outskirts of Adlington, I pulled into a gas station. Jake got out to pump the gas and I went in to pay. When I came back out, he had moved the car over to the edge of the lot and was unloading boxes into a big red dumpster. It hurt me to watch him throw his entire childhood into that dumpster, I was with Barbara in that. His art, the drawings he'd made as a boy! I noticed a laptop. "That's e-waste," I said. I carried it back to the car, and he let me do it. "Keep the sports gear for Quinn's kids," I said, and he did. He kept the paddle too.

In the car, he said, "Just to be clear, I haven't had anything to do with Reg Bevaqua for years. Since before I went to art school. So I'm not sure why this is such a big deal."

I didn't answer.

At the house, he said, "Isla. Don't let on to Bevaqua that you know me. Okay? Please?"

"That I *know* you?"

He reached in a conciliatory way for my arm and I shook him off.

NINE

I walked into the salon one night to see the Bevaquas on their last course. Eve had declined the dessert, pannacotta with basil and roasted strawberries, but Reg was working his way through his. They weren't talking. Rita, our front end manager, drifted over from the reservations desk and murmured to me, "Lady Aqua Blue didn't trust us that her coffee was decaf. She made her server bring out the can and show her."

I stood watching from across the room. Eve: her hair pale and architecturally structured, her brows strong and dark, her profile breathtaking. Her beauty was austere, it was far beyond the prettiness most women go for. Reg: there was something *brutal* about his face, I thought for the first time.

He noticed me and called me over. "We had an unpleasant experience tonight," he said. "We were accosted by a beggar out on the road."

I knew immediately who it was. Quinn O'Neil, the single mom Jake helped out. On a nice evening, while her kids played down by the creek, she would put on an orange minidress and panhandle outside The Grange. We had valet parking, of course, but people liked to take a stroll along our picturesque street and check out the lambs in the pasture, and that's where she'd hit them up, right before they settled in for their three-hundred-dollar dinner. Personally, I was grateful to Quinn. I wanted something from our customers that we weren't getting: a bit of reverence. I wanted them to have scaled a mountain to get here, to have suffered for the privilege, not to have descended from a helicopter, as happened a few times a year, not to have cruised up in their BMW Gran Coupé, or in (yuck) one of the stretch limos that occasionally clogged our parking lot. I wanted them to be worthy of the efforts made on their behalf, to bow their heads gratefully before their braised lamb, to think about what bee pollen actually *was*.

"There's not much we can do about what happens on a public road," I said.

"Of course there is," Reg said. "This town has bylaws. Somebody needs to take this up with Drew."

Drew Connaught. He knew the mayor by his first name. Of course he did.

The concept of Jake and Reg Bevaqua as best friends was mystifying. It was harder to imagine what had brought them together than what had driven them apart.

Rita Charles, our wonderful front end manager, was my best friend. We'd known each other a long time—she worked for Sheff in Toronto, and when we opened The Grange, she moved to Adlington with her two kids and lived here year-round. Rita had grown up in the Caribbean, on the island of Grenada, and her partner was a touring jazz musician named Phil. "Phil's in Philly this week," she would say as a sort of shorthand, and he almost always was. She had a long oval face, a serious, almost-sad mouth—until the fountain of joy inside her surged up and overflowed, transforming her into such a beauty that you had to smile too.

Rita chatted with Eve Bevaqua more than I did. Sometimes Eve was aloof, Rita said, other times overly friendly. "Her birth name was Nesbitt. Her family is rich. She went to a private school, and then studied classics at Oxford." Rita sensed that the marriage was essentially transactional, like in a PBS period drama: Reg had paid for Eve's old-Toronto status with his new money. He'd paid for her taste, and her connections, and her classic, understated beauty, and for what Rita called "her brought-upsy ways." Rita sensed that Reg's vulgarity embarrassed Eve. We only saw that absurd sports car once, and after that they started driving an old Jag. They had the property on Georgian Bay, a house in Colombia, and a flat on the Amalfi Coast, but their main residence was in Rosedale, the house Eve's mother had grown up in. One of the houses I'd adored as a kid, possibly. Maybe it was that childhood romance with wealth that made me so resent Reg Bevaqua's ordinariness. The teenage valet who parked cars at The Grange was smarter and funnier. Reg's speech was ridden with clichés, his efforts at wit were cringey, he had a kind of reverse charisma. He reminded me of my old swim coach. Would his wealth be more moral if he was personally exceptional? Well, no. Something basic was shifting in my understanding of the world, just from knowing Reg Bevaqua. It felt preposterous that he should exist, and more preposterous that I should know him. We let him exist, didn't we, we all let the super-wealthy keep doing what they do. Most people aspired to be them; a lot of people would trade places with Reg Bevaqua in a flash.

We saw more and more of the Bevaquas that year, because Reg had bought a helicopter and hired a pilot. He got in a fight with the Adlington hospital because they wouldn't let him use the air ambulance helipad. He had given them a donation the year before, but they didn't recognize it as a bribe.

"Poor Reg," I said to Rita and Karthik. "Why must the rich be made to suffer?" That was an Ayn Rand line, I knew it from Jake.

"Why indeed," Rita said. "Fill us in, Isla."

I laughed. "You consider me rich?"

"Yes. I do."

Our eyes met, and I saw she wasn't going to back down. Rita had grown up one of six kids in her mother's tiny sweets shop by a narrow road in Grenada. "Alright," I said. "You're right, of course." But personally, I felt totally removed from the people Barbara called "monied." I didn't yearn for money, money didn't intrude into every little decision I made in the normal drift of my days. So I didn't consider myself rich, although of course, when you thought about it, that was exactly why I was.

"I will concede that you work for your money," Rita said, lifting her lush hair with both hands and letting it drop back to her shoulders. "This dude refers to his wealth as *winnings*."

"He got that from Jeff Bezos," Karthik said.

"Haven't you noticed?" I said. "He's always dropping names like Bezos, or Musk, or Gates? He sees them as his community."

"He doesn't live in the real world," Rita said.

"No, he doesn't. He's really doesn't. He's just in competition with other psychopaths. The way school shooters are, apparently."

"Did you notice his eyes? I hate his eyes."

"I do too. They're *piggy*."

We felt no obligation to be kind about him. The rich were the only group we felt entirely free to make fun of.

Something was in the air, some peppery gas that shifted the meaning of everything. One day I was standing by the work-table making a tray of smoked trout canapés, and I could hardly go on. I said to myself, it's not like you run a sweatshop where poor women sew clothes that are going to end up in landfill after some rich girl wears them twice. It's not like you own a mica mine in India and force starving children to dig glitter for eyeshadow out of the earth. Food is a human need. But then I thought, you never cook for people who are really hungry.

Whatever it was in the air, Quinn O'Neil was breathing it too. Around that time, she upped her game spectacularly. One night, she slipped past the hostess at The Grange and began to panhandle in the salon. The entrée that night was *sou fassum*, a delicate farce made of six different meats passed through a tamis sieve and then moulded into a cap of savoy cabbage, lacquered with butter until its veins gleamed gold against purple. Quinn approached a couple who had set their plates aside after taking just a bite or two. "You're not going to finish your cabbage rolls? Okay if I take them?"

That couple was Reg and Eve Bevaqua, as it happened. Needless to say, Sheff was incensed. He called it a stunt, a malicious, ignorant stunt, he said it was self-dramatizing theatre.

If Quinn O'Neil was performing theatre, I thought it was uncannily on point.

It would have been awesome to talk this through with my boyfriend, but we'd entered a new era, Jake and I. A cold cloud had settled over our household, and it refused to move on. We did not act like children, or make a fetish of our silence. We talked to each other about domestic matters, when the router went down, for example, or if someone needed to pick up milk. But the artless chat that used to fill our days was gone. Silence is not a helpful strategy when distance is the problem, is it? I'd watch out the window as Jake walked towards the house, a little hunched, his face preoccupied, and then he'd step into the kitchen and I'd speak to him and see him flinch, like any bit of attention was an intrusion. He was hypersensitive, as though he was constantly under threat. I believed that he loved me, he just didn't have the bandwidth to interact with me a lot. I thought about the way he'd confided in me when we were first together—our conversations were more honest and personal than any I'd ever had. But strangely, this hadn't brought us closer. It had made him want to barricade himself from me.

I began to be very aware of the skylight of the shed, which you could see from our bedroom window. When I woke up in the night, I'd get up and check whether the light was still on. It always was. If Jake was asleep, I could have walked across the yard and slipped into the shed and under his quilt, caught him off guard. But given that he was awake, we'd have to contend with the awkwardness between us. And even if lust got us over that hurdle, there would be the afterwards, that cherished time of lying in each other's arms, or lying side by side with no need to touch because the air encasing you is drenched with your love. The way you talk or don't talk in those moments. Neither of us could deal with that.

The water baron was taking flying lessons, trying to log the hours for a solo helicopter licence, and after that, we couldn't get rid of him. He and Eve ate with us at least once a week. He fancied himself an amateur gourmet cook, and he started dropping in for tutorials with Sheff. Apparently, his companies ran themselves.

One day I walked into the kitchen while he and Sheff were making gnocchi. They were talking about the refurbished CT scanner the Adlington hospital had just bought, which would save a lot of people having to go into the city. It was Reg's donation that had made this possible, and Sheff congratulated Reg warmly.

"Well, I do what I can," Reg said gallantly.

"Do you," I said from across the room. The warning look Sheff gave me only emboldened me. I strolled over. "I suppose, strictly speaking, if you wanted to do what you could, if, say, you wanted to address child poverty, you could start redistributing your wealth, and personally transform life for thousands of families."

"That's how it works, is it?" Reg said, not looking at me. He had long snakes of dough laid out on the work-table, and he was hacking them into uneven pieces. "People who haven't got things sorted out for themselves, the squeegee guy at the corner, I come along and write them a big cheque, and then they're all fine?"

I forced myself to smile. "Am I getting the old I-pulled-myself-up-by-my-own-bootstraps speech?"

His face flushed. He put the knife down. "It happens to be true. My dad was a car salesman and not a very good one, thanks to his drinking. My mother had serious depression and could never hold a job. You have no idea the hustle it took for me to pull myself out of that."

"Reg, Reg, chill," Sheff said, putting a hand on his arm. "Nobody's trying to insult you."

But some sort of rage overtook him. "I'm sick of this sort of shade being thrown at me. If I'd grown up on the Kingsway or the Bridle Path, nobody would question my right to a good life. It's goddamned class snobbery." Then, in a really classy move, he started ranting to Sheff about me as if I wasn't in the room. His voice went up and up until he was shouting. "Your little partner here thinks I should give my money away. Maybe she should start thinking big picture. Does she really think we'd be better off if the world's wealth was spread out over the world's population? Has she ever considered what that would mean? Where we'd be if the entire fucking human race had the money to buy cars and fly airplanes and eat meat?"

I headed back to the office, gasping. The guy was crazy. He thought that by sitting on obscene wealth, he was sequestering carbon. He thought he was part of the solution! I could hardly wait to share this with Rita and Karthik.

They were suitably amused. Karthik and I went on to tell Rita about the day Karthik went swimming in a nearby lake and came home with a plastic bag of lake clams. One of his experiments with those rubbery bivalves was a lovely-looking seafood risotto. Reg Bevaqua dropped in just as it was finished, and in his self-appointed role as our official taster, he volunteered to try it out.

"Rita, it was *so* gross," I said. "It tasted like mud and rotting cattails—didn't it, Karthik? Reg asked us what the seafood in it was, and I said, cockles, and he sat down and ate the whole thing."

We shared another laugh. I thought about my fifteenth-century culinary Bible, *On Right Pleasure and Good Health*. It included a recipe for eel pie, and there was a special note after the recipe: *When it is finally cooked, feed it to your enemies, for it has nothing good in it.*

JAKE

TEN

The canvas for Jake's iceberg project leaned against the back wall of the shed, not even painted with an undercoat. Icebergs floating up the city streets—a sledgehammer of a premise. And totally off the mark. It wasn't icebergs that preyed on him, it was the absence of ice. The Columbia Icefields had more or less vanished in his lifetime, in his memory. He first saw those glaciers on a hot summer day as a kid, when he jumped out of the car in his shorts and T-shirt, right onto ancient, grubby ice that ran as far as the eye could see. It blew him away, a highway running over the top of the world, the heat and cold slamming into each other. Then, when he was in grade ten, his dad was speaking at a conference in Banff, and Jake, at his mother's urging, went along to Alberta to do some mountain biking. One afternoon, he and his dad drove Highway 93 in their rental car. Jake was eager to see the Columbia Icefields again, but there was nothing but a moraine of rocks and muck on either side of the road. At first he was confused. Where was the ice? A band of blue glinted in the distance. "Plans are in the works to build a glass skywalk so tourists can get closer to the glaciers," said his dad, always proud to be the insider. It was like this genius initiative would totally cancel out the loss of ice that was a quarter of a million years old.

How could a catastrophe this gargantuan ever find its way into art? Art was stymied in the face of it. Or maybe it was just that Jake didn't really want to open himself up to it, the way he would have to. He'd get a glimpse of all that loss and find himself looking away. He'd spend the rest of the day obsessing about his dad and the part men like him played in the whole thing. He knew them well, rich guys, white guys, old guys, testes shrinking, prostates swelling—he could see them, back in the days when the effects of carbon were first coming to light. They took the news in, they grasped what was coming, those genial granddads, those outdoorsmen, those sailors, golfers, heli-skiers, practical jokers, barbeque chefs, wisecrackers, limerick writers, Robert Frost quoters, first-class travellers, live-largers—they saw it, and they said to each other, go back to sleep, friend. We're going to be fine. We'll leave it to our future selves, they'll deal with it. Or maybe they said, who cares if things get a little warmer? Great news for the air-conditioning sector, right? Might finally open up shipping routes in the Arctic. *Seriously?* Jake trembled, thinking about it.

The ride back to Banff that day when he was in grade ten—he didn't actually remember feeling anguish about the icefields, he just remembered the fury he felt with his dad. Later in the evening, they talked about it for the first time. It was like they were formalizing the break that happened the year of Jake's big science fair win. His dad had a dinner at the conference centre, and Jake walked downtown on his own for pizza. On his way home, he ran into Old Jack leaning on the stone railing of the Bow River bridge. He was sneaking a cigarette. He was supposed to have stopped smoking years before and he looked embarrassed, cupping his cigarette down at his thigh as if Jake hadn't already seen it, and asking with false friendliness how Jake was doing. Maybe it was just that sliver of moral advantage that gave Jake the courage. "I'm feeling sick, actually," he said. "About what we saw this afternoon. The way the glaciers have retreated."

Something real passed over his dad's face, pain, it looked like, and Jake's hope lifted, that he and his dad were going to have an honest conversation. But then Old Jack dropped his smoke and said, "Well, ice comes and it goes. It doesn't have much to do with us."

Jake stepped towards his dad and deliberately ground out the cigarette. "It does, actually, Dad, and you've known that for a long time. But you refuse to try to change things, or even to tell the truth about it."

"Change things," Old Jack said with contempt. "You are such a child. You have no idea how the world works. You have no idea what it would take to turn this ship around."

"I guess I don't. I'm not a scientist. But you are. And you decided not to try."

"Jake, you know, you've swallowed a bunch of half-baked ideas from the greens. They cherry-pick their science. All they've got are the slogans they carry at climate marches. And how do they get to that march? They drive their gasoline-powered cars."

Jake refused to take the bait. "Dad. I don't get why you didn't do something back when you were working for Exxon. I honestly don't get it. How could you know, and then decide that we would keep right on altering the atmosphere?"

"Christ, Jake, you think I'm God?"

The two of them gazed down the river, not looking at each other.

"You know," his dad said, "there's six billion people on this planet. They've all decided they'd prefer the lifestyle oil and gas gives them."

"No. They haven't decided. A few people, a few power brokers sitting in board rooms and in government—they decided for all of us. They figured they'd be fine, and maybe their kids, and they didn't give a shit about anybody else. *They*—that's you, Dad. You knew what you were doing. That makes you responsible."

How did that confrontation end? He couldn't remember exactly—it ended the way it began, with him and Old Jack walking off in their separate paths. Now they were forty years into the new world order of forest fires and cricket meal, and everything was speeding up. That May, a whole summer's worth of rain fell on Adlington in two hours, like it was dumped out of a massive gravel truck in the sky. Tongues of brown water licked down the road. Trees lay across Bowman Avenue, their secret balls of roots yanked out of the ground. Tough luck that his father didn't live to see it.

Jake came into the house and found Isla watching news footage on TV. An oil spill somewhere in the North Sea. It was sickening. He couldn't stand it. From her troubled face, he could tell she was asking questions in the manner of a sane and practical person. How will this be cleaned up? What price should this company pay? How can we make sure it never happens again? So far her natural well-being encased her, she was healthy enough to take this in. But soon enough a realization would dawn. It is too late for practical questions. We are all truly fucked.

It was a mistake to be with her, his despair might be contagious, he was going to drag her down.

The artist is mute but Nature is not. Jake tacked his nature studies around the shed. The red womb of the sumac's seed pouch. The satin sheen of the water birch. The gills of a brittlegill mushroom. The spots on the back of a pickerel frog. And yes, human fingerprints. The swirl of black hairs on his own belly. Nature was a mimic, nature was a wit, nature was profligate in beauty. Or so we think. We only see these patterns from a human perspective. We have no idea what they mean.

Phoebe came out for another visit. "Nature," she said thoughtfully, moving along the shed. "It's hard to compete with David Attenborough in high def, though, isn't it."

Still, he kept going out to whatever stretches of untouched land he could find.

Meanwhile, Isla was spending her days at the library. She described her previous book, *The Omnivore's Alphabet*, as juvenilia.

"You mean, because of the alphabet?"

"No. I mean that when I wrote it, I was a complacent sixteen-year-old who assumed that her readers had all the plant and animal life of the planet at their fingertips." She told him she was thinking about doing a twenty-first-century version of the fifteenth century's *On Right Pleasure and Good Health*. She might even use the alphabet again. Twenty-six locally farmed or foraged foods, the twenty-six best in terms of nutrition, greenhouse gas emissions in their production, availability, affordability, resistance to drought, resistance to pests, resistance to floods. "Like, *A* is for *Apples*, *B* is for *Barley*, *C* is for *Cattails*."

"We can eat cattails?"

"Yes," she said, like she couldn't believe he didn't know.

"Do you think we could build a complete diet around twenty-six locally sourced foods?"

She didn't know. She would teach herself by writing the book.

The Hubbard Prize had kept him going for several years, but it was gone. His fee for the show in Vancouver was gone. He pushed Phoebe to do something with the nature studies, which he was calling *Crab, Primrose*. She was against it, as she said it wasn't going to build on the success of *Dreaming the Future*. But she finally did what he wanted. That's what he was living on now, a small fee for a small show at a small gallery. It was time for something else.

He came across a poignant photo of the death in captivity of the last male white rhino. A dusty, archaeological mass sprawled on a cement floor, its young keeper bent in grief over its prehistoric tusk. Gone forever from Earth. Jake began to imagine a parade of animals, a series of *lasts*. Those that have vanished or will vanish in the Anthropocene, because of the rise of the anthropoids. Death, lots of artists have done. The end of birth—that's something else. A work about extinction that included the extinction of the anthropoids: how to convey the way *sapiens* dies, wilfully taking down our shared habitat? The Dadaists came to mind. Wasn't there a Dadaist who killed himself as the culmination of a piece of performance art? Who, in the 1920s equivalent of a live-stream suicide, shot himself with a small pistol in front of an audience, first using a ruler to measure his chest to make sure the bullet went right through his heart? That would get people's attention, alright.

Jake needed to think, he needed to focus, but the invasion of his hermitage by the intimate friend of his youth, Reg Bevaqua, was death to his concentration. Isla gossiping about the guy, mocking him, complaining, theorizing, clearly fascinated by his wealth and infamy. Bevaqua, who owned three or four homes, was eager to adopt The Grange as another one. Jake tried not to be paranoid, but come on. Could this possibly be a coincidence? And if Bevaqua *was* stalking him, what was he after?

One afternoon Jake found Isla lying on their bed crying. He had never seen her cry before. She looked like an entirely different person, younger, less beautiful, her eyes and her features blunt. He stepped over to the bed and lay down beside her, but she wouldn't let him touch her. She sat up, pulling the quilt around her like a hooded shawl. It was a quilt her grandmother had made for her, blue with white triangular patches that were supposed to be sailboats. He kept wanting to reach for her, but she was fully encased. She talked passionately about how hurt she felt at his aloofness. She accused him of curating his responses to her, picking and choosing what he wanted her to know about him. Why? she asked.

"What is this 'real self' of which you speak?" he said (quaintly).

She refused to let him charm her. "It makes me feel alone. And not telling me about Reg all that time—it's hard for me to trust you. You lied without actually saying the words."

"Sorry, Geppetto," he said. "Turns out I'm not a real boy yet."

Glibness was not the answer, but he couldn't seem to find another way. He could not stand fighting with her. It filled his chest with so much pain that he could hardly breathe. He couldn't even meet her gaze in that moment. In the long silence that followed, he was saying with every cell in his body, *oh, please, Isla, don't give up on me.*

After that (it seemed to Jake), she frequently and deliberately worked Bevaqua into their conversations, like she was trying to normalize the subject. She would come home from The Grange with bits of gossip, and Jake would deepen and expand on them from his past experience. Jake told her about the online research he did into Bevaqua's business in India.

"I don't believe the guy has a conscience," she said. "How do you grow up without a conscience?"

"We played a role in that," Jake said.

"We?"

"My parents and me."

"How is he *your* fault?"

"Competition was enshrined in our home. It was our religion, as expressed in, say, Monopoly. You know, where the whole point of the game is to bankrupt, humiliate, and destroy your friends. Second place is the first loser, that sort of thing."

She was making Ukrainian cabbage rolls, deftly tucking them into a dish in a herringbone pattern, and she paused and turned towards him with great interest. She had recently listened to a podcast about how Monopoly was developed. A guy made a fortune licensing and marketing the game, but he'd actually ripped the idea off from a woman who had invented the game as a moral lesson. Children, be warned. This is what happens if we let capitalism run rampant.

"Sorry to say, that's not the lesson we took away from it."

"Who did you play with?"

"Noah, Jason, a few other guys—but mostly it was like this endless, drawn-out, gladiatorial thing between me and Reg."

"All kids play Monopoly."

"I don't know if they play it the way we did. We played for real money. At the cabin we'd take a lantern out to the tent and play all night. We had our own rules. If two of you landed on the same property, you had to fight until one of you started to bleed. And then the loser had to not just forfeit the property, but also reach into a jar and pull out a punishment. Drink the other's pee, for example."

"Drink the other's pee?"

Walk over hot coals. Jump off the cliff in the dark. Stand in front of the archery target while the other one shot.

"Yes," he said. "Or, steal my grandpa's filthy undershorts and wear them for a day."

Okay, he had her laughing. But he resented this sort of conversation, if he was being honest. She wanted everything said out loud. It was like he'd amputated a limb to stop the gangrene from spreading, and was doing just fine without it, thank you, and she was poking away at it, waking up the phantom pain.

Phoebe joined the board of Jake's old art co-op, and she started calling him for support and advice about their renovation of an old church. It was a very cool project; Jake was glad to be her sounding board as they lurched from one budget crisis to the next. But one evening when Phoebe called, she was over the moon. "You will never believe what just happened. We've had a massive donation. *Massive*. Jake, it's so awesome. This is going to get us over the hump." She wouldn't divulge the sum, and she said the donor insisted on remaining anonymous. Then, being Phoebe, she dropped her voice and said, "Your girlfriend has access to mega-money through that restaurant. Tell her I called, and we're very happy over here, and I'll be in her debt forever and ever."

Jake sat on the front step and waited for Isla to come up the road. It was fall, the last week before The Grange closing. He got colder and colder sitting there, but he was too rigid with wrath to go inside for a jacket. When Isla came around the corner and saw him, she did a happy little skip. She had a jacket on over her whites, her hair was up in a dishevelled bun.

"Isla, tell me you didn't talk to Reg Bevaqua about the art co-op."

She stood still on the gravel driveway, her eyes big. "What?"

"You told Bevaqua about The Ark. You hit him up for a donation."

"He came through? Oh, my God! I can't believe it. I've been his least favourite person in the world lately, and I never thought he'd actually do it."

"So you did tell him."

"Jake. I didn't utter your name. He has *no* idea you're involved. I walked into the kitchen thinking about The Ark and all its problems, and there was Mr. Moneybags in a great mood, talking and laughing, and I thought, why not? He couldn't care less about art but he cares about building his image. So I talked about well-known patrons through the ages, the Guggenheims and the Medicis, how they ended up more famous than some of the artists they supported, and I said what you always say, about the social importance of art when the world goes to shit. But Jake, he didn't know I was quoting you. I texted him Phoebe's number, just in case—and he called her? Unbelievable!"

"Isla, are you out of your fucking mind?"

"What? It had nothing to do with you. Why not put his ill-gotten gains to good use?"

Jake had no words.

ELEVEN

He moved into a space where everything he saw hurt or offended him. The trashy images little Brie sat watching in a trance—he said something to Quinn about monitoring her screen time, and Quinn said, "Why exactly are you hanging around?"

But one day not long after, she called Jake to complain that her cellphone contract was about to expire and the assholes were trying to double her rate. Jake said he would come over and try to sort it out with her. He stopped by her place that evening and found that she had company. A guy of about forty, a thin guy with a furtive face. Jake had seen him before. One day when Jake cycled past The Grange, the guy was standing in the doorway of the barn talking to Kurt Altenbach. He was shirtless now, and he and Quinn were sprawled on the couch in obvious post-coital languor, her legs across his lap. The kids were nowhere around. Jake couldn't see a joint, but weed was thick in the air.

"Roger is a helicopter pilot," Quinn said, all proud.

Jake had heard a copter a few hours ago, but hadn't realized it had landed in town.

"You just flew up from Toronto?"

"I'm riding shotgun. My boss has his license, and he's trying to log the hours to fly solo."

"Where do you dock?"

"We're in a shitty field beside that big restaurant."

"Your boss at The Grange for dinner?"

"Yeah."

The guy gave Quinn's thigh an affectionate squeeze, and said, "Excuse me, baby." She swung her legs down and he got up and walked to the bathroom, hitching his jeans up on the way.

Jake smiled at Quinn sitting so relaxed in her sunken old couch. She had some pink in her cheeks for once. The poor kid wasn't even thirty, and she had a daughter in junior high. "Tinder's doing whirlybird deliveries these days?"

"Piss *off*," she said, flashing her happiness at him.

He said goodbye and got back on his bike. He took a circle around town before he cycled towards the pasture, approaching it from the east so he couldn't be seen from the restaurant. An access road ran parallel to the highway and Jake took it. Boys were playing ball hockey on the narrow asphalt, and he slalomed right through them while they yelled and slapped their ball at him.

And then he was at the sheep pasture, and there it sat, Reggie's boyhood fantasy. Custom painted in two shades of blue like one of his water bottles, branded to justify the business writeoff, no doubt. Not a monstrous mosquito, as people always said, but a glass and steel space pod that had ventured into earth's atmosphere and been sucked down to this sheep-bitten pasture. Jake propped his bike against the rail fence and approached it. It was a four-seater, and from what he could see through the tinted glass, the cockpit was beautifully appointed with leather seats. God. Old Jack—would he ever be impressed.

In their post-Monopoly youth, Jake and Reg went on a ski trip to Invermere with Old Jack and Jack's former Sigma Chi roommate, Keith Lundstrom, now CEO at the water giant Ganymede. A boys' trip, Barbara called it. Jake and Reg were in grade eleven. The future loomed, it was all they talked about. Old Jack and especially Keith (who did not have kids of his own) treated them like acolytes. They elaborated their theory that business was the only true meritocracy. You become a doctor or an academic and you can be a total schmuck, you can coast for your entire professional life. Only in business is everyone's worth quantifiable: just check the bottom line. Sports were a test or a rehearsal. Did you have stamina, speed, guts? Jake managed a good impersonation of a jock, but it wore him down.

In the VIP lounge in YYC, Keith made a prediction. "Twenty years from now, Bert and Ernie here will not be flying commercial. You'll own your own planes."

"Not me," Reg said. "I'm going to get a helicopter. Land in my own backyard."

"Gotta love that kid's ambition," Old Jack said. "Especially when it comes with a work ethic."

Lundstrom agreed.

"Is making more money than you need an ethic?" Jake asked.

"More than you need?" Reg said. "What does that mean?"

"He's hungry, that one," Lundstrom observed. Old Jack's failure hung in the air: he had raised a kid without appetites.

Keith and Old Jack spent the week belabouring their stupid private jokes and reminiscing about their frat hazing, when Old Jack had had his cock and balls dipped in printer's ink and Keith's humiliation was so lurid it would only be revealed at the end of the trip—if Bert and Ernie proved themselves worthy. Tom and Jerry, Chip and Dale, Batman and Robin, Shake and Bake, Bow and Arrow, Dow and Jones—the old guys knocked themselves out. They didn't ski as a foursome because Jack and Keith didn't want to hold Bugs Bunny and the Road Runner back. Not that they were slouches on the slopes themselves. Riding the chair, Reg and Jake would look down to see two upright figures meticulously navigating the moguls on a black diamond run, crossing and crisscrossing each other's paths. "Hey, Zig and Zag," Reg yelled, and they each lifted a pole in greeting, not daring to take their eyes off their trajectory. Mid-afternoon the old guys would pack it in and start drinking in the lodge, while Reg and Jake did a few more runs and worked the chairlift line for intel about private parties in town.

During dinner at the hotel, Lundstrom pressed his opinion that they should go into tech. One good idea and you were set for life.

"The good ideas are taken," Old Jack said.

Uber, Twitter, Instagram, Dropbox, Zoom, Snapchat—they were all in the future, when Jake thought about it now, but Old Jack's opinions were considered the last word on any subject.

"I'm going into oil and gas," Reg said. "That's where the money is in Canada."

What a suck-up.

The next day Keith was busy with business calls in his room, and Old Jack insisted on taking Jake and Reg up to the peak, to a double black diamond run called Sagarmatha. You took a T-bar at the end of the chairlift, and then a tow rope. Jake had been up it before and hated it, but when he said so, his dad said, "Aw, buttercup." They skied off the tow rope and then laboured up a slope facing east. They were looking at the Rockies and the gulf that divided them from the Columbia Range. Fine snow filled the air, and the scene had the blurred quality of the establishing shot in an old television movie.

"Do you know what you're seeing?" Old Jack asked.

Framed photos of this pass were on display in the lobby at their lodge. In summer it looked like a massive dry creek bed. "The Trail of the Ancient Ones," a caption read. Jake assumed this referred to the Kaska Dena, whose country this was.

Reg said, "I saw something about this trench on TV. It's so huge, the astronauts saw it from the moon."

From two hundred thousand miles away? Jake thought. Dude.

Christ, they were high. Jake dug his poles in. He could hardly appreciate the view, he was so distracted by the precipice. He pressed his weight onto the camber of his skis, trying to maximize his grip on the earth.

"What you are looking at is a monument to opportunity lost," Old Jack said. "A monument to human stupidity."

In the 1960s, he went on to say, the US Army Corps of Engineers had put forward a brilliant plan that would have transformed agriculture and commerce for the entire continent. The Peace, Yukon, Columbia, and Liard Rivers would be diverted into this trench. "You build a whole series of dams across the north of the province," Old Jack said, "and you use this ditch as a reservoir. It's eight hundred kilometers long. Can you imagine?" He gestured west with his pole. "Some of that water, you route into a canal that runs across the prairies to Lake Superior, and you've got a fantastic, cheap, transcontinental navigation route. I mean, think about that, cargo ships moving across Saskatchewan. But most of it, you divert south through Montana. You have to sacrifice a few towns, you're going to drown out Prince George for one, but you create thousands and thousands of jobs and you turn the entire US Southwest into a garden."

"Wow," Reg said. "That's radical."

"It's radical, alright," Old Jack said with the world-destroyer's placid satisfaction. "The tree-huggers were all yodelling about the wildlife corridors and the salmon runs. But the benefits would have been enormous."

Snow was blowing, the light was flat, and Jake was dreading the mogul-pocked run back down. Sagarmatha reminded him of a corpse-strewn Everest. "Dad," he said. "I'm going." He swivelled his skis downslope and, in a minute, they caught up with him.

The Rocky Mountain Water Diversion lecture resumed over supper. They ate at a diner with butcher-paper on the tables, and Old Jack took out a pen and sketched a rough map of North America among the platters of half-eaten beef dip and french fries. He indicated all the population centres that had grown up in the US desert in the last half-century, thanks to underground water. "Sad to say, Las Vegas has pretty much drained its aquifer. The whole goddamn city is sinking. California is running dry. And that is only going to get worse. But like they say, one man's misery is another man's fortune. We have forty percent of the earth's fresh water. Think about that."

"It's a whole new frontier," Lundstrom said.

"Forty percent of the earth's fresh water for a half of one percent of the world's population. We have more water than we know what to do with. And we just take it for granted. When we were negotiating NAFTA, the Yankees were prepared to pay two thousand dollars per acre-foot of fresh water. You know the price of an acre-foot of water in Canada? Go ahead, guess."

"A hundred dollars," Reg said gamely.

Old Jack snorted. "*Ten* dollars! Can you believe it? Ten dollars! That's Canada for you. We don't recognize opportunity when it bites us on the ass."

Reg said, "Is the diversion idea dead for sure?" and it was like he'd pressed Play on another half-hour lecture. Nothing gave Old Jack a hard-on like castigating environmentalists, whose ideas were all gestated in a marijuana haze in Haight-Ashbury, deliberate efforts to halt progress and bring down the man.

Jake and Reg had plans for the night that involved a downtown bar with a lax carding policy, and (they hoped) a meet-up with a couple of girls they had talked to on the slopes. When Jake tried to make a move, Lundstrom said, "You boys are not going anywhere. It's TV night!" He and Old Jack were big into *The Sopranos*. Back in their suite, Lundstrom lined up four glasses, poured them all a three-finger Scotch, and flicked the TV on. Reg sat in an armchair, watching avidly, laughing along with the old guys' stupid jokes. Through years of having airline tickets bought for him, through years of being treated to hotels, restaurants, ski passes, and bungee jumps, he had precisely calibrated his flattery of Old Jack while still privately conspiring with Jake's petty rebellion. But that night he refused to catch Jake's eye. Jake, sprawled on a bed with ski fatigue like barbells over his legs, knew exactly what he was witnessing: Reg officially going over to the other side. Not a made man yet, but well on his way.

Up in the early hours in his shed in Adlington, Jake drew a caricature of Reg in the helicopter cockpit. Water Bandit Reg, as he'd seen him on TV. Caption: *Drinkwater the Douche hovers over the wasteland in his glass bubble.*

The cartoon made him laugh—the too-groovy fade of Reg's hair, the meaty face, the macho leer. Jake scanned it and considered where to post it. He ended up setting up a new Twitter account with the handle @Shatterhand. Kurt's nickname for him, which he kind of liked. It was stupid, it was poking the bear, but he couldn't resist. After that, the ideas came thick and fast.

Drinkwater the Douche pitches water bottles from his helicopter into the Great Pacific Garbage Patch.

Drinkwater the Douche sails his yacht through an ice-free Northwest Passage.

Drinkwater the Douche offers a sip from a water bottle to a child dying of dysentery.

People got it! Within a month, @Shatterhand had attracted an amazing following and the posts were retweeted everywhere, by real media types as well as by notorious online provocateurs. Other people's memes about BevAqua's corporate depredations popped up at #EatTheRich, #IfYouSeeMeWeep, #AtrocitiesOfTheAnthropocene. @Shatterhand was way more successful than @JakeChallis had ever been.

Not exactly how Jake had wanted to change the world through his art, but it had its satisfactions. He'd like to show it to Isla, she would get a kick out of it, but given how outraged he was when she got Reg involved in The Ark . . . no.

They had a real winter for once. A long winter, with lots of snow and lots of ice. One frosty evening, Kurt Altenbach thumped at the side door of the shed and announced, with no preamble, not even hello, "I'm going camping up on the Bruce next week."

In March!

"You pack a tent in?"

"I build a lumitalo."

A quinzhee, Jake figured. He had a love/hate relationship with the quinzhee from his days as a Boy Scout. He gestured to Kurt to come in, but Kurt ignored him.

"Where do you camp?"

"On the shore, on the east side. I park at Battery Bay and ski in."

"Battery Bay. So, a little north of Comstock Cove?"

"Yes."

"My family's cabin used to be at Comstock Cove. Before Reg Bevaqua stole the land."

"I know. And who did the Challises steal it from?"

Ah. This was why you had to like Kurt. "The petroglyphs you mentioned—is that where they are?"

"No."

"How long do you plan on staying?"

"I come back when I've had enough." Kurt stared from the doorway with his strange eyes. "It's a full moon," he said.

"The wolf moon, right?"

"No. The wolf moon's in January."

Jake had been trying to tease Kurt about his big camping story, but the guy didn't do humour. "Okay," Jake said, after a minute, although Kurt hadn't exactly invited him. "Yeah, I'd like to come. It sounds cool."

Adlington was still asleep when Kurt pulled up in his antique Ford on a cold Monday morning. He had scraped an oval porthole on the windshield, but the side windows were solid with frost, and it was like they were riding in an armoured tank. The truck had very short headlights, and Kurt drove too fast. The nighttime low was forecast to be about minus twenty all week. Jake's sleeping bag was rated to minus thirty and he had a thermal mat rolled into the Velcro loops of his pack. He'd packed five Ziploc bags of lentil stew, courtesy of Isla, who'd rolled her eyes when she gave it to him. She thought they were nuts. He had oatmeal, trail mix. A WhisperLite stove and a canister of white gas. He had a short-handled shovel, a flashlight with fresh batteries, and a stash of those chemical heating pockets you can activate if your extremities start to freeze. The biggest danger he faced was a hernia, schlepping in all that gear. The idea was to be at the Battery Bay parking lot shortly after sunrise and then ski in to the shore, a two-hour run. They'd mound up snow to make the quinzhee, and then they'd let it cure for two or three hours before they excavated their cave within it.

Anticipation, a distant acquaintance from the past, settled over Jake as they drove north. The silence. The chance to fix his eyes on the horizon. He put the heel of his hand to the frosty glass beside him and melted his own porthole. Out the window, fields and trees sped by, numb under the spell of winter. They passed the gas station where they had always stopped for ice cream. He knew every landmark on this road, and he actually found himself missing Reg. The two of them used to travel with peashooters. They'd crank down the back windows of his dad's Buick Riviera and spend the drive shooting at everything they passed. His dad pretended not to notice. His dad was more mellow when Reg was along, he had somebody to show off for. Old Jack loved going to the Bruce Peninsula. It was in the Challis genes, Barbara said. She said the sale of the Comstock Cove property broke Jack's heart—he'd always thought the cabin would stay in the family. Grandpa sold it without consulting anyone. They didn't find out until the deed had transferred. It was like the final nail in any pretense of affection between Grandpa and his children.

Why was Grandpa Challis such a mean old SOB? There was a story to explain it. When Jake's father was a boy, Grandpa Challis kept a strongbox on the top shelf of a bedroom closet. The children were forbidden from looking in it. Jake's dad was always curious, and one day when he was left alone, he climbed up and opened the strongbox. Inside he found his dad's souvenirs from the British army. Ribbons, certificates, a pocket watch, some German coins—but also an envelope of photographs. He opened it. What he thought at first glance was a huge pile of firewood turned out to be bodies. Naked bodies, thrown with monstrous callousness into a heap. Long rows of bodies lying in ditches. Grandpa Challis had never told them anything about his war experiences. But based on those photos, the family believed he had been in the unit that liberated one of the concentration camps, probably Bergen-Belsen, and these were some of the terrible things he saw. It must have been an awful experience for Old Jack, finding those images when he was only a boy. The point of the story (as Barbara told it to Jake and his sisters) was not the atrocity of Bergen-Belsen, but what the photos explained about Jake's grandfather, the horrors he carried around within him.

Jake's family didn't see the old man the whole winter after he sold the cabin, not even at Christmas. In spring, when the new owners drove in to Comstock Cove, they discovered a car behind the cabin, and they called the OPP to report that they'd found John Challis's body. He hadn't been dead long. The coroner said he'd died of a stroke, but that it was likely connected to the fact that he had advanced cancer, undiagnosed and untreated. He had smoked a pipe for decades, and they said his bottom lip was purple and swollen and that a huge sore had bloomed on the spot where the pipe rested. But by then he had nobody around him to say, "You need to see a doctor." And he still had the strength to make it up to the cabin. Where did he die, where was his body found? Jake's parents didn't know, or they wouldn't say.

The sun was up when they passed the familiar turnoff to Comstock Cove. Kurt didn't acknowledge the turnoff and neither did Jake. Then they were at the Battery Bay parking lot. It was empty and had recently been plowed. Jake judged the temperature to be about minus ten. He pulled his skis out of the truck box and scrawled blue wax on them. When he swung his pack onto his back, his knees buckled. His partner didn't bother with wax. Kurt was carrying even more weight than Jake was—a full-sized shovel bungeed obliquely across his pack and all manner of wares dangling below, a hatchet, an ice saw, a canvas bucket, a fishing rod, a coil of rope. He looked like a tinker selling goods from village to village, but he took off like a jackrabbit.

It was a great trail with just enough elevation to make it interesting. Weighed down by his gear, Jake broke a sweat by the third herringbone. Kurt was astonishingly agile on the hills, in spite of his antique skis and gargantuan pack. In two hours of skiing, he never once looked back. He led Jake to a site sheltered by a band of pines. They were on a gorgeous overlook, facing a white and blue vista. The bay was frozen about a kilometre out.

The snow was knee deep in places. They marked out the best spot for the quinzhee, and when they had heaped up a mound as high as they were tall, they left it to cure and searched around for deadfall for a fire to dry out their jackets. Once their jackets were dry, Kurt cut a hole in the ice and hauled up a bucket of water. Wolf-killed venison seemed unlikely to materialize, so Jake pulled out a bag of lentil stew and squeezed it into his cooking pot, and while it warmed, he dug a nearby picnic table out of the snow and dragged it closer.

After they ate, they excavated a pleasing cave, six feet long and about four feet wide. By the time they finished, the light was seeping out of the sky. The cloud cover was dense. They would not be seeing the moon tonight. Jake built up the fire and made tea in tin mugs. Kurt accepted his without a word or glance. The guy's silence was not monkish, not contemplative, just—he didn't give a shit about you. Alright, good. Jake had everything he needed, this little circle of firelight and the wilderness crouched in the dark around them.

In the morning, he woke up slowly, a hibernating animal in his cozy sleeping bag. Sunlight filtered through the walls of snow. Whatever language *lumitalo* came from, it was a great word. The pine branches they'd stacked over the doorway made an ornate ferny pattern on their den. He fell back to sleep, and when he woke up next, Kurt was staring expressionlessly at him, his eyes about a foot away. Jake rolled over and tentacles of cold invaded his sleeping bag. He lay without moving while Kurt crawled out of the shelter, lay listening to Kurt's piss hiss into the snow. He couldn't get warm again. When he hauled himself out, Kurt was standing with binoculars trained along the peninsula to the south.

"Morning," Jake said.

No answer. He was starting to find Kurt's silence unnerving. No grunts during the night, no sighs. The dude didn't even snore.

He set up his little stove and boiled water for coffee and porridge. The sky had cleared, the blue was dazzling. The cold air felt metallic in his lungs. All Earth's scars were covered by snow, all its fevers quenched by the cold. It was like the north country had been put into an induced coma until it could recover. As he cleaned up the breakfast, he hatched a plan. He would go off on his own. He'd carry his skis down to the lake and explore the shoreline. He had a grid map, and he got it out and sat at the picnic table to study it.

Kurt was again scanning the lake with binoculars, still focused on the shoreline to the south. Jake finally asked him what he was looking for.

"Signs of life on Comstock Cove."

"You can see the lodge from here?"

"You can see smoke if they have a fire."

"They're not on the grid?"

"No. They have a big generator. And solar panels on the south roof of the workshop. They run heaters all winter, just to keep things from freezing up, but if somebody was there, they'd be using the fireplace."

"You think Bevaqua might be there?"

"No. They're in Colombia. They have a place in Cartagena."

"How do you know?"

"From Roger."

Reg's pilot. "Ah. You two are friends?"

"Used to be," Kurt says. "Before I knew what a fucking *Arschkriecher* he is."

Okay then. "Does he come up here on his own when Bevaqua's away?"

"Sometimes."

"He can land at the lodge?"

"Yeah, they built a pad."

They had dreamed of a helipad at Comstock Cove, Jake and Reg. When the cabin was their spy-ring hideout. Jake was the pilot in those days, Reg the wielder of the laser gun.

"So do you see smoke?"

"No."

Kurt handed over the binoculars. Jake scanned the shoreline, but he couldn't identify any landmarks. "I'll take your word for it," he said, handing the binoculars back.

"It's an easy ski in from the marina at Scalloway, Shatterhand." Kurt was staring at Jake, impudent, challenging.

"What? Seriously?"

A little shrug. "Bevaqua might think he owns the wilderness, but it belongs to all of us."

"Does it?" Jake thought about that for a minute, and then said, "It's a fact that the dude enjoyed a lot of fine holidays on my family's dime." He stood looking out over the ice. A chance to see Comstock Cove again. Check out what Reg had done with it. "What does he have for security?"

"Motion-detection cameras. Solar-powered. I know where they are."

"Could we drive in?"

"No. The lane's locked. And somebody would see our tracks. We can ski. The ice is solid in Comstock Cove. There's a snowmobile trail."

Without another word, they geared up. Jake put a few essentials in a day pack. They stashed everything else in the quinzhee and then hit the trail to the parking lot. It had snowed an inch or so in the night, and the base was perfect. The trail felt half as long without the weight of their gear. There were two other vehicles parked in the lot, both covered with snow. Kurt's old truck was reluctant to start but eventually it shuddered to life and they were on the road. Sunlight shone through the astonishing frost designs on the side windows, it lit up the fierce etching of Kurt's face. Was this why Kurt came up to the Bruce? Had he planned in advance to take Jake in to the lodge? *Why?*

They'd had a very weird exchange last spring, the day Jake first saw Reg's helicopter in the sheep pasture. Jake was snooping around, checking it out, when he heard Kurt's voice: "You could sabotage it." He looked over to see Kurt standing at the gate to the garden. He was pushing a wheelbarrow laden with sheep shit, and he set it down and walked towards Jake, carrying his pitchfork. "It wouldn't be hard. They are very basic machines." He lifted his pitchfork and used it to indicate various elements in the power train. He pointed to a disk, low-down in the rotor shaft. "All you need to do is drain the oil out of the gearbox."

"Why would I want to bring this helicopter down?"

"You tell me, Shatterhand. Maybe the guy who owns it is after your wife or something." He looked directly at Jake, all feral knowing.

He was so fucking weird. Jake did not for a second believe that Reg was hitting on Isla, or that she would look at him twice. But Kurt had picked up some sort of vibe.

Again they drove past the turnoff to Comstock Cove without a word. A couple of miles south was the road to Scalloway. It was a tiny settlement, hardly a village, mainly just the marina that serviced the shore between Lion's Head and Wiarton. Kurt turned off the highway and drove to the waterfront, where he parked on the side of the road. He leaned over and opened the glove box and pulled out a pack of Nicorette gum. Then they got out and stood on the road for a minute, surveying the scene. It was Tuesday morning. Not a single person in sight, and most of the parked cars and trucks were snow-covered. The drydock area of the marina was a sea of blue, patched with snow: boats shrink-wrapped in balloon-blue vinyl tarps. Skis and poles over their shoulders, Kurt and Jake walked past it and down to the dock. It was almost noon when they finally struck off onto the lake. An ice road led to a fishing camp, and they followed that for a while. Then they took a snowmobile track that ran north. When it ended, they had to break trail. The snow had blown into drifts, it had a brittle crust that snagged their poles, so it was hard work and they took turns leading. The wind was in their faces and Jake's glasses frosted up. He paused and took them off and dropped them in a pocket. Within ten minutes, frost had crusted his eyelashes.

But bit by bit, the beloved rock faces of Comstock Cove took shape ahead of him. The beautiful harbour where three tiny cabins had had their dock, where the cliffs rose in tiers from the lake like a citadel. A lodge was poised now against that rocky backdrop. Stolen land, and here Reg squatted. In a huge mansion with a stone foundation, planks stained a pale willow-green, cedar shakes. He had a boathouse, a massive stone pier. It was all new and it looked austere and weathered, like it had grown from these rocks. It was perfect, the Platonic ideal of a wilderness lodge—you could imagine that Comstock Cove had been waiting for this home. Jake had never envied Reg. Never. Now he felt a kind of awe. If his tears had not been frozen, he might have wept. That Reg had *this*.

TWELVE

It was dark when Jake, ravenous, came down the stairs of Reg's lodge to see Kurt moving lithely around the kitchen in home-knit red socks. He was wearing a cap with a row of LEDs clipped to the brim, and he had battery lanterns on the counters. This kitchen, Jake thought, stepping into its warmth. Isla would love it.

Kurt was heating things up on the stove. He'd set out a bottle of Glendronach and two heavy-bottomed glasses, and Jake poured himself a drink. On a granite counter sat a neat cardboard box reading *The Tiffin House, Lamonte Street, New York*. A sticker said *Tout le Lapin*. Kurt had pried open four or five of the stainless steel tins it contained. He'd plated a rabbit pâté and some crackers. The pâté had green peppercorns in it and it was delicious.

"Hey, Shatterhand, find us a red wine," Kurt said, and Jake made his way to the liquor cabinet, where his old friend King Drinkwater had a huge collection. A solar heater had been cleverly installed on either side to keep the booze from freezing. Jake ran his eyes over the wine lying cork-out in rows, and reached for the oldest-looking bottle he could see. He didn't bother to wipe the dust off and check the label. Let's hope it was a Château Margaux, maybe a wedding gift, a vintage they were saving for some big anniversary. He found a corkscrew in a drawer and the cork eased out cleanly. Kurt was laying plates and cutlery on the coffee table in the living room. Candles, he lit candles. Jake found glasses. He settled on the couch and sat gazing out at the lake, sipping his Scotch.

The living room was two stories high, the lodge's whole fourth wall extravagantly open to the sky and the frozen lake. Comstock Cove, he knew every plane and angle of this scene. Now in winter it was the luminescent white of a movie screen. Just one band of colour, a dilute navy blue in the lower quarter of the sky.

How ludicrously easy it had been to get in. Kurt had climbed the rocky rise and jumped onto the roof of the boathouse, crawling commando-style along until, after a bit of blind groping, he located a security camera under the eaves and stuck a wad of chewed Nicorette over the lens. Then he was down off the boathouse and, neck warmer pulled up to his eyes, moving methodically up the approach to the lodge in a zigzag track, stealing behind particular trees, disabling the cameras one by one. A large two-story outbuilding stood behind the lodge. It had a modern lock, and Kurt knew the code. They stepped into a workshop with a cement floor—a table saw, two Ski-Doos, lots of storage barrels and boxes and gear Jake couldn't make out in the dim light. They climbed the stairs. Numerous doors along the second-floor corridor. Kurt opened one to a neat, nicely furnished apartment. Roger's, Jake guessed. Kurt went straight to a drawer and pulled out a key ring.

They went back across the yard to the lodge, and they were in.

What a place. This window had been built to scale with the magnificent view. A massive hearth of local dolomite. The furnishings, beautiful. No huntsman-rustica for Jake to sneer at, just leather, wool, stone, and wood in subtle rapport with the landscape. Jake and Kurt dropped their jackets on a couch and prowled around without speaking. Everywhere, Jake saw items he knew. A Mission chair with a worn leather cushion—his grandpa's chair. A pillow with the worried face of a Boston terrier stitched onto it in needlepoint, his grandmother's handiwork. On the mantel sat Grandpa Challis's Odd Fellows cigar box. The motto Jake remembered from when he was little: *We command you to visit the sick, relieve the distressed, bury the dead, and educate the orphan.* Miraculously, a souvenir like this had survived the in-between owner. *And the gun.* Reg Bevaqua owned Grandpa Challis's gun. There it was, the .303 Lee-Enfield rifle John Challis had bought from an army surplus store because it was the model he'd been issued by the British Army during the war. It rested on two wooden pegs on a wall, just as it had in the old Challis cabin.

Upstairs, in what was clearly Reg and his wife's bedroom, Jake found the bureau his grandfather had made. Framed pictures of Reg's kids on it. The little girl had Reggie's sassy face. A professional photo of Eve. She looked poised but lifeless. He turned towards the bathroom. A sunken tub was surrounded by glass so you could bathe among the treetops. He used the toilet without thinking—thankfully there was enough water in the tank to deal with his turd. Afterwards, he stood looking out, trying to get his bearings. A wide snow-covered path ran straight into the forest. Over the trees to the northwest, he could see a big clear-cut—that would be the helipad.

The house was chilly but not really cold, thanks to solar-powered heaters. Oh, Water Baron Bevaqua was on the cutting edge. In the closet Jake found a stack of folded quilts. He tossed a couple on the bed and lay on his back, resting his eyes on the beautiful ceiling fan. Sleep was tugging him down. Here Reg lies with the beauteous Eve. His buddy Reg, Reggie, who knew what it was to be a little boy in the Challis house. First is worst, second is best, third's the one with the hairy chest, and fourth's the golden eagle. The times Jake's dad locked them out of the cabin overnight—because they'd left garbage where bears could get it, or taken the boat around the point and let it drift away while they swam. Or because they were up on a cliff with their archery bows, and saw Jake's grandma out watering her petunias and started shooting around her, to freak her out. It was blackfly season, and he locked them out all night. He wouldn't even let them have the tent. They built up a pile of brush in a rocky enclave and wrapped towels from the clothesline around their heads. In the dark, Reg began to sob. "You're lucky your dad cares. Mine's a useless drunk. He doesn't even know I'm alive." He grabbed the flesh of Jake's upper arm and twisted it brutally. "That's for not listening to your dad."

Jake stretched out luxuriously. Reg wants me to see this, he thought. It doesn't mean anything to him if I don't see it. That's why he's hanging around Adlington. To lure me here.

Kurt came out of the kitchen and set a terrine on the coffee table, a brown clay dish that was likely an antique. It had the head of a rabbit on the lid, its long ears drooping back. Isla would be charmed by it. Jake leaned forward and lifted the lid. Rabbit stew with root vegetables. "I'm glimpsing the future. Foraged food, eaten by candlelight."

Kurt sat down at the other end of the couch. "That's what this place is for. It's his bolt hole for when things get bad."

"You think?"

"You should check out the storeroom. He's got supplies to last through the apocalypse."

"Seriously? Like dehydrated food?"

"Yes. And fancy food from New York restaurants. Think about it. This lodge is perfect. It's isolated, but you've got access by land, by boat, by air. Lots of fresh drinking water."

"Did Roger tell you this?"

"No. Nobody had to tell me."

They finished the stew, which was pretty good for tinned food, and Kurt took their plates away and came back with the second course. It was a delicate roulade, the rabbit's loins pounded velvet-thin. The light was dim, and they ate this course more slowly, their eyes on the snowy lake. The wine was magnificent, and the roulade with its tiny pink heart of prosciutto was tasty, flavoured with rosemary. You could unlawfully enter a house built by obscene wealth, you could eat a stolen dinner with a silent companion, and still the joy that Isla set out to create for strangers every night would muscle its way in. It was the wine. Jake rarely drank these days. That was a mistake. He was going to start drinking every night.

The last dish was the roasted haunches of the hare in a grainy mustard sauce. Their dinner was done. The *lapin* had given its all. Kurt reached over and pinched out the candles, and they watched silver light take over the lake. They couldn't see the moon, but it was surely rising. Was it behind the lodge? Saturn had eighty moons and Earth had one, yet Jake, a creature of Earth, had never bothered to unravel its moon's mysterious habits.

Kurt got up. "One more course," he said, and headed for the kitchen.

It was starting to get cold. Jake switched on a lantern and carried it to the big stone hearth. The woodbox was full. Spruce logs, nicely split. Kindling, birchbark for tinder. He knelt at the hearth and set to work. Open the damper, his grandfather said, and he did. The hearth drew beautifully. Flames from the kindling began to lick at the logs.

"Not clever," Kurt said when he came back.

"Oh well," Jake said. Hard to believe anybody was going to notice one little strand of smoke this far from any town.

Kurt sat back on the couch.

"Didn't you say there was dessert?"

"It's warming. So, what do you think of this lodge?"

"I'd rather be in my grandfather's little cabin." Its spidery windows, its log walls, its iron beds with their saggy, smelly mattresses.

"What did you do here when you were a boy?"

"We played games."

"What sort?"

"Feats of strength. Duels. Truth or Dare."

"I have never understood that game. Why would anyone choose to perform a dangerous stunt, rather than tell the truth?"

"You might be ashamed of the truth."

Kurt shook this off.

"Okay," Jake said. "We'll play while we wait for our dessert." The cork from the wine was still on the coffee table, and Jake palmed it and put his hands behind his back. "If you pick the cork, you go first."

Kurt picked the cork. He took it out of Jake's open hand and held it as though it was a powerful talisman. "Truth or Dare."

"Truth."

Kurt looked pleased. After a minute he said, "Why do you hate Bevaqua so much?"

"What makes you think I even know him?"

"You went by on your bike one day, and he called you a piece-of-shit loser."

"Nice." So Reg did know he lived in Adlington. Jake sat with his eyes on the fire for a long time, and then said, "I hate Bevaqua because one summer, when I had the chance to be someone better, I slept with his girlfriend."

Kurt smiled. He did not question Jake's logic. "We could punish him for trapping you like that. We could burn this place down to pay him back."

"Don't be stupid," Jake said. He swung his legs up onto the coffee table. "Okay, my turn. Truth or Dare?"

"Truth."

"Why did you leave Germany?"

Firelight made a warm study of Kurt's face. "Annalise made me. I was on the needle."

Jake was not surprised, except maybe at Kurt's openness in telling him. "Have you been on the needle here?"

"It's not your turn." Kurt picked up the cork again. "Truth or Dare."

"Truth."

"What are you so afraid of all the time, Shatterhand?"

Jake was warm now and inexpressibly comfortable. Kurt might be trying to insult him, but he was primed for the question. "When I was in psych in university, I read a case study about a man who came to see

Sigmund Freud because he was ashamed of his great cowardice. Freud listened to his story, and then said the man had turned into a coward when he glimpsed his own rage. Because it terrified him so much. I remember that analysis because it felt true to me. So, to answer your question, what I am most afraid of is my own anger."

"That's very cute," Kurt said. "Shatterhand has a cute way of thinking."

"Thank you."

"But I reject the answer as bullshit, and I issue you a dare."

"I don't think that's how the game works," Jake said.

But Kurt was up and headed for the kitchen. When he came back, he was carrying two white mugs. They were half full of a liquid the colour of old sticks, thick and murky. Jake raised a mug and sniffed. It was foul. "What is it?"

Kurt had a brown bottle tucked under his arm and he passed it to Jake. The type on the label was tiny. Jake got up and retrieved his glasses from his jacket pocket so he could read it: *Banisteriopsis caapi. Diplopterys cabrerana. Mimosa hostilis.*

"I have no idea what that means."

"Roger told me they picked up ayahuasca last year in Colombia."

So. He'd had the impression earlier that Kurt was searching for something. The vine of the dead, the vine that brought your ancestors back to visit.

"Are you supposed to drink it warm?"

"I don't know. I had to warm it to get it out of the bottle."

Jake knew two things about ayahuasca: that it made people vomit (wasn't it sometimes called La Purga?) and that people who did it in ceremonies said they saved themselves years of psychotherapy. But wasn't a Quechua shaman supposed to spend the day selecting vines in the forest and brewing them up, then act as your guide on the journey?

Kurt picked up the mug and handed it to Jake. "I dare you, coward," he said.

Jake laughed, it was such a little-boy thing. If Reg had sourced this stuff in Cartagena, it was bound to be tourist-grade. So he took the mug and drank it down. He knew it was stupid, but he did it. It was awful. Earthy like the tinctures his friends at art school used to press on him when he was coming down with a cold, but worse, thick and more bitter. It was like drinking a dose of nausea. But he drank it all except for the sludge at the bottom, and by focusing on his breathing, he managed not to gag.

"Alright," he said to Kurt, setting the mug down. "My turn. Truth or Dare."

"Truth."

It was a pretext, of course—Kurt had every intention of drinking the other mugful. But Jake asked a real question. "Why are you trying to make me believe Bevaqua is hitting on my girlfriend?"

"Because he is."

Jake laughed. "You know, if you want to stir the shit, you have to have some shit to stir. You are facing a dare, my dude."

He shoved the second mug in Kurt's direction. Kurt swallowed its contents without flinching. His expression didn't change; it could have been tea. He reached for the cork and again held it like a talking stick. "Alright, Shatterhand. Truth or Dare."

"No, I'm done," Jake said. The brown guck had coated his mouth and tongue—he was already slightly regretting it. Although, why not? Ayahuasca had the reputation of making people better. He pictured his psyche as a hollow space within his rib cage. A narrow room, with debris on the floor. Ayahuasca would break the floorboards, and he would crash through to a larger room. From what he understood, this change would be permanent. You felt yourself forever expanded.

He needed to get them set up to make sure they were safe for the journey. He went to the hearth and built up the fire, shoving three big logs close together to slow down the burning. He went up to the master bedroom and brought down two quilts. In the kitchen, he found two bowls in a cupboard. "We're likely going to puke," he said to Kurt. Kurt took a quilt and bowl over to the fireplace, where he lay on his side on the rug, staring into the fire. Jake took his glasses off and for safekeeping put them in his grandpa's Odd Fellows box on the mantel. Then he settled into a chair, draping the quilt over his shoulders.

The fire was burning nicely. Kurt was motionless in front of it. Dreaming, possibly, about wolves with blood-darkened muzzles loping over the cobblestones on Wilhelmstrasse. Jake shoved the quilt off his shoulders. So far he was not sick in the least. He felt nothing unusual—in fact, the haze of alcohol was lifting and the world was a little clearer. Maybe you could have conscious input into your vision. Invite a spirit guide. A bear—though bears might not be kindly disposed to Jake, given how many had met their end with a blast from his grandfather's .303. Invite Isla. She was healthy and she walked in trust through a wholesome world. She would lead him. He saw her following a trail through the woods. She had her hair in a ponytail and there was a lovely line to her back. He started after her, and a voice said, Leave her alone. It was a disembodied voice, but Jake recognized it. It's doomed between you, Dr. Coltrane said. It's a cross-species pairing. It's unsustainable.

The moon had sailed into sight, its pocked face stared in the window. The snowy lake gleamed in its light, and gazing at it, Jake understood that his father would not be coming either. His father's work was done. His role had been to set a task for his sons, to see which one was the true heir. Reg had this house with its wonderful window. But Jake had his paintings. They came before him now, the four canvases from his major show. He saw them as he had never seen them, not even in the days when they lived only in his imagination. One by one they filled the screen, and he was moved by their beauty. By the light and colour. The faces of the dreamers—he ached with the truth he saw in them. He had more or less disowned these paintings, but the loathing he felt for himself—he saw now that his work was untouched by it. His work had its own darkness and its own light.

His grandfather leaned against the hearth in a red and grey plaid shirt and braces, waiting. His hair was thick and brown, he was the exact age (to the day) that Jake was now.

Where did you die?

I'll show you.

His grandpa walked vigorously through the house and Jake followed. They opened the back door and went out into the yard. All was white around them. They came to an opening in the woods and entered it. The path they were on was wide and straight. Trees on either side had snow blown onto their trunks. Snow was deep on the path, and Jake soon fell behind his grandfather. Then the bush ended abruptly, and he was in a clearing, where nothing moved but the vapour plume of his breath. An expanse of perfect white lay open to the spangled sky. It was utterly beautiful, soft and languorous, it invited him to enter. And he did. He stood and watched himself pass through that layer of snow. The crystalline structure of each flake—it was as though he had never used his eyes before.

This is what we are after, all of us. Seeing this.

Noise battered the silence, and he opened his eyes to daylight. He was lying on a couch, he was in the lodge, in the living room, and he staggered up and went to the window. A helicopter hung above the cliffs to the south, pounding along the shoreline towards them. Blue. Low in the sky. Roger, responding to their smoke signals. Jake saw that the fire had burned down to coals in the hearth. He saw that he was alone and that he was himself, in his right mind and in the ordinary hard-edged world, though he felt weak and exhausted and the taste in his mouth was foul. He stumbled around the room, snatching up his jacket and day pack.

He was in the mudroom, fumbling with his ski boots, when the helicopter went over the house. He crouched under the monstrous weight of the noise. Oh, what a mess they were leaving. He'd sworn to himself that he'd clean everything up, leave no trace. His feet were tender, his socks were damp. How long would it take Roger to land? He scrambled to the back door and opened it just in time to see Kurt pelt past him in the direction of the lake. He had been in the other building, the workshop, where Roger's apartment was. He'd left its door wide open.

As Jake made for the shore, the copter throttled down. His skis and poles were still leaning against the boathouse. Kurt already had his skis on, he was already out on the lake. Roger will use a snowmobile, Jake thought. He'll chase us down like a bloodhound. We should have hidden in the bush. But he'd see our tracks. What a pair of losers.

It was all white, the lake, the sky. Kurt was a black scrawl on the snow. Jake couldn't get a rhythm. He didn't have his glasses, he didn't have his mitts or toque. Silence now, the bellicose roar had ceased. His panting, the crunch and squeak of his skis. The taste in his mouth. The dreams of last night were just a breath away, he could fall back into them at any moment. Why were his socks wet? He remembered a field of gleaming snow—he must have been outside without his boots. He was lucky to be alive. It was cold, they needed to get to the truck. If he didn't want to lose his fingers and toes.

He dug in with huge strides. He'd almost caught up to Kurt when the world exploded. A massive boom. It rocked the cove and the shoreline tossed it back, and Jake froze within the echo. "What the fuck?" he heard himself yell. In his mind the ice cracked open and the two of them went down, but he was still standing. He looked round. It was the lodge, or it was behind the lodge. Three more enormous blasts. Smoke cauliflowered against the rock face. Kurt had frozen in his tracks too. Clouds kept building, black and surly now, into the white of the sky. Kurt was staring at the billowing smoke, his face transformed by shock. What in hell? It was a reply from the cosmos, far beyond even his cravings for mayhem.

THIRTEEN

The only science course Jake took in university was Anatomy of the Human Body. He wrote his major paper on The Hand, how its nerves give us greater manual dexterity than other apes enjoy. He did his own graphics, drawing the hand from various perspectives, delicately labelling the receptors that register movement, finger position, temperature, pain, static touch or stroking, whether an object is soft or hard, whether a surface is gritty or smooth.

The day Jake skied away from the lodge on Georgian Bay, clutching his poles with bare hands, those sensory receptors packed it in early, and by the time he and Kurt reached the truck, the nerves had entirely ceased communicating with his brain. He could hardly pry his ski poles free, and Kurt had to release the bindings of his skis. His hands were mostly white and (presumably) solid to the touch. Kurt unzipped his jacket for him, and when they got into the truck, Jake stuck his hands into his armpits. The pain he began to feel as they thawed was ominous.

He should have walked straight over to the marina at Scalloway, where there was lots of life that morning, thanks to the blast up the shore, but Kurt made for the truck, and Jake was too freaked about his freezing extremities to hesitate or argue. The truck started with no trouble, but it wasn't going to generate much heat just idling, so they headed for the road. Jake said, "There's a police station in Owen Sound. We'll go there." He pressed Kurt to tell him what he'd been doing in the workshop. Sleeping, Kurt claimed. He was sleeping in Roger's apartment. Then he heard the helicopter, and took off. He seemed genuinely perplexed about the explosion. Did the helicopter crash? he wondered. No, Jake said. We heard it land. The explosion was at least five minutes later. Ten. It was the workshop that blew up. Jake didn't know enough about construction infrastructure and fuel storage to begin to guess what had caused it. They speculated as to whether the lodge had burned too. Jake was pretty sure the two buildings were far enough apart. "But last night," he said, "you talked about burning the place down." Kurt denied this vehemently. Jake studied his face, but couldn't decide if he was lying. One detail stuck in Jake's mind: the door of the workshop, gaping open when Kurt fled.

"Why didn't you close up the workshop?"

"Oh, fuck off, *Arschkriecher*," Kurt said.

When they got close to Owen Sound, Kurt suddenly announced that they needed to turn around, he wanted to go back to Comstock Cove to pick up their camping gear. He couldn't be dissuaded. No way was Jake up for a two-hour ski, so Kurt dropped him at a little motel at the edge of town. Jake had a credit card in an inner pocket, and he booked a cabin and lay down on the hard bed. The blast played over and over in his mind. The slowly burgeoning puffs of smoke, debris tossing cartoon-like within them. It felt *farcical*, so disproportionate to their petty crime of unlawful trespass. Also, he kept being pulled back to a memory of vomiting in the snow. That was the ayahuasca. Both events were surreal, it was hard to uncouple them. He eventually fell asleep with the light on. Darkness had fallen by the time Kurt pounded on the door. Jake grabbed his things and stumbled out into the truck. Kurt had both their backpacks. What a guy. But he refused to stop at the police station, he said they should go in Adlington, where they were known and would be believed. There was a logic in that. As they drove, needles of hurt ran from Jake's extremities (his hands, his big toes, the tops of his ears) to a nerve centre at the base of his skull. His elbows ached, his hips ached, his knees ached like hell. Even if he salvaged his frostbitten fingers, this pain was going to settle into his bones. When he was an old man, it would flare up and remind him what a fucking idiot he was. What had he been thinking? He tried to reconstruct the moment they decided to do it, and really, he couldn't say what was in his mind. Was he after some sort of revenge? No. Nothing was in his mind. It just sounded like a fun idea. God, was he twelve?

When they got to Adlington, Kurt drove right past the OPP station.

"Hey," Jake said.

"We'll go in the morning. I need to sleep."

"No. We need to go now. It looks bad enough that we drove away from Scalloway."

But Kurt just turned up Armitage Street and stopped at Jake and Isla's house. "I'll pick you up in the morning," he said as Jake got out of the truck.

Isla heard him and came sleepily to the door. By then skin had lifted in oblong bubbles from the purple flesh of his fingers. Isla was shocked, she wanted him to go straight to the hospital. In their bathroom was a first-aid kit with antibacterial ointment, gauze, painkillers. "That's all they'd have at the hospital," Jake said. Isla gave in and helped him bandage his hands, fretting the whole time. She said they'd have to guard against infection. She wondered who thought winter camping was a good idea. She asked how Kurt was. "He's fine," Jake said. "He had his fur cap and mitts." She couldn't grasp how Jake could have lost his gear. He said something vague about a hole in the ice. And his glasses, where were his glasses? "I honestly can't tell you," he said, and the instant the words were out of his mouth, he remembered: they were nested neatly in his grandfather's wooden Odd Fellow's box. On the fireplace mantel in a lodge on the far side of a smouldering crater. Isla rummaged in a drawer and found his old ones. Her concern made his eyes sting.

By ten o'clock the next morning, Kurt hadn't appeared. Jake pulled on his jacket and walked over to The Grange and rang the doorbell for the upstairs suite. No answer. He went around back and found Annalise shoveling the snow that had drifted behind her car. Kurt's truck was gone.

"I'm here for Kurt," Jake said. "We have plans."

"He's away for a bit," Annalise said.

"What do you mean?"

"We've had a family emergency. Kurt's dad is very ill."

"In Germany?"

"Yes."

"Kurt's gone to Germany."

"Yes. He caught a flight to Munich early this morning. He drove into the city and left the truck with someone there."

Jake was speechless. Was he going to call Annalise a liar to her face? There she stood with the shovel in her hand, like she was waiting for him to express a little concern, but he refused to be part of this charade. "Will you let me know when he's back?" he said, turning to go.

How naive, to imagine Kurt was going to walk into a police station and admit that he was the one in the workshop that morning. Instead, he'd dropped Jake right in it. What a dangerous fucker the guy was. You only had to look into his eyes to know. Jake and Isla were always trying to figure him out. He's just a troll, Jake would say. But as Jake walked up the snow-packed road to their house, a new image took hold in his mind—of clams lying in the muck at the bottom of a lake. *Concentrators*, people called them. That's what Kurt Altenbach was! He was a concentrator, like the bivalves that breed in fouled water and absorb its arsenic and trace metals. Everybody's dark ideas collected pungently within him, and he gave them back to you in toxic doses.

Jake needed to do this properly, to ensure that he stepped up for the portion of the crime he was actually responsible for, but no more. He needed to ask a lawyer to go with him to the police station. Adlington had just one lawyer, Priya Sinha. He knew her by sight, though he'd never spoken to her. It was Friday. He went out to the shed to make the call. Priya Sinha was out for the rest of the day, they said, but she'd be in the office Monday. Yes, he could make an appointment for Monday morning.

He hadn't slept much last night, so he stretched out on his futon. But anytime he drifted towards sleep, his miserable self would stoop down and shake him awake, insisting on attention. The pain of his burns was part of it. *Burns*—he kept thinking that way, like it was the blast that had got his hands. What's it going to be, fire or ice? This whole debacle threw him into a familiar place, where he was just doing what came naturally, something he vaguely knew was stupid but considered unimportant, and it turned out it was a capital offence. He could see his dad, sniffing and pinching his nostrils, the ugliness of the turned-down corners of his mouth. "Why is Daddy disappointed, Jake?" Jake would have to stand in the searchlight of that grave disapproval and guess. Sometimes he confessed to crimes that weren't even on his dad's radar. Then it would turn out he'd left the garden hose sprawled across the yard, or something equally trivial. But small things were tests of character, weren't they.

When he went to the police, he would need to guard against being pulled into that vortex of shame. The facts were bad enough. If you held this trespass up beside his other great crime against Reg (sleeping with Reg's girlfriend in Reg's house when they were twenty), you started to see a pattern; he looked really malicious. He sat up, feeling suddenly sick.

The summer he slept with Rebecca, he'd had the sense of being in an in-between place where anything was possible. Their first hook-up he considered a stupid mistake, and afterwards he made an effort never to be alone with her. It wasn't easy, because she worked evenings and was home on her own all day. He still didn't have a summer job, but every morning, he'd get up resolutely and leave the house when the others did. He'd cycle hard for an hour and then go to the library and read or sketch for as long as he could force himself to. It wasn't entirely sex that eventually pulled him back to the house. It was her. Her kindness the day he sank into her arms and wept about his father's death (the only time he ever cried about it). She kissed him with great tenderness and smoothed his forehead, and they lay on the bed for hours, talking in low voices. She told him about her grandmother dying. "I know it's not like losing a parent, but I really loved her. Afterwards, I kept thinking, my heart is broken. Like, not broken in pieces. Broken like it didn't work anymore. I would feel all this emotion for stupid little things, and I wouldn't feel it when I should have been feeling it." He had his hand under her left breast by that point, feeling for the rogue heartbeat. He was twenty, how else could he be? It was her instinctive kindness, but it was also her ass, a perfect Valentine heart, and her breasts, which were round and full, and her general sleekness and warmth. He had thought he liked skinny girls, but in this he was mistaken. The fourth time they made love, it moved them to a different place, and it seemed to him that neither of them would be able to pretend it hadn't. He was back in his room when the others came home. It was Rebecca's night off. Hannah and Amy made a stir fry, and they all ate together. No one was talking. The pleasure Jake and Rebecca had created in the master bedroom crept through the house like a fog, they were all enveloped in it. Rebecca was wearing a turquoise shirt with deep pink and orange flowers on it. She ate her stir fry reflectively, as if she was savouring the separate taste of each vegetable. Jake watched Reg through the fog, forking rice into his mouth, and a sick feeling came over him—he felt the full force of the mess they were in. He finished his dinner and loaded the dishwasher, and then he went for a long ride, all the way along Bloor to High Park.

When he rode up to the house afterwards, he still hadn't figured out what to do. But Reg had. The front door was open and Reg was on the step, and before Jake realized what was coming, something hit him hard on the shoulder. He saw Reg stoop to re-arm. It was stones from the flower boxes by the door, he was firing them as hard as he could, aiming for Jake's head. "Hey, dude," Jake yelled, dropping his bike, putting up an arm to protect himself. "Get off my property, you fucking cunt," Reg yelled, and kept pelting stones as Jake flung himself back on his bike and onto the street.

The next morning Jake had two sore spots on the right side of his head and a serious bruise on his shoulder. He was worried Reg would get a locksmith over before he could collect his things, so by eight he was in a little park half a block from the house, where he waited until he saw the Trans Am go by. The front door was locked, but his key still worked.

Rebecca was under the covers in his bedroom. She sat up when he opened the door. She was still wearing the turquoise top with the flowers, and she looked like she might have cried all night. Jake went over and sat on the edge of the bed and asked her how in hell Reg had found out.

She pressed one hand over her eyes and started to sob. "He's not stupid."

"So he asked you, and you told him?"

"I'm not a very good liar."

"You're moving into this room?"

"No. I just didn't have anywhere to go last night." Her family lived in North Bay.

"You have to come with me."

She shrugged up a shoulder to blot her tears. "What are you talking about?"

"You can't stay here."

"I know that. He gave me until tonight to get out of the house." She pushed the cover down and sat up, and then it was like she ran out of energy. "I'm not going to go. He won't stick with it. He doesn't want me to leave—he's nuts about me."

"That's a terrible idea. Let me help you pack up your things."

"What would we do? Move in with your mother?"

"No, of course not. We'll figure something out."

"Jake, Reg and I have all these plans. He's paying for me to go to art school." She looked at him fiercely. "You might just be having fun, or looking for comfort or whatever, but this is a very big deal for me." She started crying very hard, like some horrible realization was dawning on her. "God, I must have been out of my mind to let this happen! Oh, God, I'm such an idiot!"

He got up. For the past two weeks, he'd been terrified Rebecca would see how crazy he was about her. But in that moment, what he thought was, it's a big deal for *you*? You met him at *Christmas*. Reggie and I have been best friends since kindergarten.

Jake sat for a long time on the futon in his shed, his bandaged hands on his knees. His recent crime, the demolition of real property, felt flimsy compared to that. It was such a shitty thing to do, blowing up Reg's relationship with Rebecca, and he'd never entirely understood how he could have done it. How close he and Reg were, for so long. Then, that summer, Reg conspired to cheat Jake out of a brilliant job; that summer, Jake learned that Reg and his dad were secret besties. Maybe the thing with Rebecca was payback. But honestly, at the time, Jake wasn't thinking about any of that. He wasn't thinking about Reg at all. He was thinking with his dick. He was thinking, Rebecca is a free agent, she can be with whoever she wants. Or, Rebecca is so much more than Reg will ever be, he doesn't deserve her. Or, Reg is (on some level) nothing, his feelings don't matter (does the guy *have* feelings?). It was taken for granted in their home that Jake would always have the best. Jake never recognized this as arrogance or entitlement, it was just the natural order of things. Fuck, it was astonishing. No wonder Reg hated his guts.

In the evening Isla unwound the gauze on his hands and applied fresh ointment.

"Does it hurt a lot?"

"Yes. I can't lie."

"What about your ears?"

"What about them?"

"You haven't looked at your ears?" She dragged him to the bathroom to look in the mirror. Blisters lined the tops of his ears like a row of grubs. "Nice," he said. He couldn't look her in the eye in the over-lit bathroom. It was the closest they had been in a long time, he was afraid she'd see how much he wanted her.

"It's shocking," she said. "But hey, winter's still got its bite."

She'd made bean soup with chunks of sweet potato in it. "Sleep in the house tonight," she said as she filled his bowl.

"I can't," he said. "I'm too restless. I'll be up all night. I want to be able to move around and listen to music."

Would sex even be consensual, if your partner had no idea who you were?

Saturday, Isla and Rita went into the city. They were taking Rita's kids to a show. In the evening, Jake pulled out his laptop and googled Reg's name to see what the media were saying about the explosion. The first thing that caught his eye was a YouTube interview called "How I Built It." Turned out that bit wasn't about building the lodge, but about building capital. Reg Bevaqua and the host sat in white leather chairs that looked like open palms, and the host asked, "How did you get your start? Not by working at Burger King."

Jake was just about to select a different tab when he heard Reg's answer. "Day trading. About fifteen years ago."

Day trading. Jake's breath abandoned him. In grade twelve, Reg was fed up with Burger King, and he used to rave about the money you could make day trading. But the tech bubble had burst, the heyday of the day trader was over, so he did other things. He harassed his father's boss at the car dealership until the guy agreed to give him a chance, and then he became some kind of boy wonder in the import car world, undercutting his own dad for commissions.

"You must have been in high school at the time," the host said.

"Yeah. Even my parents had no idea."

Or his best friend. Though when Jake thought about it, Reg had that massive hard drive in his bedroom, he had three monitors, and he was weirdly secretive about why he needed them. *Of course* he was trading stocks. Unbelievable. Unbelievable that Jake didn't catch on. It was so weird that Reg didn't tell him. How could the guy not have bragged about it?

The host of "How I Built It" was an intent guy in his forties, the shaved head and the two-day beard. "How much equity did you need to open at that time?"

"Twenty-five K."

"Pretty steep for a high school kid."

"I had a partner. He put up the cash and I had the tech know-how. And the guts—I wasn't afraid of high-volatility properties. Also, I had the time. I mean, who does fuck-all in high school? We were a little late to day trading, so early on we started putting our earnings into real investments. We developed an excellent portfolio. Those were tough years, just before the recession, but we had some fantastic properties. Force Protection—ever heard of it? They build armoured vehicles, and in 2007 their stock shot up sixteen hundred percent. 'God bless Dubya,' my partner used to say. 'God bless the war in Iraq.'"

Jesus H. Christ.

Old Jack's laptop was still on a shelf, right here in the shed. Jake's bandaged hands were shaking as he plugged in the charger. He hadn't booted this thing up since the summer his dad died, since he first discovered the crypto-bromance between Reg and his dad. Password? Windows 98, you didn't need a password. This system was so old it didn't even try to update itself.

Reg: "Thanks for dinner last night. Beat watching my dad pass out in his La-Z-Boy. Jake doesn't know how lucky he is."

Blah, blah.

Then, there it was.

Jack: "Did you see Apple this morning? Sinking like a GD stone." He was gloating, they must have just dumped their Apple stock.

Reg: "Yeah, that was a near-death experience. God, are you good, Jack. Love that Nestlé bump."

"Call me," they'd write, specifying a time. They were doing their business mainly by phone. Looked like they were having a really good year.

Reg: "I was driving by the BMO on Bloor this aft and I saw the roof lift when that chunk landed." That was December 19, 2006.

Darkness had taken over the shed, the only light was the computer screen. Jake got up and walked out into the yard. He went into the house. He hadn't eaten since breakfast, and he opened the fridge and stared into it for a few minutes, prying a few things open and smelling them and putting them back. I'll go for a run, he thought, closing the fridge. It's not as cold as it was. He crossed back to the shed and put on his running gear. He bent into a stretch, and he could hardly breathe. But he set off all the same, into streets where the bluish light of LED lamps was pooled on the snow. Every joint in his body hurt. Nausea swamped him after a block; he had to stop and lean over and wait until it passed. There was Quinn's little house. Quinn didn't have blinds, and through her living room window you could see young women in evening gowns weeping together in the courtyard of a European villa. *The Bachelor*. Maybe the kids were watching with her, cuddled in a heap. He thought of himself lying in bed when his dad would come home from the week in Ottawa. Nestled in the litter of his nerdy preoccupations, his modelling-clay monsters, his diagrams and drawings (the flying cars, the labyrinthine cities, the people with their interior organs visible, the people with brains like labyrinthine cities), worlds that were more real than his own. Footsteps coming up the stairs, his door opening. "Son," his dad says softly. "Son." Jake lies faking sleep. Call me by my name. What is the difference between being an actual son and an honorary, chosen, "like-a-son-to-me" son? The way everything about your father tears at your stomach and fills your nostrils with rage. Only a real son will feel that.

A train was approaching the level crossing in front of him. The signal bell began to ring, the lights were flashing, and Jake ran towards the lowering arm and ducked under it. On the other side he stood, savouring that little spurt of adrenalin, watching the freight cars hurtle by, delivering the town to him in stroboscopic slices. It was a long train, he felt the din to his bones. Maybe this was why Old Jack had cultivated Reg all along, he thought. Jake never understood it, he always assumed Reg was a charitable project for his parents, like adopting a needy kid overseas. *Educate the orphan*, the Odd Fellows motto said. But no. Jake's dad was industry minister in 2006. He'd be worried about the optics of being active on the market. Turned out he'd found a useful idiot to front him. Not such an idiot, actually. Where was the money? The Bank of Montreal on Bloor. It must have been a joint account. What happened to it when Jack died so suddenly? Did Jack's accountant know about it, or did Barbara? It should have been part of the estate.

Next thing Jake knew he was back in the shed, wiping the sweat from his forehead with his wrist. The boxes of junk he'd dragged out of the house when his mother moved had ended up in a dumpster, but he had important papers in one of his plastic storage crates. His fingers were tender as hell, but he started to plow through the crate. In an envelope that held his university transcripts, he found it. The page listing all his dad's assets, the balance sheet his mother had printed after his father's funeral, when Sarah was whining about money. Jack Challis had accounts at two banks, but not at the Bank of Montreal. It was a secret account! *Maybe the old man was involved in insider trading!*—the thought went through Jake like an electric current. But instantly he knew it wasn't true. Jack

Challis self-identified as a law-abiding citizen, it was integral to the way he saw himself. Not because he was a good person by nature, ha. Because it entitled him to all the inequality the law enshrined. The money piling up in his accounts would be *virtue*, as far as his dad was concerned. Validation of his work ethic, conservatism, uprightness, genetic and moral superiority, predestination-as-a-leader-of-man, etc. He wouldn't compromise all that by doing something outright illegal. It was just that for a cabinet minister, the optics were bad. Would he have cared enough about the optics to let Reg hold all their earnings in his name? He might have. And then he died, and no one knew. If Reg got away with a shitload of his dad's money, did it matter? Yes. It mattered. It wasn't just the initial stake. It was all those earnings. Nobody'd ever been able to account for Reg Bevaqua's meteoric rise. Reg had been taunting him from a distance all these years. Jake wanted to howl. He wanted to howl that they had got him caring about money.

The door of the house slammed. He heard the crunch of Isla's boots on the driveway, and then she was at the side door. "I just wanted to see how you were doing," she said. She walked across the shed towards him. "That's your old computer."

"It was my dad's."

He'd closed the email he was reading, but she was staring right at the inbox. "Reg Bevaqua?"

"Yeah, like my mom said, the old man was kind of his mentor."

"You're reading their emails?"

He reached over and closed the lid. "Just checking to see if this old thing still works. Might be something Quinn's kids would want to play with."

All her hurt and perplexity was on her face. But they were past the stage of fighting about it.

"I was just about to go for a run," he said. His hair was still damp with sweat, did she notice? He eased his way towards the door, and she walked quickly ahead of him and went into the house without a word. Shit, he should have asked her how her day was. Pelting down the road again, his sore feet pounding the hard-packed snow, he tried to empty his mind, reaching for his running mantra, fuck, fuck, fuck, fuck, fuck, fuck, fuck.

Spring arrived that weekend—the ill-fated camping trip had broken the back of winter. The warmth was thick, stifling, like a malfunctioning radiator was to blame. The snowbanks gave in and turned to slush. Sunday morning Jake took off the bandages and looked with curiosity at his hands. His fingers were sloughing off the old skin now, like stiffened and opaque Scotch tape. The flesh was the maroon of country ham, but his hands were functional. There'd be no working for the foreseeable future, though. Oh, the self-inflicted wounds that drag you down.

Twenty-four hours until his appointment at the law office. Tomorrow he'd walk into the police station with his lawyer, making the high-minded but self-protective gesture. In fact, that high-minded gesture was going to involve ratting Kurt out, getting him charged with arson or vandalism or mischief. Jake googled arson. Damages over $5000—maximum sentence fourteen years. Christ. His testimony (if it was believed) might break up a family, or even get Kurt deported. But what was he supposed to do?

Isla was out somewhere when Jake went to the house. He made a plate of sandwiches and took them to the shed. He checked his social media, and then idly knocked a cartoon together and posted a Drinkwater the Douche entry. Then he settled into a bit of prep for the appointment with the lawyer. The difference between an indictable offence and a summary conviction offence. Intention in common law. Wilful and Forbidden Acts in Respect of Certain Property. Rules of evidence. He'd left a piece of physical evidence at the lodge, his glasses. And he was in possession of another. It was folded into the inside zip pocket of his jacket—a beautiful photo of Isla.

On a shelf in the lodge, Jake had come across a hardcover book, the sort of souvenir you can get printed with your own photos. It had been made after Reg and Eve's tenth-anniversary dinner at The Grange— Reg wearing a tuxedo and looking flushed and expansive, Eve in a lovely Daisy Buchanan gown. Posing with various friends, with Rita, with Sheff. And Isla, in The Grange kitchen, sautéing chanterelles, her face lifted in warm surprise. Kurt noticed Jake studying the album, and he reached over and ripped Isla's photo out in one quick motion. "A little remembrance of your winter camping," he said. He folded the page and put it into Jake's jacket. Jake got the photo out now and gazed at it. It was the most beautiful picture of Isla he had ever seen, and he had taken quite a few himself.

Oh, Isla. He needed to tell her. Tomorrow, they'd charge him with something (just trespassing, if he was lucky) and send him home while they investigated. Then he'd have a better idea what he was facing. He'd tell her then, when he had the moral cred of having turned himself in. Imagining that conversation, he saw instantly what else he had to do. He had to go and talk to Reg. He hadn't seen Reg in the flesh since the day the guy pelted him with stones from a garden planter. But they had been true friends for a very long time. Reg had eased Jake's way through school, he saw now with a surge of gratitude. Because of Reg, he had passed as an ordinary boy. Their friendship had shaped both of them. Not that the explosion at the lodge wouldn't still be a matter for the police, but if he went to see Reg, he could maybe prevent the whole thing from spiralling further. What a hideous thicket of betrayal and guilt they were caught in—it was going to be tough. But he could take responsibility for his part of it. He needed to apologize, and he wanted to. He thought of how Reg had wept when Old Jack died, and in that moment, his fury about the money retreated and the will to make things right glowed inside him.

Towards dark, he dressed up and walked the slushy street into the heart of the town. Light was drawing away from the ground, filling the sky. A stunning Prussian blue sliding through mauve into old rose. As Jake walked, the blue darkened and the rose paled and the streetlights came on. He wanted to get out of their range and the shadows they cast, so he turned up the access road that ran by the highway. He started imagining talking to Reg. If they were going to totally clear the air, he had to raise the subject of the stock windfall. What would he say? What was his purpose in raising it? Did he want Reg to pay the family back? Trying out various scenarios, imagining Reg's response, he walked himself into a realization that slowed his footsteps and then brought him heavily to a stop.

He had no proof that Reg had stolen money from his dad. He had zero proof. His dad could have been rolling his own share into his own accounts all along. The Bank of Montreal account might legitimately have been Reg's. Reg's alone. Reg may have paid his dad back for the stake. Jake had no evidence of theft. All he had was his fury at being shut out of their secret life. His mind had jumped to the worst possible explanation—and he'd even posted a Drinkwater the Douche meme about it. Because he relished the idea of a crime, because he wanted to see Reg as corrupt, as a thief and a user. It let him occupy the moral high ground. He, who thought he could challenge the sins of the capitalist state—competition was still his default.

Jake walked by The Grange, the pile of colonial brick where Isla practiced her culinary arts, the venue that had drawn Bevaqua like a magnet into his life again. He turned up Quinn's street, and then he was back under streetlights, in a black and white world, the ditch decoupaged with sodden garbage. We don't change, he thought. We would rather die than change. We think we can change the world without changing ourselves. You're still a piece-of-shit loser, he said to himself reflexively. But then the image of his paintings as he'd seen them the other night came back to him. The light in them that was beyond what he saw in the world. With his own hands and his own eyes, he had created something true. If he'd had trouble these last few years looking at his paintings, it was not because they were bad. It was because they were good, and he didn't know what to do with that. Maybe that's what he needed to figure out.

Jake was pulling on his clothes in the morning when Isla appeared in the doorway of the shed. She was hesitant, he'd done a masterful job of making her feel unwelcome. Maybe he should invite her in, tell her now, before he went to the lawyer's office.

"I was just talking to Phoebe," she said. "I wish you'd pick up, Jake. I always end up having to deal with her."

"I guess my ringer's off. Sorry."

"She's really upset. The Ark's in another cash crunch, no surprise, huh. The electricians have hit a snag, and they're asking for payment up front, and she's worried they're not going to finish for the opening. She called Reg Bevaqua, hoping he'd step up again, and somehow your name came up, I guess because of your show, and he told her that you guys used to be close friends. She's *so* pissed off that all this time she didn't know. Maybe she thinks she could have monetized your history with him, I don't know. But she says Reg was too preoccupied to really talk. Apparently, there was a huge accident at his lodge. You haven't heard anything about that? A guy died, it's terrible."

"A guy died?" he said, turned to stone with his sweatshirt in his hand.

"That's what she said. I asked her what happened, but she didn't have details." Isla stepped back outside and lifted her head, scanning the sky. "I guess we need to start watching the news. We are right out of the loop." She looked at him, smiling ruefully (I'll leave you alone now, Jake, because I know that's all you want from me), and turned back towards the house.

ISLA

FOURTEEN

It's close to midnight on a Saturday night in April when I walk away from an artists' party with a tall, long-haired stranger. My life in chaos behind me, a blank slate ahead. From the quick pace we set, a watcher might assume we're used to walking together. Not so. We've exchanged maybe four sentences, but between us is a rare and galvanizing force field.

"So that was weird," the guy says.

"Yeah, what the fuck happened?"

"Somebody threw the main breakers, I'm guessing."

"Well done, I say. Jesus Christ, the noise."

"I know. It was an audio death-spiral. You need these." He shows me a pair of industrial earplugs on his palm. "Never go to a party without them," he says, dropping them back into his pocket. "It's a great space, though. I'm glad they finally got it open."

I see something husband-like in this man—he wants to debrief the evening. "Yeah," I say. "It's fantastic for young artists."

"You know Mary Attica." He makes one carnivalesque word of her name, the way everyone does.

"Not really. But I love her work."

"Yeah, she's brilliant."

I want to ask him what he thinks about Jake Challis's work—a wife-like impulse, and I squelch it. Instead, I ask him how he knows Mary Attica.

"I'm in audio. I've worked with her on a few projects."

"Not the birds."

"Yeah, the birds."

Oh, the birds.

I know Mary Attica for that major work, a series of installations that depict what I can only describe as a religion for birds. It appeals, I guess, to people who long for ritual but hate doctrine. I'm in awe of the various art forms and media she mastered—ceramics, textiles, video, decoupage, metal work. Part of that show is an audio tapestry of bird calls, as grave and gorgeous as a medieval canticle. Jake and I heard it in the AGO, standing transfixed in the middle of the room. We left the gallery right after, walking up the street in silence. People are usually humbled by birdsong, they say it puts human music to shame, but Mary Attica's work left me worshipping both.

"So that was *you*. I loved it. I would love to know how it was done."

"I don't think you would."

"Like, it was all synthesized?"

He shrugs and laughs. "I do actually have a thing for birds. I'm not, like, a real birder, but I've done some recording in remote places, and I used some of that material. I'll tell you what my dream project is. It's to do a linguistic study of birdsong. To analyze the musical language and the influences. For example, there's a European thrush that weaves African songs into its call."

"Seriously."

"Yeah. Songs it learns during its migration. It's a fusion artist."

How cool.

He asks me what I do.

"I'm kind of between things right now."

He grins, like, *okay*. We walk in silence for a bit. We meet two men being pulled down the street by pugs on leashes. A kid on an electric scooter. In my mind, Toronto's streets have a film noir glamour at night.

"You're not an artist," he says.

"No. But I've only ever dated artists."

"Sounds like you really dig art."

"It's the poverty I dig." He thinks I'm joking. "Consider *birds*," I say. "And their ancestors. I used to think the dinosaurs got smaller, more birdlike, after the meteor hit. I pictured them transmogrifying, like in that M.C. Escher print where the fish transform into geese as they lift into the air. But that's not how evolution works, is it. It's just that the ones that became birds were the tiny dinos. They survived after the meteor hit because they needed less." He's still grinning. This is my new self: I see that going forward, I might be susceptible to stoner thoughts and to expressing them freely.

A guy in a Jays cap runs past us, backwards. This is called *retro* running, I happen to know, and it's supposed to be very good for you, but it's weird to have his eyes fixed on us as the distance between us gradually increases. I worry he's going to crash into something.

I hear my phone ping. I ignore it.

"You should take that," the audio artist says. "Might be your husband."

"Yeah, I don't think so," I say. "You ever been married?"

"I lived with someone for a long time. I almost proposed, actually."

"Seriously?"

"Yup. I had a ring and everything."

This amuses me. "*Everything*."

"Well, I told my parents, I guess that was the big thing. I went home—my family lives in Kingston—and asked my mother for my grandmother's ring. My mother was so thrilled. She went running to get it—she still had the little velvet box. She adored my girlfriend and she was, well, I guess that day she thought she was going to end up with grandkids after all."

"Your grandmother's ring," I say. "You're a romantic."

"Nah. I knew my girlfriend wanted . . . well, the whole thing. And I didn't care. Or I thought I didn't."

"So what happened?"

He tells me he decided to propose in their favourite restaurant, where he knew the maître d', a guy named Sheldon. "So we get there," he says, "and Sheldon's not there, a strange kid is standing at the desk, and I give him my name and he says, 'Sorry, you're not in the book.'" My new friend lets out a rich laugh, remembering. He does not strike me as a man who gets off on the role of the storyteller, but apparently this story is capital he's willing to spend tonight. "So we end up going to a different restaurant. Later I find out Sheldon had a nickname for me, and that's what he put in the reservations book. I'm not sure why I'm telling you this part of it, but somehow it fucked the evening right up and threw off all my plans."

"You were planning to get down on one knee?"

"It was in my mind at one time." He looks so melancholy that I think of penitents on their knees in a cathedral. "Anyway, we managed to find a restaurant, and we ordered our dinner, and the night went on, and I didn't do it."

I write the rest of the story in my mind. During that dinner, he saw his girlfriend in a different light. Boring, or self-absorbed, and he was grateful for this new insight, and bailed out.

As if he senses what I'm thinking, he says, "Just to be clear, my girlfriend, my ex, is a really lovely person. That night it was like I was seeing her for the first time, how great she was, how beautiful and kind. I don't know how to explain what happened. The restaurant we ended up in—it was Cibo's on Euclid Avenue, do you know it?—it's a long, narrow room, with one row of small tables on either side. It's exactly like a dining car on a train. That night, I had the weird impression that we were on a train. And it freaked me out. It was like—wherever we were going, I didn't want to go. I couldn't stay for the journey. I was terrified. I only wanted to get off." As they walked outside, he was filled with tenderness towards his girlfriend. She thought it was an ordinary night, she had no idea what he'd saved her from. A week later he moved out.

"Did she ever know you almost proposed?"

"No. She accused me of having commitment phobia, and I guess she was right."

"I think it's a brave decision," I say. "Not to, you know, let the stream just carry you along." But what do I know about his life?

We've turned up Avenue Road. The towers above us seem as old and as wise as cliffs. We walk past a mirrored building, and I turn my head and take in my reflected self, walking quickly the length of the lobby windows, a bag slung over my shoulder, and a tall man keeping pace beside me. And then the man turns his head too, and we catch each other's eyes in the glass and laugh. I think again about the priest who deconsecrated the old church, and it occurs to me that for a while my new life will be a *deconsecration* ritual, whisking all traces of Jake out of it. Claiming it for other purposes, bit by bit.

After that the audio artist and I stop talking. Because the deal is sealed, and we don't want to jeopardize it. We've looked at each other and said, this is what I want tonight. Just this.

There is a parkette at Boswell that takes you into the quiet streets of the Annex, and we turn into it. The audio artist lives a few blocks over, in a brownstone subdivided into four suites. He's on the ground floor, on the left side. He puts his key into the lock and opens the door, and when he steps in, he ducks his head a little, though the doorway is high enough, and I think he must recently have lived somewhere with low ceilings. His bed is the first thing I see when the light comes on, a big bed, nicely made up with a linen-covered duvet. It's right in the middle of the living room. "Yeah, I've switched things around," he says. "I don't like having my bed against a wall."

He leads me past the bed and into the next room, where he turns on a table lamp. "Sit down," he says. "I'll get us a drink." He goes to the kitchen and I sit in an armchair. He doesn't have a lot in this room. The chair, an end table and lamp, a couch, a coffee table, and a turntable on the floor. No art on the walls, no books or plants or tchotchkes. Except a ceramic plaque on the end table that says LISTEN in Times New Roman. It's hard to tell whether his design principle is asceticism or poverty. I'll know better in the morning, when natural light pours in. There are no curtains or blinds. He's willing to be open to the street, to make an Edward Hopper painting of his life. But when I get up and walk to the window, I see that of course this room is on the side of the building, so the window faces a brick wall.

He comes back with a drink in each hand and a bottle stuck under his arm. "Is this good? I don't have mix." He hands me my glass and I sit down again. It's rye. He has a stack of vinyls on the coffee table, and he bends down and puts a record on, and then he sits on the couch, at the end farthest from my chair. His eyes stay on mine rather too long, not minding when I notice. Just looking as long as he wants to look, feeding his curiosity. And so I gaze back, and gather up my impressions of him. His shoulders angle down, I notice for the first time. His force is more subtle than if he were square-shouldered. He has the sort of frank, bony head that might have inspired the Easter Island carvers, his features not proportionate. He's like a large bird in his posture, and very still—like an owl, attentive and not giving much away.

"Ain't No Sunshine" drifts over the room, and he nods almost imperceptibly to it. I can't see where the speakers are. He asks me again if I'm an artist.

"I was with an artist for a long time," I say.

"And what was that like?"

"Amazing. Instructive. Hard. Artists have already unhitched their wagons from this star."

"Well, some of them," he says. But obviously he's travelling light. Maybe he's a Buddhist. Maybe his joy is just in being alive in the world.

We listen to the music. It's not Stevie Wonder, it's somebody else. My friend lifts his glass, discovers that it's empty, reaches for the bottle of rye on the coffee table. "Music was better when they let ugly dudes make it," he says.

He hasn't touched me. We've missed the movie moment of ripping our clothes off at the door. We're not even really flirting. I figure he's about my age or a bit older. He has to have some sort of game.

Then he gets up and comes towards me—to pour me another drink, I think, but instead he sets the bottle down and bends to do what (it seems from his face) he's been wanting to do all evening, which is pull me to my feet and tip my face up and kiss me, deeply, fitting his body to the contours of mine, reaching a hand to my breast to take just the quickest feel, the heel of his hand against my nipple, so that the shock of it jags brilliantly through me. The kiss finishes and his face is six inches away.

"I don't actually know your name," he says.

"No, I guess you don't," I say.

In the bigger room we undress each other fully. I like his body, its rounded corners, its heft. We crawl under the covers because I've begun to shiver. On the bed, the island of his bed, he shows some deliberation, the same deliberation with which he held my gaze in the other room, until my senses are all tuned to him. It's cave sex, under that duvet. In a world of shite, the simple engorgement of blood vessels opens a channel to glory. At the end of it our cries hang in the air. "That's my favourite sound," he says after a minute.

We break apart and lie in silence while our breaths settle. I'm warm then, and I kick the cover down to our feet. After a bit I slide onto him and lie along the length of his body. He laughs softly and puts his two hands on my ass. It's like floating on a lake on a sun-warmed air mattress.

"What did you have that night?"

Miraculously, he gets what I mean. In the restaurant, the night of his thwarted marriage proposal. "I had the cassoulet."

"Oh, cassoulet," I say. "I *love* making cassoulet. I make the sausage myself."

"Yeah?"

"Yeah. And I make the duck confit. From my own ducks."

"Oh, you do, huh."

"Sort of. I have help." I kiss his luxurious mouth, and then I roll off him and lift my shoulders so he can fit an arm around me. He reaches down with the other hand and pulls the cover back over us. "Did you ever find out what Sheldon the maître d' called you?"

"Yes. I forced him to tell me. He called me the Raptor."

Sheldon no doubt had a bird in mind, or a basketball player, but in my mind the word takes on the force of *rapture*. I slide a hand across his groin, wondering what's next. But his breath is deepening, soon he'll be asleep.

This room (being the living room) has three big windows fitted with venetian blinds. Stripes of light ride the length of it when cars turn the corner. I lie nestled within the raptor's wing, stunned by how straightforward our coming together was, and how wonderful. It's all there with a kind stranger. It's all there as the world burns. His breath begins to puff out, approaching a snore, but I'm nowhere near sleep. I slide to the edge of the bed and put my feet on the floorboards, bending down to grab my clothes. I head in the direction I figure the bathroom must be, detouring to the sitting room for my bag. I don't feel around for a light switch. My recent orgasm glows in the dark like the hologram of an orchid.

My phone. The text that we heard come in—it was Sheff. *Call me*. It will be early morning in Madrid. So after I've peed, I turn the light on and get dressed and slide to the floor to call him. He picks up instantly. I can hear a lot of traffic noise—he's drinking coffee in a sidewalk café. He's been in Spain since we closed in the fall. He landed in Madrid, happily anticipating a winter spent drinking *tinto de verano* on the Costa del Sol, and got into a taxi that thirty minutes later was T-boned by a truck. It was five or six days before the news reached me. An English-speaking nurse called me at his request. He was in ICU, his jaw was broken. He'd suffered a concussion, broken ribs and femur, and a ruptured spleen.

They had upgraded his condition to stable, but he'd be a long time recovering. That was October. In fact, Sheff got out of the hospital in November, but he's still in Madrid.

He asks if he woke me up.

"No. I was at a party." I'm trying to keep my voice down. "Hey, it's great to talk to you."

"Yeah, listen, Isla. We've got a prospective buyer." So that's why we're talking. "He's really keen. The agent is going to give him the tour tomorrow, and he wants to sit down with you and talk through the business end of it. Noon your time. On site."

"Who is it? Is it somebody we know?"

The briefest of pauses. "It's Bevaqua. He phoned me an hour ago."

"In the middle of the night?"

"Well, that's why he phoned me and not you. I think it was a sudden impulse. So we need to act fast and take advantage of it. Isla, it would be a great solution. He'd keep everyone on, he'd be a hands-off owner. You could reopen next month without missing a beat."

I lean my head against the tiled wall, feeling its coolness. Fucking Bevaqua. "I don't want to sell The Grange to that asshole." Why was he even interested? Doesn't he have enough on his plate? Someone just *died* on his property. There's a long silence. Sheff is giving me time to get on board. For years he's turned his charm on Bevaqua. He never liked the guy, but he sees the super-rich as worth cultivating, and now he's cashing in. "Why does he want it? What does he want to do with it?"

"It's just a vanity project. But what do we care?"

A vanity project. Reg is remembering evenings driving up "in the gloaming," as we jokingly called it at the Grange, the top down and Eve with a white scarf over her hair. He wants to swan through the salon, playing the dining impresario to media magnates and actors and musicians, lingering traces of Sheff's charisma lighting on his shoulders.

"So I can tell him you'll be there?"

"I'm in Toronto."

"You've got time to get up to Adlington."

"I don't, actually. I could take the train to Brampton, but then what?"

"Rent a car or something. I'll let you figure that part out."

"Sheff, listen. You're not hearing me."

"No, you're not hearing me."

We sit in stubborn silence. It's Jake I'm thinking of, how he'll react if Bevaqua ends up being my new boss.

For once, Sheff breaks first. "Okay, I'm going to get someone to pick you up in the morning. Are you at Sullivan?" He means his place in Chinatown.

"I'll be there in a bit."

"Okay. I'll work this out for you. You need to leave at ten. No, nine-thirty. Be out in front of Lucky Foods at nine-thirty in the morning. A friend of mine will pick you up. She drives a blue Kona."

"Sheff. Why don't you FaceTime with the guy?"

But my phone has gone silent, the whine of motorbikes on a Madrid street sucked back into the ether. As always with Sheff, resistance is futile.

I have to creep past the raptor to get out of the apartment. You'd think an audio artist would have very acute hearing, but he's slumbering hard. I pause in the dim light and admire his size and form. Oh, a man who makes his bed up with clean linens before he goes to a party—has he really gotten off the train? Can you get off the train as long as you draw breath?

Outside I walk quickly away from the house, not checking its number. I know my way around the Annex, and I cut through to Bloor Street, still humming to my sacral chakra, recalling the hard-soft feel of his penis afterwards, the curve of it lying against his thigh. Out on Bloor, I lift my face to the towers. They're swaying slightly, alive like trees. Garbage trucks roll past me in a convoy, and I see that the city is collecting itself to do what it has always done. I'm visibly exhaling CO_2 as I walk. I think of the photo you see online of a little bird singing its heart out in the cold air, its song unfurling against the sky in the exhalation of its breath. The littlest birds sing the prettiest songs, I say to myself. I see that, having lost my business, having left my boyfriend, I might be required to build up what I know about the world bit by bit from scratch. That the property of rain is to wet and of fire to burn, that good pasture makes fat sheep, that a great cause of the night is lack of the sun.

FIFTEEN

At nine my phone alarm wakes me in Sheff's spare little *pied-à-terre* in Chinatown. Bells are ringing across the city—Christians are into this particular Sunday. I brush my teeth and my hair and wash the crud out of my eyes, and then I go downstairs to Lucky Foods, where I buy a banana and break it open. Back on the street, I see a blue Kona at the curb and walk towards it. The driver beeps as I approach. I stuff the last three inches of banana into my mouth and climb in. "You're early," I say. "So are you," the driver replies. She's maybe sixty, dressed in worn jeans and a blue puffy jacket. We introduce ourselves. Her name is Penny. I've never known a Penny before, and I picture bright copper hair, but this Penny is wearing a grey toque with no hair showing under it. I wonder if she's undergoing chemo. "I see you've had your potassium for the day," she says, referring to my banana. "Let me get you a wrap for that peel." She angles her shoulder down to dig under her seat and pulls out a Subway wrapper for me, and then we set off.

I want to sink into my thoughts, and I'm cautious about being too friendly with strangers when hours of enforced closeness lie ahead of you. But Penny has kindly agreed to drive me all the way to Adlington, and her hunger for human companionship is like an aura around her. I ask her how she knows Sheff. They were next-door neighbours growing up in Hamilton, she says, and they've never lost touch. I ask her if she still lives in Hamilton, and she tells me she moved to Mississauga two years ago. She has a little stash of business cards in the console, and she hands me one. *Dog Kennel, Driver*—one massive *D* for both, so that at first glance I read *Dog River*. Penny has two employees. She moved her business to the outskirts of Mississauga because she has a daughter there and she needed a fresh start. Her son Trent was prescribed opioids after a motorcycle accident, and then lost his life to illegal drugs at the age of twenty-two. I tell Penny how sorry I am, and she thanks me warmly. She says that every week you see three or four obituaries in *The Star* for kids who have died of fentanyl overdoses. Not that the obituary will spell this out, but you can always tell because the deceased are young, and they passed suddenly, and in lieu of flowers, the families ask for donations to the Humane Society. Animals are the only beings these kids trust. "But that org has gotta have a name change," Penny says. "*Humane* doesn't cut it anymore."

"Dogs were invented by humans, don't you think?" I say, looking for a place to stash my garbage. My stomach is a little upset and the smell of the banana is getting to me.

"What do you mean, invented?"

"Well, bred, all the different breeds. Their traits were selected for what we wanted them to be."

"I guess you're right," she says. "Well, maybe we should start doing that with people, you know, what do you call it?—genetic engineering. Because the old way sure as hell isn't working."

I finally shove the Subway wrapper under my seat and we fall into silence. When we turn onto Highway 6, Penny pulls off her toque and tosses it into the back seat. I revise her age down to fifty. I see that her hair is chopped short, and very sparse, with bare patches. "I've got alopecia," she says. "All the stress."

"Oh, that's tough," I say. "You'd think our hair would hang around to keep us warm when we're having a hard time. But you rock the look. You have a very nicely shaped head."

After a bit, Penny asks me when I expect Sheff back.

"I'm not sure he's coming back," I say. "He's got a new guy in Madrid."

Around Christmas, I thought Sheff was being strangely vague about how things were going, and whether he'd be back for a May opening, and finally he told me. He had met someone—his physiotherapist! I think he was broadsided by it. "He won't do long distance," he said about the new guy. "He just won't do it. But he's open to the idea of immigrating. Do you think you and Rita and the Altenbachs could keep the place going for a year while we work this out?"

"We can sure try," I said, having felt the shaft of middle-aged joy that arced over the curved planet as we talked.

But then, one spring morning, Annalise came to the door. I made us both a coffee and asked how Kurt's dad was. Not well, she said. Annalise and I hadn't really talked since Jake and Kurt's winter camping adventure, since Kurt went to Germany to be with his dad, and I told her about Jake's bad frostbite. Then I grabbed the chance to raise something else that was on my mind.

"Listen, I don't want to pry, but someone mentioned—" I paused, but she was looking at me neutrally, so I went for it. "Well, I've heard that Kurt has substance issues—or did have, in the past—and I guess I've been worried recently..."

"Kurt is not my problem anymore," Annalise said. "We've separated."

"Oh, Annalise," I said.

After a minute she pulled a folded letter out of an inside pocket of her parka. "I thought I would give this to you in writing."

"What is it?"

"It's notice. I've got a new job, in Guelph. I've found an apartment there for me and the kids. They're going to go to school."

Then I was *really* sorry, but all she would say was, "We're fine. We're going to be fine."

That afternoon, I walked over to Rita's to talk this through with her, and she broke the news that she was planning to look for a new job herself, a day job. Her oldest kid was starting school, and if she kept working summers and evenings, she'd never see him.

So that was that. We would not be reopening. When I called Sheff, our conversation was short and matter-of-fact. We agreed I would contact the real estate agent who sold us The Grange five years ago.

That winter, the life we knew was swiftly dismantled chunk by chunk. Jake—when he came back from his awful winter camping trip, he and I had a few days of feeling closer, but it didn't last. Nights, I'd stand at the kitchen window after dinner and watch him walk across the yard and slip into the shed, and the light would never come on. He'd just be out there, lying alone in the dark. His misery was so evident that I actually talked about it with my parents. About a week before The Ark opening, I caught a ride into Toronto, and as we sat drinking tea in the living room, I told them I was worried Jake was suffering from depression. My mother was surprised. "He's always so witty that I just assume he's happy," she said.

My dad asked me to tell him more. I was afraid I was going to start crying if I really talked about my worries, so instead I fell into analyzing Jake. "He had a very cold and judgmental childhood, and I think he's still recovering from that. And of course, there's his father's politics. He feels ashamed, or somehow responsible. Like for the whole climate denial thing."

"Has Jake ever considered seeing a therapist?" my father asked.

"We've never talked about it. But I think I can guess what he'd say. He'd say it's self-indulgent to pour all that energy into your own individual problems. Given, you know, the bigger issues."

My dad nudged the bridge of his glasses with his middle finger in a way he had. "Well, I'll just point out that the damaged psyche is very dangerous for the world. One person can have a hugely disproportionate effect, as he's apparently aware. For good too. It works both ways."

I was skeptical. "You think we have time? To fix humanity on a case-by-case basis?" But I so wanted to believe him.

Penny and I pass the turnoff for Guelph. The closer we get to Adlington, the worse I feel. It's like I've just had a holiday from my life, and it's over. I can still tune in to the warmth of that hook-up the night before, and it's hard to know where to shelve the residual pleasure. Even my bravado in going to the art show—this morning it looks like a betrayal. I've never actually known myself in this light. I think about Jake. What he looked like the morning before, sound asleep on his futon. How thin. And the skin between his eyebrows, he's scratched it all off. I turn my head towards the window, and with no warning, tears begin to slide down my cheeks. I'm not a crier, I cry about once a year.

Possibly Penny thinks I'm crying about Sheff not coming back. She doesn't say anything, but she reaches over and puts a hand briefly over mine, and then she pulls a cotton handkerchief out of the console and hands it to me. It's like, life is shit but you are not alone. I'm very close to falling into a deep trench of grief, so I press her handkerchief to my face, and will myself to calm down, grateful for her silence.

When Penny pulls into the pass-through in front of The Grange, the agent's Lexus is parked off to the side. It's the only car there, so I assume Bevaqua flew up.

I get out and ask Penny what I owe her, and she says Sheff took care of it. "What time should I pick you up?"

"Oh. Sorry, I should have said. I'm not planning on going back to Toronto."

She drives away before I can thank her. Or give her back her handkerchief, or retrieve the banana peel under the passenger seat. I stand for a minute, collecting myself. It feels like a long time since I've seen our beautiful property. The bronze letters on the stone wall, the vines beginning to fill in green.

"Isla."

It's Rita, getting up off the stone bench just inside the courtyard. I didn't realize Sheff was going to get hold of her, and relief floods through me.

"Where are the kids?"

"Over at Lizzie's. The dog just had her pups, so they were in heaven when I left."

"Oh, cool. How many?"

"Five. Too cute for words. You should see."

"I'll go over soon." We sit down. "So. Bevaqua," I say.

"I know. Why the fuck does he want it?"

"The guy doesn't know what to do with his money."

"He could hire a chef and eat every night the way we feed him."

"It's a vanity project," I say, quoting Sheff. "The rest of us try to squelch our vanity, but not Reg Bevaqua."

It's fun to fall into one of our routines, but before we can really get off the ground, the agent comes out the front door. Then a darked-haired young woman I don't know, sunglasses already in place. Reg follows her out. I haven't seen Reg since last fall. I'm shocked by how much more hair he has. He's heavier, he's leaning into middle age in a way that Jake is not. Possibly his wealth is weighing on him.

"You're early," he says unpleasantly.

Rita gets up and brushes the dust of the bench off her butt. "Are you not conducting an Easter egg hunt this morning?"

"Eve has it under control. That's why kids have two parents."

Rita's eyes meet mine. *It starts.*

Reg mimes *one hour* to the young woman in the Maui Jims, and she says, "I'll be at the copter." To our surprise, he also sends the agent away. The guy doesn't want to leave, but Reg says, "I'll call you later," and then ignores him until he walks to his car. "Come on in," Reg says to us then, as though he already owns the place.

•

We sit around a table in the salon, surrounded by chairs and tables piled together and covered with dust sheets. Reg doesn't look good to me, on closer examination. He looks hungover, his eyes red and puffy, which is interesting because part of his schtick is that he doesn't drink. Just a water guy. "I guess I could have had my people meet with you," he says. "But this is personally important to me." He wants to be congratulated for showing up to a meeting he himself insisted on! He looks around him with distaste. "I'm really glad I know The Grange when it's hopping in the summer, because this is a bit of a downer."

He's right. The heat's been off now since Annalise moved out, and the place is dusty as well as chilly. We should have picked up the blue blocks of rodent control, spaced out along the baseboards. And someone left the industrial vacuum in a corner. Sheff would not be pleased at how poorly The Grange shows.

"Where did you spend the winter?" I ask Reg.

"We were in Colombia through most of January and February and part of March. I take staff with me. I can do my job from almost anywhere, right, and we had the au pair with us, she's a qualified teacher. We planned on staying longer but—well, you must have heard about the terrible accident at the lodge."

"Yes, Phoebe told me. She mentioned that someone died?"

"We lost our pilot and mechanic, Roger."

"Oh, how terrible!" Rita and I murmur our condolences.

"It's such a tragedy. Roger had a wife and three little boys in Etobicoke. She's a sweet girl, used to be a figure skater. Of course, I'll do what I can to help out, but it's going to be tough."

"What happened?"

"Nobody knows exactly. One night the guy at the marina in Scalloway saw smoke coming from the chimney at our lodge. The cove was solid at the time, and he had seen a party of snowmobilers go by. He figured they must have broken in. We'd asked him to keep an eye on the place, so he called Roger and Roger texted me. We decided he would go up in the morning to check things out. Next morning, people heard the helicopter pass over, and ten, fifteen minutes later, they heard a huge explosion. We had a two-story auxiliary building with a workshop on the main floor and staff quarters above. It was brand new last fall. It blew up, and sadly, Roger was in it."

"Why would the building blow up?"

"There were explosives in it. And a huge tank of propane."

"You were storing *dynamite* in your workshop?"

"It was a slurry, ammonium nitrate. Long story why it was there, a contract dispute with the blaster who worked on the foundation. Luckily there was no wind or we might have lost the lodge too. Chunks of flaming debris landed on the lodge roof, but the snow was deep enough that they didn't burn through."

"How terrible," Rita says. "Do you assume Roger somehow set it off? Or was it the snowmobilers?"

"Probably the latter. The lodge was a mess, they had definitely broken in and trashed the place."

"Have they identified the guys?"

"The police are still pursuing leads."

"You don't have security cameras?"

"The SOBs disabled them." He abruptly drops the subject, swinging his elbows up onto the table and looking at us over his clasped hands with the artful friendliness of a mall kiosk salesman. "So. It's not an ideal time for me to be taking on a new venture, obviously, but when I heard this place was on the market, well, I knew I needed to act."

I reject his segue. "I thought I might see you at The Ark opening last night."

"Ah, you went. How was it?"

"Noisy. Phoebe was sure you were going to show."

"Yeah, I guess I should have given her a call."

"Why didn't you come?"

"What?"

"Why did you not show up?"

"I was at a conference in Montreal, if it matters."

"You flew here from Montreal this morning?"

"Is it your week to watch me?" he says, like we're eleven-year-old siblings.

On the left side of his forehead is a scrape about as big as a Christmas postage stamp. Not fresh-fresh, not oozing, but not scabbed over either. He notices me looking at it, and in the split second before he looks away, his eyelids lower and I catch something ugly behind them. I'm shaken by it. In that moment, I grasp that he knows who I am, he knows Jake is my partner. There is no other way to explain a look of such pure hatred. The fact that he continually pretends he doesn't know—it feels sinister. Although, of course, I've been pretending too.

Rita steps in. "It's great to know you're interested in The Grange, Reg. Do you have a particular vision for it?"

He sits back and makes an effort to smooth out his face. "I'm glad you use that word," he says to Rita. "Because from the first time we had dinner here, it was obvious you folks had a vision. If your server was out in the garden, if she just ran out to get some greens and she has a little dirt under her fingernails, well, we get that. It's what we love about this place. Most folks have no idea where their food comes from. So we'd like to keep that tradition going and build on the goodwill you created. We hope to retain your customer base."

Breathe, I say wordlessly to Rita.

He asks if we can start by going over the assets. Sure, we say.

The preserves?

Stocks depleted.

The livestock?

We didn't winter livestock this year.

The wine collection?

Sold to a dealer in Toronto. "Did the agent not tell you?"

"No. When I asked if I could see the wine cellar, he said he didn't have the key."

I'm annoyed that the agent wasn't straight with him. "We sold the cellar as a unit when the Altenbachs left last month. We didn't want to keep heating the building." And we wanted a lump sum to pay the property taxes. "Whoever takes over will have to start collecting again. But it's a fun job."

"Your agent let it drop that there's been very little interest in the property. Not too clever. But I want you to know I'm not going to lowball this offer. I respect what you did here."

I'm surprised by how unstrategic he is. Strangely scattered for a business wizard. He should be asking to see the accounts and tax returns. Then he floats the idea of hiring us. Same vision, same team, different owner. "Any hope of Sheff? When I talked to him yesterday, he was dodgy about his intentions."

"I don't expect him back," I say. "He's met somebody in Madrid. I wouldn't be surprised if he went into business there. He loves Spain, and he's pretty fluent in Spanish."

"Well, that's too bad. What about the Altenbachs—do you think they'd run the farm for me?"

"No. They've quit, and they're not together. Annalise has moved to Guelph. She's working as a ward clerk in the hospital there. Kurt went back to Germany a while ago."

"What's that about?"

"His father is sick," Rita says.

I watch the guy's face closely. Rumours have floated around the kitchen that Reg Bevaqua was supplying Kurt with drugs, or more likely his helicopter pilot was. The evidence was purely circumstantial: Kurt's lapses seemed to coincide with Bevaqua's visits to Adlington.

"Well, that's too bad," he says neutrally. "I was hoping they'd be on board. But they are not the only farmers in the world." He looks from one of us to the other, trying to make this a moment. "I want you to be honest with me. You have some stakes in who buys this place. You want the legacy to be preserved. You don't want to sell to some bozo who's going to come in and turn it into a whatever, an Elephant & Castle. So give it to me straight. What would I be looking at here? Practically? Financially?"

If The Grange has to shut down for a season, its value will plummet. A sale right now would be an answer to what some people call prayer. But I spread my hands in a where-do-I-start gesture, and Rita sees it. "Well, you know the pipes burst in early March," she says, before I can speak. And just like that, we are working together to sabotage this deal.

"The plumber patched things up, but he hasn't replaced the major joints," I say.

This has no weight with Reg Bevaqua whatsoever. Money is everything to him, but it's also nothing. Rita sees this, and she jumps in with both feet. "Our last year was a little rough, to be honest. The animal rights people were really onto us. You'll have to budget for graffiti removal. Sheff kept a sandblasting company on retainer so they could come right away when we had an attack."

That part is true, although I would have said *if* and not *when*. "Property insurance is through the roof right now because the whole industry is such a target for activists."

"It is?"

"You must have heard about guests at high-end restaurants in the US getting sprayed with liquid manure. Sad to say, incidents like that are only going to get worse. Last year we were named in an article by PETA. Sheff was called out for glamorizing meat."

"It's weird how they've gone after us," Rita says thoughtfully. "I mean, Sheff and Isla are nobodies, relatively speaking. No offence, Isla."

"Maybe Lionel Sheffield doesn't know how to play hardball," Reg says. Clearly it troubles him, though, that Sheff never said a thing about any of this, given the intimate relationship he assumes they have. "I need to know whether you would both be on board," he says after a minute. "That would be a big factor. You know this business like the back of your hand. If I was to offer on this place, could I count on you two to run it?"

Rita speaks up first. "Sorry, not me. My kids are at an age where they really need me. I've already given notice to Isla."

He names a salary—it's about twice what we paid Rita. "You could hire a good caregiver with that," he says. The second Rita says no again, I see that she ceases to exist for him, she vanishes right out of sight.

He turns to me.

"My partner and I are separating," I say. "I need to leave Adlington."

I sense Rita's quick inhale. Under the table, her cool fingers reach for mine. I think this registers with Reg too, I see something move across his face, but I don't know what it is. I expect him to bug me again about coming to cook for him at his lodge, but he doesn't. Having set this meeting up, he seems anxious for it to be over. He gets up abruptly and says, "I'll talk it through with my people, and we'll be in touch." He doesn't thank us, he just nods curtly and walks through the passage between the cloaked tables.

After he leaves, Rita leans her chin in a palm and looks tenderly at me. "You and Jake?"

"I was just trying it out, to see if I liked how it sounded."

"And did you?"

"Not very much."

"Well, you better go home." She takes The Grange keys out of her bag. "I have to pick up the kids. Come and see the puppies, and then we'll all walk to your place and say hi to Jake."

"No," I say, getting up. "Thanks anyway, but I'm going to go straight home."

I've walked the streets from The Grange to our house maybe five hundred times, but never feeling quite this stressed. Yesterday morning, when Jake was sleeping, I stood by his futon, and I could see his eyes move under his eyelids. It was almost like waking a sleepwalker, which is supposed to be a dangerous thing to do. And yet I woke him, I woke him up and I spoke cruelly to him. I said things I did not even know I was thinking. I said, "You think it's the problems of the world that drag you down. But if all this wasn't happening, you'd find something else to be bummed about. I'm sick to death of it. You think tormenting yourself makes things any better? Maybe you're just into suffering."

He shook this off, like it was no doubt true but irrelevant. "You have no idea what a piece of shit I am," he said. "You'd leave me if you knew. So I think you should leave."

Remembering this, I begin to run. Church bells are ringing again, I run through their clamour. Just as I arrive at the house, Reg's helicopter goes pounding over. Quinn O'Neil's little girl, Brie, is in our driveway on her tiny bicycle. Her mouth is smeared with Easter chocolate and her pink plastic purse dangles from the handlebars. Jake always calls her The Queen because of that purse. She's saying something to me. I wait until the noise dies down and she says it again.

"Where did you go, Isla?"

"I was in Toronto."

"Was Jake with you?"

"No."

"That's not him in the helicopter," she says. Not a question, just to confirm what she already knows.

"You're right, sweetheart," I say. "That's not Jake, that's Mr. Bevaqua."

I don't bother going into the house, I go straight to the shed. To my surprise, it's locked. I have to go to the kitchen for the key. When I step back outside, Brie and her tricycle are gone.

Light from the skylight fills the shed. The smell of oil paint has finally displaced the smell of sawdust. I smelled fresh paint when I was in here yesterday, but the easel was turned away from me, and I would not have dreamed of asking to see what Jake was working on. The easel's been moved—it's under the skylight, facing the side door, with a stretched canvas about two feet by three feet on it. I'm shocked to see that it's a portrait of me. I step over to look. I'm in the kitchen of The Grange, wearing my whites, sautéing chanterelles in a cast iron frying pan. The portrait is in Jake's typical style—it fully articulates a few elements and alludes to the rest. Naturally it's my face he lingers on, and the chanterelles with their fleshy orange convolutions. Steam has softened my hair. He caught me looking up, startled out of my work, and the loving expression on my face—it's a lover's look, brought to life in paint by a lover's talent.

The morning before, I'd stood in the doorway of this shed, watching Jake as he slept on the futon. He'd looked so young to me: for a minute, before my anger took me over, I was like a mother watching her child wander unprotected in the world of dreams. Now no one lies on the futon, no one stands at the easel. The workshop is empty.

SIXTEEN

"When a child goes missing," I say, "everyone in the county volunteers, and people form a cordon and tramp the bushes around town. The police post an Amber Alert and stop traffic on the highway. They drag the creek."

"What *are* they doing?" Rita, in her red bathrobe with a fuzzy purple jacket over it, hands me a mug of coffee at the picnic table in her back yard. Her kids are asleep inside.

"Nothing. They just say to wait." Of course, Jake is not a child. He has a credit card, he could get on a plane, his range is the world. I tell Rita that the sergeant at the OPP detachment thought he might have grabbed the chance to tie one on while his girlfriend was out of town.

"That guy's got a brilliant future as a psychological profiler," Rita says. Then she goes on to ask me exactly the same questions he asked, whether our place was locked up (the shed was, but the house was open), whether Jake's keys were around, and his wallet, and his phone (they weren't).

"You know, his phone probably has a GPS signal."

"I doubt it. He's had the same phone all the time I've known him."

I'm trying so hard to be casual. It's important to reassure the universe and everybody in it (except possibly the police) that this is nothing. Rita responds to my news in the same comforting spirit. "He's off in the bush. He's lost in his work. He's having a great time."

"Yeah, I'd like to think so. But you'd think he would have left a note. If he planned to stay away overnight."

"Well, you were away. Why would he leave you a note?"

"True enough."

"Did you check if his passport is where it's supposed to be?"

"That's a good idea. I'll check. And I hope to hell it's gone. I hope he's somewhere he really wants to be."

"How did you sleep last night?"

"Not great. I woke up about five and I was really panicky."

Her long, lovely face is so full of warmth that I drop the pretense and tell her what I'm most afraid of. "He's been in such bad shape all spring. And I keep remembering, one night a few weeks ago, I was watching a movie about a married couple. The husband was deeply depressed, and he put up a noose in the stairwell. Jake came in just at the point where the wife opens the front door and sees the husband. You know, how they always just show the guy's dangling feet? I heard Jake come in and without thinking, I said, 'I don't ever want to walk into the shed and find you like that.' I was *joking*. But when I said it, I felt something terrible rise up between us. He said 'That will never happen, I promise.' His voice was flat and serious. I don't know what he meant, Rita. Did he mean, I promise I will never take my own life? Or, I promise you will never be the one who finds me?"

She looks stricken. "What do you think?"

"Well, the fact that I don't know—that's what scares me. The fact that he took me seriously. I should have pushed it at the time, but I felt so horrified at having opened the idea up, like I was allowing this, this *unspeakable* possibility. It was just, you know, a bit of stupid banter."

Rita sits for a minute taking this in, and then she leans over the table and looks steadily at me with her beautiful, kind eyes. "I don't believe Jake would take his own life," she says. "I don't believe Jake wants to die. I truly don't, Isla."

She doesn't give a reason, but her certainty is like a life raft for me. It holds me up as I finish my coffee and walk down the street and even as I open the door to our silent little house.

The sun is warm, the lilacs are coming out purple. I want to savour this beautiful world—it's just that this terrible thing is (possibly) happening. What am I supposed to do with myself? The police don't want me to file a missing person's report for a few more days. Rita and I agree that if Jake is not back by Friday, we'll make up an online poster, and also get it printed. Drew Connaught says he'll mobilize people to drive around the county with it.

Self-harm. Accident. Foul play. I wear myself out going over the alternatives. Sometimes I think of how he's been withdrawing from all of us, and it's like he just took that last step, right out of sight. I spend a lot of time studying the portrait of me, like it's going to contain a message. But all I see is that, in spite of everything, he really loved me. He left his brushes standing in turpentine, and I clean them up for him, as thoroughly as he would. They're expensive, and he's not going to want them to be ruined. And of course I text him repeatedly and drive myself crazy checking my phone every ten minutes. Honestly, I say to myself, if you would just stop fretting, he'd be back.

My parents want me to come into the city, and on Friday, I finally do. Rita offers me her car. I write a note to Jake and put it on the kitchen table and I leave the house unlocked. Walk right in, world, help yourself to whatever you want. There's nothing here we care about. At my parents' place, I feel worse. My mother looks at me so closely that I can read what's in her mind. Could Jake be involved with someone else? *Please.* I check my phone. It's almost four o'clock. I was planning to go and see Barbara, but I'm having a hard time making a move.

"You look exhausted," my father says. "Why don't you take a nap and we'll have dinner together before you go."

I go up to my old bedroom, still cluttered with stuff from my teenage years, and I hardly remember lying down. When I wake up, I sense a long time has gone by, but my brain has trouble rebooting. Downstairs a mechanical screaming starts and stops. That's what woke me.

My dad is hunched over the coffee grinder on the kitchen counter. He cherishes peace in the mornings, so grinding his beans is part of his evening routine. The clock on the stove reads 11:20. Dad sees me and straightens up, turning the grinder off. "Your mom just went to bed," he says.

"You should have woken me up."

"We figured you must need the sleep. You can see Jake's mother tomorrow. Mom left your dinner in the microwave."

It's under cling film, a mound of something vegetal I can't identify. I carry it over to the compost bucket, and he watches with a conspiratorial smile as I scrape it in.

He dumps his fragrant coffee grounds into a little canister. "So, sweetheart. How are you coping?"

"Oh, you know." I sit on a stool. "It doesn't seem real. The worst thing is, the last time I talked to Jake, I was very harsh. He has so much going for him, and he can't seem to get things together, and I was fed up. And now I feel like, well, he was having a major breakdown, and the last thing I said to him was, 'Have a nice life, Jake.'" My voice is steady but my eyes fill with tears. The very night Jake was dealing with whatever it was this was, I was crawling into bed with a total stranger.

My father whisks spilled coffee grounds off the counter and into his palm. "I'm not a doctor, but Jake doesn't strike me as mentally ill. Life can be hard for people who are highly conscious. But they can develop coping strategies." Then he sees my tears, and looks at me with immense tenderness.

"Like what?" I manage to say.

"Learn to compartmentalize, for one thing. Don't give yourself over to anxiety about things you can't control."

My dad wrote the book on living consciously—literally. "You consider it healthy to avoid reality?"

"I consider it necessary. We all do it, all the time. We sit down for a nice dinner, and how could we take any pleasure in our food if we insisted on thinking with every bite about the children starving in Yemen?" He touches my hand, and then he picks up the kettle and turns towards the sink with it. The copper light on the kettle's curves, the silver cord of water. The ping of the stove's ignition, the tiny roar of the flame. Then, as if to demonstrate the mental trick he's describing, he says, "Your mom discovered a new rooibos tea at Guthrie's. The green kind—it's unfermented, it cost an arm and a leg. But it's supposed to be full of antioxidants. Want to give it a try?"

I wipe my tears and watch him make the tea. I survey his fleece-lined shirt, his worn jeans, his friendly moccasins, his overlong hair streaked with white and grey, and I think how decent and good my father is, and how much of his life has been devoted to making my life good as well. But at this point, I'm on my own.

At Barbara's, a grey-haired man in shirtsleeves and brown leather slippers sits on the couch, newspapers around him. It's Gordon, the lawyer for Barbara's condo strata council. It seems they are an item! Jake will be so interested. They ask all the pertinent questions. About the missing person's report, which I filed yesterday morning, about what actions the police will take. Barbara says, "Jake does tend to forget the real world when he's absorbed in something," a comment that I think Jake would take great exception to. They say I shouldn't worry, none of us should worry, there has to be a simple explanation, and I say more or less the same things back to them, and all the time we talk, I see Barbara moving her fingers, counting. Seven days. Seven days with no word.

Phoebe has someone in her office, her star client, Mary Attica, wearing the grey dress she wore at The Ark opening a week ago. They're talking about her current project, and when I step in, Mary Attica warmly includes me in the conversation. "I don't know who I'll get to work with me on audio. My old audio artist—he's a friend of yours, isn't he, Isla? He and I had lunch yesterday. You might not have heard yet—he's finally had a diagnosis. The doctors say it was a virus that attacked his eardrums, something he contracted in the tropics."

"So he's—"

"His hearing loss has plateaued, but they think the damage will be permanent. He's got new hearing aids, and he manages just fine with them, but it's a problem for someone who works in audio. Sort of like colour-blindness—not a huge disability, unless you happen to be a painter."

She sees how upset I am by this, and she says, "I think he'll find his way. He's so passionate about art, and you know, these individual griefs—you can use them."

Phoebe is staring at me, she senses something wrong. So I go ahead and tell them both. Their concern made me feel worse. Phoebe fixates on the fact that Jake seems to have vanished the day of The Ark opening, like his prolonged disappearance was part of his effort to dodge that event. Then she says, "You know, that morning, Reg Bevaqua called and asked me for Jake's cell number."

She mentioned this at the party, I remember. "Did you give it to him?"

"I did. Sorry—was that bad? I just thought—well, they're old friends, and maybe he can persuade Jake to come to the party."

I can't quite process this. I promise to keep her in the loop, and turn to go.

"I was just leaving," Mary Attica says. "Let me walk you out."

We step onto the street in front of Phoebe's downtown office and stand and look at each other, consternation and worry moving wordlessly between us. The traffic noise bombards us. The city is a gargantuan concrete installation never intended for humans. Mary Attica tilts her head, and I follow her eyes and see a tiny helicopter silently cross the patch of sky between the towers. "The monuments of the bourgeoisie," she says. "That's what Walter Benjamin called modern cities. We know them as ruins, even while they're still standing. I've always wondered whether Jake's *Dreaming the Future* was influenced by *The Arcades Project*."

"What is that?"

"It's a treatise on an abandoned shopping arcade in Paris. Benjamin writes about us as being asleep, still dreaming the old dreams of capitalism."

"I wish Jake had had you around to talk to this past year," I say. I love her face, the way life has shaped and scored it. As she turns to walk up the street, I think about what she said about the audio artist. These griefs, you can use them.

SEVENTEEN

Our little rental house in Adlington is four furnished rooms, all square, all painted a colour Jake calls sauerkraut. It has a persistent and inhospitable odour—chemical, not organic, Jake and I agreed. Embalming fluid, we used to joke. The owner was proud of how he'd remodelled the kitchen, but he actually made it worse by installing cheap particleboard cabinets. The appliances are junk. We brought in our own couch and bed, and I cooked a lot of fine meals in that ugly kitchen because that's what I do, but we never made much effort to decorate. It's almost like we dug the ugliness.

We always saw it as transitory, I see now.

Anyway, I don't really miss Jake in the house. But out in the yard and shed, I sometimes catch glimpses of him, I see him in the corner of my eye and swing eagerly around. I don't take this seriously. It's just what you do when something is lost, right? You picture it somewhere. When I glimpse him, he's so *himself*, and I do hold on to that. I know, deep in my bones, that he's okay. The alternatives are too preposterous.

The second week after Jake goes missing, I move to the shed to sleep on his futon. I turn nocturnal, like I'll have a better chance of spotting him on the prowl if I inhabit his territory. In that oil-paint-smelling darkness, I channel the way he sleeps, I lie on my back on the futon and ask myself which chapter of the book of the world's sorrows I should open in the night's dark hours. I'm still awake when the skylight begins to pale.

Eventually the sun starts shining down on me, and I get up and wander around the shed. There's Jake's grandpa's beautiful paddle, mounted on the wall like the work of art it is. There's the portrait Jake painted of me—I stop and study it again. He must have painted it from a photograph, but I don't remember a photo like this one being taken. Back when we first knew each other, he always used to say he wanted to paint me, but he never did. And now, when he was so sunk in misery, he created this. It's so beautiful that I want to cry when I look at it. I don't look *that* amazing, it's just what Jake felt for me. Maybe he thought I could save him or something. But it speaks of the life in *him*—you would need to be fully open to the world to paint this wonderfully.

Jake's current sketchbook is lying on his workbench. I pick it up. Once in a while he'd show me things he had sketched, but I always regarded his sketchbooks as private and I've never looked through one. I do now. As I flip the cover over, I find myself thinking of my own childhood notebooks, the details that drew me. If I looked through them now, I wonder what I'd see.

Jake's are a catalogue of all the news that breaks his heart. Animals, threatened and extinct. Two abstract compositions done in charcoal—after a minute, I realize that they're not abstracts. I'm looking at maps of the Arctic, showing the way the ice has vanished. They're beautiful, like woodcuts. Maybe that's the dilemma he was wrestling with, how to portray loss and terror when your whole aesthetic tends towards beauty. We could have talked more about all this, I think. We were walking the same road. Here's a familiar image, the woman who was hit by a meteorite back in the 1950s—I was the one who came across her photo online and showed it to Jake. The woman lies in a bed, stunned. The bruise on her upper hip is huge, pitch black, and shaped like a mouth. A kiss from the universe, Jake said at the time.

Here and there through the sketchbook, he drew cartoons with captions. All in the same style, all featuring a recognizable figure named Drinkwater the Douche. I flip through and study them all.

Drinkwater the Douche, pouring contaminants into a stream on First Nations lands. Reg's high forehead, the hard, downturned mouth.

Drinkwater the Douche is sentenced under the Corruption of Foreign Officials Act. Reg behind bars.

Drinkwater the Douche absconds with a fortune belonging to his dying friend and mentor. In this one, our mutual acquaintance is creeping out of a bank with a big sack of money slung over his back. It's the last entry in this sketchbook.

I stare at it in shock.

One night shortly after the winter camping trip, I came in to find Jake reading old emails between Reg and his father. He seemed very worked up about something. His dad's laptop is still there, on the workbench, and I pick it up, thinking I'll take it into the house and have a look.

As I turn to go, my eyes are caught again by the portrait on the easel. The white flowers pinned to the front of my uniform—suddenly, I get it. That flower is *freesia*. The night of Reg Bevaqua's anniversary dinner, Eve came into the kitchen before the guests arrived and pinned sprigs of freesia on all of us. The chanterelles I'm frying in the painting, Kurt foraged for them, for the sauce we served on prime rib. Jake painted this from a photo Bevaqua's event photographer took that night. Where did he get that photo? I don't remember Eve or Reg giving me a copy, so how did Jake end up with it?

You would leave me if I told you everything, he said. That afternoon a whole other train of thought opens up for me.

After dinner I cycle to the OPP station. The tires on my bike are low so I take Jake's, standing on the pedals the whole way because I can't be bothered to adjust the seat. Through the glass of the police station, I can see that it is as I hoped: Siobhan Ealing is on duty. I don't know her, but Jake and I often admire her running along the railway tracks, with her golden ponytail streaming out behind her and her golden retriever at her side. The very way she moves says, I've got this.

She takes me into an office and closes the door and looks at me with the appropriate mixture of calmness and concern.

I start with something small, just to test her. "I stopped in to let you know that I found Jake's palette. Jake must have been painting the day he went missing, because his palette was in a plastic bag in the freezer compartment of our fridge. I just never thought to look there before."

"He often put his palette in the freezer?"

"If he's finished for the day, he will clean his brushes, wipe his palette, and oil it with linseed. But if he's just leaving for a bit, he sticks his brushes into a can of turpentine and puts his palette in the freezer to keep the paint from drying out."

"So you think he figured on just being out for a bit."

"Or that he left in a hurry. Whatever he left for, it must have been too urgent for him to take the time to clean up properly. But he took a bit of care. So he wasn't, you know, abducted at gunpoint."

She seems interested. "You know, we really should do a thorough search of your house and shed. What about tomorrow afternoon? Around two?"

I say sure, no problem, but what I'm thinking is, thanks for the heads-up. I ask her if she knows who Reg Bevaqua is. She says yes, of course. "Well, he's an old friend of Jake's. Although they haven't been on good terms for years. You need to question him."

"What do you mean, not on good terms?"

"They were very close as kids, but all the time we've lived here, they've refused to have anything to do with each other."

Now she looks distinctly *un*interested.

"Siobhan, the day Jake went missing, Reg Bevaqua phoned Jake's agent and asked for his phone number. The next day, Easter Sunday, I had a meeting with Reg at The Grange. He struck me as very uncomfortable. And he had a laceration on his head."

"A laceration?"

"Well, a scrape. Just here."

She thinks I'm out of my mind, I can see it in her face. I rode over here with the idea of telling her about Jake's cartoons, and possibly about the relationship between Bevaqua and Jake's father. But does anyone in this building have the imagination to grasp a nuanced backstory or the chops to deal with a clever operator like Bevaqua?

On the other side of the door, in the lobby, a commotion starts up, a woman shouting.

I get up. My motivation in talking to the police is seeping away fast. "Siobhan, given that Reg and Jake are old friends—you will question him, right?"

She asks me if I know how to get in touch with him, and I give her the only number I have. As we talk, I recognize the voice in the lobby—it's Quinn O'Neil. I've been meaning to go over and see her, just in case Jake said anything to her about going away. I don't want to talk to her when she's upset, though, so I drag out my goodbyes.

But when I step out onto the street a few minutes later, Quinn's still there, standing under the lamppost beside Jake's bike. She scowls when she sees me. "He's not with you?"

"No. It's just me."

"I saw his bike, so I waited. He's not picking up his fucking phone."

"No. Jake's actually—well, he's missing. No one has heard from him in over a week. I've been meaning to come over and talk to you."

She looks sullen and angry. "He's not exactly stepping up for me right now."

I'm annoyed that she's making this all about her. I bend to undo the lock, and as I'm straightening up, my eyes track along her skinny jeans and I see the bulge of stomach on her thin frame and realize for the first time that she's pregnant. She is maybe five months along. And then insanity descends on me, it's like a siren blasting in my brain.

"When is your baby due?" I ask over the scream.

"September."

I start wheeling Jake's bike away from the police station. She follows me. "You don't have to say what you're thinking," she says. "I can see it in your face. But I'm clean and I'm working really hard to stay that way for this baby. It would just help if Jake was here for me."

I hardly know what to say. "What were you doing at the police station?"

"I was asking them about that freaky guy from your farm. The guy who makes the sausages. Everybody lets on they don't know where he is."

"Kurt Altenbach. He's in Germany."

"He is?" she says in surprise. "Nobody tells me anything. I can't get that dickhead at the front desk to take me seriously. The police need to be checking him out."

"Kurt? Why?"

"He's the one that set off the explosion up at that rich guy's lodge, Bevaqua. I know for sure. And nobody wants to listen to me. But Roger took that dude up to the lodge more than once. They would get wasted together up there. And I *know* he was there when the place blew up. It was cold that week and Amber went skating with the guy's daughter, Mathilda, and Mathilda says to Amber, all proud, "My dad is camping up at the lake." Amber comes home and tells me this, and I figure right away that her dad is up at the lodge with Roger. Because who sleeps out in the snow when it's that cold? I'm really pissed that Roger went up to the Bruce without even stopping in to see me, because, just a week before, I called to tell him about the baby. He seemed happy about it— and then he flies right over. And after that he stops answering my texts, and he never picks up when I call. I'm just going crazy, I don't know what to do, and then one day I'm in Steve's café with the kids and I hear this guy talking about Bevaqua, and this explosion at his lodge, and how his helicopter pilot died. So all this time, I'm thinking Roger's a deadbeat asshole, and I'm planning to take the bus into Toronto and track him down, and tell his fucking wife if I have to, and here he's—" Her voice breaks. "I looked it up online, and it was true." She begins to sob.

I'm shaken at what she's been through. I had no idea she even knew Reg's helicopter pilot. I put my free arm around her shoulders, and tell her how sorry I am, and how sorry that she had to find out the way she did. The sirens in my brain have gone quiet. "You were with Roger for a long time?"

When she can talk again, she says they met the first time Roger flew Reg up to Adlington. "I took the kids over to see the helicopter, and he and I fell for each other right away. He was so great. When I told him about the baby, he took it really well. He wasn't the usual asshole! He said he was glad because it would give him the push he needed to leave his wife, who was, you know, a toxic bitch. His mom was moving into a nursing home, and he said we could have her house in Hamilton. So that's what was supposed to happen. And now here I am on my own again, and even Jake is not helping out. This is not how it was supposed to be."

We're in front of her house. Her kids will be asleep in their beds, and she didn't leave a night light on for herself. I feel overcome with sadness for her, I feel her pain and mine together—and oh, how fiercely she carries hers. "Quinn," I say. "You are the bravest person I know. You are going to get through this. I'm in a mess right now myself, with Jake missing, but when he gets back, we will both do our best to help. The O'Neil family is going to end up with another great kid." I watch until she gets the door open and turns a light on. *This is not how it was supposed to be.* Her words feel profound to me. There is such a thing as *supposed to be*. I turn around and walk Jake's bike along the street towards our place. The sirens have started up again, but, waylaid by emotion, I'm half a block away before I grasp what they are screaming.

Back at the house, I go straight to Google. The first article that comes up is from *The Star*. "Police have identified the victim of a March 21 explosion at a vacation home on the Bruce Peninsula as Roger Lafontaine, 43, of Mississauga."

March 21. When exactly did Jake and Kurt go camping? There was a full moon that week, we talked about it before he left. I check a calendar. The full moon was March 20. I'm seeing Jake when he came home from that trip, how weirded-out he was. I'm seeing myself standing at the door of the shed, saying, "There was a terrible accident up at Bevaqua's lodge. A guy died," and Jake is standing half-dressed, his frostbitten hands in bandages, and I am as blind as a fucking bat.

Everything changes that night. I've been nursing the idea that this is a stupid misunderstanding, a comedy of errors—but that fantasy dies an instant death. I'm filled with horror at all Jake hid from me. What is he, some sort of domestic terrorist? All these old grievances, I never took them seriously. I lower my computer lid and get up. What now? I open the back door and stare out into the dark yard. Then fear overtakes me and I slam it shut and lock it.

Maybe Jake did leave the country—he was fleeing from the law! Check for his passport, Rita said a week ago.

It's there, in a shallow kitchen drawer we jokingly called "the safe." I flip it open to the photo ID. Glasses off, no smiling allowed—and Jake is his lovely self, looking at the camera with his usual thoughtful interest.

Also in that drawer is a family photo of the Challises. It was taken last Christmas, in front of a fireplace in Whistler. Jake didn't go to Whistler, but his oldest niece Photoshopped him in. He's in the back row, a little off-scale, wearing a ski toque.

"Family joke," Jake explained when that photo arrived. "Every year Mom had a family picture taken for our Christmas card, and they'd always take it outside in the snow so I'd be wearing a toque. My dad didn't want his constituents to know he had a long-haired degenerate for a son."

"He couldn't persuade you to get a haircut?"

"He sure tried."

"Well, sounds like you won that battle."

"Yeah, right."

"You didn't?"

"One night I had friends over, and we were in the basement watching a movie, and the three of them jump me. They're all over me with these fucking big scissors. They hold me down and start hacking chunks off my hair. They chop it right down to the scalp in some places. I'm fighting them like crazy, it's a miracle they don't jab my eyes out. While they have me pinned, I catch sight of somebody on the stairs. My dad's standing there grinning. Turns out, he put them up to it. No doubt he paid a fee-for-service. So, no, I can't say I won that battle."

I was stunned. "Reg was part of it?"

He shrugged. *Of course.*

"You stayed friends with those guys after that?"

He laughed, like, what can you do but laugh at your young self?

I feel a little weak in the knees, and sink onto a chair. Those grievances are not in the past, they're reaching their ugly tentacles into our beautiful present. The answer to this mystery is going to lie in the backstory, it always does.

Annalise. We worked together for years, and she's always been straight with me. I reach for my phone, and then realize it's after midnight.

First thing in the morning, I call her. She picks up on the second ring. She has absolutely no idea where Jake could be, she says. I believe her. She also says she doesn't know anything about Kurt being up at Bevaqua's lodge the weekend a man died there—and then I stop believing her. She refuses to give me contact info for Kurt. "I'm just trying to keep things together for my kids these days," she says. A wall comes down between us. Annalise and I are not going to be figuring this out together.

Rita. I walk over and sit at the picnic table in her greening yard, dreading telling her. She catches sight of me out her window and comes out. I see the scene from a distance, a long shot, from above. Our heads together. Shock, consternation in our postures. The camera zooms in. "But you didn't suspect anything?" Rita is saying.

"I didn't know they were anywhere near Bevaqua's lodge. I assumed they'd gone to Inverhuron—that's where Kurt usually camped."

"You need to tell the police."

"They're coming over this afternoon. I'll tell them then."

"Why are they coming over to your place?"

"They want to search the house and shed."

"They made an *appointment* to do a search?"

"I know, it's totally stupid. What if I was involved? What if I had evidence I wanted to hide?" I do, actually. Jake's sketchbooks. "I hate to think of Jake's beautiful sketchbooks locked forever in a damp evidence shed."

"Hide them," Rita urges me. "They're not going to help the police, and you don't want to lose them. Take my car home with you and put whatever you want in the trunk."

Siobhan really needs to watch more police procedurals, I think as I shove Old Jack's computer into a case destined for Rita's trunk. This is obstruction of justice, no doubt, and I feel totally outside my body while I commit it. The camera lingers on the mess in the kitchen, the cups of tea that went cold, a half-eaten omelet. I haven't had a full meal in days, I'm sleep deprived, but my mind is totally focused. Looking for clues, recalling reactions and scrutinizing them, coldly sifting through minutiae. I have a job to do, and it eases my terror a little. Mysteries have conventions, you can count on them. Things are always solved in the end, often in a way you would never predict.

I step outside with a duffle bag, and there is Quinn's little girl, sitting on her pink bike, her purse dangling from the handlebar. "Are you looking for Jake, sweetheart?"

"Yes."

"I'm sorry, I don't know where he is. I'm hoping he comes home soon."

"In a truck," she sings. In a *tru*-uck.

"Why do you think he'll come in a truck?"

"I just do," she says coyly.

Rita's car is in the driveway, and I drop the duffle into the trunk. As I'm opening the driver's door, Brie calls, "He might be waiting for the truck driver to drive him back."

"Truck driver? You saw Jake with a truck driver?"

She nods.

I walk over and crouch beside her. "He was on the highway?"

"No. At the gas station. He was talking to the truck driver, and then he got into the truck."

"What kind of truck?"

"A big one."

"And did you see it drive away? Did you see which way it went?"

"Yes. It went over the bridge."

So, north.

"Did the truck have writing on it?"

"It might of," she says.

"But you don't know what it said?"

She shakes her head.

"When was this?"

"It was in the afternoon," she says, very seriously and responsibly. "Just after I watched *Larva Island*. I was riding by the railroad tracks when I saw him."

"But what day?"

"On taco night. But not at night."

I stare at her. I could ask Quinn about taco night, but it had to have been that Saturday.

"Did he have, like, a backpack, or a duffle bag?"

She shrugs and makes a sullen face just like her mother's. "I waved at him but he didn't wave back."

Siobhan and her partner arrive at the house shortly after I've run the car back to Rita's. I tell them what Brie said. This news changes things, but still, they look around. In the shed they poke through Jake's gear and shine their flashlights into the rafters. I feel compelled to say, "I never thought of the shed as a crime scene, so things might not be exactly how they were the day Jake went missing." Siobhan just smiles reassuringly. Jake's computer is on the counter, and they take it. They glance at the portrait of me and move on. They find a stack of sketchbooks I missed and take them. Jake dates his sketchbooks on the inside cover. Maybe eventually the police will notice that the recent years are missing.

I ask Siobhan whether she's talked to Reg Bevaqua.

"He's not picking up at the number you gave me."

"Did you check whether he's in the country just now? He has properties around the world."

"Oh, I didn't realize that."

The amateur detective is always smarter than the police. I watch in silence as they bag up Jake's things and make their way out to their car. I'm heavy with dread, watching them. A man died. But I have no idea what went down. Why should I implicate my boyfriend without knowing what actually happened?

I spend the rest of the day thinking about what Brie said. Eventually I call Rita and tell her my theory: Jake went to Bevaqua's lodge on Easter Saturday. That's where he was headed when Brie saw him.

Just because he went north? Rita thinks it's a crazy leap. "You think he hitched a ride up to Bevaqua's lodge, and what—he's still there, and not getting in touch?" I'm silent, and she gets it. "You think something happened to him there. Isla, come on. Bevaqua met us at The Grange the next morning. If I'd just committed a terrible crime, I'm not going to show up right afterwards at a real estate meeting with my victim's girlfriend."

"That's exactly what he wants us to think. That's why he booked an appointment with the agent. Like, in the middle of the night. Who phones a real estate agent in the middle of the night, who insists on a viewing on Easter morning? Supposedly flying in from Montreal? And remember how weird he was?"

"He's always weird, Isla."

"No. He had zero interest in buying The Grange. He put on a show, but I could see right through it."

It is a crazy leap. I can't imagine trying to convince the police. But I am filled with a certainty as heavy as lead.

"He'd have to be a sociopath," Rita says.

"No. He's just very strategic. Well, I can be strategic too."

When I step outside about an hour later, little Brie is back, sitting on her bike in the middle of our driveway.

"I'm pretty sure Jake *is* mad at me," she says, resuming our earlier conversation.

I try to reassure her. I'm on my way to Rita's to pick up the duffle bag, and I ask her if she wants to come with me. But she wrinkles up her face and says, "Well, he's *gonna* be mad when he finds out." Turning down the corners of her mouth dramatically, she pulls her pink purse off the handlebar of her bike and lifts the flap to show me. "It doesn't work anymore."

His phone! She has his phone! His phone was in her purse!

"Where did you get it?"

"Off the ground."

"Where, sweetheart? Show me."

She gets off her bike. She's wearing plastic shoes that match her purse, and they're so big she can't lift her feet. She minces and slides her way towards the shed. "Here," she says, pointing to a spot in the grass near the side door of the shed. "It was just here."

"When was this?"

"It was after we all found our Easter eggs."

"So, not the day he got into the truck?"

"No, the next day. I came over because I thought he might be back and I was going to show him my chocolate bunny. But the shed was all locked. I waited and waited and finally I had to eat it." She sighs in resignation at the thought. "Then I saw his phone on the ground and I put it in my purse. And then the helicopter flew over and you came home. But he wasn't with you."

"Did you think, I should give Jake's phone to Isla?"

"Yes, I did think that. But you just went running by, and then I thought, no, I should give it to *Jake* when he comes home."

The phone is dead, of course. I watch Brie ride up the street, and then I dash into the house and stick it on a charge cord, my hands shaking. I used to know his code. I do know it, it's 1881, I punch it in. There are a lot of recent messages (phone, text, email), mostly from me. I scroll back to the middle of April. Jake got two texts April 20, the Saturday of The Ark opening. The first at 1:30, shortly after I left for Toronto. *I know it was you you little cunt.* Not a number Jake's phone recognized. It has a video attached.

Jake did not reply. A few minutes later, a second text came in from the same number. *Grow a pair and say it to my face.*

EIGHTEEN

Snow, a forest, the sun is low. A bizarre creature picks its way along the edge of a clearing. A Darwinian joke, warty bits dangling from its tiny head. It's a wild turkey. It plants its feet deliberately, like a model walking a runway. It tilts its head. Possibly it sees or hears the camera. Then it's out of the frame.

The video someone sent Jake is trail-cam footage. The camera must be motion-activated. Solar powered.

The next shot is night. The same scene, a snow-filled woods and a clearing with snow banked up along its edge. But sinister now, like night-vision footage on a battlefield. A short-legged, long-tailed animal prowls the clearing and then climbs the bank back to the woods, pausing to rub its belly furtively, sensuously, against a snowy log. It's scenting, I think. Is it a marten? No, I decide, it's a fisher. Fishers are very shy creatures—this seems like a terrible invasion of its privacy.

A winter's animal activity compressed into a couple of minutes. Day flickers into night and night into day. No bears, the bears are sleeping. Raccoons, all dapper and careless. Ravens hopping or flopping by. Grouse. A beautiful red fox, clearly hunting, though I can't see what. A deer, the same lovely deer several times, its eyes lit up like in car headlights. Rabbits on the sunlit snow.

And then we have another night shot, and there he is.

He walks along the edge of the clearing, a dark form on the snow, a blanket wrapped around his shoulders. His head is bare and he's not wearing his glasses. He's not wearing boots either. At first I think he's barefoot, and then I can see he has socks on.

His face is blank and intent at the same time, as though he's sleepwalking. He moves slowly but without hesitation across the snow. I feel a wrench of longing at the sight of him. I feel what I felt about the fisher, that I'm intruding on a private and unguarded moment full of meaning I might not be equipped to grasp. He lifts his head and looks right at the camera, and it's like our eyes meet. Then he moves out of the frame and the video ends.

FISSURE

NINETEEN

Sheff's childhood friend Penny Schroeder is friendly, reliable, and prompt, just as her business card promises. Only a few weeks have passed since she drove Isla from Toronto to Adlington, but the toque in gone and her hair is coming in nicely—although, Penny complains as they barrel north in the blue Kona, turns out she's suddenly grey.

"What colour did it use to be?" Isla asks.

"Bright as a new penny," Penny says.

Isla relaxes a little into the seat, having this confirmed. She unzips the hoodie she's wearing. It's Jake's hoodie, the one he often wore running. He'll be missing it now that the weather is so warm. Two weeks ago, when he disappeared, he was dressed in a dark grey padded jacket, at least that's what Isla assumes—it's not in the closet. She feels some trepidation at the prospect of sitting so close to Penny for several hours. Last time she rode in this seat, she sobbed her heart out, and that was Before (before Isla knew, at least).

And there's no riding in silence, not with Penny. Penny knows who Reg Bevaqua is, and she's intrigued that Isla is headed for his lodge. "It's beautiful up there on Georgian Bay. But I'm not sure I'd want to spend much time with a guy like him. The atmosphere is going to be toxic."

"Why do you say that?"

"Richard Cory, right? Filthy rich and he shot himself in the head."

"Right," Isla says. "I know the poem. But I think it might be a myth, that the rich are always secretly unhappy."

"You think?"

"I question whether people like Bevaqua are all that different from you and me. It's kind of a human trait, isn't it? To want to push things to greater and greater heights. One day you're a bunch of amateur gymnasts doing triple flips on the street in Montreal, and the next thing you know you're leveraged to a billion dollars and you have a permanent stage in Vegas."

Penny actually agrees. "It's not just humans who push the envelope," she says. "Think of the rack of antlers on a moose. The muscles in that boy's neck must be screaming."

"True," Isla says. "Or peacocks. That tail is irresistible to peahens, but it must be hell trying to flee from a jackal."

Penny reaches over for the GPS. She's preset it for the little village of Scalloway, just south of the lodge, and she minimizes the display so they can see the whole peninsula. "So this lodge—it's at the middle knuckle of the big finger."

"Yes," Isla says, though the peninsula doesn't look at all like a finger to her. She spent quite a while on Google Earth yesterday. The escarpment is the spine of a gargantuan reptile, surfacing from its burial site, and the peninsula is its saggy flanks. Bevaqua's lodge is nested like a tick in one of those flanks. It seems that Jake visited that lodge twice recently. He went in mid-March, when he was supposed to be camping with Kurt Altenbach, and he went wandering around in the night, and the place exploded. Then (this is Isla's best guess), he went up again on the Saturday before Easter, provoked by two vicious texts from his former best friend. And he has not been seen since. And Bevaqua is there now, as Isla learned last night.

Rita was the one who discovered that Bevaqua was again advertising for a chef at his lodge. She was searching employment agencies on her own behalf, and she came across the post, which offered a two-week bonus if the successful applicant could start immediately. That had to mean Reg was up there now with a gang of people. They got the idea that

Isla should show up at the lodge, using the chef job as pretext. If Eve was there, she'd be keen to hire her, and that would put Reg on the spot. He'd find a way to refuse, but Isla might glean something from her short visit, and might get the chance to ask a few questions. Her presence would rachet up his anxiety—whether this was a good thing or bad, she wasn't sure. Rita offered Isla her car, but Isla thought it might be smarter not to have her own means of transportation. She'd be harder to get rid of.

"You look tired, love," Penny says.

"I was awake most of the night."

"Want to tell me what's going on?"

Isla tips her head against the window. She's told herself not to talk about it, but Penny's warmth is irresistible. "My boyfriend is missing," she says. "He's been missing for a few weeks. Since the weekend you drove me to Adlington."

"How does the Bevaqua lodge come into it?"

"Well, that weekend, someone sent Jake some security footage taken at the lodge in March. Jake is in it. It suggests he was involved in a crime. So my theory is that he came up here to sort things out."

"Someone sent it?"

"Bevaqua sent it."

"What was the crime?"

Isla tells her. Penny recalls hearing about the blast on the news. They end up talking for a long time about Jake and Reg's history. About Jake's father, about Reg's connection to Jake's family, and how hard (seemingly) Jake tried to extract himself from all that. Not surprisingly, Penny has some wisdom on the subject: You carry around the bricks of the past, you're going to end up building the same old house.

"That's from a poem?" Isla asks.

"No, I saw it on Facebook."

After a minute, Penny says, "What did the police say when they saw the video?"

"Well, I haven't actually shown it to them yet."

Penny shakes her head in disapproval.

"I'd like to have some idea what I'm giving them first. It's a very weird video. Jake is outside in the dark in a shawl and sock feet. And I'm not sure I trust them." So far, when Isla thinks about it, the only good intel they have came from a child on a pink bike. "The police don't seem inclined to take Bevaqua on. People in town say he was storing a shitload of explosives illegally in that building, that's why it blew up, and as far as I know, he's never been charged."

"You should go to the police all the same. If you seriously think Bevaqua might have done something to your boyfriend, well, you must realize he's going to be a danger to you too."

"I will go, eventually. I'd like to be able to take them something they can't ignore." Something implicating Bevaqua, she means.

Isla turns her eyes to the window. Nearby trees fall backwards as they spin by, while, on the horizon, faraway trees dash forward, as if they're in a desperate race to beat the blue Kona to the lodge. Penny's worry is heavy in the air, but neither of them has put into words the gravest danger Isla faces in going into the lodge: that it might lead her to a conclusion she dreads. Or there's the other terrible possibility, that it won't lead anywhere, that she's facing a future in which this is never solved. Life will just go on. What will she do? She'll go on too. She'll settle into something, she'll have to. From time to time, she'll be filled with wild hope, she'll get glimpses of Jake, and he'll be so alive that she'll know he is somewhere, though hope is—what is it? It's the thing with feathers, she thinks helplessly, hopelessly, as the gentle hills slide away behind them.

Yesterday the real estate agent called and told her he'd shown The Grange that morning, to a guy who wanted to open a casino. The guy didn't divulge his intentions before the viewing, and Adlington doesn't license casinos in the town limits. Another waste of time, like the Bevaqua showing.

Isla was on her way into The Grange when she took the agent's call. She dropped her phone back into her pocket and stepped into the salon, and into a sharp memory of the day she first toured the place with Sheff. Back then, Kurt and Annalise were being forced to abandon their dream. They'd wanted to fill the place with kids. As Isla walked through the main dining room, she pictured it filled with her friends. Rita and her kids, Quinn and her kids, Annalise and her kids (Annalise was still her friend, no matter what). And Isla herself back in the kitchen—she saw herself cooking for all of them.

It was cold in the office. She turned on a little heater, and sat down and powered up the computer. She needed to pay some bills, and to get in touch with some of The Grange's long-time suppliers to let them know what was going on. The florist. The printer who did their menus. As the computer booted, she lifted her eyes to the whiteboard on the wall and saw the ghostly trace of their last dinner, back at the end of September. Cassoulet. She saw herself in a stranger's bed, talking about cassoulet, about making duck confit, and dread pulsed through her. There are a lot of taboos when someone you love is missing. Don't dwell on the bad parts of your history. Never imagine a future without them. Don't ever say "he was" instead of "he is." Don't dig too far into their things, as if they no longer have a right to privacy. But that afternoon as she settled into her work, Jake's absence felt non-negotiable. All the spells she'd been casting to make it not true—they were irrelevant. She didn't have the power to jinx his survival. She hardly knew him, apparently.

There were members of The Grange team she still hadn't been in touch with this spring. She'd start there. She clicked on the staff contact list, staring idly at the first entry, *Altenbach*, when her eyes snagged on a phone number she didn't recognize. It wasn't Annalise's. In all the years Kurt worked at The Grange, he would never agree to carry a phone—it was a constant source of aggravation. But at some point, he'd apparently given them a number.

Isla picked up her phone and punched that number in. One ring, and a male voice said, "*Ja.*"

She was so astonished she almost dropped the phone.

"Kurt?" she said.

"Annalise, *bist du es?*"

"Kurt, it's Isla. At The Grange."

Silence.

"Listen, I really need to talk to you. Where are you?"

"That's my business."

"Kurt, listen, Jake is missing."

"I know. Annalise told me."

"And now all this stuff is coming out. That the two of you broke into Bevaqua's lodge the day of the explosion in March."

"Untrue," he said forcefully. "We did not break into that lodge."

He was being pedantic about her word choice, the asshole. "Kurt, I'm not going to debate it. Jake was caught up there on camera, and the footage is date-stamped March 21. You need to tell me what you were doing. You tried to blow the place up?"

"No, we did not."

"Well, maybe you didn't *try*. Maybe it was inadvertent. You ignited something without realizing the building was full of explosives."

"Why was it?" The way he blurted this out—Isla knew she was on the right track and that he was truly freaked.

"Bevaqua was storing them for some reason. It's against the law, but he thinks he's above the law. Kurt, I don't assume you and Jake planned to kill a man. I assume you set off that blast in all innocence. You heard Roger coming and you were trying to distract him. Or you were trying to get rid of something, or pay him back for something, so you started a fire. Am I right?"

She waited a minute. He didn't speak, and she thought, I'm totally right.

"Then, because of Bevaqua's recklessness and disdain for the law"—she leaned on this part—"a man lost his life. And now you and Jake are facing very serious charges. It's not going to be simple unlawful entry or trespassing, it's going to be arson, criminal negligence, manslaughter, maybe even second-degree murder."

She paused again, expecting him to argue, but he didn't. "Listen, Kurt. You need to contact the police. Wherever you are. You need to tell them your version of events before they discover you were there and fixate on their version. Find a police station and ask to speak to an officer and tell them everything."

He made a contemptuous noise.

"This is excellent advice I'm giving you, Kurt. It would be a lot better for you and your family."

"Only a fool would put himself into the hands of the police."

"Well, then, tell *me*."

He didn't answer, and she gave it up. "At least tell me where Jake might be. Do you have any idea? You're not helping him hide, are you?"

"No. I have no idea. But he has been a friend to me, and I will tell you this. He was not responsible for the blast at the lodge. He had nothing to do with it."

Gratitude and relief washed over Isla. "Thank you," she said fervently. "I so appreciate you telling me that, Kurt. I didn't think he did, but it feels good to hear you say it. But you have no idea where he could be now?"

"Why ask me?" Kurt said. "Bevaqua is the one you should be talking to. If Jake is missing, Bevaqua's behind it."

Isla felt her heart begin to pound. "Why do you think that?"

"You said he knows Jake was up at the lodge when the workshop blew up. He won't let that go. Bevaqua will always come out on top."

They hung up, and she sat stunned. Was Kurt even in Germany? His phone had picked up the call so fast. He was likely in Toronto, hiding in somebody's basement. Maybe he and Annalise hadn't actually broken up—it might all be a lie. But on the essential question, whether Jake was responsible for the explosion, she found herself believing him. He had no reason to cover for Jake. And she'd never been able to imagine Jake as the Unabomber. If he'd caused the blast inadvertently and knew it was his fault, he would have turned himself in. Not just because he was a decent individual. Her mind reached for a less tangible but more powerful reason: because he always thought he deserved to be punished. He had a morality she didn't quite grasp—he felt responsible even for things he couldn't have done anything about. It was still bad, not going to the police with what he knew. But his reasoning was probably more complicated than the police would appreciate.

Isla once visited her uncle Paul in Muskoka, and she'd always pictured the Bruce as that sort of country, granite cliffs and spruce trees. But when she punched Bruce Peninsula into her search engine, Google Earth rolled out a mostly level green carpet, interspersed here and there with farm lands, fringed with deciduous trees. Google Earth had it right, she sees as they drive.

"It's not Canadian Shield, this side of Georgian Bay," Penny says. "And it was all logged out a hundred years ago. I don't know how much old-growth forest is left."

"And before the loggers and farmers?"

"I think Ojibway lived here. They defeated the Iroquois to take it over."

Right. A long time ago, Jake told her about this being treaty land, a treaty that was violated when white squatters moved in. They drive through bush until they see the sign for Comstock Cove, and then Penny turns east onto a narrow paved road. Bevaqua's property, Isla figures from a surveyor's map she found online, is a little pod of forest between the escarpment and the lake, one of very few privately owned pieces of land along the Bruce Trail. It's shaped like a section of mandarin orange. The lake is the straight edge, and the escarpment tracks along its rounded outer edge, until, at the north and south ends, it curves close to the shore and pinches the property off.

She and Penny drive a couple of miles up the paved road, and suddenly they're in a dense forest. Isla finds herself imagining Jake as a boy, his excitement as they drive up this road. He's wearing his swim trunks under his jeans, his eyes are eagerly picking out familiar things. That rock shaped like a sleeping giant. The falling-down wall of an old log cabin, covered in moss.

The road rises then, and they're at the escarpment. This is where the paved road ends, at a parking lot for the Bruce Trail. From the parking lot, an unpaved lane leads further into the forest.

"That will be the private lane to Bevaqua's lodge," Isla says. "It has to be." She didn't expect the property to be guarded by a chain-link fence and a locked steel gate with a Private Property sign on it. "Oh well," she says. "I can walk from here." She gets out of the car and reaches into the back seat for her pack.

Penny gets out too. "I don't like this. I don't feel great leaving you here. Check your phone. See if you have service."

To Isla's surprise, she has five bars. Penny looks around and then gestures. A cell tower, a hundred metres to the south. Bevaqua. The dude has his own cell tower. Of course he does.

Penny says she's going to drive up to Tobermory. She'll hang out there for a couple of hours. "Call if you want a ride back," she urges. "Okay? Be careful. I mean it."

The gate's not hard to climb over. On the other side of it, Isla turns to give Penny a thumbs-up. "Don't forget to drop your breadcrumbs," Penny calls. She gets back into the car, does a capable three-point turn, and vanishes.

The lane Isla follows is earth and gravel, giving way occasionally to flat rock with fingers of moss running through it. It runs between massive trees with green on their trunks, the occasional paper birch. Nothing is fully leafed out yet; sunlight slices easily to the forest floor. She walks for half an hour, feeling better and better. As she warms up, Jake's smell rises faintly from the hoodie. She feels a sort of welcome, like he's pleased that she's seeing this.

Gradually the light grows and the lane starts to slope down: Isla is getting near the lake.

First thing she sees through the trees is the blast site, a massive, uneven mountain of rubble. Beyond it is the gabled cedar roof of the lodge. She steps back off the lane to collect herself. No reason to be afraid. Reg won't dare to be openly antagonistic—that would be a huge giveaway. But still, she's not in a hurry to encounter him. She spies a path angling northeast off the lane towards the lake, and on impulse, she takes it. When she comes upon a blue rectangular marking on a tree, she goes in that direction. These blue markings are signposts for Bruce Trail digressions. She's not afraid of getting lost—no matter which way she walks, she'll come either to the lake or to the Bruce Trail.

She follows the path for a long time, gradually climbing. For stretches it runs along a cliff edge, then a secondary cliff rises to her left like the second tier of a wedding cake. Jake will know and love this trail. He'll have wandered it with joy when he was a kid. No doubt he ran down it terrified more than once. Having arrows shot at him, maybe. Hurting each other seemed to have been a game for him and Reg. Jake has *scars* as mementos of his friendship with Reg. And yet he hung in.

The path steepens sharply and delivers her to a high lookout over the lake. Georgian Bay in all its beauty. The Open, locals call the water outside the cove—she read this on a website last night. The Open is royal blue, and the water close to shore is a brilliant turquoise. The contrast is astonishing. Then Isla gets it: the band of emerald-bright water along the shore, and the white scalloped foam, and the deep blue further out—it's the BevAqua Blue brand. Bevaqua put this vista on his water bottles.

She's turning to head back to the lodge when she notices a faint path down to the water. That path was made by animals, she hears Jake tell her, deer going to drink from the lake at sunset. Isla follows it. It's steep, she has to step carefully. It takes her to an inlet with a rock ledge about two feet above the water. A tiny inlet within a cove within a bay within a massive lake. She squats on the ledge and leans out to look at the water. It's heartbreakingly clear, probed by the midday sun: you can see the pebble-paved floor far below. A few waving weeds. And something lurking, shape-shifting in the prism of the water. Something oblong. Blue, the colour speaks in fractals through the crystalline water.

Before Isla has time to think, she's pried off her shoes and yanked off her hoodie and jeans and she's in. The water slams her, it knocks the breath right out of her. It's so icy it registers as hot. Stupid, stupid—she'll have to be quick. She puts a hand against the rock face, forcing herself to focus through the bubbles. One giant kick, and she's down.

It's not a body, it's bigger than a body, it's the size of a manatee.

It's a canoe.

TWENTY

A white refrigerated van is parked by the back door of the lodge—*Morgan's*, Isla sees when she gets a little closer. Morgan's is a high-end grocery supplier. And there's Eve talking to the driver. Eve in a blue silk Japanese robe, the chic cap of her hair gleaming in the sun.

"Isla, my goodness! What a surprise!" Eve steps towards Isla and offers her the two-cheek pseudo kiss. "What in the world are you doing up here?"

She's never seen Eve without makeup before. Her skin is so lovely. "A friend of mine was driving up to Tobermory, and I thought I'd grab the chance to stop by and see your place. Sorry, I should have called." She's still shaky from her plunge into the lake. Not from the cold, she warmed up walking to the lodge, but from the terrifying effort it took to heave herself out of the icy water and onto the ledge.

"Did you *walk* in?"

"My friend dropped me off at the Bruce Trail."

"Oh!" Eve is studying Isla curiously. Well, of course, her hair is wet. She pulled it up and into a bun, but Eve can still tell. It's not Eve's way to ask, though. "I do apologize. It's not the best day for you to stop by. We're so short-staffed, and our weekly delivery has just arrived, as you see. Reg isn't here, he had to go to the city. He'll be *so* sorry he missed you."

Isla feels a little uplift of relief. Eve will be much easier to deal with on her own.

Eve gestures towards the orange hazard fence enclosing the rubble from the blast. "Isn't this terrible?"

"It is. It's just awful. It's like a war zone."

Two corners of the building still stand to about the height of the first floor. Within them is a wasteland of cement, glass, burnt planks, twisted pipes. Semi-melted plastic, the rinds of storage barrels, scorched drywall. This is Kurt's handiwork, Isla thinks. Isla imagined more of a crater, but of course the building didn't have a basement.

"People heard the explosion all the way down at Wiarton," Eve says. "It was a brand-new building, just finished last fall. Can you imagine? A state-of-the art maintenance shop with a ton of valuable equipment. All gone. The top floor was comfortable living quarters for six staff. We had solar panels on the roof. And of course, we lost Roger Lafontaine, our pilot. He and Reg were so close. It's been an absolute nightmare."

"Reg told me about Roger," Isla says. "I'm very sorry."

"Thank you," Eve says. "And thank God Reg got his solo licence before this happened."

The uniformed Morgan's driver is shoving cartons and insulated sacks at someone in the doorway, a woman wearing surgical scrubs. The woman casts imploring glances in Eve's direction. Eve clearly has a lot on her plate. Still, she has those brought-upsy ways, she remembers to ask how Isla is. "I was surprised to hear you and Lionel are selling The Grange. It's such a gem."

"It's true, we've had a good run," Isla says. "But everybody's lives are kind of in freefall just now." I, for example, have wandered onto your property in search of my boyfriend, who's been missing for weeks. And you, Eve, have a beautiful new canoe swamped on the lake floor just up the shore. Canvas-sided, wood-ribbed. It's weighted down with four or five big rocks. What is that about?

Eve doesn't ask about Isla's boyfriend. She clearly doesn't know, how would she? "Yes," she says fervently. "It's been a strange year for us too.

Reg and I had all these great plans. We had finally decided we were going to—" Just then the Morgan's driver thrusts a clipboard and pen at her. "Someone really should be checking all this," she says as she signs. The driver gets into the truck and backs slowly around the blast site. The woman in the aqua scrubs is still trying to get Eve's attention. Eve raises a hand to cut her off. "Helen, you're just going to have to do the best you can," she says, turning back to Isla with a smile, trying to make her complicit. "Helen is daily cleaning staff from Lion's Head—sorting out the grocery order is not remotely her job, but what am I going to do? As I was saying, things are beyond chaotic here. Our chef quit last week with no notice. Then on Monday, our au pair tore the ligaments in her knee. She's in the city having that seen to—who knows when she'll be back. William is supposed to be in school. She's a certified teacher, and we were counting on her to teach him. It's absolute chaos. We're down to a skeleton crew, and still, with the staff quarters gone, people are sleeping in the rafters." She touches Isla's arm. "But let me give you a quick tour, seeing you're here. I'm horrified when guests come in by the road, and that mess is the first thing they see."

She leads Isla along a stone walkway, graceful in her blue silk robe and leather slippers. Those childhood ballet classes. Why in hell are they staying here through all this chaos? Eve replies to Isla's thought. "We're having a major rebuild of the house in Rosedale. It belonged to my grandparents, and it's been terribly neglected for decades. Reg and I should have tackled it sooner, but we wanted it done right, and we were thrilled to be on a waitlist for *Mark Ellison*." She stops walking and looks at Isla expectantly, like Isla should know who that is. "Of course, Mark's call came at the worst possible time. Isn't that always the way? He had all his tradesmen lined up—he's rather more a choreographer than a contractor, isn't he?—so we couldn't possibly postpone." There's a high-falling pitch to her speech, an affectation Rita says Eve smuggled home from her years at Oxford.

Isla takes note of a security camera under the eaves at the corner of the lodge. "I guess you could have rented in the city?"

"That was the plan. But a few weeks ago, Reg suddenly changed his mind. He said we needed to be here. Because of the explosion, you know. Why we don't just lay on more security—I can't explain it."

Her resentment sounds genuine. Whatever happened here, Isla thinks, Eve doesn't know.

They're in front of the lodge now, on a headland higher than the point where Isla stood earlier. "It was so hard to decide whether our home should face the forest or the lake," Eve says (impressing people who drive up the lane versus impressing people who arrive by boat, Isla takes this to mean). In the end, the waterfront visual of the lodge rising out of the cliffs proved irresistible. A gorgeous, though not huge, yacht floats beside the pier and Isla gazes down at it, so fucking impressed she's in danger of fainting. "The *Sequana*," Eve says reverently. "Captain just sailed her in from drydock yesterday." *Captain*. Against the white hull of the yacht, the vivid water looks almost toxic, like blue icing on a birthday cake.

A limestone staircase leads to the water. The stairs were meant, Isla learns, to evoke the Spanish Steps in Rome. Eve descends them and Isla follows, out onto an imposing stone and cedar pier with a floating dock. The kids are playing in a roofed area on the pier—the pergola, it's called. Isla says hi, but they're too preoccupied to greet her. Lark's hair is tangled and she's still in pajamas. She's wailing because William threw her plastic unicorn in the water. They're being watched by a thin young man, Yann, the IT technician. He's elfin, almost ethereal, with huge, iridescent eyes. He's desperate to get back to work, he needs to send out a link for a meeting. "Go, go," Eve says. She and Isla gather up the children and climb the steps. At the door of the lodge, a brown dog bounds over to greet them. Eve sends the kids to their playroom to watch a video, and then she and Isla stand in the spectacular living room, where Eve absorbs Isla's wonder serenely. When the lodge was featured in *Architectural Digest*, she says, the editors didn't have to stage the place, which is most unusual. The only thing they did was bring in a black Lab to lie by the hearth. "They didn't think you were a proper dog for the northern wilderness, did they, Tutty," she croons, bending over her big-eared dog. He's a pharaoh hound, a dog Isla's never heard of. Eve tells Isla about their marvellous family adventure, flying to Malta and then driving to the tiny village where the Amarna-ra pharaoh hound is bred, and choosing King Tut out of a litter of squirming puppies.

The kitchen is wonderful, state-of-the-art, as Reg always brags. Eve gestures towards the espresso machine. "I'd offer you a coffee, but frankly, I'm not sure how to use that beast. One of the staff always acts as barista."

"Let me do it," Isla says. "Why don't I make us both a nice latte?" She reaches for the coffee canister, thinking, I am *so* in. Eve sinks into a chair, touching her fingers delicately to her eyelids. Then, over the scream of the milk steamer, she calls, "I do realize why you're here, Isla," and Isla (suddenly registering the dampness of her bra and T-shirt under her hoodie) flicks the steamer off.

"You do?"

"Yes. And frankly, I'm glad for the chance to talk to you about it on my own. Reg gets these enthusiasms. He and our COO, Hashem, were at a water conference in Montreal that weekend, and it turned out not to be very useful, and over dinner, people were talking restaurants. Someone mentioned The Grange near Toronto, that it was on the market. Reg wanted an excuse to escape, so he made a few calls and decided to take a spontaneous little trip over to Adlington. The helicopter gives him that sort of freedom, it's wonderful. He and I hadn't even discussed it. But just to be clear, I don't think the restaurant business is in our future."

"Eve, don't worry in the least," Isla says, setting Eve's latte in front of her. "I knew it was a *very* long shot. Actually, I came because—well, I understand you're advertising for a chef."

"Oh, Isla. Really?" Eve glows at Isla with uncharacteristic warmth. "You'd be open to it?"

"Yes, I would. I'm kind of at loose ends at the moment."

"Honestly, I wouldn't have dared to dream. That's wonderful. Absolutely wonderful! Oh, Reg will be over the moon. When would you be free to start?"

Isla smiles and shrugs. "I'm here now. I've got my toothbrush and a change of clothes. I can't wait, actually, to try out this grill."

"Seriously? Oh, Isla! We've been ten or eleven for dinner all week, and I am *so* over trying to manage!"

Isla glances around at the cartons of gelato melting on the counter and the mess left from lunch. "Let me deal with the grocery order so Helen can get back to her job, and then you and I can sit down and talk menus. Once I know what you have."

"Listen, I'm happy to leave all that entirely up to you. Ordinary home cooking is fine. We're a family here. And frankly, you have never served me a meal that was less than first-rate." She finally takes a sip of her latte, blind to its perfect foam rosette. "I'll call the agency right away and get them to send a contract up. We haven't talked money, but—"

A young woman comes into the kitchen, and Eve breaks off. "Luna, we have just landed ourselves a fabulous chef. This is Isla Coltrane, Lionel Sheffield's partner from The Grange in Adlington. Isla, Luna is Reg's EA."

"Hi," Luna says, barely glancing their way. She opens the fridge. She's glamorously made up, dressed in a business suit and four-inch heels.

"I've been admiring that piece all day," Eve says. "Alexander McQueen?"

"Akris punto."

"Ah. Of course."

Luna pulls a carafe of what looks like cucumber water out of the fridge. Her hair glistens like sunlight on black water.

"Did Yann get the link up?"

Luna nods. She goes out without another word. She's so beautiful she doesn't have to be friendly, not even to the boss's wife.

"They do so much video conferencing," Eve says, picking her coffee up again. "And the international partners expect formality. People see Reg, and they think the money just drops out of the sky. They have no idea. He's up at five a.m., he's still taking calls at midnight. That's the reality of a global enterprise. And look at me. It's almost noon and I still haven't showered."

Isla asks Eve whether she expects Reg for dinner.

"No. He's meeting someone for an early dinner in the city. He'll fly up after. The helipad is lit for night landing."

"And are there food sensitivities in the group I should know about?"

Eve fills her in on a few. "And Monday, a demolition crew is coming in to clean up the blast site. It's a local crew, three, I believe, and we agreed to provide meals."

"All good," Isla says. Will she be here Monday? This is Friday. It seems unlikely.

Eve heads upstairs with her latte. Isla finds Helen in the walk-in fridge and introduces herself, and then she locates the inventory binder and sets to work, trying to keep her mind on what she's doing. Avocados, asparagus, fennel, lots of greens. Porcini mushrooms. Wonderful fresh scallops. She's yearning to snoop around the lodge, but what she really needs to do this afternoon is make herself very, very hard to get rid of.

The dining room. Its windows open onto the forest, and its furnishings evoke Japan, or at least Frank Lloyd Wright evoking Japan. When the light softens outside, William rings the dinner bell and people drift in. Helen's gone home, Captain has sailed on. It's Reg's business team, young, personable, their teeth over-bleached. They've been living on freezer pizzas and Yann's cowboy stew, and they're ecstatic about

Isla's chowder and biscuits. A guy named Alessandro moves around the table filling everyone's glass. He's a built guy with a buzz cut and a fine if unoriginal dragon tattoo on his right forearm. He's Bevaqua's driver and bartender. These jobs are often paired, he tells Isla, because the driver is always on standby and has to stay sober.

"Isla, sit with us," Eve says, and Isla goes to get another plate. Witticisms fly around the table about the previous chef, who night after night served slabs of charred meat. Isla laughs along with everyone. Be natural, be friendly, be a person they will talk to. Good luck with engaging Luna, who doesn't laugh. Before dinner she took off the Akris punto jacket but not the studio makeup. When your eyes are the uncanny green of a luna moth, well, why ever lose the volume lashes?

Second course: fettuccine primavera with a salad of arugula and fennel. More jokes about the old chef, who hitched a ride out last week in the Morgan's van, claiming he'd heard a rattlesnake in the explosion debris. "Don't laugh about it!" William cries. "There was a rattlesnake. Nobody believed Duarte, but I *saw* it!" In his excitement he knocks his milk off the table and the glass smashes. "Move fast and break things," Yann cheers, scrambling to clean it up. Luna hitches her chair out of the way, Isla smiles in her direction—really, it's hard to take your eyes off Luna—and the hound lifts his head sharply, like he smells Isla's energy change before her mind can register this astonishing fact: she's seen Luna before. Easter Sunday, when Reg flew into Adlington and toured The Grange, *he had Luna with him*. She was the woman in the Maui Jims, who went straight back to the copter. No question about it.

Eve, in a Bretagne sweater and white pants, is holding forth from the head of the table, reminiscing about The Grange, apparently feeling the need to flatter Isla. "Adlington's loss is our gain," she says without apparent irony.

Isla takes a breath. "I'm looking forward to cooking for all of you," she says. "But I hope you'll forgive me if I seem a little distracted. My partner, my boyfriend Jake, has been missing for a few weeks. He vanished Easter weekend, and no one has heard from him."

Eve's shock is obvious—the embarrassment of a hostess ignorant of the biggest story in the room. She murmurs her concern along with everyone else. "You should have said something. I would never have let you—" She waves a hand, *do all this*.

"It's better for me to be working. And this place, this beautiful peninsula, is country Jake loves, so I'm happy to be here."

No one knows where to take the conversation after that. Do they reassure Isla or offer condolences? At what point will the phrase "and presumed dead" be tacked onto this story of a missing man?

It's Luna who breaks the silence. "When was this again? When he went missing?"

"Easter weekend."

Luna's lashes lower like fringed blinds. This is proof, Isla thinks. Reg *was* here the weekend he came to tour The Grange. He and Luna flew down from the lodge. He wouldn't be able to take lovers to hotels, people know him everywhere. He was never in Montreal that weekend. He was here, with his girlfriend.

Isla forces herself to look away. "Jake has the habit of trekking all over the country. So it's hard to know where to focus a search. He could be anywhere."

Eve comes alive. "Or he could be right at home," she says, like she's onto something brilliant. "It's funny, but just the other night I watched a film about a man who disappeared, his family didn't know where he was. Bryan Cranston played the lead."

"Oh, I saw that movie," someone says. "The guy was up in the attic the whole time."

"In the attic?" Isla says.

"Yes, well, they had a separate garage," Eve says, "and that garage had an attic, so he was across the driveway from his family. For a whole year, as the seasons changed, he watched them through a little window, sometimes with binoculars. His wife was played by Jennifer Garner."

"Why was he hiding in the attic?"

"He dropped out of his life. People take off sometimes rather than face up to their problems." A way to dismiss Isla's tragedy seems to be occurring to her. "But honestly, I wondered, how could Jennifer Garner not sense he was up there, watching her?"

"Jake is not watching me these days," Isla says. "I have never felt that. I wish I did."

Eve tilts her head to express concern. "What can we do to help?"

"Well, we think Jake may have headed up to the peninsula. A child in Adlington saw him hitchhiking from the gas station. He got into a truck headed north. You realize his family used to summer on this bay?"

"*Oh.* Oh, my goodness. That Jake. The artist, who just had a show at the new art centre. Of course! Forgive me—I never put it together that your boyfriend is Jake *Challis.*" Isla watches her stock zoom way up in Eve's eyes.

"Yes. So, as you know, Reg and Jake were really close as kids. And you have a lot of resources that could be used in a search. The helicopter, your boats. That was a factor, when I decided to take this job today. The police aren't doing much, and I honestly don't know where else to turn."

"Of *course,*" Eve says. "Of course, Reg will be eager to help."

Isla is serving tarte Tatin when Lark shrieks, "Daddy!" Her sharp little ears have picked up the helicopter. Yann leaps out of his chair. "Come on, kiddos, let's go out and watch your old man set that bird down."

"I did not at all expect him for dinner," Eve says. "You'll warm a plate for him?"

The first person in through the kitchen is not Reg, but a tall, dark-haired, and very handsome man in an expensive suit—Hashem, their

COO. Just up for a few days, he says to Eve, just to get them through this patch. Then Reg fills the doorway, Lark on his shoulders. He sees Isla and he stands still and slides his little girl down.

"I've got a huge surprise, Reg," Eve calls from the passage to the dining room.

"I see that."

"We've just had the most wonderful dinner. Say hello to our new chef."

Reg glowers. "Reg," Eve says softly, moving towards him, no doubt wanting to alert him to Isla's situation before he really steps in it. But he ignores her, he says, "Isla, can I speak to you in my office?"

Isla closes the microwave and follows him through the living room, down a hall, and into an area of the building she didn't even suspect was here. He closes the door. It's huge, a city centre financial office reassembled in the forest. Off-white leather, pale and polished wood. Lots of glass, a triptych of computer screens, a fireplace.

Like Hashem, Reg is still wearing his suit, though he's opened his shirt at the neck and his tie is shoved into the jacket pocket. The skinned patch on his forehead has healed. How are they going to play this? He'll have to go along with the charade.

But he doesn't. He does not sit down and he does not invite Isla to. "What are you doing here?" he says in the most aggressive tone Isla has ever heard from him, and her courage vanishes. The TV mystery is finished, the days when she dashed around murmuring *motive, opportunity, means*. That role energized her for a while, but it's done now. This is real, and absurd in its weight. When she talks, her voice is stiff. "I'm looking for Jake. I think you know he's missing."

"Yeah, the police called me today. They told me you suggested they call. I'm not sure why you thought I would know anything. And you gave them my private cell number. I consider that a serious violation of my privacy." That's going to be his pretext when he gets rid of her, the asshole.

"Don't try to bullshit me, Reg. I saw the video you sent Jake. I know he was up here the weekend of the explosion."

Reg can't hide his shock. He lifts his hands, *whoa*.

"You must have had that video since March. I've been thinking about that. On Easter Sunday, you told me the guys who blew up the building disabled the security cameras."

He walks over to his desk and sits on the edge, playing for time. He's switching tactics, he's going to pretend they're on the same side, take her into his confidence. "That's what I thought initially, Isla. We gave the police the map of webcams our security firm had provided, and the vandals had disabled all of them—but the helipad camera was just installed last fall and it wasn't on the map. Anyway, the police missed it. And so did Jake, the day he skied in and blew up my workshop. You can imagine how I felt when I came across that footage this spring. Learning that someone I knew was responsible for the death of a good buddy."

"Jake did not blow up your workshop. He trespassed on your property, which I admit was stupid and wrong, but he wasn't alone. And I honestly don't think it was deliberate. I think it was an accident—though the person storing explosives illegally on this property might want to consider his own responsibility."

"Oh, right. Fuck off, Isla."

"But I'd really like to know when you found that video."

"Why? What does it matter?"

"Well, strangely, the police don't seem to have connected Jake to the blast. Why didn't you send the file straight to them? Instead, you send it to Jake, you taunt him with it. I'm trying to figure that out." His eyes harden, and suddenly she has an answer: Bevaqua found that footage when he flew in for his Easter-weekend tryst with Luna. He didn't want anyone to know he was here that weekend. He likely planned to take it to the police later, when he could come up with a different pretext for finding it—but the day he found it, he couldn't resist sending it to Jake. And then, something happened, and he didn't want the police to connect Jake with the lodge. The implications of that thought almost blind her. "You sent the footage to Jake," she says, "and he dropped everything and came up here. And nobody's seen him since."

"Here?" he says like the idea is risible. "You think he came here?"

"Yes. I'm pretty sure he did, Reg. Which is why I'm here."

A flash of hatred—like the flash she caught the day he toured The Grange. But when he speaks, his voice is perfectly calm and conciliatory. That's what it is to be a hardcore liar. "Listen, Isla, I realize you're going through hell. I'm very sorry about your trouble with Jake, but I sense you might be making up ridiculous stories to explain it. You need to get a grip. If the worst has happened—and I hope to God it hasn't, but if it has—your paranoia is just going to make things harder. For you and for Jake's family. As my staff will tell you, we have zero tolerance for drama around here. This is our workplace. We're in a massive business crunch at the moment. It might be hard for you to grasp how high the stakes are"—("They are rather high for me too," Isla murmurs, but he talks over her)—"and I think it would be best if you left tonight."

"I don't have a car. Someone dropped me off."

"Alessandro will run you out."

She so regrets having to reach for the nuclear option before she can plan out a strategy, but what else can she do? "You might want to think for a bit before you throw me out. I enjoyed spending time with Eve this afternoon. And it was interesting to meet Luna. You didn't actually introduce her when she came with you to tour The Grange."

Rage turns Reg's face monstrous, like a mask. She doesn't wait for his reply. She walks to the door and closes it on her way out, and goes straight to the kitchen, breathing hard. The staff have demolished the tarte Tatin and wandered away. Isla serves up dinner for Hashem and Reg, putting their plates on hot pads in the dining room. She hears Reg come in as she's wiping down the kitchen. Eve joins him. He's reduced to arguing about where they will put the new chef. "You didn't foresee this problem when you asked her to stay?"

"I was planning to move Yann and Alessandro to the den and give Isla their room. I wasn't counting on Hashem coming up."

"I need Hashem."

"Well, I need a cook."

A long silence.

"She can sleep on the *Sequana*," Eve says in a low voice. She's trying to get him to lower his.

"No. Nobody's sleeping on the yacht. There's a good chance Edelman and Watson are going to have to come up. I want to keep it open for them."

"They're coming here?"

"Well, yeah. If worse comes to worst."

"Why don't you meet in the city?"

Then he does lower his voice, he says something Isla can't hear, and Eve murmurs a response.

When Isla drifts over to the dining room doorway, they're back to the question of bedrooms. "We'll have to pitch the tent," Eve says.

"We don't have a tent. It was in the workshop."

"No. It's in the boathouse. I saw it yesterday. Yann and Alessandro can sleep in the tent, and Isla can take the double room and Hashem can sleep in the upstairs den."

"Don't move Yann and Alessandro," Isla calls, not even pretending she's not eavesdropping. "I would love to sleep in the tent."

A nightcap on the water. Isla follows Yann and Alessandro down the Spanish Steps and settles on an empty lounge chair facing the lake. The *Sequana* is undoubtedly beautiful, but when you're sitting in the pergola, it blocks a big chunk of the view.

They've just spent an hour setting up the tent. It was hard to find a flat spot, with the area behind the lodge so torn up, and they finally pitched in the middle of the path just to the north, on a ridge above the lodge. It's a great location. You can lie on your stomach with the tent door tied back and watch everything going on at the lodge. Yann and Alessandro brought out two air mattresses, two big warm sleeping bags, a little flashlight and a big one. They were determined to move into the tent, but Isla dug in and they finally agreed to flip for it. Isla reached into her jeans pocket for a quarter, and there was the big Brazilian coin the busker gave her at the Ark party. She called heads and she won. She's never slept in a tent, though she didn't tell them that.

Alessandro has lowered the bridge of the *Sequana* and he's moving back and forth along it, bartending from the yacht's bar. When he brings Isla a gin and tonic with a generous wedge of lime, she takes it. It's one of those idyllic nights Earth is still capable of. The lake has lost its brilliance, but the sky is a perfect azure. Jake, she thinks with a pang. Water laps on stone, and an eerie cry fills the lake, as mournful as a wolf howl. It's loons. They trade their tremolo back and forth while Reg comes down the stairs from the lodge. His belligerence is visible, he wears it like armour. Hashem follows. He looks to Isla like an intellectual whose true thoughts will always be secret. Like a fastidious man you'd confide in without thinking twice. He's carrying a beautiful stringed instrument.

"Is that a lute?" Isla asks across the circle of chairs.

"It's a kind of lute," he says. "A *barbat*. It's Persian. My father was a professional musician in Iran."

He sits still, like he's centring himself, and then he leans over the instrument and begins to play. Each note is a drop of mercury spilling over the lake. Everyone stops talking. Eve turns her profile to the music, absorbing it into her pale beauty. Luna lies in her lounger, eyes closed, like she's in her lover's bed. Even the loons go quiet at notes more melancholy than their own. Only the dog is indifferent. He sits alertly at Eve's feet, not taking his eyes off her.

Isla slides her hand into the pocket of Jake's hoodie and fingers her second find of the afternoon. Grabbing a chance to search the living room before supper, she noticed a carved wooden box on the fireplace mantel. Inside was a pair of glasses. Plastic frames, black matte—Jake's glasses. The glasses he lost in the winter, stashed tidily away in that box. By him, or by someone else? Either way, Jake was here. Isla has proof she can hold in her hand.

While the notes of the *barbat*, limpid and lovely, float over the water, she senses Reg stealing glances at her. With everything that's coming down on him, he cares about whether she's impressed. This slice of paradise is *mine*, he feels the need to say. Isla looks back at him, she fixes Reg in her gaze, making no effort to hide her aversion. She keeps staring until he looks away.

TWENTY-ONE

In the tent, she dreams of having sex with Jake. He comes before her, and she feels his release like a warm alpenglow. She wakes up full of emotion and doesn't manage to fall back to sleep.

She lies thinking about what it was like when they were first together, the year she and Sheff bought The Grange. She thinks about the day they went to Gracie Lake. It was fall and the burnt-out campfires of a long summer littered the shore like eagles' nests. Jake said the beach was exactly the same as when he was a kid, a grassy bank, a long dock, the changing huts with rough pine benches and sand floors. In the girls' side, Isla stepped out of her sandals and into her white one-piece, taking in the childhood smell of pee and wet bathing suits, holding her breasts for a minute, feeling their lovely weight, and then she let the door swing closed behind her and walked out to where he was waiting in the sunlight.

"Ten feet deep at the end," he said. She trusted him and she pounded down the dock and dove deep. By the time she opened her eyes, his feet were flicking ahead of her like white fish. She buried herself in a crawl, and when she broke back to the sky, he was right in front of her, water pouring off him. Their chins at the surface, the lake glazed with light. Their limbs tangled, cold skin and warm flesh, while the far-off horizon tipped.

At the water's edge Jake and Isla stopped to admire a sandcastle some kids were building. A sister and brother, they looked to be, wearing red hoodies over their swimsuits. They were dipping their cold hands into a blue plastic bucket, drizzling a slurry of sand and water onto the towers.

"Hey, La Sagrada Família," Jake called. "Great job!"

"No," the kids shouted. "Wrong!"

They looked closer, studying the towers. "Angkor Wat," Isla said, and the kids cheered.

Jake snagged his towel up and towelled her off, wrapping her like a baby. "You are such a show-off."

"As an artist, you should take an interest in Angkor Wat. Its builders were abducted by aliens. That's where their vision came from."

"Is that right." He rotated her, turning his back to the kids and peering into the cowl around her head. His lashes were stuck together, his hair was wet-black and plastered to his skull. "So, Isla. Are you trying to abduct me?"

"Yes," she said, and she lifted her smile to his mouth, digging her toes into the sand so the tsunami of feeling headed their way didn't sweep her right out to sea.

The sun is up, she needs to make breakfast, but it's hard to drag herself out of her sleeping bag. Her nose is cold, like a dog's. It's nuts that Eve is content to let her sleep outside on the ground in April. Then Yann is on the path, calling her. "Be right down," she shouts, scrambling out of the sleeping bag.

After breakfast, Eve calls her to the living room, eager to show her the *Architectural Digest* that featured their lodge. Isla studies the photo spread, laughing obligingly about the cliché of a black Lab lying by the hearth. In the photo, a gun is mounted on the wall. "Looks like *Digest* thought you should have a rifle too," she says, and Eve says, "No, that's our rifle." They both look up and Eve frowns. There's no rifle on the wall. The wooden pegs it rests on are there, but the gun is gone. It's an old one, Eve says, a Lee-Enfield .303 that was in the Challis cabin. She's upset. She takes off to ask Reg about it.

Isla carries her own shock back to the kitchen, where she sets about trying to sort out the meals for the day. A swamped canoe. A missing rifle. Colonel Mustard in the library with a gun. William's at her side, asking if she wants to see the helicopter. "I'd love to," she says. They're heading for the back door when Eve comes out of the office.

"Did you find out where your rifle is?" Isla asks.

Eve raises her eyebrows to say, is that really your business? She asks Isla where they're off to. Next thing Isla knows, she's agreed to take Lark as well.

Sun hats. Sunglasses. Sunscreen. Juice boxes. "Don't forget the EpiPen," Eve sings out as they leave, and Isla turns back to take it from her.

"Do we have allergies happening?"

"Not so far. But there's always the worry they might manifest."

They set off along the edge of the blast site. Isla senses someone behind them and turns. It's Hashem.

"Someone's told you about the NWA?"

"The NWA?"

"You know, like an NDA. The No-Wandering Agreement." He's trying to charm her. "We've asked the staff not to go into the forest, to limit their walks to the boardwalk to the helipad."

"Oh. Why is that?"

"It's a liability issue. This is a workplace, obviously."

"Is this something new?"

"New this spring. There were grey wolf sightings on the peninsula in March. And of course, the arson attack has us all a bit rattled. And Madelaine's fall."

"Madelaine?"

"The au pair. She went for a hike and got her foot caught in a crevasse just up there. Those cliffs are a lot more treacherous than folks realize."

Okay, then, Isla thinks, smiling at him. Just watch me. And in her mind, she moves Hashem from the *Potential Ally* column to *Possibly Implicated*.

Lark begins to whine as they start down the boardwalk. Isla crouches, and Lark climbs up and settles her little body into the curve of Isla's spine. Her warm weight is a comfort.

William runs ahead of them towards a big rock. "This is where Daddy shot a bear."

Sunlight splinters through the pine trees. "He used the gun from the lodge?"

William doesn't answer. "Here!" he calls from the rock. "He shot it here." He demonstrates how the bear fell, on its side.

"Why did he shoot the bear?" Isla asks.

"Because it was coming around."

"Well, this was its home."

The helipad. A rectangle brutally hacked out of the bush, spread with fine gravel. Isla sets Lark down. The pad is huge, much bigger than she imagined, and it has light standards around it. The blue helicopter sits at one end like an offering from another world. William is jumping up and down beside it, trying to reach the door handle. The kid's an endless GIF. Isla walks over and reaches for the handle and discovers to her surprise that the door was left unlocked. William and Lark are desperate to play inside—why not? She gives them their juice boxes and hoists them into the cockpit and closes the door. She wants time to think. She wants someone to tell. She wants to tell Jake, to warn him. She pulls out her phone and calls Rita. Rita answers right away, and Isla feels her shoulders relax at the sound of Rita's voice.

"You've got great reception."

"They have their own cell tower. This is Bay Street in the woods."

"Is the lodge nice?"

"It's gorgeous. Except it's, you know, haunted by the ghosts of the farmers who died on their parched farms in India to build it."

"Yeah, no shit. But you're *in*? He's letting you stay?"

"Rita. Get this. I've got something on him. You remember when he came to tour The Grange? He had a woman with him?"

"Young. With dark hair."

"She's his EA. Her name is Luna. They're having an affair."

"How do you know?"

"Because he lied about that weekend. Eve thinks he was in Montreal with a guy named Hashem. But obviously, he was with Luna. Last night he was going to throw me off the property, and then I told him I recognized Luna from that meeting, and he realized he couldn't. Oh, poor Eve. I feel bad for her. She's being very friendly."

"Sincere-friendly?"

"Mm, no. She keeps confiding in me. She thinks it will thrill me to be taken into her world. She always says 'frankly.' Isn't that a tell? Of insincerity? *Frankly, Isla.*" Bevaqua's kids press their smeared faces against the cockpit glass, staring at her, and Isla struggles to focus. "Listen, Rita. Think about what this means. Luna is not just leverage over Reg. I think she and Reg were *here* on Easter weekend. If she was here, if Jake came up that Saturday, she'll know something. I'm going to try to talk to her."

And then she tells Rita about the gun.

"Oh, Isla." Neither of them speaks for a moment. "Listen, it might be nothing," Rita finally says, like she's trying to convince herself. "It could be anything. Maybe Reg started worrying about safety, and locked it away. But still, it's crazy for you to be there. You need to leave. You need to go to the police."

"What can I tell them? A gun used to be on display, but the owner moved it?"

In the helicopter the kids are scuffing up the leather seats with their mucky shoes, they're fiddling with the presets and dribbling pomegranate juice onto the dashboard. Isla stands on the edge of that gravel patch cut into the woods, and her eyes drift to the row of light standards, and then, about six feet up, she sees it. A webcam strapped to one of the lights.

Just here Jake walked on a snowy night—in his sock feet, with a shawl over his shoulders. Here's where she saw him pause and look right at the camera with animal frankness. That was the moment she stopped believing that solving this mystery would be a good thing.

That day Luna never once comes into the kitchen. When Isla has a free moment, she stations herself in an alcove in the living room where she can see the door to the office. Luna comes out eventually, heading for her room upstairs. Isla says her name, and Luna turns her head, expressionless.

"Do you have a minute?"

"Sorry, no. Catch you at dinner?"

"Sure," Isla says.

But Luna doesn't come to dinner.

While Isla is cleaning up afterwards, Eve fills her in on Sunday. It's their family day, a sacred Bevaqua tradition, and staff day off. Everyone will fend for themselves for lunch and dinner. If Isla will, you know, just put out a selection of items they can fend from.

"Reg wants to cruise around the cove in the *Sequana*," she says. "It's supposed to be a very warm day, and we want to take advantage of it." Her eyes fall on Isla, and she adds, "But I'm sure his old friend is absolutely on his mind. We'll keep our eyes open for anything out of the ordinary along the shoreline."

"Maybe I could come with you? One more pair of eyes."

"Actually, it's going to be a family outing. We don't get a lot of time together, just the four of us. We plan to stop for a picnic lunch at Prospect Point, up the shore to the north. It has a beautiful little sandy beach. Can I ask you to put together a picnic lunch for us?" Eve opens a few cupboards, scanning their contents. "We have a wicker picnic basket—I so hope it wasn't in the workshop."

"Maybe we could ask the staff to form a search party and check out the woods around the lodge?" Isla says.

Eve pauses in her search and looks at Isla coolly. Something in her has hardened against Isla, it's obvious. "Reg tells me you and Jake Challis had separated."

"No," Isla says. "Reg got that wrong."

"Oh. He says you told him yourself."

Isla shakes her head. "Jake and I are very much together."

She's mashing chickpeas for their hummus when Reg stops by the kitchen. Eve found the wicker basket somewhere, and he drops it off for Isla to pack.

"A day out with the children," Isla says.

"That's right."

"So Luna's going on the *Sequana* with you?"

"Fuck off, Isla." He gets a beer from the kitchen fridge and snaps it open.

"She's what, twenty-three? You are such a cliché, Reg." It's probably stupid to provoke him, but she can't stop. "Hashem tells me you just made a rule that people can't go into the woods. Bit of a red flag, isn't it?"

"What do you mean?"

"Must be things out there you don't want the staff to see."

"Isla, you're sounding a little unhinged." Reg sets the beer on the counter and goes into the walk-in fridge. Unhinged? Yesterday he called her paranoid. This is classic gaslighting.

He comes back with a vacuum pack of beef jerky and drops it into the picnic basket. "Just to be clear," he says. "I don't make any secret of my opinion of Jake Challis, but that doesn't mean I had a hand in whatever's happened to him."

"I don't know what you think of him, actually."

He shrugs. "I pity him. Poor guy. Born with everything, the old silver spoon in the mouth, and he couldn't make anything of it."

"Seriously? That's what you think? His art is nothing?"

"Well, he needed outside help to get it shown, apparently."

"What are you talking about?"

He stands there, smirking. It takes a minute for Isla to get it. She can hardly speak. "That's why you got involved with The Ark? To mess with Jake?"

He just laughs.

"How long have you known we were together?"

"I've always known. Come on. You live in a hamlet."

"I don't get it. I don't get why you don't leave Jake alone. What are you hoping to accomplish? Like, what's your end game?"

"You don't think he was messing with me? He blew up my property. He harassed me for months, smearing me on social media."

"He'd never do that. He couldn't care less about you." Then she remembers the cartoons in his sketchbook.

"Challis was always a jealous little prick. He hated me for my success. He could never get over the fact that I've done so much better than him."

"Jake didn't give a shit about your money."

Reg laughs again, like this is genuinely funny.

"He *didn't*. He despised you for it, actually. And if you want to talk about jealousy—well, you're the one who built your house on his family's property." She sets down her masher, hoping to make this the last word, and heads for the walk-in fridge. "Excuse me. I need a lemon." Inside the fridge, she realizes she's trembling. We're talking about him in the past tense, she thinks. Reg is, and so am I.

She scoops a lemon out of a bowl and turns back to the kitchen. But Reg followed her, he stands blocking the doorway of the fridge.

"Isla, if you want to know what a total fucking loser your boyfriend was—that cunt slept with my girlfriend in my own house."

She stares at him.

"I invite him into my house, I give him a bed, and he seduces my girlfriend. *In my house.* He didn't give a shit about Becky—he just did it to get at me."

Then he's the one making a dramatic exit from the scene.

Isla sets her phone alarm for eight, but she hardly sleeps, and as soon as it's light she gives up trying. In the night, the thing about Jake and Reg's girlfriend felt very big. Around maybe three, she was overwhelmed with sadness and hurt and she turned her face into her sleeping bag and cried for a long time, as if Jake's lust for this girl Becky took something away from her. But as dawn seeped into the tent, the story shrank back to size. When did this happen? Jake was living in Reg's house just before he went to art school, it must have been then. Reg delivered his accusation like it was going to be the final blow to all the esteem Isla feels for Jake. But in a way she feels glad—that at one time, Jake was so reckless with desire.

She gets dressed and sticks her arms into Jake's hoodie, digs out the binoculars. She creeps out of the tent to tie her shoes. Last night she brought some bread and cheese up to the ridge, and she sits on a nearby rock to eat. While she eats, she thinks about what Reg said about Jake harassing him online. *Drinkwater the Douche,* she thinks in a flash of certainty. She pulls out her phone and does a search. There's Jake's cartoons, alright, on Twitter. In an account called @Shatterhand. Shatterhand, what is that? She scrolls down, studying the posts. Reg stealing money from "his friend and mentor"—that caption troubled her when she saw it in the sketchbook, and she intended to dig into Old Jack's laptop, but she never got around to it.

Oh, Jake. Obviously, she's failed in the basic task of any relationship, learning to know your loved one. But then, how well does she know herself? She's got her night with the audio artist to consider—a night that was good and beautiful in itself, a joyful response to something she truly felt. And also a betrayal. There's a knot here that she can't untie.

She sits for a long time, watching a chipmunk dart back and forth between the roots of the trees, and then she sticks her phone in her pocket and forces herself to get up. Every day on this property may be her last, so she really needs to be smart about how she uses this one. With the Bevaquas out of the way, she could make another attempt to talk to Luna. But Luna does not want to talk, and that might mean the day is totally wasted. Isla's instinct is to keep her eye on Reg. Boat ride or not, he'll be keeping his eye on things too. Why does the criminal return to the scene of the crime? Because there's something he needs to fix, or hide, or guard. Or maybe just brood over.

It's a beautiful morning, sunlight filtering through the woods. There's still no movement at the lodge when Isla sets off, the binoculars around her neck and a day pack with a water bottle on her back. She walks north, along the trail she followed the day she arrived. She stops often to take in stunning vistas of the lake. She has time. It's going to be a while before the Bevaquas arrive at their picnic spot. When she slows down and pays attention, that's when she senses Jake's presence. She may as well admit why she's not going to the police: because she wants to be here. Jake's voice in her ears. Her sense that when she looks at things, she's seeing what he saw. New growth a lime-green haze in the treetops. Tiny red mushrooms. Spring has been quietly taking over the forest while they were all caught up in their feverish drama.

She walks as far as the overlook where she stood the first day. At the base of the cliff, white foam plays over sculpted brown rocks, rocks that were shaped by the water the way wind shapes a snowdrift. She sees the little trail down to the water, and takes it again, down to the tiny inlet where she dove off a ledge. The canoe is still there. It's in deep shadow now, but she can make out its shape. She forgot to tell Rita. Rita might have had some idea what it meant. And if you never come back (Isla finds herself thinking), Rita could tell the police about it.

She climbs back to the main trail. At first it was packed earth, but now it's a chain of rocky stepping-stones. Many of the stones are scored, as if they were clawed by a bear. Or a raven's claws, like a raven preened itself on the rock before it hardened. They're like hieroglyphics or logographs. Occasionally Isla crouches and runs her fingertips over one, trying to read it. They won't surrender their meaning to her. This is what drew Jake out to the bush, she thinks. This is what he was trying to read.

The *Sequana* nestles up to the shore, and the bridge powers down to a rocky ledge. From her perch on the cliff, Isla watches the family traipse off and follow a trail onto the beach. Then she can't see them, she just hears snatches of their voices carried on the wind. She assumes they're on the rocks close to the base of the cliff, eating the lunch she prepared.

After maybe fifteen minutes, Reg appears on the sand, followed by his kids and the dog. He's carrying a mid-sized drone. White, four-propellers. Maybe he's *filming*, Isla thinks. Is there something particular he wants to check on? But if he was filming, would he get William involved? The drone crashes on their first try and William starts to wail. Isla lifts her binoculars and pulls their happy-family masquerade into focus. William, choking back his tears, doing a brave impression of the son Reg Bevaqua wishes he had. Eve in a red sarong, picking her way across the sand, playing the loving wife. The faun-coloured dog, watching with his faun-coloured eyes—evolutionarily, he mimics a deer. Poor Reg. Everyone around him is impersonating someone else. Except Lark, the little darling, who is just being four.

The warmth of the sun is like a drug. Fatigue overtakes Isla and she sinks onto her back and closes her eyes. Over the rustle of pines and the lapping of waves, she can hear the terns calling. The white yacht, the white drone, that bloated plutocrat playing with his stupid man-toy. Everything stolen. Stolen from his friends, stolen from the poor and desperate. What is that? That's the mystery she really needs to solve. A bird begins to tweet nearby. Isla opens her eyes and turns her head, and that's when she sees it, on the moss under a low pine branch: a small, bright, metal tube, the brass casing that powered a bullet manufactured with the sole purpose of ripping flesh. She lies and stares at it in disbelief. Don't touch it, Jake says in her ear. So she doesn't. She just sits up and takes careful note of its location.

And then she flounders out of the clearing and strikes off into the forest. Almost right away, the earth falls away on the lake side, and she's walking the edge of a breathtaking drop. She stops, squats, steadying herself to look down. It's thirty feet at least to a lower ledge, a ledge that slopes down to the lake. Last fall's leaves are scattered at the bottom, but nothing else that she can see. A crashing in the bush startles her. A big animal. She scrambles to her feet.

It's the dog, it's King Tut. He's snuffling through the woods, a real hound that's picked up a scent. His eyes, his coat are the same warm brown—he looks eyeless, he's all nose and ears. Isla calls him and he comes to her and she scratches his head. He's interested in her, he smells her eagerly. "Don't you have an NWA?" she asks softly. Apparently not. He turns away from her, he's preoccupied, he wants to keep going. So she follows him. He turns away from the lake too, moving deeper into the forest. Tail up, nose down, he doesn't falter or hesitate, and she struggles to keep up. He leads her around rocks, over fallen trees. To a feature even more dramatic than that cliff—a deep crevasse, where the earth has split open. The gap's about two feet wide, it's like two cliffs are facing each other. What would break the earth open like that? King Tut noses along it and Isla follows. She thinks of the trenches they dig in England on the edge of a meadow to contain livestock, when they don't want to mar the view with a fence. What is a trench like that called? —a ha-ha. This is a ha-ha that bisects the woods, like a lightning bolt laid itself down on the forest floor. Made in an instant, the lightning sought out weakness and severed the earth along that seam. The dog stops, whining urgently. Isla can't see what's at the bottom of the ha-ha because detritus from the forest has fallen into it. Oh, Jake, Isla breathes. What is this hound after? Should I look? No, Isla, Jake says, don't look. She turns blindly and cuts through the forest in the direction she came, scrambling back around rocks and over fallen logs. Jake, she cries silently. She's on the trail then, stepping from rock to rock, not letting herself think. She slips, recovers, keeps running, her own panting filling her ears. The trail is earthen now, the light grows. Then she's at the clearing and the lodge is below her and her tent with its door neatly zipped sits in the middle of the path.

Isla spends the afternoon in the tent. The ache in her heart relocates and sharpens—she starts to feel pains in her stomach. She pictures police cordoning off Prospect Point, turning their searchlights into crevasses and down to the feet of cliffs. She hears a shout, and sees a police officer crouching on the rock, just where the dog started to whine. All along she's been thinking, I don't have enough proof to go to the police. Now she thinks, I don't want to know what they will find.

A lot of yelling and laughter in Comstock Cove, people running back and forth between the lake and the lodge. Staff day off and the boss is away. The utility boat starts up, they're going fishing. The yard falls quiet. A squirrel begins to scold, she can see his tiny enraged shadow twitching against the tent wall. He's hated Isla being here from the beginning. At a certain point she rolls off her air mattress, wanting to feel the stony earth under her. But the floor is springy, she's cushioned by the moss and cedar under the groundsheet.

A long time goes by. Maybe she sleeps, because when she next looks out, the *Sequana* is docked, and she didn't hear it arrive. Soon after, she hears the utility boat come back, and she unzips the tent and positions herself to watch. Luna was out fishing with Alessandro and Yann. Reg walks down to the pier and admires their catch. Now they're making their way up to the kitchen, they're going to fry everything up. They've been drinking, it's obvious. Well, maybe not Alessandro. Reg and Luna trail behind, their faces close together in an intimate exchange. Isla lies back on her sleeping bag. People have started to discover a poisonous mushroom on the Bruce. It's spreading north as the climate warms. A classic white, although it may have an olive-green tinge to it. Death is slow but inevitable.

After a time, she hears everybody head back down to the pier. Music starts up—the sound system on the yacht. It's Jack White, "Seven Nation Army." She sits up again and pulls on her warmest sweater, crawls out of the tent, makes her way to the lodge. The kitchen stinks of fish and she turns the fan on. She uses the bathroom and then walks back outside and around to the terrace. It's a beautiful evening on the lake. God-rays slant down from the clouds. A party on the pier. Hashem is dancing with Luna, Reg is in a lounger, she can't see his face. Dock lights dot the shore in both directions. The rich love nature too. They drive up from the city to worship. Nature's their god. Their cathedral, their ashram, their therapist, their treasure-cache, their slave, their nemesis. She stands for a while at the top of the Spanish Steps, considering what sort of grenade she can toss into the scene. After a minute, she goes back into the lodge.

Eve is alone in the living room, a cup of tea on the table beside her. The kids must be in bed. She's scolding King Tut, loving him up, wicked little Tutty. "What a scare this boy gave us!" she says, cradling his muzzle with one hand, scratching behind his ears with the other. She lifts her head, smiles. It's Friendly Eve tonight. "We let him roam free at Prospect

Point because we didn't think you could get up the cliffs there, but then he was gone! He just vanished. So we hurried home in a panic to put a search party together. And there he was, lying by the back door!"

If only it were that easy, Isla thinks.

The music cranks up, it blasts over the lake. Their neighbours must love them.

Eve makes a rueful face. "Reg has a bespoke sound system on the *Sequana*. He helped design it and he is so proud of it. The subwoofers are in the cushions of the sofas on the back deck. Boys. Honestly, what can you say?"

"Eve, do you own a canoe?"

Eve pauses to mark Isla's rudeness.

"Yes, we do."

"Is it in the boathouse?"

"Actually, it was stolen a few weeks ago. Our driver ran it up to Scalloway—it's a classic canvas, and it needs annual maintenance—and then the folks at the marina called to say it had disappeared from their yard." She sighs, she lifts helpless eyes to Isla. "Whether our insurance will cover it, or theirs will, I don't know. Just one more thing to deal with."

Isla is still standing in the middle of the room. Eve takes a sip of her tea and says, "You're not going down to the pier?"

"I'm not much into partying these days."

Eve tilts her head in sympathy. "I've been wanting to say, Isla, I'm sorry we didn't make it to your boyfriend's show at the art centre on Easter weekend. I had a hospital benefit, and of course, Reg was in Montreal at the water forum with Hashem."

Isla looks at Eve's elegant, vacant face, and she accepts that slender cord of sympathy, and remorselessly she braids it into a weapon. "Well, I appreciated Reg's interest in The Grange. Coming all that way on a Sunday to meet with us. I wonder what Luna thought. She went straight to the copter after the tour and I didn't get a chance to talk to her."

Eve's control is astonishing. Her expression does not change. She does not say, Luna was with him?, she does not say a word. But her eyes darken—Isla actually sees her pupils dilate. She sets her tea down, and reaches over and straightens the magazines on the coffee table, and then she gets up and walks to the window and tips her face close to cut through her reflection. Then she just leaves. The dog follows her. A minute later, Isla goes to the window too, and sees Eve out on the front terrace. She has her phone to her ear. She's phoning her husband, who's sprawled on a lounge chair on the pier thirty metres below. Isla watches him fish his phone out of his jacket pocket and lift it to his ear.

The signs of all hell breaking loose on Comstock Cove: The music goes off. Reg climbs to the terrace, and he and Eve step back and Isla can't see them from the window. The pergola lights go out. Hashem, Yann, and Alessandro come up to the lodge, singly. They each say a polite good night to Isla as they pass through the living room. Luna comes through, stony-faced. Doors close. This is how hell breaks loose in Eve Bevaqua's world: quietly.

Isla picks up a muffin and some yogurt in the kitchen and takes them to the tent. She ties back the screen door and resumes her surveillance while she eats. After about ten minutes, two people make their way to the parking area beside the blast zone. When they pass under the security light, Isla sees that it's Luna and Alessandro. Alessandro is carrying Luna's suitcase. Unintelligible bits of her tirade float up towards the tent. There are two cars on the property, a black Mercedes SUV and a black BMW sedan. They get into the SUV. There goes my best witness, Isla thinks. She had fun, tossing that grenade, but what did she accomplish? Alessandro starts backing up and Reg comes out of the lodge and holds out a hand. Alessandro rolls down his window. Reg gestures towards the tent.

Oh, Christ. He's throwing her off too. She's got nothing on him now. She grabs her hoodie and scurries up the slope. Outside the range of the lodge's yard lights, where the darkness is close and dense, she sinks to the ground. The night is cold, and she pulls the hoodie on. She left a flashlight switched to low on her sleeping bag, and below her, the tent is lit like a paper lantern.

For ten minutes or so, she watches Alessandro and Yann run back and forth between the house and the tent. *Is-la*, they call from time to time, and she thinks of neighbourhood games of hide-and-seek when she was a kid. The lights in the lodge go out one after the other. Soon the second floor is dark, except for the glass-walled en suite. A white apparition crosses that square of light, and then it goes dark too. There's a family in pain down there. Maybe this is nothing new for Eve, maybe it's a familiar humiliation, but Reg is going to be hurting. Isla and Jake have each cost Reg a girlfriend, when you think about it. Isla feels a twinge of something you'd normally call pity. How do you think of people who behave like scum, where do you put them in the human family? You hold them accountable, don't you. But it's hard to do that with Reg. He's got his fame and his money and his lawyers—who can touch him?

Last year's leaves are a damp mulch under Isla, the cold creeps into her thighs and butt. She pulls her hood up and she's still cold. Then it hits her—how stupid! She can't hide forever. If she lets Reg kick her out of the lodge tonight, she'll get to spend a couple of hours in the car with Luna! She scrambles to her feet.

But maybe the same thought occurred to Reg too, because just then the door of the SUV slams and its red tail lights vanish around the debris site.

For a long time, Isla sits motionless on the ridge. She sits while the generator goes off and the yard lights dim. Other nights the stars have been like thistles stuck together, so thick their light blurred, but tonight, there's no stars and no moon. She can't see the lake, it's just a restlessness around her. And the breathing forest, the earth with all its secrets. The cliffs, the fissure in the rock, she's attending to it more than thinking about it. If it was a moonlit night, she'd go there now, she'd hold vigil. If she had the courage.

In the dark, the night reveals itself as noisy. Waves slap the hull of the yacht, sections of the floating dock bang together. Her fear rises, and her grief, and she struggles not to cry. She's going to need courage to go forward. The world is not what she thought. It's cruel and confused and wilfully blind. She slides her hands into the opposite sleeves of her hoodie, trying to smooth out the goosebumps on her arms. Her eyes stray back to her lit-up tent, an incandescent shrine in the forest. She digs her heels into the earth. This is the world Jake loved, in all its pain and terror and joy and beauty, hurtling towards a version of itself she doesn't dare to imagine. It was sacred to Jake, this world. He loved it and he's gone from it, and here she is.

TWENTY-TWO

An ugly pounding wakes Isla up, a helicopter pummelling the sky. She unzips the tent door to watch it go over the lodge and sink behind the trees. It's about the same size as Reg's, but black. After a bit, three men appear on the boardwalk and disappear into the lodge. Two of them are in suits and carrying briefcases, and the third is in uniform. Isla watches from the ridge with narrowed eyes, as befits a fugitive. Bevaqua has called in reinforcements, he's trying to seize control of the narrative. Or a different drama has swallowed up Isla's, something more consequential to Reg than the life of an old friend.

Monday morning. The forest is blanketed in smoke, the wind blew it in while Isla grabbed a few hours of sleep in the tent. Woodsmoke, it's so thick you can't see across the cove. A few minutes after the helicopter lands, a houseboat pulls up at the pier: a neat little log cabin on a barge. It floats behind the elegant *Sequana*, they're an uncaptioned cartoon. Then a truck with a flatbed drives up the lane, carrying a huge metal container and a little Bobcat. Three men in hard hats and hazard vests look the blast site over. One of them backs the flatbed close to the site, another drives the Bobcat down a ramp. The Bobcat sets to work. It grabs up rubble in its iron bucket. Pivots, drops its load into the container with a thunderous crash. The smoke and noise, it's hell.

Isla endures it in the tent until about one o'clock. When the yard falls quiet, she gets up and dresses. As she walks down to the lodge, one of the removal guys steps onto the little houseboat. He powers it up and pilots it slowly across her line of vision. She watches it disappear around the point to the north, and then she goes into the lodge to use the bathroom. No one's around. The door to the offices is closed. A tray of frozen Danishes sits on the counter, and she eats one. Drinks a glass of milk, puts her phone on charge. Goes back outside and stands on the patio, listening to the silence. What if she was someone who could do something? She thinks for another long minute, and then she walks back around the lodge and climbs to the shore ridge.

The houseboat is moored in an inlet five minutes up the shore, where it fits sweetly into the landscape. Window boxes with plants growing in them. The removal crew sits drinking coffee on rocks close to the water, their hard hats beside them. They call hello.

"You moved!"

"View's better back here."

She makes her way carefully down the slope. "I'm Isla."

"Pull up a chair, Isla," says the oldest guy. He introduces himself and his crew. He's Mike Guimond, the young guy is his son Nathan, and the big red-haired guy is Owen Navalny.

"Tall, taller, tallest in reverse-alphabetical order," Owen says. He looks like a goof, but an endearing one.

"Gotcha," Isla says. She's still standing.

"Coffee?" Nathan has a wooden crate at his feet. It's a portable cupboard for their Thermos and coffee fixings. "Milk? Sugar?"

"Give her Violet's cup," Mike says.

Nathan fixes Isla's coffee in a china teacup with violets on it.

"We carry that cup around in case any nice women drop by," Mike says.

"Pretty smokey, huh," Isla says, taking the cup from Nathan with a thank-you smile and lowering herself onto a rock.

"Yeah. We've never had fires this early before."

"Do you know where it is?"

"Red Lake. Two communities have already been evacuated to Sioux Narrows."

Owen asks her who's sleeping in the tent.

"I am."

"You must be a camping maniac."

"It's a new thing for me. But I love it. This cove—Jake, my boyfriend, spent summers here as a kid. His grandfather had a cabin."

"Right where Bevaqua is?" Mike asks.

Isla nods.

"I remember those cabins. Three of them. Not much bigger than my houseboat there. They had a dock they all shared."

"Did you grow up near here?"

"Just southwest of here. Nathan and I are members of Saugeen Ojibway Nation. But when I was a kid, we sometimes came over here to fish."

"What do you do for the Bevaquas?" Nathan asks.

"I was their cook for a few days, but I'm kind of on strike at the moment."

"We noticed. They were supposed to feed us. Another broken treaty." They all laugh. "Dad had to warm up a few cans from his stash. It's going to be a hell of a long week."

"You do debris removal year-round?"

"Dad and Owen do. They just took me on when my classes finished up last week."

"What are you studying?"

"Film. I'm doing a BFA."

"My boyfriend's an artist, a painter. Jake Challis. I took this job because—well, he's been missing for a couple of weeks, and I think he came up here." Their eyes all swivel towards her. "Yeah. He and Bevaqua were friends at one time, but things went bad between them."

"What?" Owen says.

"Are you thinking some sort of foul play?" Nathan asks.

Foul play. "Yes."

"Police on it?"

"Sort of. Not much is happening."

"Wow," he says after a minute. "That's big."

They sit in silence, finishing their coffee. They believe her. She would hate it if they didn't, but it's worse that they do.

A bird calls from the bushes behind them—the rudimentary rusty-gate song Isla heard the day before at Prospect Point.

"Yellow-throated vireo," Owen says.

"So, Mike, that spool of cable on the back of your houseboat barge. What is it?"

"It's a hand-winch," Mike says. "A come-along."

"What's it for?"

"Hauling things. You can hook, say, a boat or a log and crank it up out of the water."

"Could you pull up a canoe that has rocks in it?"

"A canoe? Sure. It'll handle a ton of weight."

"If it's sunk about twenty feet down?"

"The cable's got a heavy hook at the end. You drop it, grab the canoe by the thwart. Nathan's an ace at that sort of thing. Then you crank it up. Piece of cake."

"Do you have time for me to show you something?" Isla asks.

The lodge is still deserted. The kids are watching a movie in their playroom. No sign of Eve. Come for supper, Isla said to the removal guys. Anything special you'd like? She mentioned the big box of Kobe rib-eyes in the freezer, and their faces lit up. A dinner took shape in her mind, apple pie and entertainment. This is called grabbing control of the narrative.

The steaks are thawed and surrendering to Isla's secret rub when the office door opens and Reg himself steps out. He stiffens when he sees

Isla in the kitchen. What's his recourse? His only recourse is to kill her. It seems a useful experiment on her part, to determine whether he's capable of bare-handed murder.

Instead, he says, "Three extra for dinner," and goes back. He's got guests here and he needs a cook.

"Six extra," she calls after him. "You're feeding the removal guys."

She turns back to the pie pastry, shocked by how bad he looks. Pale, and with massive bags under his eyes. He's grieving Luna, no doubt. It's need, infantile need that drives him. He doesn't really see other people around him, he just reaches for what he wants. And now he's got to deal with the horror of what happened between him and Jake. And he's here, something's keeping him here, and it's making him crazy.

It's five o'clock before the black SUV drives into the yard. Alessandro stops to talk to the helicopter pilot, who's been sitting on the patio all afternoon, playing poker on his phone. When he comes into the kitchen, he looks surprised to find Isla there. "I was sure Mr. Bevaqua would get Yann to drive you home."

"I guess he needed Yann. Turns out, he needs me too. And what about you? You were gone a lot longer than I expected."

"Yeah, I took Luna right into Toronto. Mrs. Bevaqua told me to drop her off at a hotel in Owen Sound, but Reg told me to run her home. You have to know who you're working for, right?"

"But still."

He finally admits that he went to his place in Toronto and slept. "Good thing, because there's no sleeping here. That frigging Bobcat with its back-up beep, excuse my language."

"Do you know who the suits are?"

"They're Mr. Bevaqua's main lawyers."

"Why are they here?"

"Who knows? Some sort of bad shit going down. Hostile takeover, market collapse, criminal charges. Mr. Bevaqua is going to be lost without

Luna. You might think he hired her because she's so hot, but she was a crackerjack assistant, the person you want to have beside you in a crisis. Reggie, Reggie, when will you learn?" He pulls a Coke out of the kitchen fridge and pops it open. "Anyway, it's tough. I have a bad day, I end up at the body shop. Reg Bevaqua has a bad day, he loses a billion dollars."

"A billion?" Isla is skeptical. She thinks about Old Jack's laptop. She never did get around to investigating what was on it. Looks like it doesn't matter—Reg is finding his own road to ruin.

Alessandro hangs around until she finally asks him to set up a serving table on the pier and get coals started for the barbeque.

The kids ring the dinner bell, and to Isla's surprise, the first to appear on the Spanish Steps, descending long-gowned through the haze like a figure in a Victorian ghost story, is their mother. She glides wordlessly to a wicker lounger, and Alessandro brings her a manhattan. Then the lawyers' helicopter pilot, George, moseys down. Yann arrives. Mike, Nathan, and Owen walk over the ridge. Alessandro pours them all drinks, and they wait. The salads wilt on a folding table, the barbeque coals reach their orange peak and pass it, the kids bicker. Music? Alessandro asks. No one replies, he takes it as a no.

The loons start up, eerier than ever. Mike with his grey-streaked hair—he sits on a billionaire squatter's pier in a plaid shirt and jeans, smoking and watching and listening. Other worlds have come to an end, Isla thinks. Not just this one. They're all quiet. Mike's crew was troubled by the swamped canoe, she could tell. She passes her glass to Alessandro for a refill. The gin she's drinking is having zero effect. Except that she feels a bit outside her body. She's with Jake, a little kid swimming in black water off the dock while his parents play cards by kerosene lantern on the veranda above.

Finally, the Bay Street gang materializes at the top of the Spanish Steps. The two lawyers follow Reg and Hashem down. White shirts and suit pants, they've all taken off their jackets. Trying to shake off the malfeasance of their day. The lawyers are old—Reg looks like a brash kid beside them. Quite possibly they were friends of Jack Challis. One is lean, one stout. A silver fox, a beige badger. They perform the social rituals, but Isla lets their names slide over her.

Alessandro takes drink orders, and the silver fox heads for a chair beside Eve. "Forgive us for the primitive dining arrangements," she says as he sinks into it. "My beautiful harvest table was destroyed in the attack."

"What a terrible thing that was," the silver fox says. "But thankfully, the gods were on your side. You could have lost this lodge. Now, that would have been a tragedy. It's the jewel of the western bay."

"Thank you," Eve says. "That means a lot, coming from you, Frank." She's a Greek goddess tonight in a pale caftan and elegant gold jewelry. Her hair perfectly sculped, her makeup subtle. How excessive Luna was, she's saying.

Reg inspects the steaks, tastes the rub. He takes their orders, rare, medium-rare, playing the big man. Isla grills, Alessandro serves. Reg never looks at her; their eyes repel each other's like opposing magnets. The hostess and the silver fox murmur, and everyone else eats in silence, blood pooling on their plates. Eve raises her voice, and they all look up: a baton's been lifted to signal the overture to one of her performances. "I'm trying to find a name for our lodge."

"A new name?"

"You don't like Comstock Cove?"

"Well, it refers to this whole shore, doesn't it, from Prospect Point to Scalloway. We need a name for our estate. Something, you know, along the lines of *Beechcroft*, the Anson Dodge mansion on the mainland."

"We have beech trees, babe?" Reg says.

She angles her shoulder slightly to block out the sight of him, and holds out her martini glass. Alessandro crosses the pier swiftly and picks it up. "Something that draws on the natural setting. Or a name from mythology, like the *Sequana*." Her voice loves the word. "Sequana was a Gallic water deity, the goddess of the River Seine. There's a wonderful bronze of her in a museum in Dijon, standing in a boat with a duckbill prow." She looks towards Mike, like this should mean something to him. When he doesn't respond, she says, "I'm interested to know what Indigenous people called this cove. Or *call* it, I guess I should say."

"It's not a name we share with others," Mike says. "We used to come fishing this way when I was a kid, and we always passed this shore full throttle, and kept our eyes to ourselves."

Eve wants to know why.

He won't tell her. He finally says, "It's a story you can only tell when there's snow on the ground."

"We will have to have you back in the winter," she says gracefully.

The beige badger, sitting by Reg, starts a conversation thread about the insurance claim for the explosion. "Vandalism on that scale—it should be considered domestic terrorism."

"Well, it's been a huge wake-up call, that's for sure."

Isla studies Reg's face. All day she tried to imagine the scenario, Reg raising a gun and firing at Jake. It's not believable, even for him. More likely he fired, aiming to miss but trying to terrify. That was their pattern, right? Isla could see Jake dodging to save himself, leaping in terror, moving through the air. Injured, maybe—his leg was grazed, or his shoulder, enough to catapult him into the void. If the police do tie Jake's death to Reg, if they establish that Reg was the one with the gun, and if, say, he admits that he fired a few warning shots, what will the charge be? If Jake was never hit, but fell running away in the dark, was killed in a fall? Second-degree murder, Isla thinks—by rights it should still be murder. But it won't be. Reg has his lawyers right here. At best, it will be manslaughter. Or aggravated assault. Then they'll get it downgraded to careless use of a firearm. Will Reg do time, if all they convict him of is careless use of a firearm? No, he won't. No chance he goes to jail. The gin has finally kicked in, it's delivered her to a flat plateau of rage. Her task tonight and every night is wresting power from these rapacious ghouls.

Alessandro brings Reg another beer in a mug, and he tilts it, admiring the hue. A new hotel is going up in Lion's Head, he says, lots of development around Tobermory. The locals don't like offshore investment, they're having fits about a Chinese company that wants to build a big resort. But the real threat to the area is the feds, who would gobble up the whole peninsula if they could. Luckily, Reg was able to outbid Parks Canada for this property.

Mike sets his plate down under his chair. "Reg, word in town is that you're building a survival hideout. A bunker. This is for when the world blows up, is it?"

"I don't know how stories like that get started," Reg says.

"Well, we watched a chunk of your property go up in smoke this winter, and I guess all that slurry lying around got people thinking."

Everybody's interested in the bolt-hole thing. They recount anecdotes they're read or heard. Concrete bunkers built on sheep farms in New Zealand, retrofitted Cold War missile silos in the US Midwest. With bowling alleys five stories down, shooting ranges. Nobody looks at Reg, they've cut him right out of the circle.

The badger's phone peeps. Four phones whip out.

"It's nothing," the badger says, sliding his back into his shirt pocket.

"Daddy, can we go out in the paddleboat?" William asks.

"It's past your bedtime," Reg says. He looks at Eve, who steadfastly ignores him.

Owen can't let the doomsday bunkers go. "What's up with rich white dudes anyway?" he asks tactlessly.

Isla jumps in to help. "I know. They want to blast themselves a pit into the ground, or they want to shoot themselves out into space. What *is* that?"

And they take it up again. If you have money, you have options. That's Yann, sounding pious. *Isla:* Is a bolt-hole really an option? Hiding in a cement tunnel through years and years of nuclear winter, and then venturing out when all life on earth has been poisoned with radiation? Seriously? *Owen*: They're more for climate disasters, aren't they. Floods, fires, hurricanes. *George*: Or pandemics. *Owen*: Or revolutions. When everybody's had enough, when the mob shows up at your door with torches and pitchforks.

Just then the line between grey sky and grey water vanishes—they're in a grey globe, a sensory deprivation chamber. The steaks are done, the apple pie is done (did Isla serve it?). Also, Nathan is gone. Isla saw him climb the ridge but she's not sure how long ago. It's a shocking conversation, how do they dare? But somebody has to say no to these people.

She turns to Reg. "What *is* the thinking of the One Percent, Reg? Enlighten us."

He actually answers, in his blunt, belligerent way, still not looking at her. "We've always had natural disasters, there's nothing new in that. Frankly, if a chunk of the human population died off, we'd have far fewer problems on the planet."

"You could look at it that way," Isla says. "Or maybe the One Percent could die off, the folks that prop up the old way of doing things. *Frankly*, that would make things better fast."

His hand moves beside his chair—he's covertly giving her the finger.

Two phones ping simultaneously.

"It's in," the badger says.

The lawyers are on their feet, Hashem and Reg too. They're almost at the Spanish Steps when William shrieks, "Daddy! Daddy! Look!"

Reg turns. A canoe glides around the northern point in the failing light, nosing through the spectral air like it's gliding out of the past. A beautiful blue canoe, with Nathan in the stern.

"The canoe!" William prances with delight.

"What the fuck," Reg says.

Nathan paddles up to the boat dock, does a smart ninety-degree turn.

"Where was it, where was it?" William cries.

Nathan clambers onto the dock. "It was just around that point," he says, gesturing, its rope in his hand. "At like, the crotch of a tiny inlet. Isla noticed it. Somebody piled rocks in it and sank it. Dad's got a little hand winch on the houseboat, and we managed to hook one of its thwarts, and it came right up. Somebody swamped it, but they didn't scuttle it. It's in perfect shape. It's a beauty."

"So, that's your canoe, Reg?" Isla asks.

"It was stolen from the marina at Scalloway a while back," Alessandro says.

"Somebody stole your canoe and brought it over to your property and sank it?"

Reg finally turns his wrathful face to Isla. "Go get your things."

"Poor you," Isla says a few minutes later when Alessandro looms at the tent opening. "Another midnight run to Toronto."

He doesn't answer. He picks up her duffle bag and they make their way down the dark slope to the parking lot. Nobody's around; the four horsemen of the apocalypse are huddled over their spreadsheets in the office. Alessandro backs carefully past the blast site. But when they're out of view of the lodge, he stops the car and turns the lights off. "Listen," he says. "I need to talk to you. I almost quit my job today. I almost didn't come back. Because of something Luna told me when I drove her into the city last night. I didn't know whether to believe her, because, you know, she was really pissed at Mr. Bevaqua. And there might have been an innocent explanation. Mr. Bevaqua told her the guy got back into his canoe and paddled up towards Lion's Head. So I decided to give my boss the benefit of the doubt, I decided to believe him, and I came back—but then tonight you guys found the canoe."

"Alessandro, what guy?"

TWENTY-THREE

The debris removal crew's houseboat has a two-ring propane stove, and Mike makes scrambled eggs and toast as soon as it begins to get light. By the time the four of them step out the door, the eastern horizon is notched by a splinter of light. They climb over the shore rocks and up the rise to the cliff trail. Mike is carrying his battery lantern. Nathan's got a bright LED flashlight in his jacket pocket. Owen's got a backpack with a jackknife, a filleting knife, a fishing line and hooks, a hatchet with a leather sleeve, fire starter and matches, a compass, and a coil of yellow nylon rope. Isla is wearing Jake's hoodie. She doesn't even have her phone. During the night on the houseboat, she realized that she'd left it sitting on charge in the Bevaqua kitchen.

"Let's check out what's happening at the lodge," Isla says when they get to the trail, so they turn that way first, and climb to the ridge where her tent used to be. No one's stirring below. The second helicopter is still perched by Reg's on the helipad—its passengers must have slept on the yacht. Isla's tent is gone; Yann must have taken it down. The SUV is not there either. The night before, Isla advised Alessandro to keep on driving to the city, to turn the SUV in at corporate headquarters and go home. Looks like he took her advice.

Isla gazes out over the dark water. She wants to picture what Luna and Reg saw from the window of the lodge on their romantic long weekend. Sunset, a lake that had blown up into whitecaps in the afternoon, a canoe moving along the shoreline from the south, from the direction of the marina at Scalloway. Reg was watching through binoculars, Luna told Alessandro, and Isla pictures what he saw, the paddler's intent face, pushing hard against the wind on that cold spring day.

In the night, Isla told Mike, Nathan, and Owen the entire story Alessandro had told her. Mike's floating log cabin is divided into two rooms, and they were sitting in the main room with a big battery lantern on the table. Isla was on the couch, Mike and Nathan on kitchen chairs, Owen on a beanbag. Most of this story would be considered *hearsay* by the rules of evidence, Owen pointed out. Well, Isla said, Luna herself will tell it from a witness stand someday soon.

The drama began in the morning on the Saturday before Easter, when Luna and Reg landed at the helipad and he noticed the trail cam there. He took the memory card into the lodge and checked it, and discovered footage the police had missed, footage from the weekend his workshop blew up. And he recognized a guy on it, a guy who he said had been threatening him for a while. He was really freaked about this, couldn't get his mind off it, so eventually Luna left him alone, went and had a long nap. When she woke up, he was in a better mood. Then that evening, while they were having drinks before dinner, they spied the canoe, and the guy crossing the water towards the lodge turned out to be the same guy! Reg was enraged, he insisted Luna go upstairs and lock herself into the master bedroom ensuite. She did, and a few minutes later, she heard a gunshot. She couldn't see the pier, but the shot sounded very close. She was terrified, she assumed the intruder had killed Reg and was coming for her. And then through the glass wall of the ensuite, she saw Reg running up the trail towards the north shore. It was getting dark, but she could see that he was carrying a long gun.

She didn't see him shoot, but she heard five more shots. She counted them, she was certain it was six in all. She heard them over the course of about half an hour. The first three were close, and the last three were far away.

"Do you know what type of gun Bevaqua owns?" Mike asked when Isla got to this point in the story.

"A Lee-Enfield .303. How many bullets do they hold?"

"Just one in the breach," Mike said. "But you can put a clip on. Usually a five-cartridge clip. If he had one of those, he could fire six times without reloading."

They figured Jake ran as far as Prospect Point, because of the shell casing Isla saw. Of course, that shell casing might have been dropped by a hunter, but hunting season doesn't open until October, and the casing looked shiny and new. Mike knows Prospect Point. If Jake ran there in half an hour, he was not injured by the first few shots. But then there were three more. Deadly cliffs out there, sudden drops in the dark. Isla has known for two days where Jake is.

"The boys and me will go take a look at Prospect Point as soon as it's light," Mike said. "You'll be fine here, Isla. You can lock the door."

Isla was not going to stay behind, but she didn't bother to argue. She turned her face into the couch cushions and smelled ancient smoke, and when the men moved to the bunks in the other room, she actually slept for a while. A few hours later, something woke her and she realized Mike was back on his chair by the table, smoking.

He saw her sit up. "You get some sleep?"

"Some."

"A lot to think about," he said. "Or do you have it mostly figured out, what happened that night?"

"Mostly. It's more . . . well, what was Jake thinking?"

"Do you figure he came up here to settle a score with Bevaqua?"

"No," Isla said.

"Not a fighter, your guy?"

"They had a lot of reasons to be pissed off with each other, but Jake was really trying to move away from all that. Maybe he came up here to work things out. But Bevaqua didn't give him the chance."

The ember of Mike's cigarette glowed. "Some people can pick a fight in an empty room," he said.

By the time they set off north up the trail, the sun is peeping over the lake, a sunset sun because of the smoke. Mike takes the lead and Isla follows close behind. He holds back branches for her and turns to check that she's okay when the trail is steep. They keep a steady pace, but they don't hurry, for which Isla is grateful. She's already crossed a line into her future, and whether this morning's mission is accomplished sooner or later makes no real difference.

They're on the escarpment stones with their cryptic messages, and then they're at Prospect Point. The wind-shaped pine right on the lip of the cliff—that's where Isla sat waiting for the *Sequana* to appear on Sunday morning. The four of them stand in silence, looking out at The Open. Smoke has transformed the scene. Gone is the light sprinkled on the water. Gone is the lime green of lit-up moss. The water is dark grey and surly. Isla glances around. Her eyes fall on the fungus on a nearby tree-trunk, a column of fungi like little shelves. It's called artist's bracket, Isla knows from her mother. She didn't notice it on Sunday, and for a minute she doubts they're at the right spot. Then she sees the scattering of deer turds. "Under there," she says. "I'm pretty sure."

Owen lowers himself to the rock and moss and turns his head to the side.

"It's there, alright. A .303."

Isla asks the men if they know a big crevasse nearby, where the rock has broken open—she indicates with her hands how wide that crevasse is.

"Yes," Mike says, and they turn inland, in that direction.

They see their first blue trail marker, and then they come up to the split in the earth, and the minute she sees it, Isla discovers that she knows what caused it after all: water. It didn't happen in an instant.

Water seeped into a tiny crack and expanded when it froze, forcing the rock to open. And then that crevasse filled with water and it froze again and the water muscled those walls of rock further apart. Over and over. That's how long time is, that's how strong water is. *Rock, paper, water.* That wouldn't work. Water would always win.

Mike switches his flashlight on and tracks its beam along the fissure. Twenty paces from where the ground first splits opens, the gap between the rock faces is filled with branches. They fill the crevasse to about six feet from the top. "Where's the trees they came from?" Mike asks. "That's not deadfall." Those branches were dragged to this crack in the earth and dropped in.

Owen jumps over the gap and tosses one end of his yellow rope to Nathan, and they try for a long time to loop that rope under the top branch. It's a little like the technique you use in double-handed skipping, Isla thinks, remembering a group of girls on the sidewalk when she was ten. They manage to loop something—just a small branch, but it's attached to the big branch, and it's enough. They pull that big branch up and drag it awkwardly out of the fissure. Poplar, Mike says. It was ripped off, alright, it's not deadfall. The branch has early spring growth on it, budding leaves that are shrivelled now.

Nathan and Owen lie on their stomachs and work to get another branch up. This time it's harder because the debris is deeper and made up of smaller branches. Finally, Mike goes into the woods and brings back a long pine pole. Using the pole, they shove and drag the debris horizontally along the crevasse. They only manage to move that tangled mass of branches a few feet. But it's enough. Even without a light, they can see a shape below the debris, lodged at the bottom of the ha-ha. Mike crouches and swings his powerful flashlight between the two rock faces. Nathan shines his smaller, brighter light from the other side.

Jake is lying on his side where their beams intersect. Lying like he was caught in a snare. How far down—maybe fifteen feet? You can just see his head and his left shoulder, the rest of his body is blanketed by the branches. He's wearing his dark grey padded jacket. His eyes are half-open and his face has no expression. He's gone from it, he's been gone for a long time. He's framed by the rock, he's part of the landscape. His face is very white, paper white, as though it was cut from the peeling birch-bark in the forest around them.

After a bit, Mike raises his eyes to Isla. She nods that it's enough, and he turns his flashlight off. He puts his arm around her and Isla leans into him for a moment. She's not crying. In the crevasse lies the answer to questions she hasn't even been asking.

"I've got my phone," Mike says. "Do you want me to make the call?" When she says yes, he walks a distance away and turns his back to them. They are going to find a bullet in Jake, she thinks. If he simply fell, Reg would have been the one calling the police.

When Mike comes back, he says, "They're heading straight out. They're going to come in by the road. I'll go back to the lodge and meet them there."

Nathan says, "I'll walk you back to the houseboat, eh, Isla? Owen can stay here."

Isla says no, she wants to stay. After Mike leaves, Isla keeps her eyes on Nathan, on his warm face. He reaches a hand out and squeezes her arm. When he lets go of her, she takes a step back and leans against a tree. It's incredibly solid, like it's made from the rock it grows out of.

Nathan leans on a tree too. "You okay?" he asks.

Isla nods.

"Jake Challis," he says. "It clicked with me after we talked yesterday. I saw his show a couple of years ago."

"*Dreaming the Future*."

"No. The small pieces. Really good eye. Really great. I spent a long time there."

Nathan wants to make films, Isla thinks. Maybe this will find its way into his work. It might not be a big thing in his life, but it will be one thing. Maybe he'll find the story that eludes her.

Although she's getting closer to piecing it together. As she grows through life, she will understand Jake better. Their relationship is not over.

They wait in silence. A little bird twitters like it's trying to engage them in conversation. Not the yellow-throated vireo, a different bird. Isla starts picturing the OPP arriving, two uniformed officers, Mike leading them through the trees. She sees with heaviness that they've brought the property owner, the squatter, along to check this out. He's dressed in a business suit. Apparently, he was up early, trying to do a day's work in his wilderness office, when he was interrupted by news of a troubling find on his land. He'll be smart enough to keep his mouth shut. His lawyers are on standby. Is it easier to convict a person of a single murder or of contributing to the ruination of thousands? That remains to be seen. When Isla pictures Reg coming up the trail, he's moving so stiffly you can imagine he's already in handcuffs. His magical powers are gone. His face is blank, none of his fury and self-pity visible on it. But in his heart, he's blaming Jake for this. Jake didn't give him any choice, he'll be saying to himself.

Don't think about him, Jake says urgently to Isla. Don't give him another thought. What you have is this. With time you'll want to recall it, so you need to be alive to it now. The budding branches, and the fallen logs giving themselves back to the earth. A little clutch of yellow mushrooms breaking through the moss. The sky, that today is cloudless but grey. It's not one of Georgian Bay's idyllic days. But we need to break our expectations of a certain kind of beauty, don't we, and she tips her head back against the tree and takes it in.

ACKNOWLEDGEMENTS

Thanks to the Manitoba Arts Council and the Canada Council for the Arts for financial support in the years I worked on this novel.

Joy Cooper and Martin Reed, my warmest appreciation for many wonderful experiences in shield country, and for a particular stunning moment on a frozen lake that made its way into this book.

Elizabeth Philips, Pauline Conley, Lana McGimpsey, Patricia Robertson, and Susan Israel, you may hear echoes of our conversations in this book. Thanks for being so interesting and provocative. I learned the history of Monopoly through John Green's amazing podcast, *The Anthropocene Reviewed*. And thanks to artist Shirley Brown. It's been almost two decades since I saw *Vestiges* at the Winnipeg Art Gallery, but once again it left its imprint on my fiction.

Sam Baardman, I'm deeply grateful for your astute early reading of this manuscript. Your insights illuminated my work for many months.

Martha Webb, I'd be lost without your unfailing support, feedback, and good sense. Thanks to Dean Cooke for timely help, and to all the staff at CookeMcDermid.

And warmest thanks to my editor, Jennifer Lambert, for your enthusiasm for this book, and for so often seeing beyond what I see. Working with you is a gift. Thanks to Natalie Meditsky and Peter Norman for a stellar copy edit, and to all the staff at HarperCollins Canada for being such pros.

Thanks to my father, Ralph Thomas, for what you teach me about resilience and grace, and to Caitlin, Carlos, and Bill for love, comfort, and fun.